Tillian's Isle

A tale of lost treasures

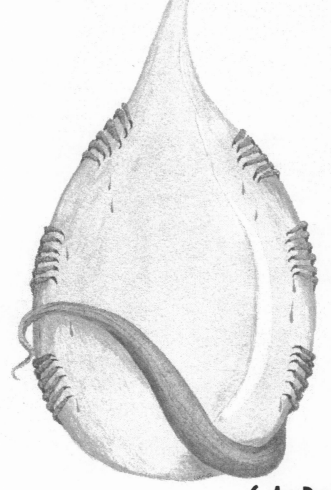

S.A. Davis

For Suraya and Simon, my greatest treasures.

And for all who hear the knocking on the door of their heart...

... rise and answer!

Oct. 13, 2010

Brianna,
Enjoy!

S. a. Davis

"... sin is crouching at your door; it desires to have you..."

- Genesis 4:7

It's unfortunate, the ways the world has come to know. Time marches forward, strolling along hand-in-hand with Life, though the relationship between the two is far from perfect. Life never seems truly satisfied with the pace at which Time advances, and Time, without emotion, exchanges partners every other generation, leaving the old to death and decay, while embracing the young and carrying on with them instead, at least for awhile, until that batch of Life is spent and a new one is born. What's most unfortunate about this struggle is that it didn't have to be like this...

W.W. 17 10 402

Iman's Isle – A Tale of Lost Treasures

chapter one: ·the island·

Tilden, October of the year 303...

An early autumn breeze rustled colored leaves as the sun began to set. Three men walked side by side, completely crowding the mile long path that ran from the sea to the village. Their somber appearance contrasted with the vibrant forest surroundings: each had long hair, tangled and snarled, and scruffy beards. They were old, relatively speaking, but their tanned faces wore no wrinkles, there was no gray on any of their heads, and their bodies remained strong and supple. Justin, the eldest of the three, walked between his lifelong friends, Warrick and Elson. Their gait was unsteady and they often stopped altogether, as their focus was on their conversation rather than on returning to the village to light the fire.

Warrick placed a hand on Justin's arm; "Did you say there was a mountain in your dream?"

"Not just *a* mountain – it was Rigid," replied Justin. Warrick released Justin's arm when he raised his hand to point in the direction of the village and upward toward the highest peak of the mountains ranging in front of them. "In my dream, I'm standing at its base, and I'm filled with excitement, but I don't know why," said Justin regretfully. "It's nice, though, to have had a pleasant dream."

"Did you see anything unusual?" asked Elson. "Do you think something secret was concealed there?"

"I don't know, but nothing happened and..."

Warrick interrupted; "I've had a number of dreams about Rigid."

Elson and Justin looked surprised and a bit upset, but they waited for Warrick to explain before they rebuked him.

"They're always the same: I'm chasing Lucy through the forest, just as I used to do through Hettered Forest when we lived on..." Warrick didn't finish. "She keeps turning to look back to make sure I'm following. I can see her smiling and hear her laughing. She runs surprisingly fast and eludes my grasp. When I get to the section of trail that passes by the foot of Rigid, she disappears."

"Why didn't you tell us about this before?" asked Justin.

"I thought it was just another haunted memory of things lost, nothing more," said Warrick. "But to hear you speak that you dreamt ..."

Elson interrupted; "Don't think too much of it, for what things have ever come to pass that matched our visions?"

"Let's keep walking, it's getting late," said Justin.

The three men moved forward again, walking more swiftly now as the light along the path grew dim and they were barely halfway back to the village. Their walking sticks drummed firmly into the hard, well-traveled path. Their long brown coats swayed back and forth as the cold air nipped at their exposed skin.

Suddenly Warrick stopped and stared at two trees on opposite sides of the path. There was nothing unusual to note about them, except perhaps that they were very straight and thin and stood relatively close to each edge of the path. "We can't give up," he said, more to himself than anyone. "Promises have been made."

Elson prodded his friends and they began once more along the path. In spite of their delays, they arrived at the village in time to start the fire as the last bit of sunlight disappeared.

*   *   *   *   *   *   *   *   *   *   *   *

Justin did not sleep well that night. His mind was not full of pleasant visions of Mount Rigid; in their place were familiar images that brought him dread, scenes that had taken place long ago...

In his dream, Justin awakes to shouting outside his island home. He sits up in bed and sees flashes of white light through the window. He gets out of bed, throws on the clothes he had worn the previous day that are lying on the floor, and rushes outside, leaving his wife, Evelyn, inside and alone.

Two large men, each holding a long whip, are shouting at the people and herding them away from the village. He can't understand what the two are yelling amid the screams of the islanders. He looks to his left, behind his house, where he had seen the flashes of light, and begins to walk in that direction. Loud cracks erupt, and as he gets closer he sees more large figures brandishing whips, hammers, rods, and blades of all kinds, driving the islanders away, and is forced to return to the village.

One of the men notices Justin and approaches him with swift, long strides. Justin is frozen in fear. The giant reaches out a long arm and grabs Justin's shoulder, lifting him off the ground. "You, especially you, must leave! NOW!" With little effort he throws Justin into the air.

The village becomes smaller, his house falls out of sight, and the very land beneath him slips away. The shouts and cries of his fellow islanders become faint and finally silent as he plunges into dark water...

The sensation of being submerged caused Justin to wake, covered in sweat and his heart pounding. He sat up, reached to his bedside table, opened a drawer, and pulled out a small cloth, mostly white but red stains of a past injury could still be detected, and wiped his forehead and the back of his neck. He got up, dressed, and went outside to discover that the sun was beginning to rise.

Warrick and Elson often had similar dreams, but they weren't as intense, for their guilt was not as great as his. They all had different methods of recovering from the nightmares: Elson liked to work with his hands on projects around his house; playing music is what soothed Warrick; interacting with others helped Justin. His wife was always willing to sacrifice some sleep to comfort her husband, but Justin didn't like to disrupt her sleep, and unless the dream had been so awful that he was in sheer mental anguish, he wouldn't wake her. Instead, he would venture outside and wander around, looking for anyone to talk with. If nobody was found, the motion of walking was effective in distracting his thoughts from the awful images. Tonight's dream wasn't so bad and he had gone outside without waking his wife.

He walked aimlessly and tried to fill his head with joyful memories. He thought of his wife and how much he loved her and she him. But this made him sad when he considered that the time they had been together was filled with more hardship than happiness.

Sooner or later, when Justin searched for fond memories, thoughts of the island came to him. So many years had gone by since he had been there that he'd given up hope of ever seeing it again. He made his way back to his house and retrieved a scroll kept beside his table and went outside to read it. He unraveled it carefully and let his eyes revel in the text as if they gazed upon the isle itself...

<u>The Island</u>

A description of what we once knew, written so that we will never forget

The island was the most magnificent place. The land was nurtured by heavy morning dew and gentle afternoon sunshine – it was always sunny and warm. A slight breeze flowed occasionally across the island, but the wind never blew violently against the shores, and never did a dreary rain fall.

The island was located in the narrowest section of the great sea that separated the vast countries of Marland to the north and Tilden to the south. Islanders traveled often to Marland to gather lumber, stones, and any other needed building supplies; Corliss Lake, as this channel between the island and Marland became known, was calm and easy to cross with any kind of vessel. The southern channel was also easy to cross, but due to the island's rugged southern mountains, most traffic to a mainland occurred between the northern island port and Marland.

Except for the southern mountains, the landscape of the island was tame; rolling hills and broad fields of soft, rich grasses covered most of the isle. In these open areas many gardens had been planted, tended by the servants of the Island Caretaker. The soil continually produced food, and there was no need to toil excessively in the summer to store provisions away for winter. Weeds were never seen in any of the gardens, and it was not known whether they could grow on the island or if the Caretaker's servants plucked them all, so meticulous were they in their care for the gardens. A few dense forests were scattered about; their tall trees bore many kinds of delicious and unique fruit. Walking through the forests was pleasant; there were no harmful obstructions, such as thick underbrush with thorns and barbs to rip skin and cloth. Streams of icy water flowed steadily from their origin in the high mountains down to the bays of the island, their water clean and clear as glass.

The island was teeming with wildlife. Colorful birds of song and swift birds of strength flew overhead. The surrounding sea seemed to quiver, it was so full of underwater life. In the forests dwelt creatures of all sizes, and in every field multiple herds and flocks grazed freely.

Spectacular though they were, climate, landscape, and wildlife were not what made the island special. It was the nature of the island life that made it magnificent: all living things were at peace. The underwater creatures swam as friends of the sea. The gentle animals grazing in the fields had no need to watch for predators lurking at the edge of the woods, for the woodland animals prowled around, preying not on the weaker animals, but on the plentiful crops of berries and fruits. Surviving wasn't only for those that were strong; survival was what all island life knew.

The islanders weren't exempt from this; they were all full of genuine respect and care for one another. Consistently joyful, they knew only pleasure and peace, but by no means were they to be considered lazy. Certain times of the year were set aside for relaxation, but mostly they were busy building projects to enhance the quality of the island. The youth spent their nearly inexhaustible energy playing in the mountains, forests, and sea, often engaging with the wildlife. And everyone enjoyed an adventure once in a while, for the isle possessed a great many wonderful and hidden things.

The fruits of the land were delicious, but some offered more than nutrients and pleasant flavor. Some varieties afforded a tremendous, though temporary, physical enhancement to those who ate them. Among the islanders' favorites were the renden that grew in a large orchard near the southern mountains. Once the tough purple skin had been peeled away, the fleshy inside provided unnatural strength to its consumer. Yallup were another favorite - tiny brown beans, speckled with white, provided a prolonged rush of energy.

Every year during the first week of August, the Island Tournament was held in celebration of the Fruits of Ability. Some contests of the tournament were simple enough and a few competitors who possessed significant natural talent preferred to compete in them without the aid of the fruit. Thirling, a contest which measured accuracy and strength in throwing hatchets and axes, and The Archerion, a contest of bow and arrow, were such contests. Puttining, a distance throwing contest, and The Runrining, a race around the island, could be done without enhancement, but no one competed in these without the fruit, for they would not be competitive. But some events were extraordinary, impossible to perform without the aid of the special fruits. The Launtrining was such a contest: one person would stand at the end of a thick plank, its center hinged to a round steel bar, while their teammate slammed down their end of the plank, throwing the other into the air over Corliss Lake. Tremendous altitudes were reached - the highest launch was deemed to be over five hundred feet.

Another contest that required the use of the fruit, held in the lake itself, was Wavelling. Contestants used a variety of methods to propel themselves from the bottom of the lake through the water's surface and into the air as high as they could. This contest allowed for the consumption of two varieties of fruit: one fruit of choice and meer, ruby red berries that were necessary for prolonged underwater activity.

The Ascentining was a race up the sheer face of the cliff on the south side of Mount Manor, whose base formed the coastline with the South Sea. The last of the eight events was the Luggerrun. Prior to the commencement of the tournament a number of logs were prepared on the coast of Marland. The objective was to bring them across Corliss Lake as fast as possible and deposit them at the island's north port. The

Luggerrun was not performed during the first few years of the tournament, but was added when the islanders decided to bring necessary building material to the island in a more exciting fashion.

People participated in these activities throughout the year as much or as little as they pleased, but the beginning of August was the only time when the entire island set aside everything to partake in them collectively in the formal setting of a tournament. It was a rule that no person younger than thirteen could compete, and so reaching the age of thirteen was something that all of the island children looked forward to with great anticipation.

When the tournament was finished, the islanders enjoyed a period of calm, spending the following weeks in playful relaxation. They reflected on the past and planned for the future, but most of all they enjoyed the present. They embraced the island by walking its beaches, climbing its trees, swimming in its streams and bays, climbing its mountains, reclining in its grassy fields, and enjoying the company of their neighbors. They were thankful and content and lacked nothing that was good.

It wasn't by chance that the islanders had such cheerful dispositions. Three rivers, their colors yellow, blue, and white, flowed across the island. The Rivers of Power, as the islanders called them, were not like the rivers of clear water that flowed down from Mount Manor; each of these affected the natural tendencies of the island life. Like the Fruits of Ability, each river benefited those who partook of them, but unlike the skills afforded by the fruits, the enhancements were permanent. The blue river, Azor, and the yellow river, Candra, flowed openly across the island and the people had full access to their waters. To drink from the Candra resulted in one obtaining a desire for peace, while drinking from the Azor allowed one to experience life's joys in fullest measure.

The most powerful of the three rivers was the white Icyandic, which prevented death from conquering any living thing of the island. Yet, although it flowed close to Epidomon, the island's main village, the Icyandic was the one island river from which the people did not drink. Nor could they feel its gentle currents - it flowed beneath a thick layer of glass, unbreakable by any means of the islanders.

The affect of the Icyandic was most dramatically observed during the island games when an unfortunate competitor, such as a Launtriner or an Ascentiner, fell from a great height to the ground instead of into the soft waves of Corliss Lake or the South Sea as intended. Their bodies would break, but after a few moments, they would recover, being reassembled if necessary, by the power of the white river. Spectators who observed such tragedies were not heard wailing and moaning sorrowfully; instead, they cheered wildly for the most impressive displays of destruction and dismemberment. Mock trophies were even awarded to those whose crashes and recoveries most spectacularly demonstrated the mighty healing power of the Icyandic.

And all of the islanders knew of the time when the rivers were called from deep springs to the surface of the isle from the annual telling of the Legend of the Island Caretaker, recited by the island servants.

In addition to caring for the gardens and telling the legend, the servants of the Island Caretaker tended all of the natural features of the island. They walked through the gardens and forests to prune the trees and plants and observe the quality of their fruit. They ventured into the mountains to perform a census of the wildlife. They dove into the sea to measure its depth and observe the great fishes.

The servants were constantly busy, but were always patient and friendly, well liked by all. One of the first projects that the islanders undertook was to build a great mansion for them, constructed near the Icyandic, to show great appreciation for their care of the island. The servants, however, did not require shelter and they preferred sleeping outside under the starry sky, which was their custom. In the end though, they accepted the gift of the mansion for the islanders' sake, some say at the request of the Caretaker.

There were many servants; wherever the people went they were likely to cross the path of at least a dozen of them. Most stayed on the island for only a short time before they were called away by their master to tasks elsewhere.

Two servants, however, were permanent residents of the isle, Durwin and Baldwin. They enjoyed being among the island folk and were never seen without jolly smiles on their shining faces. They were always together, were very similar in personality and build, and many of the islanders were convinced that they were twins, but Durwin and Baldwin said they weren't related. The islanders knew them well, but found it necessary to inspect them closely in order to determine which was which. None of the servants ever divulged their tasks to the islanders, not even Durwin and Baldwin. Most of their responsibilities were obvious enough, but the people surmised that one of the regular duties of the twins, as they were called, was to report back to their master and inform him of all things happening on the island.

The Caretaker himself did not live on the island, even though he treasured his friendship with the people there. When people first came there he visited them often. He enjoyed their company and walked with them across the island and revealed to them some of its secrets.

The Caretaker required much from his servants. He asked only one thing of us.

Justin stopped reading there, as he always did, rolled up the scroll and wiped a tear from his eye.

chapter two: ·the highest dive·

Previously,
Iman's Isle, June of year 272...

Two hundred seventy two years had passed since the first islanders arrived on the island. Justin was nineteen, newly married, and in love with his wife, Evelyn. Warrick was also married and he and his wife, Tanya, had a single child, a four-year old daughter, Lucy. It was common for the islanders to marry before reaching age twenty, and the marriages were arranged by the parents of the couple: a firm tradition of betrothing had been established. Elson was not yet married, nor betrothed, and spent most of his time searching for adventure with his two best friends, but today he preferred to sleep, although he found it difficult to ignore the sounds coming from outside.

Early morning work was underway in the front yard of the Verrill house. Two hammers thudded into handles of sharp carving tools, dropping wood shavings onto the soft grass that had been scythed the day before by Elson's father. Two twelve year old boys were patiently carving large slabs of wood on makeshift tables.

"This is the best one," declared Conroy Verrill, Elson's younger brother. Conroy didn't look like Elson; he had hair the color of sand and bright blue eyes. Conroy took a break from carving to admire his work.

Keelan Tilman, Conroy's best friend, tall and lanky with black hair, inspected Conroy's sign. "Nice, but I like the Launtrining one best."

The door of the house opened and Conroy's father came outside. Ansen Verrill was of medium height and average build, and had lively blue eyes that matched Conroy's. He finished eating a piece of fruit and tossed the core into a clump of nearby trees where some deer were grazing. "Looking good, boys." Ansen came over to make a closer observation. "How many have you finished?"

"This one's about done, which will make five," answered Keelan.

"Six, this one's almost done too," added Conroy.

"Good!" said Mr. Verrill firmly. "Would you like to put some up this afternoon?"

"What do you mean?" asked Conroy. Neither he nor Keelan understood why Mr. Verrill seemed so pleased with their progress; he'd never talked about hanging them up before.

"I've got some news for you," Mr. Verrill revealed his secret; "Wendel Wright paid a visit last week and I showed him the signs. You might recall that Wendel is a leading member of the Island Council. He was quite impressed and made a recommendation to the Council to hang them permanently as an island project."

Mr. Verrill paused for the boys' reactions. Having a project selected for permanent installation was an honor. Projects that were considered had to be recommended to the Council by a member, who must demonstrate its ability to enhance the quality of island life, and approval came only from a unanimous Council vote.

"Really!" exclaimed Keelan, staring hard at Mr. Verrill.

"Are you teasing?" asked Conroy.

"No, I'm not, and the Council wants to put them up right away - the tournament is in less than a month."

"Can we start today? Can we hang these?" Keelan pointed toward the stack of finished signs in the nearby shed.

"I'll go and make arrangements. You two finish the signs you're working on."

The boys couldn't see the smile on Ansen's face as he began to walk into town, but it was there, and joyful pride filled him as he thought about Conroy. He had watched Conroy create many wonderful wooden crafts since teaching him the basic techniques of woodcarving. Their house was full of many of these creations. He had often thought that the Island Council might one day recognize his son for his skill, but he didn't think recognition would come this soon, before he turned thirteen, before he participated in his first tournament.

Meanwhile, the boys continued to work. "Do you think we're the youngest people to have a project selected by the Council?" asked Conroy.

"What about Idris? You know, he designed the bridge that spans Corliss Lake."

"Of course I know." Conroy sounded insulted. The bridge was one of the most celebrated island projects, and everyone knew that it had been Idris Wincrest who had thought of it. "No, the bridge was installed just last year and Idris is the same age as Elson. We're definitely younger than he was."

Each sign was unique, fashioned to symbolize its respective event. Conroy inspected the Wavelling sign he was working on; the black letters were thick and wavy, symbolizing how writing would look underwater if viewed from above the surface. A variety of sea creatures were intricately etched into the aqua colored background. The Launtrining sign, Keelan's favorite, had tall and thin letters; 'l-a-u-n-t-r' ascended from left to right, while the letters 'i-n-i-n-g', descended back down, forming a gentle arch. A thick, horizontal, dark blue line was placed below the letters and the bottom part of 'g' dipped below the line. The intent was to symbolize a launched contestant flying high into the air, then falling down into the lake. On the top of the sign were carved some white clouds and the sun above them, and in the space between the blue line and the ascending and descending letters was carved the launtrining apparatus.

"Are we going to practice today?" asked Keelan. The two boys, besides making the signs, had done little else for the last few months but train for the tournament.

"I'd rather put up the signs," answered Conroy, uncertain if Keelan would be willing to let a day pass without practicing for at least one of the contests.

"Yeah, alright. Maybe it won't take too long and we can practice later." Keelan returned his paints, brushes, and carving tools to the shed, then Conroy helped him carry the heavy, but now complete, Thirling sign and place it next to the other five finished signs.

"Did you ask Allison to be on our team yet?"

Conroy twinged. "No, I ... uh, haven't had a chance yet." Even as the words came out of his mouth, he remembered how he had seen Allison the night before and had a perfect opportunity to ask her, but he'd been too shy. "I think she might already be on another team. I heard my brother say that her sister asked her to be on her team."

"We've got to find a couple of more teammates; maybe we can ask the Pantison brothers?" suggested Keelan.

"No, don't ask them yet. I'll ask Allison first."

Keelan looked doubtfully at Conroy and prepared to scold him for procrastinating, but before he could a voice called out loudly; "Conroy! Keelan!"

Durwin and Baldwin, two island servants, were walking toward the boys. Durwin had called out to Conroy, and Baldwin to Keelan. In their usual fashion they took turns speaking.

"We just spoke with your dad, Conroy. Great news about the signs!" said Durwin.

"He asked if we'd help install them," added Baldwin.

"It turns out that we do, in fact, have time to spare this morning," said Durwin.

"We're glad to help," said Baldwin. "Your father instructed us to get the signs for the Archerion and Thirling and meet him near Hettered Forest."

Conroy was delighted at the arrival of the twins, not so much for their willingness to help with the signs, but because the subject of him not yet asking Allison to join the team was dropped, at least for now. Keelan went back to the shed and attempted to pick up one of the signs. His thin frame tensed as he started to wrestle with it.

"No, no, we'll carry them," insisted Durwin.

Each of the twins grabbed a sign and lifted it with ease. All of the Caretaker's servants were renowned for their strength.

"We're also supposed to bring nails and a mallet," said Baldwin. "You two can carry those."

Keelan found the pouch of nails and slung it over his shoulder in an attempt to mimic the twins. Conroy chuckled and followed suit by doing the same with the large hammer. And so the four of them began to walk toward the center of town, each carrying a burden on their shoulder.

They had only gone about a half mile when they came into sight of a couple lounging in a clearing. The fine-featured young man called out to them with a strong voice; "What have you got there?" Idris got up and came to investigate, leaving the girl with nothing to wrap her arms around.

They stopped and explained what they were doing. Idris took a peek at the signs and said, "My plaque has lost its value, even so, congratulations. I'll be anxious to see all of them." He wished them well and resumed his place next to the girl, who immediately returned her arms around him.

The route to Hettered Forest ran west through a short section of the central town, Epidomon, before turning northwest and running across a few hundred yards of fields. People in the street watched and cheered as they passed - it seemed that everyone knew what they were doing, a possibility since Ansen Verrill had passed through only a short time before. The boys were thrilled at the applause, but when Conroy heard a familiar voice say, "Nice signs! Can I come with you?" his heartbeat quickened.

A girl with brown hair in a ponytail that descended to the middle of her back came bounding across the street. Conroy turned around quickly to face Allison, nearly striking Keelan in the head with the heavy end of the mallet.

"Sure." Conroy tried not to sound too excited.

Allison glanced back across the street to a swarm of her friends and beckoned them to follow.

The twins, Keelan, Conroy, and now Allison, proceeded to leave the main street of Epidomon to follow a neatly kept path that ran through several grassy fields to Hettered Forest. About ten yards behind them followed the group of kids that Allison had invited, and behind them came some adults from the village. Mr. Verrill and a short, bushy haired man were part of this last group.   Keelan glanced back to see the large procession and realized that the raising of the first sign would be a well-attended event.

Conversation between the three youth flowed smoothly, mostly due to cheerful and lively Allison. Conroy knew that he couldn't let this opportunity slip by, but he needed to wait for the right moment, and currently Allison was inquiring about the signs; "Why did you want to make them?" she asked.

"It gave us something to do this summer. My father showed me how to do it and gave me some tools when I was pretty young. I like making something out of a block of wood; it makes me feel good to make things beautiful. Maybe that sounds strange, my brother, Elson, is always teasing me about it." Conroy shrugged as he finished his awkward response.

"He just wishes he could do it half as good as you," said Keelan. "Conroy has all the talent, I just did some of the easy stuff, but I *can* take credit for the idea. At the beginning of the summer I was so excited about being able to finally compete in the tournament that I was going crazy. All I did was practice. One day I wanted to practice launtrining and I set up a makeshift launch device. I put a big rock on a plank and launched it, but it went straight up and crashed through the roof of my house."

Allison's eyes and mouth opened wide. Conroy smiled and nodded to confirm Keelan's tale.

Keelan continued; "My mother came running outside, yelling that if I did anything like that again she was going to make me live at the top of Mt. Manor until the tournament."

Conroy and Allison laughed as Keelan caught his breath. "Lucky for me, the next day was when Conroy and I decided to make the signs. I went to Conroy's house and found him outside etching something into some wood. Seeing Conroy carve wood was hardly unusual, but when I saw that he was drawing people launtrining, I got the idea for the signs. Conroy thought it was a great idea so we started right away. Working on the signs has been fun, and I was even able to stay home for the summer after all."

Conroy felt more comfortable around Allison and leaned in close to her and whispered, "His mother really would have sent him to the top of Mt. Manor, you know."

Allison giggled. "My sister says that you two are the youngest people ever to have a project selected by the Island Council."

"Maybe," said Conroy, "Are you going to be on your sister's team?"

"She wants me to be on her team, but..." she paused, unsure how to answer.

Conroy didn't know what to think of her incomplete response but carried forward with his invitation; "We need two more people. If you want, you could join our team." He felt a sense of relief to finally unload the question. He felt even better after hearing her response.

"Can I really?" she said gleefully, then composed herself and said, seriously, "You need *two* people, can I ask Megan to join too?"

Neither Keelan nor Conroy was surprised at the mention of Megan Prendt. Allison and Megan had been best friends since they were born and were hardly ever apart from each other.

"Yeah, maybe," said Conroy.

Keelan wasn't as eager. "What's she good at?" he asked bluntly. Keelan was team captain, in charge of deciding which person would participate in each event. He was determined to have a good team, even a team capable of contending for the championship. Winning was unlikely considering that they would be competing against teams with years of experience. One such team was the one that Elson was on – his team had won the last three years.

"She's really good at the Archerion," answered Allison, sensing Keelan's desire to fill the roster with only quality competitors. She could see that he needed further convincing and so she expanded on Megan's skills; "I've seen her hit the center mark six times in a row, and usually seven out of ten tries. I know she wants to do well. This is her first tournament, well it's going to be the first for all of us, and she's been practicing a lot."

This impressed Keelan. He was planning on participating in the Archerion himself, but he typically hit the center only three out of ten tries.

Conroy knew that Keelan would question Allison about her own skills next, and knowing that Keenan could be a bit too forward, especially when it came to the tournament, he posed the question to her as gently as he could so that she wouldn't be uncomfortable; "What game is your favorite?" A quick glance at Keelan revealed that he had indeed been preparing to query Allison.

"The Launtrining," she answered immediately. "Do you think I could be part of a launch team? I don't want to be the launcher though, I want to be the person who gets launched."

Conroy looked at Keelan and saw that he was pleased. "The spot is all yours," answered Keelan. It was one of the positions that had yet to be filled, not because no one else wanted to do it, for it was tremendous fun, but because Keelan had strategically assigned the others to different events where their skills would be most utilized to benefit the team. So, in spite of not practicing that afternoon, Keelan was delighted with the development of his team: the two needed players were secured; the vacant Launtrining position was filled; and they improved their potential to do well in the Archerion. Every teammate is required to compete in two contests, Keelan knew, and he'd have to find where else to use the girls, but he didn't have a chance to press Allison on the matter – the twins stepped off the path, walked into the field and stopped.

The boys and Allison followed, then the rest of the people began arriving in clusters. They were about fifty yards from the edge of Hettered Forest; this was where the Archerion was held. Two long poles, each about eight inches in diameter, sanded smooth and sealed with a dark stain, lay on the ground beside two holes.

Durwin and Baldwin put down the signs, placing them gently on the ground out of the way. Then they each grabbed one end the first pole and lifted it up.

"Wait!" cried someone from the back of the crowd. It was the short, bushy haired man who had come with Ansen Verrill. He scurried across the short stretch of field that remained between him and the twins. "The Council must see this done - you know of our traditions: it is the strict policy of the Council to have at least one member present at all times during island project construction." Wendel Wright came to a halt between the two island servants as he finished scolding them.

"We were just getting ready," explained Baldwin.

"Shall we begin now?" asked Durwin.

"No. Not yet."

The twins continued to bear the weight of the post; it didn't take much effort from them, while Wendel turned to address the crowd; "Thank you all for coming. It is my great pleasure, on behalf of the Island Council, to recognize Conroy Verrill and Keelan Tilman for their design and creation of these magnificent signs for the island games. Their craftsmanship and artistry are spectacular. Let us commend them for their contribution to this island tradition."

The crowd erupted as Wendel presented the boys with awards: wooden plaques, each with a silver hammer and a silver rod, and on the bottom the words "Signs of the Island Games" were etched, along with the boys' names and the date.

Conroy and Keelan were overwhelmed by the unexpected praise. It had only been a few hours before when they learned that the Council had chosen their signs for installation. Now they were being honored by a large group of islanders for their work. Neither of them had ever received this much recognition in their lives.

Wendel continued; "One thing more must I say before our beloved friends begin," he glanced at Durwin and Baldwin standing by patiently, still holding the post. "Conroy, Keelan, it is the Council's wish to grant you another token of recognition. You are the youngest people to ever have a project selected. As such, please accept these."

The crowd cheered again as Wendel presented them with new awards; gold plates decorated with four jewels, one at each quadrant, and in the center were engraved their names and ages below the words `Youngest Island Designer`. A few murmurs could be heard from the crowd about how Idris Wincrest had been the previous holder of the title.

"Now, let the work begin!" shouted Wendel. With nothing else to say, he patted the boys on the back and nodded for Baldwin and Durwin to start.

The twins went quickly to work. Baldwin placed his end of the post into one of the holes and Durwin stood it up straight, then grabbed the hammer and nimbly climbed onto Baldwin's shoulders, where he stood with amazing balance and prepared to strike the top of the post.

"Don't hit it too hard and bring up another river!" cried a burly, rugged man at the front of the crowd.

"No need to worry about that, Lachlan!" replied Baldwin.

"There'll be no more rivers on this isle," added Durwin, and with a single blow he smashed the head of the mallet into the post, driving it several inches into the ground. Just two more blows and the post sank down nearly thirty inches. Using the same method, they erected the second post, then hung the Archerion sign.

"It looks a little bland, don't you think?" said Allison, coming up to the twins with Megan Prendt at her side. Megan was slightly shorter than her and wore a navy blue ribbon in her straight, blonde hair.

"Yes, young lady, it does" said Wendel, "but we're not done yet." He addressed the crowd again; "Folks, we could use your help. If you wouldn't mind, the Council has prepared a number of flowers and shrubs to decorate our new sign. Please look toward the forest, see where Ansen Verrill is standing, you'll see them. Could you please bring them here and help us plant them."

Ansen had slipped away and pulled from the forest about a dozen plants that had obviously been placed there in anticipation of being needed. With a large number of volunteers, the task of planting them was soon complete and the Archerion sign was transformed into a decorative monument.

*   *   *   *   *   *   *   *   *   *   *

The spot chosen for the Wavelling sign was unique in that it was located on the water rather than on the island. A float had been constructed by the Island Council and anchored to the bottom of Corliss Lake. The islanders rowed two dozen boats across the gentle waves and secured the sign to the float.

Wendel, who took it upon himself to represent council oversight for all of the installations, adjourned the ceremony; "Thank you, friends, for coming here today. Let's commend our young craftsmen once more for their contribution." The people applauded Conroy and Keelan before departing. By now the boys had gotten used to the attention and fanfare, and they smiled and waved to acknowledge the disappearing crowd as they returned to shore. "They have two signs yet to complete," called Wendel, "and we'll be anxiously waiting for them. Good day everyone!"

Conroy, Keelan, and the rest of their team, which by team vote now included Allison and Megan, pulled their boats onto land and prepared to practice Wavelling, or *Reverse Diving*, a term that some of the younger islanders had begun to call the activity.

"Oh no!" exclaimed Conroy. His teammates looked up to see food and towels strewn about the ground where he stood with his empty bag upside down and wide open, but the package of meer that he was supposed to bring wasn't there. "I forgot the meer! Does anyone have some?" He looked desperately to Keelan, who seemed unusually calm, thought Conroy, considering they wouldn't be able to practice without the fruit.

Keelan let Conroy look through his empty sack once more, then walked over to him and said quietly so that only Conroy could hear,

"I thought you might forget - distracted by Allison a little?" He held out a cluster of scarlet berries.

Conroy took the meer. "Thanks," he said, embarrassed but grateful, then passed around the berries.

"We've never used these before," said Megan, referring to herself and Allison.

This didn't upset Keelan since he planned on having these two girls compete in other events, and he kindly explained their function; "A few berries will allow you to be underwater for about two hours. But beware, when you go under it takes a few seconds for your body to adjust, and you won't be able to talk."

Megan and Allison nodded, and everyone tossed a few meer in their mouths.

"Strength or speed? Strength or speed?" asked Conroy as he presented renden and yallup to his friends, having retrieved the fruit from the ground where he had dumped out his pack. Each of them took either a few yallup or a chunk of a peeled renden, except for a tall, blonde boy who selected both.

"What're you doing, Brant?" asked Conroy.

"Strength *and* speed for me!"

"Both aren't allowed," challenged Keelan.

"Aren't allowed during competition, you mean," said Brant, "this is just practice. And come on, everyone knows that Derek and Mahrlee are going to be competing in this, not me. There's no need for me to practice like it was the real thing."

Derek, a muscular boy with curly brown hair, and Mahrlee, a black haired girl with a perfect smile and a sharp, thin nose, looked at Keelan, but neither spoke.

Keelan sighed and shook his head gently, but didn't press the matter further – he had already decided that Derek and Mahrlee would be the ones competing.

"Relax. If you need me to compete, I won't let you down, trust me." Brant tossed the handful of yallup into his mouth and then quickly took a huge bite of the southern grown rendan. With his mouth stuffed, he attempted to smile, but his cheeks were so full that he could hardly close his lips and his contorted face was so ridiculous that everyone laughed, even Keelan.

"Fine," consented Keelan, only slightly frustrated. "Let's go!"

Everyone else ate whatever food they had selected, ran to the water, and dove in. Megan and Allison resurfaced instinctively after several seconds. The rest of the team, experienced with using meer, remained below the surface and waited for them to make another attempt to join them. Megan and Allison dove back underwater and spotted Conroy beckoning them deeper. They started to go to him, but turned back as their air supply diminished.

Knowing that their instincts would cause them to resurface, Keelan swam up and grabbed hold of Megan, wrapping his arms around her from behind. Conroy grabbed Allison in the same manner, pinning her arms to her sides. Both Allison and Megan had eaten yallup, while Conroy and Keelan had eaten renden, and the girls were unable to free themselves from the boys' strong grips. The girls flailed their legs and hands (as much as they could while the boys held their arms), making the water around the struggling pairs swirl and churn furiously. They couldn't hold their breath any longer; their reflexes made them exhale and draw in a new breath. To their amazement, and relief, they found that they could breathe, but not in the normal fashion. Their lungs were dormant, and speech was impossible, but oxygen was being delivered to their muscles somehow. The girls smiled.

Sensing the girls relax, Keelan and Conroy released them and led them further out and down to the bottom of the lake where several concrete platforms came into sight. Each platform was square, about four feet long on each side. Keelan, Conroy, and Brant swam straight to the platforms and prepared for their first dive. Each stood in the center of a platform and, at a wave from Keelan, jumped simultaneously. Tremendous waves moved through water, rocking the onlookers as they watched the three wavellers explode upward. Two of the figures were streaking through the water holding a fixed position, as straight as could be with their arms up over their head, pointing to the surface.

The motion of the third was quite different and his speed was much faster than the others: Brant had launched upward with the same super strength as Keelan and Conroy, but his legs were kicking and his hands were moving back and forth so fast that they were only a blur. He reached the surface a few seconds before Conroy and Keelan, and the spectators watched from below as he vanished into the air.

Keelan and Conroy approached the surface moments after, but before they flew from the water, each cupped their hands and pushed down hard to throw themselves up as high as they could.

All three came plunging back into the lake at about the same time and they swam back to the platform area, grinning at the others. Brant's smile was largest and he kept trying to gesture how incredible his reverse dive had been. His jerky movements were not exceptional means of communicating, but everyone understood what he was trying to convey.

Some of those who had watched the first series of dives moved into position on the platforms to have their turn. And so Wavelling practice was underway. Megan and Allison's first few attempts were not very high, but their skills were quickly improving and they were both enjoying themselves. Some, having eaten renden, launched from the platforms with tremendous strength, while others, having eaten yallup, swam from them, propelling themselves with rapidly moving limbs. Both techniques were effective; some of them reached elevations over a hundred feet above the lake. By far, the two best wavellers on the team were Derek and Mahrlee. The height of their dives surpassed even Brant's, and the grace by which they traveled through water and air was fascinating.

After about thirty minutes of wavelling, some sea creatures came into the area to get a closer look. One curious fish was a large Mako shark. The friendly beast was like a missile gliding through the water, swimming about halfway between the lake floor and the surface. As it swam the sunlight shown on its tensing muscles, revealing the source for its incredible power.

Another underwater animal that had come to observe wavelling was an Orca. The black and white colors of the whale contrasted so beautifully in the glassy water that all of the people became enthralled and paused from diving to stare at it as it circled above them and below the shark.

Conroy caught Allison's attention and motioned for her to follow him upward. She followed him a short distance and then saw him gesture again, this time pointing to himself and then to the shark, then at Allison and next to the whale. Allison understood: sometimes wavellers used the aid of the powerful undersea creatures - this was Conroy's intention.

Conroy swam up higher to a spot that would intersect the shark's path if it remained on course. The shark, three times as long as Conroy was tall, veered only a little when it swam past him. He lunged at the fish, reached out his hand, and grabbed one of its pectoral fins and held on tight. The Mako didn't appear to be disturbed by its passenger, and it continued to swim around the platforms to watch the wavellers, who had resumed practicing. Conroy swung himself below the shark and grabbed the other fin so that he held one in each hand, his front side pressed against the shark's belly. In this position, he discovered that he could manipulate the shark's swimming by moving the fins, and by squeezing them he could make it swim even faster. But its skin was rough, and if he gripped the fins too firmly it cut his hands.

Allison saw that Conroy had succeeded and prepared to do the same with the Orca. She positioned herself in front of the whale and prepared to grab hold of it when it came near. As the whale approached, Allison was amazed at its size and beauty and she desperately wanted to swim with it. She had never been so close to such a large animal before. The top half of the beast was as black as the darkest night, while the lower portion of the whale was as white as the purest snow. But her first and second attempts to grab hold failed; unlike the shark, the whale had skin so slick that its fin slipped easily out of her grasp. On the third attempt she decided to try a different technique; she straddled the large dorsal fin with her legs and wrapped her arms around it as far as she could. It worked! The dorsal fin caught her and she was able to lie with her stomach against the whale's back, her arms pressed into its sides firmly enough to hold her in place. Just like the shark, the whale didn't seem to be influenced by Allison's presence. "How magnificent a creature!" she thought.

Having mastered control of the shark, Conroy directed it to swim swiftly around and come beside Allison and the Orca. She glanced at Conroy to see him suspended under the fish's belly, gesturing to show her how he was able to maneuver. Allison understood what he was doing, however, she was unable to reposition herself on the whale, so she decided to remain as she was and ride it wherever it wanted to go.

As Conroy swam alongside Allison and the whale, he noticed something zooming toward her. Brant, wanting to participate in the interaction with these two spectacular sea giants, had launched himself directly at the whale. Allison could not see Brant since her hair drifted into her face and covered her eyes when she turned her head to look at Conroy, and she wasn't willing to move to clear it away for fear of falling off, but the whale noticed him and was able to move forward and avoid the reckless youngster with a single stroke of its mighty tail. Allison used the rush of water to move her hair out of her face while strengthening her grip on the whale's sides. The whale, naturally playful, became enthusiastic after dodging Brant, and Allison found herself focusing on holding on rather than on enjoying a leisurely ride.

Brant went sailing past them at full speed with his legs kicking and hands twirling, now headed for Conroy and the Mako. But Conroy had time to react and maneuvered the shark into a rapid dive to easily escape a collision with Brant.

Conroy and the Mako recovered from their descent and pulled up beside Allison and the Orca again. He indicated that he was going to make an attempt at a dive and Allison nodded that she understood as she watched them swim away.

The whale became even more excited after seeing the shark pull swiftly away, and it began to circle the diving area quickly; its tail moved repeatedly up and down as its massive muscles flexed. Allison repositioned her hands for a better grip, and when she did some yallup residue rubbed off her fingers and entered the Orca's mouth and eyes.

Meanwhile, Conroy gave the shark's fins a good squeeze and pulled back. Spectators below watched the Mako shoot upward with Conroy holding on tight. Shark and human left the water together, but returned separately. The Mako seemed to have had enough of reverse diving and swam away, while Conroy swam back to the diving platforms; his face beamed with excitement as he rejoined his teammates there. Although it had been his highest dive of the day, he noticed that the others weren't paying him much attention; in fact they weren't even looking at him. He didn't understand why until Keelan grabbed him and spun him around to face out into the sea. Then he saw what everyone else was staring at – Allison and the whale.

The Orca was continuing to gain speed. Allison held on as tight as she could as the whale swam down to the bottom and raced past the gawking onlookers. Then it changed course, tilting rapidly upward into a vertical climb. She was barely able to hold on, and kept her face pressed into the whale's black back.

Captivated by Allison and the Orca, the others hadn't noticed Brant's return. None of them saw him until he was zooming upward from one of the platforms again, having launched himself toward Allison and the whale for a second time, still wanting to be a part of their union. He wasn't able to catch them before they breached, but as he rose out of the lake and looked up he caught a unique view of Allison's dive.

She still clung to the Orca, though she wasn't sure whether she should continue to hold on or let go of the animal. When the whale reached the pinnacle of its leap, it arched its back and rolled over, preparing to fall backward into the lake. As it did this, Allison was unable to hold on to the Orca's twisting body and her momentum carried her further upward. Now several inches above the whale, she looked down to see its black top roll away and be replaced by its white belly. But before parting, the whale gently lifted its tail to meet her, and for a split second, she found herself cradled in the Orca's tail, before a single flick sent her shooting up even higher.

She screamed with excitement, her lungs functioning again. Her eyes were wide as she flew higher than any of her teammates had that day. At that high altitude she had time to enjoy the view: she glanced down to see the whale reenter the water; she saw a group of people running down the beach, diving into the water; and then she saw something else.

If she was fast enough there might be a chance, she thought. When she finally fell into the lake, she swam as hard as she could down to the platforms. Her lungs were dormant again, but she knew that she somehow had to communicate what she'd just seen to the others.

Beneath the surface of Corliss Lake, a quarter of a mile to the west of the Wavelling platforms, a low, long, thick cloud formed as the feet of two massive animals pressed deep into the soft floor. Awkward and lumbering on land, they were nimble, even graceful, under water. Two jolly hippos trotted swiftly along the lake bottom, saddled with packs and carrying Durwin and Baldwin atop their rotund backs. Normally these creatures avoided such depths due to their need to surface to breathe, but the twins had fed each of the robust (and ever hungry) animals a handful of island meer, and they had no need to remain in the shallows. Although other means existed for the twins to journey across the lake, this was the preferred method, allowing them greater secrecy than any floating vessel could afford them, even under the cover of night.

Secrecy on this trip would be spoiled. No person on the island saw the twins climb on the backs of the hippos and enter the lake, for the twins took every precaution against that happening. They did not, however, consider a thirteen year old girl reverse diving so high over the lake that she could look down and see them through the crystal clear water.

Her dive with the Orca was far from her mind now; twin servants trotting along on hippos consumed Allison's thoughts. A vortex of swirling water trailed behind her as she sped down to the platforms. Even high in the air, she had recognized the four islanders entering the lake as Conroy's older brother, Elson, and Elson's friends Warrick and Justin, accompanied by Justin's wife, Evelyn. No sooner did she reach the diving area than the newcomers arrived. Elson Verrill, Justin and Evelyn Nickols, and Warrick Spenser had come to practice reverse diving.

Elson swam stealthily up behind his younger brother and grabbed him by his feet, hoping to pull him helplessly backward. But Conroy was still powered by renden and he kicked to free himself from whatever had hold of him, sending Elson violently down into the lake floor.

It took a few moments for Elson to recover, and while he did, all the others doubled over with quiet laughter and clutched their stomachs. Most of them had been victim to Elson's trickery before, and whenever his pranks backfired, though they rarely did, it produced more laughs than his intended foolery would have. Even better, the fact that it was Conroy who foiled Elson's mischief this time was cause for extra intense, albeit silent, laughter. Elson rejoined the crowd, rubbing his sore head, and bowed sarcastically to his friends, glad that he was able to amuse them.

Allison realized that she was letting too much time slip away. She swam into the middle of the group and waved her arms, but when everyone looked at her, she realized that she had no idea how to communicate what she needed to say using only gestures. She pointed upward, then swam to the surface in hope that someone would follow. Conroy, Elson, and Warrick went to join her while the others stayed behind, not sure what was happening and determined to continue wavelling.

With her head out of the water, Allison was free to speak. "I just saw them leave! Only a few minutes ago! I saw them on the bottom of the lake!"

"What are you talking about?" asked Conroy.

"Durwin and Baldwin!" she replied.

This caught the full attention of Elson and Warrick. Long had it been a mystery to know where these two servants ventured and what they did when they left the island.

"I bet they're going to see the Caretaker!" exclaimed Warrick. "Where did you see them?"

"Over there," she said, pointing west. "They were going straight across the lake toward Marland."

"How far away were they?" asked Warrick.

"I don't know, about a mile, I guess. It looked like they were riding on hippos."

"Hippos?" questioned Elson. "Hippos aren't very accommodating to carrying passengers. Are you sure?"

"They were definitely riding on large animals, and it seemed to me that they were hippos," replied Allison, fairly confident of what she had observed.

"It doesn't matter, let's go!" said Warrick. Without hesitation, he dove down into the water to pursue the two servants. With unnatural strength, he launched himself in shallow arcs through the water, pushing himself off of rock formations on the bottom.

Allison and Conroy followed close behind, but Elson returned to the diving area to collect Justin and Evelyn; they would not be pleased to be left out of an adventure.

Although uncertain why Elson was waving frantically at them, Justin and Evelyn consented to follow. The three departed the diving area and swam northwestward.

Keelan and Megan observed that Allison and Conroy had not returned, and they spotted Justin, Elson, and Evelyn swimming away. They looked at each other and pointed toward Marland. Both nodded, then moved as fast as they could to follow, suspecting that by doing so they would find their missing friends.

    *   *   *   *   *   *   *   *   *   *   *   *

Baldwin, Durwin and the two hippos stopped just short of the Marland shore, remaining in water deep enough to keep submerged. In spite of their nature, the two robust beasts waited patiently while the twins removed their gear, then the twins gave each of the hippos a gentle slap to send them back to the island. Immediately, as if a spell had been revoked, a noticeable change occurred to the animals; all patience and docility was replaced with their natural belligerence as they turned to journey home.

Warrick arrived on the scene in time to observe the servants unloading their packs. He took cover behind a rock formation to avoid being seen. Conroy and Allison joined him, and all three had to crouch low behind the rocks to avoid being trampled by the heavy animals as they trotted past.

Unaware that they were being followed, the twins emerged from the water, climbed up the short section of beach that isolated the dense Marland forest from Corliss Lake, and disappeared into the woods.

Just after the twins entered the forest, three wet heads popped out of the water. Warrick, Conroy, and Allison came onto the shore and their lungs filled with air again.

"I don't think they saw us," said Allison excitedly, her hopes high that the mystery of these expeditions would soon be revealed. The sound of water splashing nearby startled her. Elson, Justin, and Evelyn had arrived.

"What's going on?" asked Justin, wanting to know why he just swam the considerable distance between the island and Marland.

"Shhh!" whispered Warrick. "It's Durwin and Baldwin! We followed them across the lake. They went into the woods just a few moments ago. We need to go now or we'll lose them."

Justin and Evelyn smiled. They waded onto the shore and were about to enter the woods when more splashing came from the lake. It was Keelan and Megan. Keelan was about to speak when he observed the entire party on the beach holding fingers against their pursed lips, urging silence. Conroy and Allison beckoned for their two friends to join them. They obeyed. Keelan tried to walk out of the lake as quietly as he could by lifting his feet out of the water and placing them softly back down. His long, lanky body struggled with great effort to maintain balance as he proceeded toward the shore in this fashion. Conroy had to turn away in order to avoid laughing at his friend's ridiculous strategy.

"Is anyone else behind you?" Warrick asked.

"No," answered Keelan. "Why do we need to be quiet?"

"You'll see." Warrick turned and led the group into the woods. Justin and Elson went next, followed by Conroy and Keelan, then Megan and Allison. Evelyn brought up the rear of the group. Each of them stepped carefully to avoid making noise as they walked through the forest along a narrow and winding path, and Conroy and Allison quietly informed Keelan and Megan that they were following the twins.

Exploring Marland was not an unusual thing for the islanders, and the three leaders, as well as Evelyn, were familiar with the trail. About a minute had passed since the twins were last seen, and Warrick led the group as briskly as he could along the path. He knew that if the servants got too far ahead they would likely not be found again; even now he was losing hope of recovering sight of them. The path wound through the trees in a serpentine manner, hindering them from seeing very far ahead, but the terrain was fairly level and the convoy proceeded down the trail at a good pace.

The islanders approached a rare straight section of the trail where it ran through a low, narrow valley, and Warrick was relieved to finally see Durwin and Baldwin in the distance. To the left was a tall rock ledge. Warrick paused when the twins took an abrupt turn and left the path, starting toward the ledge.

Justin and Elson came up beside Warrick. "Where are they going?" asked Elson. "There's nothing there."

At the base of the ledge were two large boulders, broken pieces of the tall rock wall that had come loose and fallen from far above, and between these two rocks the twins disappeared. The curiosity of the three men grew quickly, and they nearly came out into the open to approach the rocks and discover what had become of the two servants. But keeping stealth a priority for a few more moments, they remained where they were and waited for the twins to reappear.

Durwin and Baldwin did not emerge from the rocks.

"What should we do?" Warrick's patience was at an end.

"Maybe they're taking a rest?" suggested Elson.

"Has any of us ever seen an island servant resting at midday?" replied Justin rhetorically. "Maybe they've spotted us - maybe they're hiding behind those boulders, watching us right now to see what we'll do."

"Then we might as well go and find out," said Warrick, anxious to act.

The others caught up to the three leaders as Warrick moved into the open valley. Departing from the trail at the spot where he had seen the twins do the same, Warrick cautiously approached the two boulders at the base of the ledge. He found himself facing a wall of smooth stone: Durwin and Baldwin were nowhere to be seen.

"Why are we leaving the path?" asked Evelyn.

Quickly, Elson explained to the others how he, Justin, and Warrick had seen the twins leave the path and disappear between the very boulders that they now stood between.

Warrick knew that every second that passed meant that they would be less likely to find Durwin and Baldwin. Hope of discovering the secret behind their mainland tasks again dwindled. He touched the rock and began feeling for anything unusual. Then, not out of anger or frustration, but meaning to further inspect the solid wall before him, Warrick clenched his fists and slammed them into the wall. Still empowered by the island renden, Warrick struck with tremendous force. The sound of the blow echoed off the wall, and the others winced and took cover for fear of falling rock from above. No rocks came crashing down, but something did happen: Justin noticed a very thin, straight crack form in the wall just above Warrick's head. Inspection of the crack revealed that it spread horizontally for a few feet and then joined two other cracks, at opposite ends of the first one, running vertically downward.

"Look!" exclaimed Justin, pointing to the cracks. "Warrick, do that again."

Warrick slammed the rock with his hands again. Another loud crash echoed off the rocks and the cracks grew deeper, in fact a large rectangular slab of rock moved backward into the ledge.

"It's a door!" realized Justin excitedly.

"Quick, everyone push!" commanded Warrick. "We need to get this open fast or we'll lose them for sure!"

They all found a place to push against the rock door. Justin and Elson, like Warrick, still possessed unnatural strength, but Conroy and Keelan were no longer under the influence of the island renden. The rock moved slowly as the group struggled against its mass. Conroy, Keelan, Megan, Evelyn, and Allison all stepped back while Elson, Justin, and Warrick continued to move the rock on their own. Finally, after the door had been pushed about a foot and a half into the mountain, it came free and slid into a pocket, creating an opening in the side of the ledge that was easily passable.

Warrick's excitement was renewed and he walked quickly inside, determined to find Durwin and Baldwin. The others proceeded one at a time behind him, keeping their previous sequence unchanged. The passage through the cave was not long, and light from the far side illuminated the interior enough to allow them to see where they were stepping. When they emerged they looked upon land that no islander had ever seen. Had they hesitated a moment longer before passing through the cave they would not have caught sight of the twins again, but as it was, Warrick spotted them disappearing around a distant bend. He motioned to the others and once again the pursuit continued.

The islanders walked for several minutes along a new path, following the twins deeper into Marland. The excitement of the journey faded slightly for Allison and Conroy as they walked along and their thoughts drifted to other things. Allison thought of the girl walking behind her. Evelyn's beauty and adventurous nature had always impressed Allison. She had known Evelyn as far back as she could remember, and she often came to the Krunser household due to the fact that she was a close friend to Allison's older sister, Bethany.

Allison remembered how Evelyn often told of wild experiences she had; they were always incredible, fantastic tales. One story in particular involved an encounter between Evelyn and an unusual creature she met while swimming in Corliss Lake. Evelyn had been hunting for jewels and shells on the lake bottom one summer day. She had gathered a large collection and placed them in a metal basket on the floor of the lake. The gems reflected the sunlight shining down into the clear water, attracting a passing dolphin. It came to inspect the basket and picked it up by taking the handle into its mouth and began to swim away.

Evelyn was determined not to lose her newfound treasures and she pursued the animal. The dolphin was not swimming very fast, weighed down by its purse, but Evelyn could not overtake it and she was about to turn back toward the island when, for no apparent reason, it released the basket and swam away. The heavy basket sank down to the floor and fell into a crevice. Evelyn dove to recover it, but she was unable to grasp the handle before the basket disappeared into darkness.

Disappointed, Evelyn turned to go home, but as she did, she was startled to see an enormous creature in front of her. With six limbs, six digits on each, and covered with fins, scales, and webbing, the creature was between her and the island. Puzzled, but unafraid, she stared at it and offered a friendly wave. Without responding, the creature looked at her for a few moments and then swam away, as if displeased for having met the young girl, and passed by her as it headed toward Marland.

Allison's thoughts came back to the present as she stepped on a trunk of a large tree that lay across the path. She realized too late that the spot where she had placed her foot was bare of bark and its exposed skin was slippery. Her footing gave out and she landed hard on the tree before falling to the ground. Two strong, but soft hands took hold of her and raised her to her feet.

"Be careful," said Evelyn. "We'd better hurry up; the others are almost out of sight."

Allison realized that she might be in the middle of one of Evelyn's adventures right now, and this exhilarated her. She smiled at Evelyn, thanked her for her assistance, and raced ahead to catch Megan and the others.

Meanwhile, Conroy's thoughts strayed from Durwin and Baldwin to Elson. His brother was always teasing him. Conroy found this annoying, even though he knew it was Elson's way of showing him affection. Now that he was thirteen and in just a few days would participate in the island games as an adult, he hoped Elson's teasing would stop.

If Elson possessed anything that Conroy admired it was his friends. In spite of the fact that Elson was on the most winning team of the island games, Conroy knew that the team's success wasn't founded on Elson's contributions, but mostly on the skills of Evelyn, Justin, and Warrick. Conroy knew each of them well, for the amount of time they had spent at the Verrill house was considerable.

Conroy glanced ahead to see the three men walking proudly, purposefully through the forest. Justin's shoulder length brown, wavy hair brushing against leaves from branches crowding the path. Warrick's determination showed in his rigid expression, seen in the dim light of the forest. Elson's plain, straight, brown hair swayed slightly back and forth as he leapt over a small stream. Justin and Warrick might as well have been his brothers, for they had both influenced him as much as any little brother has been influenced by a big brother. Likewise, Evelyn might as well have been his sister.

Conroy thought back to a special memory. The group of five had gone to Handellen Pond. Hippos were always present at the pond and the young islanders found it quite fun to go swimming in the pond and play with the large water beasts. One activity that they found amusing was to stand on the back of a hippo and see how long they could remain standing as the hippo walked, swam, and eventually started bucking in an attempt to rid itself of its unwanted passenger.

The group had finished *hippo gliding* for the day, Evelyn was declared the victor, and they reclined at the edge of the pond, engaging in light conversation while they dried in the sun. Elson's playful antics were not limited to Conroy and he teased Evelyn about which one of the three she would marry, since she had not yet been betrothed. Evelyn smiled and replied defiantly that she would never afford any of them the honor of being their bride because she had already chosen Conroy. She smiled and winked at Conroy with her emerald eyes as the waves of her flowing blond hair glowed in the sweet sunshine. Conroy blushed as the three jilted young men sat quietly without response. He treasured that memory, feeling victorious over three admirable opponents, even though it had been in jest.

Suddenly, Conroy saw Justin halt a few yards in front of him and the joyful memories were put back within his mind. Justin held up his hand in gesture to stop. Justin, Warrick, and Elson huddled together and spoke amongst themselves, peering out from the underbrush of the forest at what lay before them. Conroy couldn't see what they were looking at, but he could tell that they were looking down into some kind of a clearing, for up above the canopy of trees disappeared. The rear members of the group approached the three leaders and joined them in crouched stances.

"Look, it's the Renfrew!" exclaimed Justin as loudly as he dared. "The red river really is here!"

The view before the islanders was spectacular for two reasons. The first was due to the fact that they were looking down upon the Renfrew, the hidden River of Power. It was a wide river, flowing smoothly, its water a deep red color. The other site that caught the islanders' attention was a new figure standing beside the river. None of them had ever seen this person before, but they knew at once who he was. Handsome beyond compare, he had hair as black as darkness itself and deep blue eyes that sparkled. His stature exuded supreme confidence and his tall frame suggested great strength. The twins walked toward him.

The spies remained hidden in the trees. They could see very clearly from where they were, but were too far away to hear the words spoken between the three at the river. They watched as the twins got closer to the man and fell to their knees before him.

Only a few seconds passed until Durwin and Baldwin leapt back to their feet. They were irritated but unafraid.

"Not willing to greet me properly?"

"Those days are gone!" retorted Durwin, boldly.

"Don't do that again," said Baldwin.

The twins knew the Island Caretaker well. They had served him their entire lives. The person they now spoke to at the river's edge, however, was not the Caretaker. Their jolly faces transformed into rigid countenances.

"Still faithful to the high king?" he asked in a ridiculing tone. "Why do you continue to come here to perform these trivial chores?"

"You have chosen your path, Kavan," said Durwin.

"And we have chosen ours, and they are not the same," said Baldwin.

Kavan spoke with a sincere tone; "But you are worthy of so much more! So much responsibility and recognition you deserve! And what have you been given for your service?"

The twins were silent.

"Join me and rule the isle! It will be yours! That's how it should be!" declared Kavan. "Surely you know it better than anyone."

Still, Durwin and Baldwin did not reply, but continued at their work, retrieving flasks from their packs.

The red river guardian grew impatient with their lack of attention. "Your efforts to this point have been in vain! Again, I say there has been no reward for your toil, no payment for your service from your master. Can you deny this?"

The twins filled the flasks with water from river and returned them to their packs, but they didn't answer.

"Under me, your payment would be regular and worthy of your efforts! Listen to reason!"

Finally they responded; "At first your words are sweet to our ears, and we think that your motivations are from a genuine concern for us, so well hidden is your deception," said Durwin.

"But then our minds digest them and weigh them with your real motives and we know your proposal is corrupt, as you are," said Baldwin.

Kavan was offended, but he didn't reply immediately; instead he turned and walked away.

Back in the forest, the eight islanders continued to spy on the three at the river. They watched Kavan march away from the twins, then, with a single pivoting motion, he leapt up and over the river.

He did not descend into the water, but flew into the air above the Renfrew.

The spies were in silent awe as they saw Kavan soar toward the middle of the river and descend until he floated in a prone position just above the surface of the red water, then he reached down and grabbed something. He rose upward and pulled from the river a long, thick, silver, steel chain, each link about a foot in width and a foot and a half long. He flew upward, far above the tallest tree, elevating higher and higher in order to pull the last link of the long chain from the water. Finally it came free and Kavan flew back to where Durwin and Baldwin remained at the riverbank and lowered the chain into a large pile on the ground beside the twins. The links clinked loudly as the pile of metal grew larger and larger as Kavan descended until he stood on the ground beside his chain. He tossed the last link of the chain onto the pile.

"Do you know what this is?" asked Kavan.

"A chain, of course," said Durwin.

"Yes, but not just *any* chain," said Kavan, boastfully confident. "Each link of *this* chain belongs to a general of significant power, each with authority over twelve thousand. Every link of *this* chain was given as a pledge of loyalty to me in the coming war."

"You've spoken of war for ages, yet it has never begun," said Baldwin, brushing off Kavan's boasting.

"You accuse me of being deceptive? You deceive yourselves if you think war isn't coming! It is! And soon! You may not have another opportunity to become my ally," warned Kavan.

The twins swung the packs over their shoulders, their chores at the river's edge complete.

The islanders had seen the twins put on their packs and they backed away from the edge of the trees, expecting Durwin and Baldwin to make their way back to the woodland path.

"The twins must not know that we are here," said Elson. "I am sure they would not be pleased to learn that we have followed them to the Renfrew."

"Should we hide or flee?" asked Warrick. "Justin, what do you think?"

No response. Justin and Evelyn were still watching the action at the river. It seemed that Durwin and Baldwin were not yet ready to leave.

Kavan stretched the chain along the riverbed so that the twins could see more accurately its full length. As the last section was made straight, they could not help but be amazed by the number of links. Then Baldwin spoke, redirecting their attention away from Kavan and his chain, "Ready to take the measurements?"

"Wait, Baldwin, the power of the Renfrew might be of use to us now."

Baldwin agreed. They knelt down and lowered their faces to the water and drank.

Evelyn and Justin couldn't believe what they had just seen and they looked at each other with shocked expressions. Evelyn was about to speak, but before she did, Warrick called to them.

"What are you doing?" he asked. "We need to take cover before we are found out." Warrick waved for them to join the others behind a clump of trees. Evelyn held up her hand for him to wait; she and Justin would join them soon enough. Helpless to make them come, Warrick remained where he was and looked around for a better spot to hide.

"You measure the depth, I'll check the rate of flow," said Baldwin.

Justin and Evelyn were surprised further still when they saw the twins leave the ground and fly over the river as Kavan had. Near the center of the river they turned and flew upstream. After flying about ten yards Durwin paused, but Baldwin proceeded past him.

Below the area where Durwin hovered, a square silver shaft rose up from the river, its top reached thirty feet above the water. Justin and Evelyn watched as Durwin approached the shaft and stared at it for several moments. They didn't understand what he was doing, for from their view they could not see the fine markings engraved in the tall shaft.

"Forty feet and six inches," said Durwin, before departing from the shaft and flying toward Baldwin.

Justin watched the square shaft disappear back into the river, then turned his attention toward Baldwin. Beside him rose another tall silver shaft from the river, this time cylindrical in shape. Even from their remote vantagepoint Justin and Evelyn could see that this shaft was rotating. He watched Baldwin fly close to the spinning cylinder and place his fingers on it.

"Forty feet every minute," declared Baldwin.

"Good, let's get back to the island," replied Durwin.

Baldwin nodded and the two started to float back toward the river's edge. Kavan met them in the air, smiling. "Are your chores all done? I'm sure your master will be proud of you. Think about what I said. I assure you, your master will be in for more than he expects; more than he can handle, I think." He gestured at the chain.

"Our master will be prepared for whatever you bring against him," said Baldwin.

"Wisdom would have you remember the outcome of your last attempt to challenge him," said Durwin.

A fierce look came over Kavan, his eyes narrowed and his lips pursed in restrained rage. He reached out his arm and the nearest end of the chain flew into his open hand. He flew high into the air again so that the chain lifted off the ground, then carried it over to the center of the river where he proceeded to let it sink back into the water. When the final link was submerged, he latched it into place and righted himself. Then he began to take strides.

Justin and Evelyn stared at Kavan in amazement as they realized that he was walking on the waves of the Renfrew. Kavan paced toward the twins at the riverbank, but stopped short of them and cast a glance to the forest where Justin was hiding. Evelyn had her back to the river and was conversing with Warrick, assuring him that she and Justin would join the others in a moment.

But Justin's attention was still focused on Kavan, who was looking right at him through the trees. Their eyes met. Kavan's gaze was so piercing that it grabbed hold of Justin's mind and prevented him from looking away. He remained standing on the Renfrew, however, and did not approach the islander. After a few moments, which seemed to last for days, Kavan released Justin and soared upward, swiftly ascending above the trees on the opposite side of the river and disappeared.

Justin felt a hand on his shoulder and sprang nervously around. It was Warrick. Warrick had had enough of waiting for Justin and Evelyn to join the others and he came to bring them away to the hiding spot.

"What have you been doing? We need to hide," said Warrick. "Here they come!"

This time Justin and Evelyn agreed and they followed Warrick to the clump of trees where all of the others were quietly hiding. Here they would wait for the twins to pass by.

No sooner had she crouched beside Allison than Evelyn remembered how she had been the last one through the cave entrance, "We have to go! We didn't put the stone back! At the cave! ...They will know that they were followed if they get back there and find the door open."

"Let's go, hurry!" Warrick did not hesitate to give the command.

Immediately, they all took off, running as fast as they could along the path back to the cave. By now, all of their enhanced speed and strength had dissipated and Warrick wondered if they would be able to pull the heavy door back into its place, even if they were able to reach it without being spotted.

As Justin ran, his mind could not release the image of Kavan. Justin had been very frightened when Kavan had looked at him, so much so that his muscles twitched and shivered. His body was now alive with adrenaline as he took the lead in the race back to the cave. He glanced backward as he ran, pretending to check on the others, but his true motive was to look to see if Kavan was pursuing him.

Warrick, running behind Justin, stopped and turned to beckon the others to hurry past. Megan was last, and just after she rounded a bend the twins came into sight.

"They must have been delayed," said Warrick out loud to himself as he ducked down and moved around the bend. He chased the others back toward the cave, which was only fifty yards away.

Through the passageway and out the other side went the islanders. At the entrance, they stopped and attempted to close the large stone door. They were surprised that they were able to close it; they expected it to close as hard as it had opened, but the stone moved lightly from its pocket and came flush with the smooth face of the rock ledge, leaving no visible indication of a doorway. Elson and Warrick pushed with all of their natural strength to see if they could budge the door, but could not; without the strength brought on by the island fruit, no islander would be able to open it.

The group left the cave entrance and moved back into the forest where they could take cover and discuss what they had seen as they waited for the twins to emerge. Justin tried to unravel the mystery of what he had seen. Everyone knew from the annual telling of the legend of the Caretaker that a former servant of his, Kavan, had been placed in charge of caring for the red river and the surrounding mainland. *"Why did Durwin and Baldwin kneel before him? Why would they take water from the river? Why did they drink the water?"* These questions, especially the last one, raced round and round his head as fast as he had raced from the river to the cave. Then an answer came - *It was to fly!*

On the other side of the cave Durwin and Baldwin lingered.

"Do you believe what he said about the chain?" asked Baldwin.

"Telling the truth is not Kavan's specialty," replied Durwin, "but I think there might be some truth in his boasting this time. Remember the day of his rebellion, and how many of us were lost then - one in three fell from the master's service to join him!"

"We should report to the king at once," declared Baldwin.

The twins picked up their pace, walking not back through the cave from which they had come, but along a different path that provided them with a more direct route back to the island.

The islanders huddled together and talked quietly amongst themselves while Warrick kept watch, continually looking at the cave entrance for Durwin and Baldwin to emerge. He dared not let his focus shift to the conversation, though he was aware of an avalanche of questions...

"Was that Kavan?" asked Keelan.

"It had to be," replied Allison, "Who else would be guarding the Renfrew?"

"Didn't you see his chain?" said Conroy.

"Why would they bow to him?" asked Megan.

No one offered an answer.

"I didn't know he could fly," said Keelan, "I've never seen any of the Caretaker's servants fly, not even Durwin or Baldwin."

"Didn't he just see the twins fly a few minutes ago?" thought Justin. Then he remembered that when Warrick had summoned him away from his hiding spot that all of the others had already abandoned their spy posts. He wondered if he was the only one who had seen the twins drink from the river and then fly. A glance at Evelyn gave him reason to believe that she'd seen this as well, and he gestured for her to keep quiet.

"Why would the twins collect water from the Renfrew?" asked Allison.

"*What are they doing,*" thought Warrick, "*they should have come through by now.*"

Evelyn noticed that something was strange about her husband. She took Justin's hand - it was cold and clammy, then released it and placed her hand on his arm to feel his muscles twitching uncontrollably. She looked into his distant eyes and said softly, "What's wrong?"

"I don't know," replied Justin quietly so that only she heard him. He was still shivering from fright. "I, ...I want to get away from here."

"Don't you want to keep following the twins?" she whispered.

Justin responded by timidly shaking his head. The thought of seeing the twins would have been normally very comforting, but he was deeply troubled by what he had just seen them do.

Evelyn acknowledged that his desire to get away from there was real, but found it very odd to see Justin so feeble. "Justin and I are going home now," she said to the others. She was as surprised as anyone to hear the words come out of her mouth.

"What?" exclaimed Elson, "I've never seen either of you walk away from an adventure, especially one as grand as this!"

Evelyn didn't know what to say.

"Keep following the twins and let us know what you find out," said Justin.

Elson and Warrick agreed, and then they all watched in disbelief as Evelyn and Justin left.

They walked about two miles along the coast until they came to a long floating bridge that led back to the island. Idris' Bridge was one of Evelyn's favorites of all the island projects. The boardwalk and railings of the bridge were made from a beautiful dark wood that had been sanded, sealed, and polished smooth. It was well traveled, but as far as could be seen, they were the only people crossing it at the moment. The sound of the waves against the sides of the bridge was comforting to Justin, and as he walked along his nerves began to calm.

"What's wrong with you?" Evelyn finally demanded.

"It was Kavan, did you see him?" answered Justin.

"Of course I saw him, we all did."

"He walked on the water, did you see *that*?" Justin was barely able to believe that he'd seen it.

Evelyn nodded.

"He looked right at me, even through the cover of the forest! I think he saw me! No, I *know* he saw me! I couldn't escape his gaze until he let me, and I've been shaking since."

"How come you're the only one of us who's trembling?"

"I'm the only one that looked into his eyes. I felt his desire and power, they're tremendous!"

Evelyn had not had the same experience, and didn't know what to say, so they walked on in silence for a few moments.

It had been several hours since they had eaten, before going reverse diving, and they were hungry. Justin was glad, for the hunger pangs distracted him from dwelling on Kavan. They were about a third of the way across the bridge and his condition seemed to be improving with every step closer to the island. As they approached the midpoint of the bridge, Justin's trembling stopped and his fear began to transform into curiosity. In fact, he became excited and ignored his hunger and recalled the twins flying.

"Tell me what you saw the twins do at the river," said Justin, hoping that she'd seen everything he had.

Evelyn slowly recounted what she'd seen in the proper sequence; "I saw them each carry a pack to the water's edge where they bowed to Kavan. Then I saw them draw some water from the river into their flasks and put them back into their packs. They then put their packs back on and it looked like they were getting ready to leave. At that point, everyone except for you and I went back into the woods to hide."

"Go on. Then what?" Justin's fear was gone, replaced by the excitement of the adventure.

Evelyn was glad to see Justin back to normal, and she continued speaking about what she had seen: how she watched the twins drink from the river; how she saw them flying in the air above the water to inspect the two tall obelisks that emerged from the water; and how she watched Kavan return the enormous chain back into the river. She shared how she saw the twins return to the ground, and that she saw Kavan walk on the water, and lastly that she saw the twins start to walk back toward the woods. She had not seen Kavan look at Justin, and she did not see him fly upward over the trees on the opposite side of the river and disappear.

"You saw it too!" Justin exclaimed when she was finished. "You saw them drink from the Renfrew!"

"Yes, but how could they? How could they do what they have forbidden us to do?" She stopped walking and stared out across the water. She looked at the island and back toward Marland.

"Well they did!" exclaimed Justin. "And then they flew!"

"We need to find out what they're going to do with those flasks." As she continued to look toward Marland, she was surprised to see others following behind them. "Here's our chance. Do you want to be direct, or should we spy on them some more?"

Justin didn't know what she was talking about until he turned around and saw two familiar figures walking toward them. Durwin and Baldwin were walking briskly over the wooden bridge, their packs slung over their shoulders. "I suppose it can't hurt to try and get some information out of them, but we can't let them know that we followed them."

"They must have passed the others. They might already know."

"Hey, you two!" Durwin's voice boomed over the soft sound of water lapping wood.

"Are you ready for the Island Games?" asked Baldwin.

"It's only a few days away," reminded Durwin.

The twins stopped when they reached Justin and Evelyn.

"We'll be ready," answered Justin. "So what have you two been doing? It's rare to see you away from the island." Justin thought a direct approach would be the most effective and least suspicious.

"Keeping on top of things," answered Durwin.

"What kind of task takes you away from the island?"

Baldwin didn't hesitate to answer, "Caring for the island sometimes requires us to tend to things elsewhere that affect it."

"Did you go see the Caretaker?" asked Evelyn, probing into their affairs more aggressively. "You know that's what everyone thinks you do whenever you leave."

"Yes, we know," said Durwin, smiling.

"It's not necessary, or beneficial, for you to know all of our activities," explained Baldwin.

"We must be going now, our work for the day is not yet finished," said Baldwin.

The two servants bid farewell to the couple and proceeded south across the bridge toward the island.

"That went about as I expected," said Justin after the twins had departed.

"They obviously don't want us to know what they're doing."

"All the more reason that we should follow them."

They turned to pursue the twins once more, but Durwin and Baldwin had already gone a considerable distance and were almost to the island. Evelyn and Justin walked as quickly as they could, but their effort to follow them this time was to no avail, and when they finally reached the island the twins were nowhere to be seen.

They spent several minutes running about in the woods looking for the twins, but they couldn't find them anywhere. They gave up and went back to the shore. Warrick, Elson and the others were running across the bridge toward them. After a few moments the entire group of eight was together again.

"What happened?" asked Warrick. "We saw you two talking to the twins on the bridge. What happened?" he asked again.

"Didn't they pass by you?" asked Evelyn.

Elson answered, "We were waiting for them to come out from the cave, but they seemed to be taking too long, so we decided to come home. When we reached the bridge we saw the twins talking with you. They must have taken a different route."

"Where are they now?" asked Warrick.

Justin and Evelyn shrugged their shoulders and shook their heads.

They searched again, all eight of them, unsuccessfully, to find Durwin and Baldwin. Eventually they gave up, tired and hungry from their adventure. But it wasn't for lack of effort that they didn't find the twins; in fact, no islander saw them that evening - they had once again left the isle.

    *   *   *   *   *   *   *   *   *   *   *   *

In a remote place far from the island, two servants bowed deeply, willingly before their true master. Several others stood around them as they rose to report to King Iman.

"Master, we have seen Kavan today in Marland beside the Renfrew," said Durwin.

"He spoke of waging war against you," said Baldwin.

Durwin spoke, "Today he showed us a great chain and boasted that the links had been given freely to him by generals in command of thousands as a pledge of loyalty to him."

"We knew not whether to believe him," said Baldwin.

King Iman rose from his throne and approached the twins. "I am pleased with your loyalty and service to me. I know that Kavan offered you much to ally with him. You deserve great reward. Tell me, are you content?"

The two answered together, "Yes, Master."

"We consider it a great honor to hold the positions that you have given us," replied Durwin.

"All of your servants, even those who have turned from you, know how much you care for the islanders," said Baldwin.

The king sighed. "It is for that very reason that I am concerned. You have come here to bring me news, but I am troubled with news that *I* must give *you* now." Durwin and Baldwin looked at each other. Their faces became somber as they awaited grim words from their king. "Some of the young ones of the island followed you today to the Renfrew."

The twins hung their heads, feeling that they had failed their master.

"Do not be hard on yourselves. We knew that someday they would find a path to the red river, and that hiding it deep within the Marland forest was but a delay to this moment. A delay that has allowed me many years to delight in these pleasant folk."

"Who? Who was it, Master?" asked Durwin.

"It was Justin and Evelyn Nickols and their friends, Warrick Spenser and Elson Verrill. Also, Elson's younger brother Conroy and his friends Keelan Tilman, Allison Krunser, and Megan Prendt."

The twins were truly embarrassed by having been followed by so many. "Master, what should we do now?" asked Baldwin.

"There has never been a more appropriate time for the telling of the legend. Return to the island and perform your regular tasks. Tell the legend and give the usual warnings, ensure that the stone pillar is intact and that nothing hinders the islanders from observing it. Nothing more can be done for them at this time. They are not in danger yet, but only a few steps more and they will find themselves in great need."

One of the others stepped forward and spoke, "Master, what should be done about Kavan?" His face was as firm as the rock ledge of Mt. Manor and the seriousness of his countenance was unmatched by any of the other king's servants.

"He *is* planning a war, Sandor," said the king, very plainly. "He has been plotting against me from the very day that he became as he is. Even now he is giving orders for those loyal to him to assemble. He will come against us soon. It is time for you to gather my city's army and prepare for battle: it is your duty to guard Casilda. Kavan wants my throne, but I am not concerned about losing it to him, for if it were possible for him to overthrow me, he would have done so ages ago. Yet, I *am* concerned about what he might do when his assault against me fails."

"You are concerned for the islanders, Master?" asked Sandor.

"Yes. As Baldwin has stated, Kavan knows how much I care for them. When he realizes that he cannot harm me, he will choose to harm those that I care for. Though I have ordered the Gemstones to guard the islanders, Kavan has access to them indirectly. As weak as they are, the islanders have the ability to resist him, but they may not realize this. We can only wait and see if they fail."

The king finished speaking and some of the crowd left. Durwin and Baldwin bowed once more to their master and departed to return to the island. Sandor also bowed to the king and then approached a group of other servants who had gathered together. They were all very impressive, nearly as massive and as serious as Sandor. After a few minutes, Sandor led this group from the king's palace.

King Iman remained in his throne room in the center of his majestic castle, which was itself at the very center of the great city of Casilda. Here he continued to pace slowly about as thoughts of the islanders consumed him. "*It is not yet their time to possess what the Renfrew will bestow upon them. Yet they are close to taking hold of it. If they should fail, what assistance could I offer them? If Kavan succeeds in making them slaves, what price could I pay to free them? Would it be possible to restore what would be lost?*"

The days following on the island were filled with the business of tournament preparations. Those competing in the tournament practiced throughout the day at their respective events, while those who were not made ready for the festivities by baking, setting up the scoring boards, finishing the trophies and plaques, and the like. All island projects were either completed or put on hold during the week prior to the games in order to provide everyone with a full week of preparation time.

After their adventure to the Renfrew, the eight islanders met the next morning to discuss whether to reveal their secret to anyone else. Since they could see no benefit in doing so, and because they were uncertain why the twins had bowed down to Kavan and brought back with them water from the red river, they resolved not to tell anyone else, at least not until they understood what they had seen.

Conroy and Keelan worked diligently to complete the two last signs for the tournament, signs for the Runrining and the Puttining. Wendel Wright was pleased with the finished products and the two signs were installed at once.

Homes were decorated with team banners, which rose and fell slowly in the gentle breeze. Some houses had multiple flags flying; such as the Verrill house, where flags flew in honor of Elson's championship team and also for the new team to which Conroy belonged. The flag for Conroy's team had been recently designed in tribute to Allison and the Orca. The flag was almost entirely black except for an oval shaped white spot in the far lower corner of the flag, resembling the whale's white false eye.

The flag for Elson's team was the most popular banner flying on the island. In the center of their turquoise flag was a fierce creature, dark green and covered in scales, with three rigid fins running from its forehead across its scalp until they combined into a singe fin at the back of its neck, then proceeded down its back and into a long thick tail below its waist. The four armed figure stood dominant and fearless on two thick legs. Its eyes were dark and lidless, like a serpent's, and his hands had six long fingers with sharp claws at the end of each. It was the creature that Evelyn had met several years ago in the clear water of the lake. She was the only islander to have ever encountered this creature. Her teammates were so inspired by her description of its appearance that Elson had created a sketch of it. The sketch was impressive; Evelyn was pleased with its likeness to the creature, and it was decided that this would become the symbol of their team.

It was the day before the games were scheduled to begin, but it appeared that they had already commenced. Nearly everyone on the island was involved in one of the contests that afternoon, whether as spectators or contestants, making the most of their last opportunity to practice their skills. The *Unknown Creatures* were no exception; they had gathered at the shore of the South Sea to observe the final Ascentining practice runs of Elson and Justin.

Although Justin had practiced this event, as well as his other event, the Wavelling, for many hours each day, his thoughts were mostly on trying to understand what he observed the twins do at the Renfrew. He did not think much about the fear that he had felt when Kavan looked into his eyes; instead he thought about what it would be like to fly.

Justin grabbed the rope and began the long ascent up the face of mighty Mount Manor. He was now faster at climbing it than he had ever been, and he was sure to be the favorite to win the contest again. Justin finished his climb and looked into the sky over the South Sea. Then he leapt off the edge of the cliff and began to plummet toward the large bay below.

As he fell, he imagined that he could stop himself from falling, deny gravity its right, and fly as the twins had. He pictured himself turning upward, his arms spread wide and his legs tight together and straight. Traveling at speeds faster than he had ever known, he would shoot through white puffy clouds in the blue sky toward the sun. Then he imagined diving down toward the earth, passing the swiftest of birds on his descent. Evelyn would join him in the air and together they would circle the island and look down on their beautiful home and their friends.

Justin was still far above the bay and falling. His daydream fled as other thoughts pressed into his mind. "*Durwin and Baldwin drank from the river,*" he thought, "*Why can't I?*" This question had burned inside him night and day, and all of his efforts to find the answer had failed. He had consulted his wife and found that her uncertainty matched his own.

Justin rolled over so that his feet were below him as he finally entered the water. He thought about how he might confront Durwin and Baldwin and question them further, more aggressively than before. Then he remembered that the legend would be shared that evening. This time, more than ever before, Justin looked forward to hearing the ancient tale.

"Wonderfully done!" Justin heard Evelyn's voice as he reappeared from under the water. Evelyn and his other teammates waited for him on the shore. "Are you going again?"

"No, that was my last one. I'm ready," he called as he swam to the shore. A loud splash sounded behind him as another competitor finished a practice run. Justin walked up the sandy beach, grabbed his towel, and dried himself off.

"Let's eat and then go to the valley," said Elson, who had already finished practicing, had dried off, and changed his clothes.

"You're really going to go and listen to that story *again*?" Russel Minns, a thick, strong young man who competed in the Launtrining and the Luggerrun asked. "Aren't you all a little old for tales of fantasy? No one has ever seen this supposed Kavan character, or the mysterious red river for that matter."

The four friends looked subtly at one another but none offered to enlighten Russel.

"It's nice to keep the tradition," answered Elson, dodging Russel's sarcasm. "Besides, what else is there to do tonight? Almost the entire island will be there."

"I suppose," said Russel, "but I'm going home to enjoy a quiet evening. A little extra rest will serve me well; I'm scheduled to compete in the Launtrining first thing tomorrow." Another islander splashed into the bay as Russel finished speaking.

After promising to meet the next morning, the teammates departed from one another for the evening. Justin and Evelyn planned to meet Warrick and Elson at the island amphitheater, *Jovian Valley*, an hour before the annual telling of the legend began.

*   *   *   *   *   *   *   *   *   *   *   *

After a light feast at their cozy cabin, Justin and Evelyn arrived at the large outdoor theater, located about halfway between the villages of Epidomon and Thiagara. About three thousand chairs had been set up on a gentle sloping hill overlooking an oval shaped, level, grassy area where numerous children were running and playing. Beyond this was a large elevated natural plateau that was used as a stage. At the back of the stage were thick clusters of trees that created a scenic backdrop and served as a partition to shield performers and props from the view of the audience. Large black tapestries were suspended in between the tree clusters; these provided access to and from the stage from behind the trees.

Some of the servants were finishing setting up when Justin and Evelyn arrived. The young couple walked through a dessert tent behind the seating area, picked up a couple of sweets, and then took their choice of seats. They sat at the base of the hill on the far left so that they were in the optimal place from which to observe but not be observed themselves.

After they had been seated for a few minutes, Warrick arrived, followed by Elson and Conroy. Conroy did not sit with them however; instead, he stood aside near the entrance until Keelan, Megan, and Allison arrived. These four took seats opposite the others at the base of the hill on the far right.

It was not long after this that the seats became completely filled. People of all ages assembled to hear the telling of the legend, the favorite story for many of the islanders. The flat, grassy area directly in front of the stage was now filled with people reclining on the cooling ground with blankets and pillows. The children that had been running about in this area had become quiet and calm as daylight faded, and they joined their families to listen to the legend.

Justin and Evelyn talked with Warrick and Elson about what the twins might have done with the water they had collected from the red river. They were all very anxious to hear the legend; they were eager to listen and analyze every word that would be spoken.

Justin and Evelyn had still not told their two friends about the twins drinking from the river and flying. He wasn't sure why he withheld this information from them, Justin had always been so close with Warrick and Elson, and there had never been a need for secrets between them. Evelyn had looked at him oddly when he suggested that they not speak of this to their two good friends, but he was able to convince her that it would be wise to keep it a secret until they had a better understanding of things. Justin wanted, needed, to learn more before sharing what he saw with anyone, even Warrick and Elson. Justin was startled when a large thick hand grasped his shoulder from behind.

"How are our favorite champions doing this evening?" It was Durwin. Baldwin followed immediately behind him.

The group had been so involved in their discussion that they did not notice the twins arrive, even though they had been greeted by nearly everyone they passed on their way down the aisle to the front of the seating area.

"Fine, just fine," came Justin's delayed response. He wanted to bombard them with questions but held back, sensing poor timing.

"Guess we'd better get ready," said Baldwin, nudging his twin.

"Hope you enjoy the evening," said Durwin. He winked at them and then both proceeded up to the elevated stage.

Several other servants arrived and met with the twins on the stage. Some carried large bags of props and clothing behind the clumps of trees. Some of them brought lanterns and placed them around the perimeter of the seating area and all around the stage and lit them. Each lantern was matched with its own servant who stood beside it. The people, while waiting for the legend to begin, engaged in loud, friendly conversation as preparations were made.

At last, a servant emerged from the backdrop of trees carrying a large metal disc in one hand and a silver hammer in the other. He wore a bright white tunic with a golden band across his chest. He came to the front edge of the stage where he stood very straight, pausing for an entire minute to allow the crowd to become quiet. The sun had set and the lanterns now gave forth all light that was present. He struck the disc a single time with the hammer. The sound was not deafening, but their wasn't a person in the crowd that did not hear it clearly as it reverberated from the stage. The servant held the disc out straight until the noise dissolved into the night air.

He spoke loudly to the audience, "Be prepared now! The telling of the Legend of the Island Caretaker begins!" He stood there for a few moments more but said nothing else, then spun nimbly about and walked from the stage. The crowd heeded his command, and the whole place was overcome with attentive silence. The servants at the lanterns adjusted shields to cover the flames to dim the light.

Two lanterns at the stage were uncovered to show that another servant, tall and thin, had come onto the stage. Anult, well known for his care of the island's renden orchards, wore a jeweled belt around a violet robe. He addressed the audience, "Let us remember when the Rivers of Power were called from the deep to flow over this magnificent island. Let us acknowledge the blessing that they are for us. Let us not forget to appreciate them." Anult paused to catch his breath, then continued, "From the northeast flows the yellow river, as yellow as the daffodil, and purer than sunlight. It is the river Candra!" Anult flung his left arm up, pointing to the right side of the stage. As he did this, a lantern was adjusted to show a yellow stream flowing down an incline that had been erected in secrecy. It flowed across a small, shallow trough in the earthen floor.

Anult lowered his arm and spoke again, "From the northwest flows the blue river, as blue as the bluebird and purer than the sky. It is the river Azor!" This time Anult raised his other arm and pointed to the opposite side of the stage. Here a blue stream could be seen as, once more, a lantern was turned to show what was hidden in shadow. Like the yellow stream, the blue water flowed diagonally across the stage floor. The blue stream and yellow stream crossed in the center of the stage; a beautiful green pool formed where the streams mixed, but, like the real rivers, as the water flowed from the pool, each recovered its original hue of blue or yellow.

Anult continued, "Where the waters meet at the center of the isle is the green pool, as green as an emerald and purer than island grass. It is the pool Verimere!" Anult held out his hands to gesture to the green pool in front of him.

"Candra! Azor! Verimere!" cried Anult. "But what of the red river? Where is the Renfrew?"

The lamps were dimmed and the stage became dark again. After a few moments, the stage was relit to reveal that the flowing streams were gone and the servant who had sounded the gong, Treece, was back.

"This story begins at a time when the island was like all other surrounding lands: there were no Fruits of Ability here; there were no Rivers of Power here; there were no people here," began Treece. "Across the South Sea, on three giant ships of glorious sail of colors blue, yellow, and red, came the Caretaker and his servants. They had sailed many leagues to reach the island, intending to form it into a habitat for all creatures to dwell in harmony, for the Caretaker possessed knowledge of mysterious and wonderful things of the world."

As Treece spoke, three majestic, but miniature, sailing vessels rolled onto the stage, containing a dozen servants each, using oars to maneuver their ships. After their boats were properly placed, they dropped their oars and walked from the ships to the rear of the stage where they stood waiting to act out Treece's narration.

"Upon arriving, the Caretaker's first act was to send out the crews of the three ships in search of the hidden Rivers of Power," said Treece. "The Caretaker knew about the powers of these rivers and planned that they would become the foundation for the nature of life on the island. The captain of each ship was commanded to lead his crew in search for one of the three mighty rivers." Three servants, outfitted in a manner suggesting authority, stepped forward.

"Sandor, the captain of the ship Aiken, the very ship on which the Caretaker sailed, was sent to search for the Azor, the blue river. Gavril, the captain of the ship Thalassa's Crown, was sent to find the Candra, the yellow river. Kavan, the captain of the ship Hypatia, was sent to find the Renfrew, the red river."

"Kavan was the most magnificent of all the Caretaker's servants," Treece paused while the lanterns were adjusted to shine brightest on the tallest of the three captains. "His cleverness was unsurpassed, and his bravery and strength were renown in the high city of Casilda. Tall and handsome, he carried himself with supreme confidence, founded rightfully on his high rank and privilege."

Justin felt for a moment the same fear that he had felt a few days ago and he looked away from the stage. He didn't understand why he should now be afraid, but as Treece continued, his fear subsided and he looked again to the stage. Walking between Kavan and Sandor, another servant came forward, this one portraying the Island Caretaker. He carried three long, silver steel staffs and three solid, silver steel mallets.

Treece continued, "The Caretaker gave to each captain a mallet and rod of steel and instructed them to go find the places on the island where the earth could be tapped to draw the precious springs forth from deep within the earth. Sandor led his crew to the northeast region of the island, Gavril to the northwest, and Kavan toward the east shore." The three captains bid their crews to follow and walked toward different parts of the stage while the Caretaker remained in the center alone.

"Upon finding the three secret spots revealed to them by the Caretaker, each captain gave the order to place the rods in the ground," said Treece. "With a mighty swing from the strong arm of each captain, the hammers crashed into the rods, three perfect strikes. Three giant pins unseen, pushed by the powerful blows, were driven into the earth where they penetrated the walls of three underground springs. Their boundaries broken, the rivers gushed up from the deep to flow across the land."

"And so it began," continued Treece, "the three Rivers of Power flowed on the surface of the world for the first time. Like a heart pumping blood to provide life to the body, so the pressures within the earth drove these waters to the surface where their powers would benefit the land." Once again the blue and yellow waters flowed across the stage. The two captains, Sandor and Gavril, and their crews left the stage. The Caretaker stood beside the pool of green water, Verimere, and Kavan and his crew remained on the far right of the stage.

Treece continued, "Yellow and blue water mixed together as the Candra and the Azor rivers met to form the pool, Verimere. The Renfrew, however, did not flow to meet the other rivers at the pool as the Caretaker intended. He looked to the east but saw no sign of the red river. Then, with extreme disappointment, he set off to find Kavan." The Caretaker began to walk toward Kavan and his crew, but disappeared from the view of the audience as the stage lanterns were adjusted so that only Treece was visible.

"The reason that the Renfrew did not come forth and join the other two rivers was Kavan's doing," explained Treece. "The Caretaker knew immediately what Kavan had done, for Kavan, like the Caretaker, had some knowledge about the Rivers of Power. He knew that if the flowing water of the Renfrew was stopped, the gift that it would offer to any who drank it would be changed. The Caretaker had given him firm warning to not interfere with the flow of the river once it was brought forth. Kavan, however, ordered his crew to construct a dam in its path."

"The Renfrew was caught by the dam and the crew of the Hypatia gathered around the swelling pool of red water, watching it grow deeper with uncertain anticipation, realizing that something significant was about to happen due to the excitement expressed by their captain," said Treece. "As they watched, a creature of great size and strength emerged from the swirling water and stood over them. It peered down on them and looked into their minds. Their thoughts became dull as they indulged in the visions the creature revealed to each of them. They desired to obey the beast in hope that it would make the fantasies become real. Kavan formed an alliance with the creature at once and declared his allegiance to it by drinking from the pool of still water that lay before him, as he desired, and this pleased the creature. Kavan's crew also knelt beside the red pool and drank."

The lamps were turned to illuminate the right side of the stage where Kavan and his shipmates gathered around a red pool. A giant figure stood at the back of the stage just out of the lamplight. Although its features couldn't be see, its large form could be detected by the shadow it cast against the trees. Some were kneeling by the water with cupped hands, others had their faces down to the water, but all were drinking. Kavan wiped drops of red from his lips and smiled as he stood over his crew. Treece remained silent for a few moments to allow the audience to observe the rebellion of the Hypatia. When the crew finished drinking, the shadow of the creature disappeared, though its presence seemed to remain.

"The effect of the altered Renfrew was immediate!" Treece spoke quickly and angrily. "The heart of each servant became inflated with pride and they each thought themselves stronger and cleverer than they were. They began to perform physical feats to display their power and prove themselves superior to their fellow shipmates. Boasting followed, then mocking, then angry threats, and finally a large brawl broke out as they fought against one another with fists, hammers, and blades!"

The stage came alive with fierce action. Servants were struggling against one another, tumbling and being thrown down. The sound of clashing steel echoed loudly in the air. The audience was enamored by the intensity of the fighting.

Treece continued to speak loudly, trying to be heard above the clamor; "Kavan circled his fighting crew, observing which ones were strongest. One of them dared to challenge Kavan himself. Drimelen, the first mate of the Hypatia, was an enormous individual, taller and wider than any of his mates. His black hair was short and thick, and he had a jaw that stuck out like a chunk of granite. Drimelen felt that he was worthy of commanding the Hypatia, and he made this known to Kavan."

The audience watched one of the crew, assumed to be Drimelen, charge at Kavan with tremendous speed, brandishing the Caretaker's rod high in the air, for he was the one who had held the rod for Kavan to strike. But Kavan ducked the blow that had been meant for his head, and as Drimelen's momentum carried him past his missed target, Kavan took the hammer that he still held and struck a solid blow into Drimelen's side. The first mate released the rod as he collapsed to the ground. With his free left hand, Kavan lifted the large Drimelen up and dealt him another solid blow with the mallet squarely on the top of his head. Drimelen fell to the ground and was still. But after awhile his body began to restore itself.

Treece continued, "Kavan did not have to defend himself again; the example he had made of Drimelen discouraged any other to challenge him, for Drimelen was not weak. Instead, they continued to assault one another to seek a position of authority under Kavan."

The struggles went on for several minutes until the servants became satisfied with the positions they had obtained, or they lay motionless on the ground beside Drimelen. At last the action on the stage slowed and the audience relaxed. Twisted faces, open wounds, and bent limbs, all still in the process of healing, were everywhere.

The lanterns were adjusted to show the Caretaker walking toward the crew of the Hypatia. Treece resumed, "As the Caretaker approached the scene, he crested a knoll and stopped to view the activities before him. He saw Kavan standing on top of the dam that held the Renfrew back, still grasping in his right hand the steel mallet that the Caretaker had given him, speaking to his crew, commanding them with unleashed passion."

Kavan was at the back of the stage, standing on a large pile of brush stacked behind the scarlet pool. He faced his crew and beyond them, the audience.

"Mighty mates of the Hypatia, listen to me now!" exclaimed Kavan, his words booming. The crew became attentive, ready to heed their master's command. "I have observed the outcomes of your quarrels and your positions under me are now determined. If you are not satisfied with your rank, there will be opportunities in the future for improvement, but there shall be no more fighting among you until then!"

The crew remained silent and accepted the regulation put before them by their captain.

Treece continued; "Kavan refrained from speaking further until all his crew were fully recovered from their injuries. He desired their complete attention and would be patient for them to heal so that he could have it. When all of them had recovered, he revealed his plan and gave them their first task."

"Disappointment broke the heart of the Caretaker as he proceeded from the knoll toward Kavan, who still stood on top of the dam," said Treece. "It was evening and as the Caretaker strode eastward, the setting sun shone brightly behind him."

"The crew of the Hypatia became aware of the presence of the Caretaker as one." Kavan's eyes gleamed with anticipation as he saw the Caretaker approach. "Now!" yelled Kavan.

The action on stage became quick again and Treece described the events; "The crew turned and raced toward the oncoming Caretaker in the hope of executing their captain's rebellious plan. Kavan, however, remained on the dam with a smug expression on his face and watched his warriors demonstrate their commitment to his agenda."

"The Caretaker's pace neither slowed nor quickened," said Treece. "He continued walking directly toward the dam in spite of the advancing crew, his eyes remained fixed on Kavan. Poised for attack, the crew flew onward, those in the front lines of the assault came within a few yards of the Caretaker, who continued steadily forward."

"Be still," said the Caretaker, the words came coolly but quickly from his mouth. All of the action on the stage stopped immediately and it became quiet.

"All of them were stopped instantly at the Caretaker's command," explained Treece softly. "Their poses were those of men caught in mid stride, balanced only on a single foot, or suspended in the air, gravity unable to pull them down. Fury and rage corrupted their faces."

"The Caretaker strode though the paralyzed assembly to the edge of the water and stopped at the base of the dam. Kavan remained confident," said Treece.

"Why have you done this?" asked the Caretaker, looking at the still, red water of the dammed Renfrew.

"Surely you know why," came Kavan's sharp reply. "Am I not worthy of my own throne?"

"You and your crew are corrupt. I commanded you to not interfere with the river's flow, least of all to drink from it while it was altered!"

"Do not pretend that I have been corrupted," said Kavan. "For I know now that my power equals yours. The reason you gave the false command against altering the river was to prevent me from claiming what I am worthy of!" The volume of Kavan's voice increased until he was shouting, "But you have failed and must now contend against me!" Kavan leapt from the dam with the hammer still in his right hand, the shining steel rod flew from where it lay on the ground and he caught it in his outstretched left hand as he landed at the river's edge beside the sad, and now angry, Caretaker.

"Kavan swung the hammer with great force at the Caretaker's head. The Caretaker lifted his hand to block the blow!" said Treece excitedly.

Kavan and the Caretaker paused on the stage, allowing Treece to further describe the scene; "With all eyes open wide, but looking into the blinding sun, the crew of the Hypatia did not know what was happening. They heard the hammer whistle through the air, then a loud crash, followed by another whistling sound, ending with a dull thud, and finally a distant splash."

Kavan and the Caretaker resumed the action while Treece continued to speak; "What the crew could not see was that the hammer, when it struck the lifted forearm of the Caretaker, shattered to countless pieces, exploding back into Kavan's face. As it did, the Caretaker grabbed the rod and pulled it free of Kavan's grasp. The momentum of the Caretaker's action spun him rapidly around, the rod now in *his* hand, which he extended horizontally. As he completed his turn, the rod crashed into Kavan just above his waist, hurling him unconscious through the air into the sea."

On stage, the actions of the two characters had been carried out just as Treece described, and Kavan lay sprawled on the very right edge of the stage where three ships appeared. Sandor, Gavril, and their crews maneuvered the ships around the fallen captain.

Treece's narration slowed, "The Caretaker stood alone beside the red water and looked east into the sea. All three ships, the Hypatia, the Aiken, and Thalassa's Crown, were sailing around from the south and quickly reached the spot where Kavan had plunged into the water. A large net was lowered from the deck of the Hypatia and Kavan's limp body was caught up into his boat where he was bound and made a prisoner on his own vessel." Kavan was lifted from the stage floor and placed into the center ship.

"The ships set anchor and Sandor and his crew from the Aiken came ashore and removed the weapons from the paralyzed hands of the Hypatia crew," said Treece. "The Caretaker saw that they were disarmed and he released them from his spell. Their freedom was brief, however, for they were all bound and taken to the Hypatia where they gathered around Kavan, who had recovered and stood at the bow of the ship with his hands and arms tied tight."

Treece paused to allow the last of the crew of the Hypatia to step into the wooden boat on the stage. "Kavan glared at the Caretaker, who was now himself boarding the Hypatia. Four strands of steel bound Kavan's arms, and four of the crew of Thalassa's Crown stood guard beside him. Fueled by hatred and jealousy, Kavan's desire for rebellion was rekindled as the Caretaker approached and with a quick summoning of his tremendous strength, snapped the strands that bound him and flung the four guards over the edge of the ship into the sea."

"Kavan picked up the broken cables and rushed toward the Caretaker, swinging them fiercely, the whirring of the metal slicing through the air was terrific!" exclaimed Treece. "But, just as before, Kavan's attack on the Caretaker was short lived. The Caretaker caught the massive strands in his hand, and with a short, sharp tug, disarmed Kavan once more. The Caretaker raised his other hand and from the tips of four of his fingers came strands of silver that wrapped around Kavan and bound him. He struggled with all of his might but found that he could not escape these new restraints."

Treece went on, "The crews of the Aiken and Thalassa's Crown watched from the shore as the Caretaker addressed Kavan. He spoke calmly, but with obvious disappointment."

"You were the greatest of my servants. You had access to my throne, and walked among the fiery rocks that decorated the floor before it, delighting me often with your music. It pleased me to bestow on you garments adorned with jewels to match your handsome features. But now you *are* corrupt, in spite of what you believe, and you've cast it all aside."

"In the presence of your crew and my faithful servants, I remove you from your high rank under my command," said the Caretaker. "You shall have no part in the tending of this isle; yours shall be the land across the water. And since this river cannot taint you further, and since you have tainted the river itself so that it is unfit to flow here, it shall be moved to that land, and you will oversee it there." He paused to let his words carry their purpose, then said, "You are free of my command, but your endeavors will not be unknown to me. My authority will be in place to prevent you from destroying what I value."

The Caretaker turned and addressed the crew of the Hypatia; "Since you have chosen the same path as your captain, so shall your fate be as his. You are removed from your ranks under me. You shall accompany Kavan to the land across the water and shall have no part of the tending of this isle."

Treece resumed narrating, "As the Caretaker finished speaking, he slowly paced around the deck, gathered all of the splendid red sails from their masts, raised the anchor, and then departed from the ship. Before the small boat could return the Caretaker to the shore, he stood and placed his hand on the vessel and pushed firmly. With slow but steady acceleration, the Hypatia began to move forward. By the time the ship parted from his hand, it was moving with significant velocity. The last light of dusk disappeared as the Hypatia became a sail-less, spiked silhouette fading into darkness."

One of the ships, which held Kavan and his crew, departed the stage. The other two ships, their captains and crews, and the Caretaker remained on the stage while the lanterns were dimmed and then revived.

Treece continued, "The following morning, on order of the Caretaker, the crew of the Aiken removed the dam that stopped the Renfrew." The pile of brush was thrown off the stage. Then the stage lamps were turned to reveal three colored streams flowing across the stage. The yellow and blue streams mixed to form the green pool as before, but now it was divided by the red stream, which flowed straight across the pool, not mixing with the other colors, but striping itself between two sides of emerald green water.

"The servants and the Caretaker gathered around to observe the pool," said Treece. "Several minutes passed while they watched, and then the Renfrew began to fail. The edges of the red ribbon of water began to fray, the red stream mixing with the green, turning the Verimere a hideous brown."

"It is as I declared," said the Caretaker. "Kavan's meddling has not only corrupted himself and his crew, but has also altered the Renfrew. See how it reacts with the pure Verimere."

"Sandor and Gavril were sent back to the east side of the island to stop the spring of the red river," said Treece. "The Caretaker instructed them to strike the land again, and the two captains took the hammer and rod and found the secret coordinates. Sandor swung the hammer as Gavril held the rod; a single blow was all that was needed. The Renfrew stopped and went back to its deep dwelling place. The captains returned to find the Caretaker waiting for them at Verimere's edge, the pool once again dazzling green."

"We have done as you said, Master," said Sandor. "What shall become of the Renfrew now?"

"It shall flow elsewhere for a time and be under Kavan's care," the Caretaker replied. "But let's get on with our work, another river is needed here."

"Having said this, he turned and walked about a half-mile to the north where there was a wide depression in the landscape," said Treece. "He carried one of the rods with him and walked to the center of the valley where sat a single stone, a miniature monadnock. It was round and tall, its peak about fifty feet above the ground. The Caretaker climbed to its top in a few easy bounds with the rod in his hand." A large rock had been placed on the stage and the Caretaker climbed to its peak and lifted the rod over his head.

"Icyandic, I call you forth!" shouted the Caretaker, slamming the rod down into the stone, splitting it in two from top to bottom.

"Immediately, a blinding white stream gushed out from the split at the base of the rock," explained Treece. "The Caretaker leapt from the rock on top of the springing river, but did not sink into the deepening white water. He walked across its surface to meet Gavril, Sandor and their crews, who were watching from the southern slope.

The servants were not unfamiliar with the white river and they raised their swords and beat them against their shields, using the flat of the blades, as they cheered."

"Icyandic! Icyandic! The white river flows again!" shouted the actors on the stage.

"The water continued to rise, filling the depression all around the rock in a giant ring," said Treece. "The volume of each of the Rivers of Power is finite, and, although the Icyandic is the most powerful, it is the smallest. The Caretaker and his servants watched the white river grow larger until they saw the last portion of it emerge from the rock, like the tail of a giant white, shining animal coming out from its cave. The Caretaker raised his hand and the two halves of the rock came together again and merged so that it was as if they had never been split."

"The river leveled in a ring around the wide rock and became still," said Treece. "Gavril and Sandor knelt on the hillside and reached to touch the water, only to find that its surface was solid."

"Will it not flow like the others?" asked Sandor.

"It shall," the Caretaker replied.

"The Caretaker walked out to the center of the river and stopped. He lifted high the rod that he still held," said Treece, "and drove it into the water in the same manner that he had driven it into the rock. A loud 'CRACK!' sounded as the rod pierced the hard surface. The water did not leak through at the penetration; instead a seal formed around the rod, and the Caretaker began to stir, moving the rod gently back and forth, making the circles of his motion gradually larger. He increased the speed of his stirring and waves began to form. The surface of the water lifted and fell with each wave, but remained solid. The Caretaker bounced up and down on top of the river to the frequency of the waves passing beneath him. He gave one final stir and pulled the rod from the water, another CRACK! sounded as the surface became whole again. The flow of the river was now obvious, as its waves could be seen in motion all around the rock island."

Treece gave his final narration; "After bringing forth the Rivers of Power, the Caretaker remained on the island for many seasons, instructing his servants how to care for them, and imparting to them the knowledge of growing the trees and shrubs which bear the Fruits of Ability. He revealed to them all of the secrets of the island so that their care for it would be complete."

"One midsummer evening, after the servants had proven their ability to care for his island, the Caretaker instructed Gavril to summon the crew of Thalassa's Crown and prepare to sail. And so they departed, leaving Sandor and his crew to oversee the isle, while they went to gather those whom the Caretaker had planned to bring here, those who would become the first inhabitants of the island." Treece was finished.

The audience watched the actors, and finally Treece, walk off the back of the stage and behind the trees. All the lamps were extinguished, even those that lit the seating area, and the whole place became dark. After an extended silence, a single lantern was relit to reveal Durwin and Baldwin standing at the front of the stage.

"This ends the legend," said Baldwin. "We assure you by all that is sacred that these events took place, for we were among the crew of Thalassa's Crown."

"The rivers Candra and Azor, as well as their product, Verimere, were brought forth by Sandor and Gavril and have been a blessing for all island life since that day," said Durwin. "And the Caretaker himself, on the following day, brought forth the mighty Icyandic."

"These unique waters ensure that all creatures of the island live peacefully, joyfully, and safely," said Baldwin.

The islanders knew full well about the powers of the rivers, yet they listened respectfully as the twins reiterated their functions.

"Water from the yellow Candra gives you peaceful dispositions," said Durwin.

"Water from the blue Azor gives you joyful hearts," said Baldwin.

"Water from the white Icyandic gives you health," said Durwin. "So powerful is this river that its mere presence offers you its benefit."

"These rivers, like the Fruits of Ability, provide you with unique enhancements. But unlike the abilities given to you by the fruits, those imparted to you from the rivers are permanent," explained Baldwin.

"Although moved to the mainland, the Renfrew retains its ability to alter anyone who drinks from it," warned Durwin.

"The alteration that the red river offers would disrupt the island harmony. The mighty Icyandic would recede from its banks and sink back down to the great deep, where its powers would be withheld from you," added Baldwin.

"As you know, before bringing the first guests to the island, the Caretaker carved a single verse on a column of stone and planted it near the Icyandic," said Durwin. "Heed the command of the Caretaker, and if you should forget it, revisit the Stone Pillar and view the words written there by his own hand."

"In the meantime, we'll recite to you this verse," said Baldwin.

So far, the presentation had been as it always was and now was the time when the twins would normally leave the stage, and be followed by Anult, who would recite the writing on the Stone Pillar. But tonight they did not leave; instead, they remained onstage with a desire to plead further with the islanders to refrain from tasting the Renfrew's water. They struggled for impossible words until they realized that no matter what they said, the islanders would be unable to comprehend the situation they were in: their obedience would come only from trust, not from understanding.

And so, without speaking, the twins finally departed and Anult emerged to take their place. His voice rang clearly out as he recited the verse:

> "Take care, young and old,
> To taste only isle rivers
> Flowing blue or gold;
> For lo, across the calm sea,
> Deep among dark woods,
> A river flows quick and deep,
> As bright as cherries;
> Quenches not; but opens wide
> Minds to self and fault,
> Concentrated, fills with pride,
> Let not your lips part
> To pass the red, red water."
> -The Island Caretaker

Anult concluded with a single farewell, "Goodnight," he said, then departed to join the other servants back at their palace.

The islanders remained for a while, conversing with each other. The group at Justin's table waited for some of those around them to leave so that they could speak privately. Conroy, Megan, Keelan, and Allison came and joined them.

Justin remained silent, but in his mind his thoughts were raging, for the struggle within him had become more intense. His desire to fly wrestled against his desire to obey the twins, who he had loved and trusted ever since he could remember, and their master. "*Who are they to tell us not to drink the red water,*" he thought. "*I saw both of them drink from the Renfrew with my own eyes.*"

Warrick and Elson urged the others to keep their discovery a secret, something that they had all done successfully to that point. Warrick suggested that they focus on the island games and seek answers to their questions after the tournament. Everyone agreed, but banishing the image of the fascinating red river from their minds was easier for some, and none planned to stay away from it for long.

chapter five: ·victory and defeat·

Lachlan awoke an hour earlier than he usually did and made his way from his isolated cabin toward Corliss Lake. He preferred living outside of town in peaceful Hettered Forest and enjoyed the quietness of his seclusion, rather than being in the midst of the hustle and bustle of busy Epidomon, the island's largest, central town. With the Launtrining competition scheduled to begin in a couple of hours, he harnessed his stout, black workhorse to his cart, into which he had placed a half dozen long steel planks and some other gear, and set off.

He was the first competitor at the lake that morning and he wondered when his partner would arrive. Idris had agreed to come early so that they would have plenty of time to make any necessary last minute adjustments to their equipment and strategy. Lachlan remembered the previous year's contest when he and Idris had disappointedly placed second. During the fourth and final launch, their plank broke and Idris barely reached the lake. Their third launch had been close to the best launch of the tournament, that of Russel Minns and Ayona Bo, and the two men were confident that first place would be theirs with one more attempt. But the tournament referees declared that the rules of the contest guaranteed each team three successful launches, but if the equipment should fail on one of the four attempts, it was to be considered bad luck and the failed launch could not be redone.

This year, however, they would do all they could to ensure that all four of their launches would be successful; they would use a new plank for each launch. Lachlan looked behind him in the cart at the planks that lay in the bed of the wagon. He had spent numerous hours in his metal shop trying to improve on the construction of the launch planks. Lachlan was known as a master of metallurgy, but he wondered if Idris would be pleased with the modifications he had made.

He would not have to wait long to find out; a group of people approached the launch site, among them was Lachlan's partner, Idris Wincrest. With him were the two reigning champions, Russel Minns and Ayona Bo, of Unknown Creatures, as well as some young rookies from the team, *Orcas*. Walking beside Idris, holding his hand firmly, was his betrothed fiancée, Kira Leta. Kira's steps were light, her smile wide, and her face glowed; she was a living definition of joy.

Idris noticed Lachlan waiting for him and went to help him unload the planks from the wagon.

"Looks like we're going head to head with the champs again," said Idris.

"Good," responded Lachlan. "I'd hoped we'd be matched together again this year." Idris and Lachlan finished unloading the wagon and moved Lachlan's horse and cart out of the way.

Because there were many teams that needed to complete the eight contests in a week's time, the officials organized the events efficiently, keeping the action of the tournament going from morning until early evening. For the benefit of the contestants and the spectators, the events were arranged to provide as much mixing among the teams as the officials could manage, so it was unlikely that the same two teams competed together in more than a couple of events.

"I don't think it was by chance. Remember how many people came to watch us last year? I think there may be even more this year," said Idris, after looking around at the gathering crowd.

Although the start of the Launtrining was an hour away, dozens and dozens of spectators had already arrived, choosing optimal spots to view the contest. Some were even brave enough to take boats out onto the lake, willing to dodge the falling players in order to get a clear view of the action. It seemed that the officials thought of no better way to begin the tournament than by attempting to recreate the duel that ended the previous year's competition so dramatically.

Next, some of the island servants arrived sharply dressed in their officiating uniforms of maroon and black with an emblem of an eagle on their right shoulder. Large hourglasses, used to measure the duration of each flight, were put into place near the newly erected Launtrining sign and the scoring board was made ready.

Lachlan remembered that he had left his team's banner in the wagon and went to retrieve it. He found the flag, picturing a three tongued flame of red and yellow burning against a dark brown background, and attached it to one of several flag posts, and hoisted it high into the air above the Launtrining sign. As he turned to seek out Idris, he had to duck in order to avoid being struck by a launch plank being carried by two boys. Behind them came two girls, one with blonde hair was carrying a black and white flag.

Megan secured her team banner to a pole and hoisted it up next to the banner of *Fire*, while Keelan and Conroy installed the plank. The whole Orcas team gathered around the launch site, watching Brant and Allison, and Conroy and Mahrlee practice their routines. Keelan had selected Brant to partner with Allison in the event even though Conroy had wanted to be partnered with her; Keelan was worried that Conroy would be too concerned about Allison's well being instead of her altitude. Not that she would get killed, but experiencing injury was never pleasant. Thus, Conroy was placed at the opposite end of a launch plank from Mahrlee.

The final two banners were raised to fly beside the others. One was a flag on which five shapely feminine silhouettes stood in various poses, one figure in each corner of the flag and one larger figure in the center. The center figure stood posed seductively with her hands on her hips, which were at the top of long, slender, slightly bent legs. This was the flag of the team *Island Beauties*, a team comprised only of women. The final flag displayed the six-limbed figure of the champions, Unknown Creatures. The sixteen competitors, four from each team, took their positions and the sound of horns signaled the commencement of the tournament.

Lachlan's fist slammed into the thick metal plank and Idris was launched straight up into the air, higher than anyone else, but his trajectory was wrong. Unlike the others, who soared upward and outward so that they would land in the lake, Idris began to drop back to the island, causing the crowd to disperse quickly when they saw the unlucky competitor descending toward them. He crashed hard into the newly erected sign, shattering it to pieces and breaking the two signposts. He lay broken on the ground and white fluid spilled from his body.

"So soon to call upon the white river!" shouted one bystander.

Laughter and cheering from the crowd burst forth at Idris' demise, for they knew that in only a few moments Idris would stand before them restored, and all that would be lost was the new Launtrining sign and a launch attempt for the team, Fire. The white blood on the ground flowed back into Idris' body through his wounds, which then closed and sealed. Those that had been successfully launched returned from the lake in time to see the healing of Idris complete.

"Thanks, thanks," said Idris loudly, getting to his feet and addressing the crowd, which was still laughing and cheering at him.

"That's going to be a contender for sure!" cheered the crowd. Every year a prize was awarded to the contestant who experienced the most tragic tournament mishap, demonstrating the magnificent benefit of the Icyandic in the most spectacular fashion.

Only one spectator seemed to be slightly disturbed by the crashed landing; Wendel Wright came forward and gathered some of the broken fragments of the sign. As he carried the largest pieces of the sign away, he looked around to spot Keelan and made his way through the crowd straight for the young sign maker.

"Keelan, I am sorry that this has happened," said Wendel, showing him the broken sign fragments. "It is made even more unfortunate by the fact that it occurred on the very first trial of the very first contest of the tournament. Such a pity, but would it be too much to ask if you could make a replacement? I'm certain that this is damaged beyond repair."

Keelan glanced at Conroy, now preparing to launch Mahrlee for the second time. Conroy saw Keelan and figured at once what Wendel was doing. Conroy nodded to Keelan.

"Of course," answered Keelan, "after all, this was my favorite."

Wendel walked away satisfied that the sign would be replaced, but disappointed that this year's tournament would proceed without it.

During Idris' recovery, Lachlan had installed a new plank and assured his partner that the next launch would send him along the proper trajectory, affording him a much more enjoyable landing in the calm water of Corliss Lake.

Lachlan's modification was a success, and Idris soared impressively high into the air, though just a few feet higher than Ayona and Mahrlee, whose flights were the most enjoyable to watch. The majority of the tandems relied on a strategy that matched brute strength with a light partner to create the highest launches; such were the strategies of Lachlan and Idris, and Russel and Ayona.

The best launches for the Orcas, however, relied on the extraordinary leaping ability of Mahrlee. It was because of this skill that she was selected to compete in both the Launtrining and the Wavelling, the two contests where the ability to jump was a weighty asset. Her long slender legs sent her flying upward with great velocity, her body moved gracefully through the air, spinning and twisting and diving into the water at last, as straight as could be with only a small splash.

Ayona was also quite graceful in the air, and her launches were aided by her leaping ability as well, but not to the extent that Mahrlee's were. Idris had no concept of grace, soaring into the air with flailing limbs, unable to stabilize himself from spinning and tumbling, he fell into the lake in an awkward position every time.

In spite of his poor form, Idris was the one who ascended highest into the sky. His fourth and final launch reached a height of five hundred twenty five feet, a new tournament record, and Fire was declared the victor of the first session of the Launtrining. Unknown Creatures followed and Orcas behind them. Island Beauties were fourth, as they had expected, for this contest was not suited to their strengths.

"Nice job!" Russel congratulated Lachlan. "I don't know what you did to those planks, but whatever it was, it was effective. I don't think that performance will be matched by anyone."

"Oh, there's nothing special about them, it's all here," said Lachlan, flexing his arm to display his large bicep muscle.

The next launch was not scheduled for another hour and the crowd dispersed across the island to watch other contests. It was the general consensus among the islanders that this year's launtrining competition between Fire and Unknown Creatures was not as dramatic as last year's, but Idris' crash made up for this, and besides, there was still lots of action to come.

*   *   *   *   *   *   *   *   *   *   *   *

Swarms filled the air, hordes covered the ground, all approaching the city of the king. Serene Casilda was under attack. So vast was the oncoming enemy that no sky could be seen above them, nor could any ground be seen below them. A more motley crew never existed, each one unique in form and the weaponry they bore. Some were armed with swords, some with spiked clubs, some with bow and arrow, and some carried no weapons at all, their very bodies having parts adorned with horns, or sharp ridges, or some other shape with which to inflict pain. Kavan himself led the legions of warriors, soaring high above in the sky at the vanguard of his company. Armed with a pair of short double-edged swords, his course was straight toward the center of the white-structured city, right for the castle of the king. He looked down at Casilda as he passed over its limits, and as he observed its magnificence his desire to dwell in the palace and rule the city overwhelmed him. In his eagerness to conquer, he proceeded so quickly that he began to distance himself from his companions.

His army was large, strong, and motivated. Like Kavan, they had all been removed from their service under the king, losing certain privileges and responsibilities as a result of their choice to fall in league with him. Possession and power is what they sought now, and there was no greater wealth than that contained within the king's stores, and no greater power than to rule the glorious city. Although they had been allowed access into Casilda in spite of their rebellion against its ruler, they were forbidden from dwelling there and were required to be escorted while visiting. The attackers desired to live within the city boundaries once more, and were prepared to fight to recover what they had lost.

The horde on the ground marched to the north entrance of the city to find the doors of the gateway closed and barred. The leader of the ground force, an extremely large creature with two arching horns protruding several feet from his shoulders, bent down to the ground like a bull preparing to gore his adversary and pressed into the solid wooden doors so that his horns dug deep into them. Then, with a long grunt and a loud roar, he lifted his shoulders and wrenched the doors easily from their hinges. With a quick heave, he sent them flying though the air behind him and into the angry crowd. The horned creature stood at the entrance and peered down the main street of the city for only a moment until its round, flat, face was met by the fist of a defender of the city.

"I've been sent to repel you, Elzib!" said Sandor as his blow sent the creature soaring into the air along the same arch that the gateway doors had flown a few moments before.

Behind Sandor came another vast army, even more numerous than the assailants outside the city walls. Unlike the unlawful horde, the soldiers of the king were dressed in uniform and marched in time with one another into battle. Each wore white cloth garments, gold vests and helmets, and each carried a single straight, long sword and large shield. Fighting commenced just outside the gateway as Sandor and his comrades formed rank at the open entrance to prevent the horde from entering. Having been stopped from passing through the gateway, the invaders spread out along the perimeter of the city's high wall and used their own bodies to provide a slope for their forces to scale the barrier and enter the city. Inside, members of the white army, poised and ready to fight for their home and king, met the trespassers in a defensive fury.

In the sky above, the battle began as well. Another branch of soldiers flew up from the center of the city in a stream of white and gold to meet Kavan, who was now well within the city limits. Kavan met the defenders with vigor, sending his foes, one after another, falling downward, broken by a single blow from one of his swords. His approach toward the royal palace slowed only slightly as he fought through his enemy. Like a great black bird consuming a swath of white cloud as he passed through it, leaving only a void in the whiteness behind him, so Kavan advanced through the soldier-filled sky toward the palace.

Kavan's success was not matched by his airborne allies, however, and their advance was halted by Casilda's army; the battle raged in the air above the city where the two forces met. Defeated soldiers from both sides fell, so numerous that their bodies crashed to the solid streets and buildings below like mammoth drops of rain.

While his troops held the gateway, Sandor advanced through the horde on the ground in the same manner as Kavan was doing above. As quickly as he could, he left a path of fallen foes in his trail. He drove his sword into an ugly beast with four arms and four legs wielding a spiked mace and large club. Although the creature was able to successfully land blows with each of these into Sandor's side, the captain was not injured, and defeated the monster with a single angry thrust of his silver sword.

"Captain!" came a cry from above. It was the leader of the troops that were attempting to resist Kavan. "The air assault has been met and the forces are being contained and driven back, and many have been captured already, but Kavan is advancing swiftly to the palace. None of us can stop him!"

*　　*　　*　　*　　*　　*　　*　　*　　*　　*　　*　　*

The second day of the island games was underway as the starting bell of the Runrining was rung. The contestants were off the line like a flash and screams of excitement could be heard from a number of the women racers as everyone jockeyed for position at the first corner. Evelyn, along with Kira Leta and Amara Dodie, both of Island Beauties, were clustered together in the middle of the pack. Warrick, the other Unknown Creature in the race, was toward the front. They rounded the corner and came to the first of several collection points, where each racer was required to pick up a token to prove that they had run the full length of the racecourse. Evelyn grasped a blue bead from one of two long troughs placed at each side of the course while remaining at full stride and efficiently placed it in a small pouch tied around her neck.

It wasn't long before they finished the first stretch of the race, passed through a long series of open meadows and then entered the first forest section of the course. The runners, traveling inhumanly fast, noticed immediately the cooler temperature in the shaded woods. The forests were the most dangerous parts of the course; a slight error in navigating through the narrow trail and a tree could easily knock a runner down, and sometimes out of the race altogether. Evelyn was careful to avoid being pushed off the track, but at one instance someone tripped and fell forward into Kira, who was directly behind Evelyn. Kira threw up her hands as she was driven into Evelyn and both girls were knocked off balance near the edge of the trail, but they were able to remain on course. Soon, Evelyn could see the brightly lit fields at the end of the wooded trail coming quickly and she prepared to make a move to get closer to the front. Looking ahead, she saw that Warrick had already asserted himself in the lead.

Evelyn focused hard on her running and felt her limbs moving fast and strong as she exited the woods, going out wide from the course to pass some of the pack. The ground below her feet felt good as she pushed against it. To her right, far to the south she saw the finishing point of the race, the peak of Mount Manor. Knowing that there was still a long distance to go until the finish, Evelyn restrained her pace and pulled back into the pack after passing about a dozen other racers. Kira and Amara had followed Evelyn when she made her move forward and they also resumed positions within the pack, remaining directly behind Evelyn. It wasn't until this point that

Evelyn realized that it was the Island Beauties' strategy to trail her, mimicking her proven racing technique; Evelyn had always been a top contender in the Runrining. "Wait 'til the bottom of the mountain," thought Evelyn, "see if they can keep up with me then!"

Warrick had been in the lead since the first checkpoint. He was thoroughly enjoying the contest and he started to distance himself from the rest of the group. A pair of cheetahs leapt out from some bushes and began to run playfully alongside him, but they could not maintain the pace of the runner and gave up the chase, choosing to play in the meadow of green and gold grass instead. He looked down at the ground and increased his speed to the second checkpoint, the round stone tower of the Island Council near the eastern edge of the isle. Grabbing a red ruby, the token of the second race station, suspended from the low hanging branches of the trees at the base of the tower, Warrick came around the tower and headed north, running in the opposite direction of the finish line.

The route from the tower to the north shore at Corliss Lake had yet to be run before the last stretch, a direct route from the north shore to the tip of Mount Manor at the southern coast.

*   *   *   *   *   *   *   *   *   *   *

The letters were finely carved so deep into the stone that Justin could not imagine a tool able to make such marks in the hard rock. The lines of each letter were perfectly smooth and the handwriting was flowing, not feminine like his wife's script, but rugged and bold. Near the ring of the Icyandic River, Justin stood and observed the solitary stone pillar. He read the words, speaking them out loud softly to himself. They were exactly as Anult had recited the night before. The verse was oft spoken at community events and was known by heart by every islander older than seven, but as he looked at the writing on the stone before him it provoked a new and powerful effect. The struggle between his desire to fly and to obey the command intensified.

Justin touched the rock and found it to be coarse and cool. He pushed the stone to see if it would move; it didn't. He walked around all four sides to view it from every angle, all the while envisioning the twins sipping from the scarlet stream, and doubting the merit of the words. On every side the same twelve lines were carved, and at the end of the script the signature of the Island Caretaker was clearly legible. He read the inscription four times, pausing at each side to examine the words closely:

take care, young and old,
to taste only isle rivers
flowing blue or gold;
for lo, across the calm sea,
Deep among dark woods,
A river flows quick and deep,
As bright as cherries,
Quenches not, but opens wide
Minds to self and fault;
Concentrated, fills with pride;
Let not your lips part
to pass the red, red water

-the Island Caretaker

Justin traced the lines of the letters with his right forefinger. The letters were wide enough so that he could press his finger into them. He felt their sharp edges and sensed that whatever force had placed the stone there was one that should not be challenged. Yet, Justin's longing to see the Renfrew again, and to touch it and taste it did not subside.

He turned away from the stone pillar and walked down the slope, across the gentle waves of the Icyandic, and toward the servants' palace. It was unlikely that Durwin and Baldwin would be there, but maybe one of the others would be able to answer some of Justin's questions. He walked up the seventy-seven wide stairs to the front entrance of the palace and pulled down on a thick rope to ring the bell within. Several seconds passed before Justin heard activity inside. Finally the door opened, revealing the smallest servant Justin had ever seen.

"Welcome," said the servant. "My name is Carollan. May I help you?"

"I am Justin Nickols and I am looking for Durwin and Baldwin. Do you know if they are here?"

Carollan motioned for Justin to come inside. Justin entered and glanced around the rooms adjoining the large entryway. He did not see anyone else there.

"I'm afraid they're not here at the moment," answered Carollan. "As you must know, the twins are busy with the Island Games."

"I see," said Justin.

"Is there anything I can help you with?" asked the small servant, again, detecting a need within the islander.

Justin was not surprised that the twins weren't there, but he was disappointed that he didn't see any of the other servants with whom he was familiar. The only source for help in understanding the matter at the forefront of his mind stood unimpressively before him. Justin hesitated for a moment, but then decided to pose some questions to Carollan; he certainly seemed harmless enough, Justin towered over the little servant by at least a foot.

"I was hoping to learn more about the Renfrew and the stone pillar," declared Justin firmly. The words came from his mouth bolder than he intended, and he thought for a brief second that he saw a flash of intensity in Carollan's eyes, but it didn't last long, if it had been there at all.

"You saw the twins drink from the red river and you are confused," stated Carollan plainly, his forthrightness matched that of Justin. "It is true that they drank from the Renfrew, but they did nothing wrong. The law of the stone pillar applies only to you islanders, not for us who serve the Caretaker."

Justin was taken aback by Carollan's response, "How do you know what I saw?"

"The twins told me."

"Can you tell me more about the Renfrew?" asked Justin, his desire for knowledge of the secret river surpassing his curiosity to find out how the twins learned they had been followed.

"There is nothing more to tell other than what has been told in the legend," replied Carollan. "And as for the difference between you islanders and us servants, we have been faithful to our master for many ages, but your relationship with him is newly formed. You must prove yourselves worthy of greater privileges."

"How?"

"By doing what has been asked of you, even though you may not understand. And as for your desire to fly, the Renfrew will not afford you with such skill."

Again the little person amazed Justin. But anger swelled in Justin's mind and he replied, "How do you explain that the twins were able to fly after they drank from the Renfrew?"

"You do not know all that you think you know," the softness of Carollan's voice had disappeared. "I am not deceiving you, but I cannot tell you more, for you would not be able to understand what the Renfrew would do to you. Only by consuming its water would you gain knowledge of the full power of the river, but then it would be too late; the effect would be permanent and irreversible."

Silence overcame the grand foyer where the two stood. Justin looked down at Carollan and saw a firm resolve in his face to divulge nothing more about the Renfrew, though Justin didn't know whether it was because the servant *could not* or *would not* enlighten him.

At last Justin spoke, he hoped not to offend his host further, but he had to speak of one last mystery, "Are you aware that I also saw the twins fall to their knees before Kavan? Why would they do that?"

Carollan did not answer and this time Justin was sure that he saw a fiery intensity in the small servant's eyes. Justin became frightened and decided to leave.

"Thanks for your time, Carollan," said Justin. "I must be going if I am to see my wife finish the Runrining." He passed through the doorway and walked down the stairs.

Carollan followed and called out; "There are those who would lead you down a path that you desire to travel, and though you think it is a path that would serve you well, at its end you would find yourself in a trap that you could not escape."

Justin waved politely to Carollan, tossed some yallup into his mouth, and started to run swiftly south toward Mt. Manor.

    *   *   *   *   *   *   *   *   *   *   *   *

Sandor glanced up to see the dark figure of Kavan piercing a giant white cloud of Casildan soldiers; he was nearly at the castle and was casting down servants of the king as he advanced. Sandor thought quickly to determine his course of action. "*The king does not need protection, but if Kavan reaches the palace he will position himself to gain more followers.*"

Sandor launched himself upward and flew quickly toward the conquering and intimidating Kavan.

"*I must stop him or many more will be lost!*" thought Sandor. He reached over his shoulder to grab his shield. He had not needed it while fighting the horde on the ground, but he would need all of his resources to fight Kavan; none but King Iman had ever defeated him.

Kavan was nearly at the castle; only a few unworthy adversaries remained to stop him. But suddenly he found himself plummeting. He recovered from his fall and looked up to see, at last, one worthy with whom to do battle. Sandor hovered in the air above Kavan with his shield at his side and his sword extended, pointing down toward Kavan.

"Sandor!" cried Kavan, almost happily. "I was beginning to get worried that I would not have the pleasure of defeating you on my way to greet the king." Kavan ascended to meet Sandor.

"You'll not see the king today!" replied Sandor.

Kavan lashed out furiously with his blades, but Sandor held his shield high and was able to withstand the blows without injury, even though he was pushed backward toward the castle with each one.

On a balcony high up on the side of the castle, King Iman stood and watched the commander of his army contend with the one who had once been his greatest servant. Sorrow and anger filled the king's heart; sorrow that one so great had chosen a path that would ultimately lead to his destruction, and anger that this same one was now causing turmoil in his peaceful city. The king knew that the outcome of this battle would have a significant impact on the fate of the other servants. Two others joined him on the balcony; the first was his son, the prince, and the other was without definite form, a glowing, fiery silhouette in the general shape of a man - a living flame.

"Observe how Sandor fights for the sake of others, as well as to please us, while Kavan fights only for himself and his own gain."

*   *   *   *   *   *   *   *   *   *   *   *

The climb up the north side of Mt. Manor was exceptionally difficult, yet it was Evelyn's favorite section of the race. Since leaving the eastern side of the island and rounding the tower of the Island Council, she had gradually made her way toward the front of the pack. Only Warrick remained in front of her as she began the long ascent up the winding mountain trail.

The two Island Beauties, Kira and Amara, still ran directly behind Evelyn, but now she would test them. She hungered to consume the slope with her pace, and she increased her speed until the passing trees became blurs in her peripheral vision. Halfway up the mountain she moved ahead of Warrick, while Kira and Amara fell behind and struggled to prevent other racers from overtaking them.

She was determined not to break stride as the peak of the mountain came within sight, and she planned to leap from the cliff into the blue sky and plummet victoriously into the bay. She was only a few yards from the edge when, for some reason, she looked to her left. Far away down the east side of the mountain, near the place where the clear mountain streams flowed, she saw two figures crouching beside the water. They were not in the open, and they should not have been easily seen, but sunlight reflected off one of the metal spouts of their flasks, catching Evelyn's eye.

Evelyn halted just one pace from the edge and Warrick went sailing by.

"What are you doing?" he shouted, his cry fading as he fell.

Evelyn had only a moment to watch the twins, but she was certain that she saw them pouring red water into the mountain streams. Then, against her will, she was driven by the oncoming crowd over the cliff, but not before Kira and Amara had passed her, claiming second and third place.

*   *   *   *   *   *   *   *   *   *   *   *

Kavan's barrage of blows finally ceased as he realized that he could not destroy Sandor's shield. The image of the large eagle on the shield mocked him, for there was not a scratch on its face. Sandor lowered his defense to gain a better view of Kavan pensively revising his offensive strategy, and saw that his adversary was still close to full strength. He decided to remain defensive, hoping Kavan would tire; then he would attack.

Kavan began another assault. He flew all around Sandor in an attempt to get past the shield. Sandor was very quick, and with one arm holding fast to the shield and the other handling his sword, he spun around to meet Kavan's blows and his defense protected him from injury once more.

Sandor was now satisfied that his opponent had wearied himself sufficiently, and he prepared to strike. But Kavan did not allow him to do so yet, for he flung his swords at Sandor. The blades whistled through the air, but Sandor spun and they passed by him, before reversing direction and coming at him again. But again they missed their target and flew back into Kavan's grasp. Again, and again, and again, the giant Kavan flung his swords at the commander of Casilda's army, manipulating them to make them move as he wished with only his thoughts. Sandor spun and darted side to side to avoid the sharp and spinning blades, deflecting them with his shield and pushing them off course with strokes from his own blade. Throughout this lengthy ordeal Sandor was able to avoid significant injury, but the exposed edges of his arms and legs were cut where the blades had sliced him. No blood came from the wounds; light emitted from them instead, but they did not hinder his defensive efforts. His gashes grew together and covered over the light that leaked from him; the power of the Icyandic was within him, as it was with all of the immortals.

Sandor determined to strike. He had been pushed back to the castle, and his feet brushed against its side. He launched himself from the wall and drew his shield aside and began violently hacking at Kavan with his sword, pushing the red river guardian backward and downward. Kavan had no shield and so he caught the blows with his swords and even used his armored forearms to receive some of the force. Light shone from within Kavan where Sandor's sword struck.

All around them other struggles continued. Outnumbered two to one, most defeated assailants regained consciousness to find that they had been bound and taken captive by soldiers of Casilda's army, while the fallen defenders recovered and rejoined the battle. Thus the number of Kavan's supporters dwindled, and it was obvious now that the king's army would prevail, if for no other advantage than that of sheer numbers.

In between delivering blows to his weakened enemy, Sandor dared a quick glance around to observe the surroundings. He saw that his army was near victory, and that multitudes of his own soldiers were watching him.

"*They are depending on me,*" he thought. "*I must prevail!*"

He continued to force Kavan down, out of the sky, until he stood on the smooth stones of the city's central street. Sandor also touched down, still swinging ferociously with his sword, and empowered by the knowledge that his efforts were for the benefit of those who watched him.

Kavan's defenses failed at last as his two swords were wrenched from his hands. Sandor swung his shield into him and knocked him onto his back. Kavan looked up from the street to see the sky full of soldiers in white glaring down at him. Sandor stood over him with drawn sword.

"Get out!" shouted Sandor, pointing to the gateway. "Take your horde and flee! Do not dare attack Casilda again! If you do, it will be the Riders' wrath you face instead of mine."

Kavan's swords flew low across the ground and returned to his hands as he erected himself.

"It's fortunate for you that the king has decided to spare you today, though I don't understand why," said Sandor. "Perhaps out of respect of who you once were."

"This is only the beginning," replied Kavan, still defiant. He lifted from the street and flew away without turning from Sandor or Casilda.

From the balcony, the king and his companions watched Kavan and what remained of his horde leave, and then they descended to the royal court. It was only a moment before Sandor arrived, accompanied by many others. The king commended Sandor on the victory, and then a large table was set with maps and scrolls. In the center of the table a parchment was unrolled, revealing an ancient and detailed map of an island. At the top of the sheet in bold lettering was written: *Iman's Isle, the Island of the King's Treasures.*

$*$ $*$ $*$ $*$ $*$ $*$ $*$ $*$ $*$ $*$ $*$ $*$

It wasn't until later that evening, when Evelyn and Justin finally returned to their home, that she was free to tell her husband what she had seen at the top of Mt. Manor and reveal to him the reason why she did not win the race. When she finished, Justin shared with her his encounter with the little servant, Carollan, at the servants' palace. The two of them talked long into the night about these things. But try as they might, they could not put these pieces of knowledge together into anything that made sense to them.

In dreams that night, both had the same vision; they were standing at the edge of a large cliff that extended to their right and left as far as they could see. The sun shone bright in a cloudless sky and there was neither water nor any kind of plant in sight. Across a wide and deep chasm they saw another cliff, also extending right and

left as far as they could see. They desired more than anything to
cross the expanse and reach the other side, but they saw no means
to do so. They glanced down into the canyon and saw nothing; it
wasn't dark, like an abyss into the heart of the earth, but there was
no bottom to the bright void.   They walked together along the edge
for what seemed hours, but found nothing that bridged the
impossible divide. At last they turned away from the chasm and
began to walk into a barren, flat, endless space.

*   *   *   *   *   *   *   *   *   *   *   *

Excitement ruled the island throughout the week as the
competition progressed. The three teams, Fire, Unknown Creatures,
and Island Beauties, seemed to have a top contender in nearly every
event, clearly becoming the likeliest teams to win the tournament.
Warrick and Justin remained confident that it was theirs to win;
Justin had not competed in the Ascentining, and Russel Minns had
yet to compete in the Luggerrun. Both were expected to win these,
but victory this year would be much closer than it had been in the
previous years when Unknown Creatures had won easily.

One other team had performed surprisingly well, keeping
themselves within reach of the champions: the rookie team, Orcas.
Derek and Mahrlee performed exceptionally well at the Wavelling,
holding first place past the midpoint of the competition; it was likely
that they would hold on to the top spot through the end of the week.
Brant had a good showing in the Ascentining, and Keelan and Conroy
both placed moderately well in the Runrining. Keelan was continually
motivating his teammates, and they were all responding to his
encouragement, beginning to truly believe, as he did, that they had a
chance to capture the trophy.

The next event for the young team was the Archerion in which
Megan was scheduled to compete. Megan and Allison walked
together from Epidomon through the soft meadows toward Hettered
Forest in the early afternoon of the fifth, and next to last, day of the
games. Megan carried a new bow that her parents had presented to
her as a gift for her first tournament. At first she was not sure
whether she should replace her old familiar bow, and she worried
that it would take her a long time to get used to the new one. But
the wooden frame of her new bow was light, smooth, and well

balanced, and the string tension was just as she liked. Her worries were put to rest the first time she drew back the string and loosed an arrow. It sailed smoothly through the air, not succumbing to gravity until it had traveled a surprising distance.

Before the games began, Megan was confident that she would have a good showing in the archery shoot. But now, with her team in contention, she wished some other Orca would compete in her stead, and she revealed this to Allison.

"Stop worrying," said Allison, "you're the best archer that I've ever seen."

"I just wish Keelan wasn't coming to watch. He's so intense. He makes me nervous."

"I haven't noticed so much," replied Allison. "Maybe it's because you like him," she mumbled.

"What did you say?" asked Megan.

Allison didn't reply but moaned softy and shrugged her shoulders.

"Allison, what did you mean by that?" Megan asked again, but again, Allison didn't answer; instead she started to run ahead.

Megan pursued her but didn't get another chance to push for an answer. The two girls arrived at the archery site just as the contest was about to begin and Megan was ushered into the shooting area without getting an opportunity to take any practice shots. Her designated shooting space was between two other women, both skilled with the bow; an extremely tan woman with short brown hair, Deryn Lani, was to her right, and a muscular, black, Ayona Bo was to her left. Further down the line she saw Idris and Warrick positioned next to each other. It seemed that the officials had uncharacteristically scheduled Orcas, Fire, and Unknown Creatures to compete together once more.

"*I don't see Keelan. Maybe he didn't come.*" Just as this thought entered Megan's mind, she spotted Keelan approaching. He walked through the spectators and went right to her.

"Megan!" he cried, handing her a bundle of freshly picked flowers. "Good luck!" He backed into the crowd, and Megan could see Conroy and Allison behind him smirking.

"*What is going on?*" she thought. That was definitely not what she had expected from Keelan, but he still made her nervous.

"Begin when ready!" called the loud voice of the official, Huxlanni, a stout servant with a thick goatee and a gold hoop earring.

Arrows whirred through the air at targets placed fifty paces ahead. Most of the archers, including Megan, had selected to consume a few island yallup to minimize the time lapse from when the arrow was lined up in the sight of the target and the moment it was released.

Megan watched the first arrows of Ayona and Deryn sink into the center of their targets, then pulled back the string of her bow, confidence growing within her every inch the string went back. She held it fixed for a split second while she lined it up to the target and then let go.

"Thuunk!" the arrow caught the edge of the target's center. One down, nine to go.

Many other archers also struck the center of their targets with their initial shot, but it wasn't long before Megan, Ayona, and Deryn gained an advantage over the others. Both Warrick and Idris had a couple of early missed shots. It wasn't until Ayona shot her seventh arrow that any of the three girls missed the center mark, and even that only missed by an inch. Deryn's shooting was perfect until she shot her ninth arrow, leaving Megan as the only archer yet to miss. She looked into the crowd and spotted her friends. They returned her gaze and offered her encouragement.

Megan watched Deryn's final arrow strike its mark, earning her a nearly perfect score of nine out of ten. Ayona missed her final shot, scoring eight out of ten, tying with Warrick and Idris. Megan drew back her last arrow. As she held herself poised to shoot, she began to think about whether she was properly aimed. She realized that she was taking much more time than she did for her normal routine. Her arms grew tired and she began to have a difficult time keeping her aim steady. Instead of releasing the arrow, she let the string slowly pull itself back, uncurling the bow, making sure the arrow remained notched to avoid disqualification.

She didn't know what do. Suddenly, she had no idea how she had managed to shoot nine other arrows into the small circle so far away. Shaken, she looked again to her friends. Allison smiled, Conroy looked calm, and Keelan winked. She focused hard and drove doubt out of her mind as she faced the target, drew back the arrow, and released it without hesitation. It flew straight into the center of the center, and the entire arrow passed through the target into the field of thick grass.

"Ten for ten!" yelled Huxlanni, "A perfect score for Megan Prendt of the Orcas!"

Allison rushed forward and gave Megan an enormous hug as the crowd cheered. Conroy and Keelan followed suit, although the hug Keelan gave was a bit longer than the others. Ayona and Deryn congratulated Megan, as did her teammate in the competition, Elleron Little, followed by Warrick, and lastly Idris.

*   *   *   *   *   *   *   *   *   *   *   *

The final day of the tournament arrived. Unbelievably, the Orcas had taken the lead, partly due to Megan's spectacular performance in the Archerion the previous day, and Elleron Little's second place finish in the Thirling that morning. But rugged Russel Minns had claimed first place in the Luggerrun as expected, bringing the hopes of the Unknown Creatures' fourth consecutive championship closer to reality. As dusk approached, all eyes were on Justin Nickols, the last person left to compete among the few teams contending for victory. In a few minutes he would lead his team to victory again, or else the rookie team, Orcas, would be crowned champions. Fire would have to settle for third place, most likely.

Justin leapt up as high as he could and took a strong hold of the rope in both hands and began climbing. Driven more than ever before, the title of champion at stake and the rest of the Unknown Creatures depending on him, he ascended toward the peak as quickly as he could. Upon reaching the top, he climbed onto the peak and grasped the dazzling blue sapphire that awaited him.

With the required token in hand, Justin looked down from the mountain, selecting his spot to dive. He thought that it would be appropriate to provide a glorious ending to the tournament and, knowing that he had time to spare, decided to jump out from the cliff as far as he could in a magnificent dive. But as he placed his foot on the edge of the cliff in preparation to jump, some rocks gave way and he slipped. His arms flung upward wildly as he fell and the sapphire came free from his grasp.

At once, Justin realized the seriousness of losing the jewel, knowing that if he did not recover it he would be disqualified. As he fell headlong toward the bay, he could see the blue gem falling only inches in front of him, and he reached his hand out to recover it. But the speed of his descent could not match that of the sapphire and his attempt to recover it was futile. The gem plunged into the water apart from him: Justin was disqualified.

    *   *   *   *   *   *   *   *   *   *   *

Because of Justin's disqualification, Unknown Creatures had to default to using Elson's score for the event. As a result, Fire pulled into second place ahead of the defending champions. The Orcas stunned the entire island with their victory.

In spite of not winning, Justin and Evelyn and their teammates cheerfully celebrated the close of the tournament with the rest of the island, for the powers of the rivers Candra and Azor prevailed, filling all hearts with peace and joy. Yet, Justin knew that had he been able to fly, he would have been able to recover the falling sapphire and would now be at the center of the ongoing celebration. He glanced toward the winning team as they sat together in the market square, while all about them people enjoyed food, music, dancing, and laughter.

Keelan was wild in victory, running and dancing all around and doing back flips from the winner's table, a large round table with seats for the nine members of the winning team. At the center of the table, on a raised pedestal, stood the tournament trophy. It would remain there until the end of the celebration the next day, then it would be placed in the trophy hall of the tower of the Island Council.

In spite of his current abandon, Megan noticed that she couldn't take her eyes off of Keelan, finding a certain charm about him. Sitting next to Megan was, of course, Allison, and Conroy beside her. Megan observed that Allison and Conroy seemed to have become very comfortable with one another. Keelan started running laps around the table and grabbing each of his teammates in turn and shaking them with violent triumph. Conroy had just picked himself up from the ground after Keelan had finished with him, moving on to celebrate with Mahrlee and Derek, when someone else took hold of him.

"Congratulations!" said Elson, "you've had a good month, I think, with the signs and now the championship."

"Yeah," was all Conroy could say.

"Don't get used to it, little brother; we'll be taking back the trophy next year. I'm going home. See you later."

"Okay, goodnight," replied Conroy. "I'm staying here."

None of the Orcas left the square that night. Some stayed up all night talking about the victory, while the rest of them reclined on the soft grass beside the square and fell asleep under bright stars.

$$*\quad*\quad*\quad*\quad*\quad*\quad*\quad*\quad*\quad*\quad*\quad*$$

After the tournament the islanders returned to their usual daily routines. Evelyn was enjoying her normal morning run, and as she came to the end of her circuit near the Icyandic, something colorful caught her attention – a large parrot was perched on the flat top of the stone pillar near the river. These beautiful birds were common on the island, yet this one seemed larger than normal to Evelyn, and its colors were exceptionally vivid. The other thing that made this sight unusual was that no animal had ever been seen sitting atop the pillar. The islanders considered the stone to be sacred, for the island servants had always declared it to be so, and they restrained from climbing on it. Evelyn's curiosity prodded her over to investigate.

It had been a long time since she had looked upon the script engraved in the stone. "Such fine writing," she said out loud as she approached the pillar.

She was not surprised when the bird replied, for parrots were very conversational. "Fine writing, foolish words," squawked the parrot. "Don't be fooled, *squawk...* don't be fooled."

"What do you mean?" asked Evelyn.

"Fooled by the words, fooled by the words, *squawk.*" The bird lifted its feathers and stepped up and down awkwardly several times, rocking back and forth as it turned on the stone to face Evelyn. "Why not drink the red water?"

"The Caretaker has asked us not to, and warned that if we did something would happen to the Icyandic."

"But *they* drink it, *squawk*, the island servants."

Evelyn's recent observation of the twins validated the bird's claim. "How do *you* know that?"

"I see much from the sky," answered the parrot. "I've seen them drink it. Can't you drink it too?"

"The Caretaker said..."

"How do you know what the Caretaker said? ... *squawk*," interrupted the bird. "The island servants put the pillar here and wrote the words."

"Why would they do that?"

"Because, *squawk*, they don't want you to become like them."

"Like them?"

"Powerful," said the bird, "they have great powers, and they know the secrets of Marland, *squawk*."

"What secrets?"

"You won't know until you drink. Then you will learn about them, and you'll be able to fly. Like me!" The bird raised its wings and leapt from the rock, flying away and leaving her mind pregnant with questions.

*　　*　　*　　*　　*　　*　　*　　*　　*　　*　　*　　*

"I want to fly!" exclaimed Justin. "Why shouldn't we?"

Evelyn and Justin discussed the Renfrew late into the night. Again. This new testimony from the parrot, combined with their current knowledge, seemed to provide ample evidence to refute the legend and the writing on the pillar. At last they agreed what they would do and went to bed.

Early the next morning, the young couple strode hand in hand across Idris' bridge over Corliss Lake to Marland. When they reached the mainland they walked along the shore until they found the trail. Curious to gaze upon the red river again, they made their way through the forest to the secret passageway, which they opened with the use of a couple of renden, and went to the Renfrew. They had intended to only look at the river, but as soon as they saw it, its appearance delighted them and they were overwhelmed with desire to know its flavor. With mild hesitation and hungry hearts, they knelt beside the water and leaned over so that the sweet stream touched their lips... and drank.

chapter six: ·departure·

Evelyn was the first of the two to draw the red water into her mouth and delight in its sweet taste. Justin watched his wife finish her initial sampling of the Renfrew, then he also *parted his lips to let pass the red, red water*. The two remained kneeling on the bank, sipping from the river until they had indulged themselves with several long draughts, then they stood up together and brushed the dirt and grass from their knees.

The only sounds to be heard were the soft chirps of small woodland creatures and the rush of the river. Justin lifted his arms to the sky and jumped, uncertain whether the effect of the Renfrew would be as he hoped. To his delight, he rose from the ground and ascended to an elevation that matched the top of the tallest trees. He hovered there and looked down on his beautiful wife and realized that she was no longer standing on the riverbank but was rising to meet him in the air. The couple embraced and smiled at one another, then they began to fly as swift and nimble as birds. They flew up and down, round and round; they zigged and zagged, twirled and spun; they darted into the woods where they soared with magnificent velocity and control in between the densely packed trees. Their laughter and joyful shouting drowned the sounds of the forest. Never had they felt so alive!

On this day their positions were reversed, as Kavan and some of his companions hid in the forest and spied on the unsuspecting islanders at the river. They were not trying to learn what the young couple was doing, for Kavan and his colleagues knew their every thought, one of the many abilities that all of King Iman's servants possessed, even those who had fallen from the king's service. Kavan smiled as he watched Justin and Evelyn play gracefully in the air like a pair of birds during their season of courting, not because their joy made him glad, but because they had given him his first victory in the war. He rewarded the islanders for their contribution to his cause by allowing them a moment of pleasure, and besides, he delighted in deceiving them; as Carollan had warned, it was not by consuming the Renfrew's red water that Justin and Evelyn were able to fly: it was Kavan's power that currently afforded them this skill. The islanders had yet to realize the real effect of the Renfrew.

On Kavan's right was the creature that Sandor had repelled from Casilda's gates, the large, two-horned Elzib. Above Kavan, perched on a high branch, was a large parrot, and directly behind Kavan, standing taller even than him, was the webbed, scaly, green monster whose image decorated the team flag of the islanders; it was the Unknown Creature itself.

None of them were more pleased at the moment than the creature, for *it* had been the one that conceived the plan. *It* was the one that convinced the bird to go and talk to Evelyn. *It* had been the one that fondled Justin's thoughts and fueled his desire to fly, for manipulating minds and kindling desires is what it ever seeks to do. *It* had been the one to stand beside the islanders when they returned to gaze upon the flowing red river and placed its long fingers around their minds, urging them to go closer. And *it* had been the one that gripped their hearts in its strong hands as they knelt down, enflaming their desires to melt away all sensitivity of consequence. It placed one of its scaly hands on Kavan's shoulder and gave a firm, excited squeeze of congratulations.

"Shall I go and speak to them, *squawk*?" asked the parrot, descending to a branch closer to his master.

"Yes, Shanahan," answered Kavan. "Congratulate them and tell them to prepare themselves to learn many secrets of Marland. And most importantly, encourage them to return to the island."

"Yes, yes!" exclaimed the scaly creature, "let them return there so the Candra can carry the Renfrew's effect to the others, all of the others, even the whole island!" The creature gave a gurgled, wheezing laugh as the large bird flew from the trees toward the airborne islanders.

"Look! Justin!" shouted Evelyn as she soared over the center of the river. She stopped in midair when she saw the parrot approaching her, recognizing it as the one she had met previously due to its unusually large size. "It's the bird that I told you about, the one I saw at the stone pillar!"

Justin finished a series of steep, descending barrel rolls then rose to meet the newcomer who glided in gentle circles around his wife.

"Hello, *squawk*," said Shanahan as Justin arrived. "I see you have both drank from the river. Well done, well done!" The bird attempted to clap its wings together to applaud Justin and Evelyn, but as it did it lost a bit of altitude. "Much is in store for you now," said the bird, rising back up to the islanders.

"Do you have a name?" Evelyn asked.

"Yes, *squawk*, I am Shanahan." The manner in which the parrot spoke indicated that it was proud of its name.

"Shanahan, you said before that there were many secrets about this land, and that we would learn them if we drank this red water. Will they be revealed to us now?" asked Evelyn.

"Soon, *squawk*, soon you will learn the mysteries of Marland," the bird circled both islanders as it spoke, unable to hover effortlessly in the air as they did.

"But Shanahan, why would the Caretaker and his servants want to keep us from experiencing this?" asked Justin. "This is amazing!"

"As I told her," said Shanahan, nodding toward Evelyn, "they didn't want you to become like they are, possessing great power and knowledge. But you *are* like them now! And so shall you always be, for the gift of the Renfrew cannot be returned. Go and tell your friends. Go and show the Caretaker's servants what you have done." With that, Shanahan flew away.

Justin and Evelyn resumed soaring wildly about for several minutes until, at last, the young couple had their fill of flying, at least for awhile, and returned to the ground. They reclined on the riverbank and looked up into the clear blue sky over the river. They talked about how they might surprise Elson and Warrick with their new ability to fly, laughing as they imagined their friends' reactions. They talked about their new friend, Shanahan, and how dazzling were the colors of his fine feathers. They talked about the island servants and why they had spent so much effort attempting to keep the people of the island from experiencing the Renfrew. Then they talked about the Caretaker.

"Do you remember him?" asked Evelyn.

"Vaguely," answered Justin. "I was only about five years old when he last visited the island; all I can remember is the image of a tall man with bright white hair and beard. I remember that he came to my house to visit my parents."

"He did have white hair and a beard," said Evelyn. "I was only four when I saw him, but I can remember his face. '*Daughter, how do you like my island? Are you finding the animals pleasant?'* he asked me. I answered him yes, and told him how much I liked to search for jewels in Corliss Lake. Then he picked me up in his arms and said, '*Yes, yes, there are many treasures here, but among them you are the most valuable.*' Then he put me down, patted me on the head, and sent me off to play with Bethany Krunser and Kira Leta."

"Why did he call you *daughter?*" asked Justin.

"He called all of the little kids on the island his *sons* and *daughters,*" replied Evelyn. "And he called all of the adults his *friends.*"

"What kind of a parent keeps their children from enjoying life? What kind of person keeps his friends from knowing pleasure?" said Justin, flinging a stone into the water. Evelyn was sure that she had never heard her husband speak in such a bitter tone.

"Now we can tell the others there's no reason to refrain from this river," said Evelyn. "Should we go and tell them now?"

"Yeah, I'm sure Warrick and Elson will want to come here right away."

"Should we walk back or fly?" asked Evelyn.

"As much as I'd like to return to the island soaring in the sky over Corliss Lake, all of the island would see us and we would lose our chance to surprise Warrick and Elson. Maybe the four of us can come back here and then we could all fly back to the island together." This plan excited them and they hopped to their feet and strolled over to the forest path and disappeared into the trees.

Kavan and his companions emerged from the woods on the opposite side of the river after Justin and Evelyn departed and stood on the riverbank. Shanahan returned and perched on the tip of one of Elzib's long horns. Kavan walked on the waves out into the center of the river and pulled his long chain from the water. As he did this, the Unknown Creature knelt by the river and slapped the surface with his four webbed hands, making a loud clapping sound that was carried through the air and the water. Soon, all sorts of creatures emerged from within the forest and from below the surface of the river in response to the creature's summoning.

"A great victory is ours today!" shouted Kavan after his loyal generals were assembled.

"As are the people of the island!" hissed the creature, lifting all four of his long arms up to cheer. A celebration of roars erupted from the warriors.

"No more will the king protect them," Kavan declared, "for the foolish people have unknowingly set themselves against those who watched over them. We have earned the right to enslave them, and with our power we shall bind those weaklings, the king's pets; there shall be no escape for them. Their time of free living has come to an end!"

The creature shook with excitement and licked its slimy mouth with a forked tongue and sliced its scaly flesh with sharp claws as Kavan spoke.

But the celebration ceased as a voice called loudly; "The strands that bind you are not yet loosened!" A lone figure emerged from the west and walked to the edge of the river. The horde parted to let him pass. He was dressed in bright white garments and had a large shield slung across his back and a sheathed sword at his side. All recognized him immediately.

"Here so soon, Gavril?" said Kavan, not surprised by the intruder. "I take it that your king has heard the good news already? Has he sent you to congratulate us? And have you come here by yourself? That would be unwise, don't you think? Perhaps you've come to join us?"

"I've come to bring you declarations from King Iman." Gavril showed no fear and strolled across the Renfrew's rolling surface to its center where he stood beside Kavan.

"Very well, let us hear what Iman has to say now," said Kavan.

Suddenly Gavril was lifted up by the spinning cylinder that arose from the Renfrew, the same one that Durwin had observed to measure the flow of the river. He stood on the flat top of the rotating shaft and addressed the crowd. As he did, the face of the eagle on his shield came to life; its eyes blinked and from its moving mouth came the very words that Gavril spoke so that his message was heard clearly by all.

"The king has declared that he will not abandon the people of the island to be destroyed by you," said Gavril and the eagle.

This angered Kavan and he did not let Gavril continue; "But he must let us have them: they are ours, all of them!" he shouted. The horde moaned with discontent.

"The first declaration that I bring is that the restraint preventing you from annihilating the islanders remains in place," Gavril and the eagle said loudly, "the king will not allow you to wreak your will upon them, for he knows that you would destroy all of them in a day. His power will act against you in this matter as it always has."

"They are contaminated with guilt and have positioned themselves against the king himself! He is obligated to destroy them!" Kavan demanded.

"No more so than he is obligated to destroy you and everyone here, and you have all been given time," answered Gavril. "Their doom is certain, but it need not come to them swiftly: they also shall be granted a number of seasons."

"A number of seasons to suffer!" exclaimed Elzib, his voice resembled the deep lowing sound of an ox. The horde cheered.

"You shall not be without spoils," continued Gavril. All of the cheering ceased as Kavan raised his hands to quiet the crowd, extremely interested in what Gavril was about to say. A sorrowful expression came over Gavril, and his strong shoulders slumped slightly. "Because they have placed themselves against the king, as you correctly stated, you shall be allowed to claim one of them each season." Cheers erupted again.

Gavril didn't wait long to issue his next statement, not wanting to hear them cheering at the misfortune of the islanders; "Secondly, King Iman has demanded that all of us who are immortal, we who have tasted the white water of the Icyandic, shall be invisible to those whose days are numbered. Their affairs shall require all of their efforts without being influenced, beneficially or detrimentally, by the things of our realm." The horde quieted as Gavril continued to spin atop the shaft.

"Thirdly, since the actions of the people have affected the animals, you are authorized to establish a new order among them." This brought a wide, sharp-toothed grin to the face of Scynn, the six-limbed, scaly creature.

Gavril's shoulders became rigid again as finished speaking; "Know that the white army of Casilda will not be idle as this war unfolds. We will ensure that these decrees are obeyed. We will oppose your efforts directly if necessary, and we shall aid those who desire to be friends of the king." The eagle's face became lifeless and Gavril shot upward into the sky. The spinning cylinder descended back into the river. None of the horde gave pursuit; instead they remained at the river to receive new instructions from their leader.

*   *   *   *   *   *   *   *   *   *   *

As Justin and Evelyn made their way through the forest, the real effect of the Renfrew's water took hold of them, making its way into their hearts and minds. Justin looked at his hands. For twenty years he had looked at them, but now, suddenly, they seemed strange to him: the skin looked so thin, and the hair that grew upon them seemed so dark and thick, like the fur of an animal. Evelyn stopped and observed her own body: she felt frail.

They looked at one another. Outwardly, their appearance was unchanged, yet each perceived that something had happened to alter them inwardly. As Evelyn looked into the eyes of her husband, she became full of fear and shame, two feelings she had never known before. Justin also became afraid, but this time the fear that gripped him was different than the fear that he had experienced during his last visit to the Renfrew, the fear that Kavan had induced upon him. This new fear was less intense but it seemed unavoidable, as if he had caused the formation of an infinite dark cloud that kept sunshine from the earth, preventing the precious rays from reaching living things that needed them. He worried that returning to the island would not remedy his fright as it had last time.

Justin walked on in silence and Evelyn followed. The image of Elson Verrill and Elson's father, Ansen, came into his mind. Justin was a young boy, picnicking by the Icyandic with the Verrill family. Mr. Verrill had taken the two boys to the stone pillar. "*The Caretaker is good and we are to trust him. Though we may not understand why he has asked this of us, we should obey out of respect for him.*" Mr. Verrill's words, spoken long ago, screamed in Justin's mind.

Next came the poem into his head. Round and round went the last two lines: *Let not your lips part to pass the red, red water. Let not your lips part to pass the red, red water. Let not your lips part to pass the red, red water. Let not your lips part to pass the red, red water.* The words were inescapable. He recalled Carollan's warning and realized that the small servant had spoken the truth; the very act he committed that enabled him to understand right and wrong was a wrongful act.

Evelyn was also in torment. She remembered the image of the Caretaker - how he had smiled at her so long ago. *"What would be his expression toward me now?"* she thought. *"Would he still smile at me and tell me what a treasure I was?"*

By the time Justin and Evelyn reached Idris' Bridge at the Marland shore, they no longer wanted to share with Warrick and Elson what they had done. Instead, what they desired was to return home as quickly as they could without being seen by anyone. As they crossed Corliss Lake, Evelyn tripped on one of the wooden planks and fell into the bridge. She stood up and looked down at her knees. She saw that they were both scraped and she waited to see if they would start to bleed. Sure enough, after a few seconds, blood started to leak though the abrasions. Her eyes went wide when she saw that her blood was dark red, not the usual white color it had always been.

"Justin!" she screamed. "Justin, look!"

Justin turned around and came to Evelyn, for he had been isolated in thought, walking several steps ahead, and had not been aware that she had fallen.

"What is that?" he asked, seeing her knees and hands covered in red; he did not yet realize what it was.

"It's my blood!"

The two stood speechless for a moment, not knowing what to do or think. They waited to see if the power of the Icyandic would heal her, but after waiting for much longer than it had ever taken the white river to heal a wound, they saw that it would not. Evelyn reached her bloody hands over the edge of the bridge and washed them in the clean water of Corliss Lake, and then washed her knees. The salt stung her, but she continued to wash until all red had been rinsed off. But still her blood continued to flow, and she stopped washing.

"Let's go home," she said, her voice shaking and tears streaming from her eyes. She took Justin's hand and they walked across the bridge for the second time that day hand in hand. When they reached the island they made straight for their home and were able to arrive there without passing by anyone. They went inside and Justin quickly shut the door and covered all the windows.

"What should we do?" asked Evelyn, still sobbing. Both of her knees were still bleeding and she used the first piece of cloth she could find to cover her wounds - a ribbon from her wedding day, hanging on the wall nearby.

"I don't know," answered Justin. He was confused. He couldn't understand how he had felt the best that he had ever felt in his life just a little while ago when he was zooming about in the air over the Renfrew. What had happened to him since then he didn't know; his wife had fallen and bruised her knees and now she sat across the room with stained blood coming from lasting wounds. Justin needed to know if he had been changed as well. He grabbed a knife and slowly pressed the tip of the blade into his left forearm and slid it backward, then waited and watched. Red! He touched the blood. The drops were thick and they clung to his finger as he pulled it away. He took the knife and cut off a piece of the ribbon that Evelyn held and covered his own bleeding wound.

A knock on the door sent them into a panic. Evelyn jumped from where she was sitting and ran into the bedroom, still holding the cloth to her knees as she crossed the room, leaving Justin to deal with the unwanted visitor.

"Justin. Evelyn. Are you in there?" called Warrick. "I've been looking for you two all day, are you there?"

Justin tossed the soaked red ribbon into the fireplace and opened the door.

"What's going on?" asked Warrick, seeing Justin pale and weak. "You look like you did before, when we were coming back from..." Warrick paused as his thoughts led him to think that Justin may have returned to the Renfrew. "Did you go back?" he demanded.

Justin didn't speak, but nodded in reply.

Warrick let himself inside and Justin closed the door behind him. "What did you do?" Warrick asked, but Justin didn't answer. "Justin, what did you do?" Warrick asked again.

Evelyn came out from the bedroom, her face covered with partially dried tears. Red marks were all over her hands and knees.

Justin went to her and helped her sit down in one of the chairs by the fireplace, then sat in the other chair.

"Sit down, Warrick, and we'll tell you everything." Justin looked at Evelyn to see if she agreed, and she nodded her approval. She was still not able to speak without sobbing and she didn't attempt to do so. Justin began, "We did go back to Renfrew, but we didn't intend to..."

Another visitor knocked on the door. "Hello, Justin? Evelyn? Warrick? Anybody home?" It was Elson. Warrick rushed to the door and opened it for Elson.

"Aha, so here you all are," said Elson cheerfully, entering the house and pouring himself a glass of water. He had found his three friends, but he failed to notice the condition they were in. "Warrick, I thought you were going..."

"They went back to the Renfrew!" Warrick exclaimed. "Come sit down and listen to what happened." Elson finally observed the poor condition of Justin and Evelyn and quietly brought a chair over and sat beside Warrick.

Justin told them everything. He spoke about how he had seen Durwin and Baldwin drink from the Renfrew; he spoke about how he had seen them fly around the river and look at the two pillars that came up from the water; he spoke about his meeting with Carollan; he spoke about Evelyn's conversation with the large parrot, Shanahan; he told them about how Evelyn had seen the twins pouring red water into the streams on top of Mt Manor; he told them how they returned to the Renfrew earlier that day to look upon it again, but when they got there were overcome with desire and drank from it; he told them how they had flown as swift and graceful as birds; how Shanahan met them there and told them to be prepared to learn the secrets of Marland.

Elson and Warrick asked the dismal couple question after question, and they answered them as best they could, though they did not know the answers to all of their questions. They looked closely at the wounds of the two, observing the crimson blood that flowed from them.

"Why are you so distraught?" asked Elson, finishing his glass of water. "You said yourselves that the twins drank from the river. If *they* did it then it has to be okay that you did it too, right? Even the parrot said so."

"Remember what Carollan said to me?" said Justin impatiently, upset that Elson had forgotten something that was just mentioned. "He said that it was all right for the Caretaker's servants to drink the red water, but not us."

"Well, what are you going to do, stay in your house for the rest of your lives?" asked Elson, standing up from his chair to get another glass of water.

"Why don't you leave!" Justin suddenly became angry at Elson's insensitivity and he stood up and pushed Elson backward into his chair.

It was the first time in the history of Iman's Isle that the power of the river Candra had failed. Elson fell backward, toppling his chair over and reaching out to catch himself as he fell. The glass that he held shattered as it crashed into the floor, and Elson's hand came down on top of some of the shards. Elson stood up, not knowing how to react to his friend's violence. He pulled a piece of glass from his palm and was about to speak, but then glanced back down at his hand. What he saw didn't make sense; red fluid was coming from where the glass had cut him. Like Justin, he also touched the red blood with his finger and smeared it about. He showed the others.

"It appears that your actions have consequences that extend beyond yourselves," said Warrick. "Look how Elson has become like you."

"What about you, Warrick?" Elson asked.

Warrick found the knife that Justin had used and poked its tip into the back of his hand just hard enough to puncture his skin. He was not surprised when a red dot emerged from where the knife had been pressed.

"We must tell the others," said Warrick. "They must know that the healing power of the Icyandic may no longer protect us."

"No! No, please don't tell anyone," Evelyn finally spoke, fresh tears forming in her eyes. "Please don't tell anyone," she pleaded again.

"Evelyn, it may be that the entire island has been infected," said Warrick. "They have a right to know. The Council, at least, must be made aware of this at once." Warrick grabbed some yallup from a large bowl on the counter. "Elson, you patrol the island and hinder any activities that might result in significant injury, but do it without revealing what Justin and Evelyn did, that should be done at the direction of the Council." Elson agreed to do as Warrick suggested and left the house. Warrick glanced once more at his two friends then followed Elson outside and proceeded to run east toward the tower of the Island Council.

"Justin, please do something!" Evelyn fell to her knees, begging her husband to act.

When Justin had seen the red blood come from Elson's hand and then Warrick's, he tried desperately to comprehend what was happening. He remained silent, deep in thought, while Warrick had decided to inform the Island Council of what he and Evelyn had done. Suddenly he realized what Warrick was going to do and, encouraged by his wife's pleas, ran outside to pursue him. "*It should only take a few minutes to reach Warrick*," he thought, bending his knees and leaping into the air with his arms raised in expectation of taking off into the sky, just as he had done that morning. But his feet lifted off the ground only a few inches before returning to the earth. He was unable to fly and unable to understand why. He tried several more times, but his efforts were in vain. Knowing that there was no way he could catch Warrick, he went back inside, tired and confused.

*   *   *   *   *   *   *   *   *   *   *

The entrance to the tower of the Island Council was on the western side of the tower, the inland side, about fifteen feet above the ground. In order to reach it, it was necessary to walk up a ramp that spiraled all the way around the large base of the tower. Warrick slowed his pace as he approached the ramp. He walked around the tower until he reached the entrance, pulled open one of the large oak doors, and stepped inside the cool stone structure. There was much activity here; the trophy of the recent island tournament was being installed in the trophy room, a large and richly decorated room on the left side of the main corridor. Warrick was familiar with the tower and knew that he had to ascend to the uppermost level where the Island Council met; at least one member of the council was sure to be there.

He found the tightly spiraled staircase that occupied the central shaft of the tower and began to climb quickly upward. Reaching the top level, he ascended into a large, open, round meeting room that comprised the full top level of the tower. On one side of the room he saw Wendel Wright and Ruth Jarison, another council member, sifting through several large stacks of paper. They seemed to be enjoying light conversation, as they were both chuckling when Warrick approached.

"Wendel, Ruth," Warrick offered a firm greeting, surprising them.

"Well, hello young master Spencer," said Ruth. "What brings you here?"

"I'm here on behalf of Justin and Evelyn Nickols," answered Warrick. While he had been running across the island, his plan to tattle on two of his best friends had diminished. He thought about the words he'd just spoken, "'*here on behalf of Justin and Evelyn.*' *Am I really?*"

"You know that the rules of the tournament are fair," said Wendel. "Just because Justin slipped and let go of the jewel doesn't mean that we should go changing the rules. Remember last year when Idris and Lachlan's plank broke on their last attempt at the Launtrining? There was no exception made for them either. No exceptions means things are fair for everyone all the time."

Warrick couldn't bring himself to expose his friends' actions, and he hadn't expected to hear what Wendel said. The words sparked anger in him and he lashed out at the councilman; "Everyone knows that Justin climbed the face of Mt. Manor faster than anyone. And he got the jewel at the top, proving that he reached the peak. Why should it matter if he wasn't holding it when he finished the dive?"

"Because that is the rule!" answered Wendel loudly, his face tense with anger. Ruth stepped back, uncomfortable by their behavior. "If he hadn't been so foolish, trying to show-off, then you would have retained the trophy!"

"Tell me who made the rules?" demanded Warrick.

"The Island Council did, of course. Why have you waited until now to challenge the ruling? Why didn't you protest before the tournament was over? I even saw you at the celebration; you seemed to have no complaint then. Why the sudden change in your attitude?"

It was then that Warrick recognized that his behavior was similar to Justin's when he had pushed Elson. He composed himself and backed away from Wendel, who was still tense. Without another word, Warrick turned and ran from the meeting room, back down the curling stairway and outside.

Up in the tower, Wendel's anger remained. He lifted a chair and threw it into the stone wall, breaking two of its legs off.

"What are you doing?" cried Ruth.

Before Wendel could respond, Bethany Krunser came running into the room. Bethany, Allison's older sister, had worked for the Island Council for the last few years as an island messenger. Never did she bring news such as she did now. She stood in between Ruth and Wendel, who was finally calming down. Her petite frame heaved for breath and her usually perfect blond curly hair was disheveled.

"I've just come from Epidomon and Thiagara," said Bethany, still trying to catch her breath. "Quarrels have broken out there and all over the island, and all of the servants are gone!"

"Quarrels? What quarrels? What do you mean the servants are gone?" asked Wendel.

"They are nowhere to be seen!" answered Bethany. "Not even Durwin or Baldwin, and their mansion seems to have been abandoned!"

"In Epidomon, Russel and Lachlan got in a fight at Lachlan's metal shop," said Bethany. "It seems that Russel considered Lachlan's modifications to his planks as cheating, and Russel went there to tell him so."

Ruth and Wendel waited patiently for Bethany to tell them what else she had seen; "And in Thiagara, Valena was angry with Cindy Richards because she is on the Council and Valena requested that the work on her garden continue though the winter. She said that she saw no reason why she should have to wait until spring to have her garden finished. Then Cindy explained that it has always been the Council's practice to suspend projects during the winter, but Valena wouldn't accept this and she shoved Cindy into the street. She was almost run over by a horse and cart, but Keelan Tilman pulled her out of the way just in time."

"Wendel, the council has to be called to order immediately!" said Ruth. "Send for them now!"

"You're right," said Wendel. "Bethany, go back to Epidomon and Thiagara and summon the council members who live there, Elleron Little and Deryn Lani will go to Littun, Sandeborough, Remishire, and Morl."

Bethany turned and ran down the stairs. Ruth followed her to go and meet with Elleron and Deryn, the other island couriers.

$*$ $*$ $*$ $*$ $*$ $*$ $*$ $*$ $*$ $*$ $*$

Elson wandered aimlessly around and it became obvious to him that the islanders were undergoing a terrible transformation. It was as if a veil had been pulled back from their minds, allowing them a new perspective of themselves and the island. Like children, ignorant and innocent and happy, they all had been. But now, suddenly, in the span of a few hours, innocence was gone and in its place crept a condemning knowledge and sadness and death. The promise of the poem on the stone pillar had been fulfilled. Imperfect physiques, improper desires, impatient attitudes, and inappropriate actions of their lives were recognized for the first time as such, and their new consciousness convicted them: guilty.

Despite the fact that it was only Justin and Evelyn that drank from the Renfrew, everyone had changed, for when they returned in their altered state, the Candra carried their condition to all things of the island. There wasn't a person or animal that was exempt from the effect, and this phenomenon was evident by the stained blood that now flowed red like the color of the river whose water had transformed them.

$*$ $*$ $*$ $*$ $*$ $*$ $*$ $*$ $*$ $*$ $*$

When Justin returned inside he found Evelyn kneeling on the floor, weeping. He went to her and lifted her up and held her tight to calm her. She stopped crying, and silence came, allowing them to perceive restlessness and fear. The day couldn't pass fast enough for them as they hid inside their home, feeling captive and anxiously yearning for darkness of night to come and hide them.

"I don't want to be here now," declared Evelyn. "I want to get out of here; I want to go somewhere where nobody will find us."

"Where?" asked Justin.

Evelyn didn't have an immediate answer, but after a couple of minutes she thought of such a place. She grabbed Justin's hand and led him outside, but not before grabbing some yallup.

"Where are we going?" Justin asked.

"To the top of Mt. Manor," replied Evelyn. "Not to the peak, but to the spot where I saw the twins pouring red water into the streams. No one will find us up there."

As they journeyed south toward Mount Manor, they passed by several people along the way and were pleased that none of them seemed to pay much attention to them. When they approached the peak of the high mountain, they veered from the trail and went to the spot where Durwin and Baldwin had emptied their flasks into the clear streams. They reclined on the grass and discussed what action the Council might take.

As they talked, Evelyn attempted to gain a new perspective. "Maybe we didn't do anything wrong," she suggested. "We *did* see the twins drink from the Renfrew, and Shanahan told us that we could also. Maybe the way we are now is the way the Caretaker's servants are all the time."

Justin considered the idea; "That would make sense, especially if what Shanahan said was true. If so, maybe the Council will reward us for discovering the command to be a hoax and for bringing enlightenment to the island."

With fresh and positive attitudes, the young couple basked in the warm sunshine and their feelings of guilt started to melt away. They talked about how Shanahan told them that they would learn the secrets of Marland, and they became excited about returning to that country. Then, as if it was responding to being summoned, a familiar creature descended upon them; Shanahan glided gently down out of the sky and perched on a branch nearby.

"Glad to see you two back here, *squawk*," said the parrot. "Did you tell the others yet? Have they changed too?"

"We only told two of our friends," answered Justin. "We're not sure that what we did will please the others."

"It doesn't matter, *squawk*," said Shanahan, "all that matters is that you've returned. Now you can all learn the secrets of Marland, *squawk*."

"Shanahan, what *are* these secrets that you keep teasing us with?" asked Evelyn.

Before the parrot could answer, Justin and Evelyn were struck with an intense fear that made them run and hide within the foliage of some evergreen trees. A large figure climbed up over the edge of the cliff onto the peak of the mountain, then proceeded directly toward them.

"Who is that?" asked Justin.

"It's him!" said Evelyn. "It's the Caretaker!"

"Are you sure?"

"Yeah, he looks the same as I remember him."

The two islanders became still and silent, hoping to avoid being noticed by the Caretaker. Then, without being touched, they found themselves swept out from under the skirts of the trees, laying face down at the Caretaker's feet. He bent down and helped them to stand up.

Justin attempted to glance at the Caretaker and found that he couldn't look upon his face for more than a moment, but saw enough of him to know that he was angry.

"What have you done?" demanded the Caretaker of Justin.

"We didn't do anything that your own servants haven't done," replied Justin bravely. "I saw them drink from the Renfrew with my own eyes!"

"But you are not like them, and they are not like you," the Caretaker said plainly. "And I know that my servant Carollan informed you of this fact, yet you still went to the red river and drank from it."

"But we saw Durwin and Baldwin pour some of the red water into that very steam, which provides drinking water to all of the island," stated Evelyn, pointing to the stream nearby.

"Didn't you listen to the telling of my legend?" said the Caretaker. "Don't you recall that the effect of the Renfrew is twofold, depending on whether its water is flowing or still? Excess pride is a terrible corruption, but the proper amount of pride is beneficial, helping you to appreciate what is good and acknowledge what is valuable. The twins were commanded to bring a small amount of concentrated, *still* water back to the island regularly."

"But Shanahan, the parrot, told us that we should drink the red water," said Evelyn.

Shanahan realized that it would be best for him to depart and he abandoned his perch. But the Caretaker lifted his arm and a shiny metal strand shot forth at the bird. One end of the strand wrapped around Shanahan's legs while the other end wrapped around the tree limb on which he had been sitting. Shanahan struggled fiercely to get loose, but his wings beat the air in vain. He was like a kite in a turbulent wind, darting quickly in one direction and then another, but never gaining altitude. Justin and Evelyn remembered the part of the legend when the Caretaker bound Kavan with strands such as this that shot forth from his fingers.

The anger of the Caretaker now focused on the bird, his eyes raged as he looked at Shanahan. "You evil creature! You have allowed Scynn to wrap its slimy arms around your mind, and now you have led these people, who I love, into harm's way with deceptive words. Don't you know that your name means both clever and wise? You should have invested yourself more to obtaining the latter rather than frolicking with the former; you would not find yourself about to be judged! No more shall you be privileged to speak of your own accord, but only to repeat what words you hear. You and your kind shall be dumb birds."

"Dumb birds, *squawk*, dumb birds," was all that Shanahan could say as he struggled to get free.

"Go and show your master how I have judged you," said the king. "Remind him that it is not long before I do likewise to him."

The Caretaker turned from speaking to the bird, and the strand that held Shanahan vanished. The parrot flew away over the island to the north, calling out "Do likewise to him, *squawk*, likewise to him."

Next he looked at Evelyn, his countenance remained rigid, but not so much as it had been when he spoke to the parrot. Still, Evelyn was desperate to avoid his penetrating gaze; she longed for him to wear the happy face of her memories, but it did not emerge. "The wages that are due from you shall be collected soon," the Caretaker said sadly. Evelyn didn't know what this meant, but sensed it was bad and she remained silent.

Finally the Caretaker looked at Justin. "I asked only one thing from you in return for this." The Caretaker opened his arms wide and gestured to the beautiful island surroundings. "But you desired even more than this, and in pursuing your desires you cast aside my instruction, deciding that you knew better than I what was best."

Justin did not reply, and it seemed to take all of his strength just to remain standing.

"This is where you are now," the Caretaker shrugged his shoulders and sighed. "The island is corrupt because of what you have done. It is true that you were misled, but you possessed enough knowledge to make the right choice. Deception is not in me; you will learn soon enough the truth of the verse on the stone pillar, and you will learn about the depth of suffering that others will endure because of what you have done."

Then it was as if the flame that had burned with anger inside the Caretaker blew out. He took Evelyn's hand and placed it in the hand of her husband. "You two do not understand what will come from today, and what great price I will have to pay for your sake. Remember how many times the twins proclaimed my desire for friendship with you?" Justin and Evelyn nodded. "As you go forward from today, remember their words, for it is true that I count you all as treasure to me, and it's my desire that not one of you should be lost. Go home and be together." With that, the Caretaker vanished.

*   *   *   *   *   *   *   *   *   *   *

It didn't take long for the three island couriers, Bethany, Elleron, and Deryn, to deliver the news of a Council meeting throughout the whole island. In only a few hours, the Island Council was fully assembled; all one hundred members gathered in the upper room of the stone tower to formally discuss the changes that had come over everyone. Tempers flared, voices roared, and emotions ran high. Most conversations, if they could be called that, resembled the shouting match that took place in that very room earlier between Wendel and Warrick.

Without knowing what had brought about the changes, they were helpless to know what action to take. Nevertheless, it was decided that, next morning, the whole island should assemble at the outdoor amphitheater to discuss the phenomena together. Then, for the second time that day, the three messengers were sent out, their purpose - to make sure everyone was invited.

*   *   *   *   *   *   *   *   *   *   *

It was nearly midnight when Justin finally fell asleep. The note pinned to the front door of his house demanding his presence at the amphitheater the next day offered no consolation. He hadn't expected to be able to sleep at all, but weariness from the day's events proved heavy and sleep overcame him. Evelyn also had trouble falling asleep, but she fell into slumber about a half-hour before Justin.

CRACK!!

Justin sat bolt upright in bed. He blinked hard and rubbed his eyes.

"Is our house moving?" asked Evelyn. The loud noise had awoken her as well.

"Not just our house, the whole island! Look outside!"

The Icyandic always offered some light at night, but visibility was abnormally good. The glow of the nearby white river, coupled with the unusually bright moon, lit up the island. Outside, other homes could be seen shivering and shaking and several stone chimneys had toppled over.

The trembling did not stop.

More loud cracking noises erupted, but these were unlike the single loud crack that had awoken them moments before. The Icyandic's illumination, normally a calm and steady glow, began to flutter.

Justin rolled out of bed, threw on the clothes that he had worn the previous day, and rushed outside, leaving Evelyn behind. Immediately he saw two large figures brandishing whips and calling out loudly. The cracking noises continued; it sounded as if thousands of stones crashed through thousands of windows. Then he realized the sound *was* that of breaking glass - the unbreakable surface of the white River of Power was breaking! He ran toward the Icyandic.

As he approached, he heard more loud voices calling out, "Back! Keep away from the water!" *Snap!* The sharp sound of a whip cracked the night air. The noise of breaking glass became louder as Justin crested the hill that overlooked the plain where the

Icyandic flowed. He saw more large individuals with whips, hammers, rods, and blades of all kinds shouting at the people to direct them away from the river and back toward Epidomon to the north.

The river had changed. Usually calm, the waves were violent and the glass cover was torn apart into what looked like thousands of pieces of jagged ice falling below the surface of the churning water. Bright flashes of white light escaped into the air as the waves broke into each other.

"Look at that one, there!" a figure holding two long rods exclaimed, pointing one of them to an islander crouched beside the exposed river. In response, a smaller figure with a short sword leapt from the large rock that was encircled by the river and landed beside the kneeling islander, who had drawn up some of the white water in cupped hands. The water never reached the islander's lips. Red blood spilled into the white river; fiery explosions resulted as the power of the Icyandic met the power of the Renfrew. The figure put away his sword and reached down to pick up the dismembered limbs, which he had sliced off above the elbows. He dipped them into the river, and though they burst into flame as the blood within them burned away, they were not destroyed and he placed them back onto the remaining stubs of the frightened man, healing him immediately. He remained standing between the islander and the Icyandic, letting his sword hang down in a non-threatening manner, but keeping it ready. The islander consented to leave and dashed away into the shadows.

A crowd rushed by, but Justin was determined to get a closer look at the Icyandic and he moved down the grassy slope. But when he saw the large figures advance toward him with weapons in hand, he turned to run with the others back toward Epidomon. The ground still shook, and he and everyone else stumbled as they ran.

Back in Epidomon, Justin saw that the first two monsters continued herding the people away, driving them out of town to the north. Evelyn came outside.

"Evelyn! Run! Go with the others, don't wait for me!" Justin shouted as loud as he could and waved at her frantically.

She obeyed.

Justin strained to hear what the two giants were shouting. At first he couldn't understand what they were saying amid all the screaming, but after hearing them repeat the same phrases several times, their message became clear. The one nearest him finished calling out, "...Prepare to leave! You can no longer dwell on the island!"

Then he spotted Justin and approached him with quick, long strides. At first glance, he was unlike anyone Justin had ever seen, ferocious and terrifying, but also magnificent and pure. After a moment, though, Justin thought there was something familiar about him.

"Durwin, is that you?" he asked. "Baldwin? No, wait! ..."

The giant reached out a long arm, squeezed Justin's shoulder, and lifted him off the ground. The other one was issuing the declaration now, and the one that had Justin was free to speak to only him, "You, especially you, must leave! NOW!" He stared at Justin so hard that his gaze caused him physical pain. "You want to fly?" And he hurled Justin high into the sky.

Justin saw his house shrink out of sight, Epidomon faded away, and the ground below him disappeared as he flew off the island. He remembered how had he flown all around at his own will at the Renfrew and attempted to take control of his flight. But, just as when he tried to catch the falling sapphire, he was helpless to maneuver in the air. The shouts and cries of his fellow islanders became fainter and finally silent as he plunged into the warm, dark water of Corliss Lake near Idris' Bridge.

Marland and Tilden; on this day their shores became the destination of all that lived on Iman's Island. Thousands and thousands of footprints marked the sandy beaches of these countries where animals had emerged from the water, escaping from the doomed island. By some means the animals of the island had known, as if they had been forewarned of what was to happen, and had crossed the sea to these lands before the sun had set. Had not that day been so unusual for the islanders, the sight of Idris' Bridge packed with animals, and masses more swimming across Corliss Lake and the South Sea would surely have drawn more attention. But this scene was just another strange event among numerous others that the people were trying desperately to comprehend, and the exodus of animals went almost unnoticed by the stunned people.

As night fell, the water came gently onto the smooth sand of the Marland beach in repeating caresses. The place for occasional adventures for the people would become a necessary refuge. The first loud rumble that had shaken the island was a deathblow to the foundation that held the pleasant isle above the surface of the surrounding water. The island was falling away, and soon the South Sea and Corliss Lake would merge to cover the island, forming a single body of water between Marland and Tilden.

The silhouettes of the trees that stood over the Marland beach were haunting as the full moon shone behind them. After the last of the island animals had crossed the lake safely and scampered into the woods, a menacing force came from deep within the forest to gather near the shore. Behind the first few feet of foliage they waited, watching with joy as the island dropped into the sea. They knew it would be only a short time more until they confronted the pitiful islanders and filled their hearts with a new despair. They could see the king's servants ushering them off the isle, directing them toward the bridge that would lead them right into the anxious teeth of their ambush.

The Caretaker's servants were urging, even commanding, the people to leave the island at once. Although the islanders had frequently observed the magnificent strength and agility of the servants, it was the first time that their powers were directed against them. Their appearance had changed: they were large and intimidating now, transformed into fearsome fighters. Even the usual jolly faces of the twins were rigid and ferocious, so much so that the islanders barely recognized them. A few people tried to resist them and found themselves thrown into the lake like Justin. So, either on their own or with the help of an island servant, the islanders moved north to Corliss Lake, all of them.

The first fifty feet of Idris' Bridge was submerged when the fleeing islanders reached the northern beach. It was fortunate for them that the moon gave forth its brightest light, allowing the islanders to move quickly across the quaking island. Russel Minns and Ansen Verrill were able to see well enough in the clear water to dive down to the end of the submerged bridge and cut the ropes that anchored it to the island. Once free, the loose end of the wooden bridge came swiftly up to the surface. No longer taut, the straightness of the walkway dissolved and the spine of the bridge bent as the currents of the lake carried it. Ropes were tied to the end of the bridge to keep it as close to the land as they could so that the people could climb on and depart dryly from the island. As they crossed, some of the men stayed in the water, swimming and hanging on the bridge, allowing the women and children to cross more easily and to assist those who were pushed off or who slipped off the bridge. Others recovered a significant number of boats that were floating nearby, drifting freely now that the water had risen to lift them from where they were kept.

The spot where Justin had been thrown was not far from the bridge and he made his way over to a boat that was drifting close to him. He climbed in and found the oars and rowed over to the bridge. Immediately, he began to search for Evelyn, hoping that she was among those traveling safely across. Evelyn spotted Justin first, right after she had climbed onto the walkway, and pushed her way through the crowd to reach the edge of the bridge. She yelled to him, but it was several moments before he noticed her due to the overwhelming chaos. At last he spotted her and moved the boat over to where she was. She jumped into the boat and embraced him. Elson had been with Evelyn and he climbed in to join them.

It had been nearly an hour since the foundation had given way, but still there was a loud rumbling noise that came from deep below the island, sounding through the water of the lake. And even though the isle continued to fall, its rate of descent slowed, giving sufficient time for the long line of people to get on the bridge. Observing that there would be time for everyone to get off the island safely, Justin and Elson began to paddle toward Marland.

As the first people reached the end of the bridge at the Marland shore, a soft, high pitched hissing sound could be heard coming from within the dark woods. Curious as it was, the people were occupied with getting everyone safely across the water and they did not think to find out what was making the noise. As more and more people arrived, the hissing became louder. By the time Evelyn and Justin's boat came near the shore, it was so loud that it hurt their ears. Finally, Ansen Verrill decided to go and investigate, but before he reached the edge of the woods, the hissing stopped and a voice spoke: "Welcome to Marland! Come learn its secrets!" Ansen halted and watched an enormous figure come out from the trees and stand in front of him; Ansen's head was only as high as the giant's waist.

Fear gripped the entire assembly. Ansen scurried back to fall in with the men of the island, forming a barrier between their families and Kavan. Constantly, the people kept looking behind them to see if the island was still visible. Only the lofty peak of Mt. Manor remained above the water. Although there were nearly one thousand men standing before a single adversary, they were afraid. Dark shadows of other monstrous creatures could be seen shifting just within the woods. Then the branches of the trees bent forward to let pass some of Kavan's followers. The hearts of the people sank into hopelessness; the women screamed, the children cried, and the dwindling courage of the men melted away.

"It is required that one of you join us this evening!" Kavan looked into the minds of the weak islanders and smiled when he observed their terror.

Fear turned to panic and all at once the people rushed to get away from the Marland shore. They grabbed the boats that had been brought ashore and threw them back into the water and climbed into them in a panic or rushed back onto the bridge, even though it would only lead them to the open sea.

"It shall be that one!" declared Kavan. He didn't point with his finger or even nod his head, but simply shifted his eyes to look out into the lake.

A moment passed and nothing happened. The children continued to cry, but the men and women became silent and watched to see who had been chosen, though they still struggled to get away from the shore. Then, suddenly, there was a splash near the boat in which Justin and Evelyn sat. A scaly creature rose up out of the water in a powerful lunge and grabbed Evelyn as it soared past. Scynn landed softly at Kavan's side, holding Evelyn firmly with two of its four strong hands. Paralyzed, Evelyn remained silent, her face pale as she stared dazedly back at the water with empty emerald eyes.

"No!" Justin jumped from his boat shouting, "Take me instead! Take me! I'll go with you!" These last words became garbled as he fell into the water. He swam frantically toward the shore.

Kavan waited for Justin to wade clumsily onto land, falling twice as he attempted to run through the waves. When he at last came onto the beach, he sprinted straight toward Evelyn, but didn't get very far before his progress was stopped; his mind was made dull by an inescapable trance that Kavan placed on him. He fell forward into the sand, unable to move his arms to break his fall. He could still see Evelyn and her captor standing beside Kavan.

Kavan didn't speak out loud, but Justin heard his piercing voice in his mind; "It is not your place to decide who comes with us tonight. Perhaps you will join us some other time."

Then Kavan and his horde disappeared into the forest; Scynn carried Evelyn away with them. No sound came from within the trees to indicate that a vast army now marched through it; there were no voices to be heard, no breaking branches or rustling of leaves. The only evidence that they had been there at all was the fact that Evelyn was gone.

Justin recovered from the trance the moment they left and he dashed for the woods. The light of the moon revealed the entrance to a forest path and he proceeded to it swiftly and vanished into the trees, all the while shouting Evelyn's name. At first the path was perceptible thanks to the bright moon, but after a few minutes Justin had advanced deeper into the forest where shadows swallowed light and he could no longer distinguish tree from open space. He ran full speed into a large oak and fell backward to the ground. The course bark had opened a gash in Justin's forehead and severely scraped his right hand. As he lie there, the blackness of the night was replaced with the blackness of oblivion.

In and out of consciousness, Justin spent the night on the forest floor. During the brief periods when he was cognizant, he heard the sound of shrieking and howling and felt the ground tremble below him. He believed that he was close to Evelyn but was powerless to move from where he lay, for every time he attempted to rise his mind went blank and he crashed back to the earth.

      *   *   *   *   *   *   *   *   *   *

Indeed the ground was shaking as thousands and thousands of Kavan's unkempt flock jumped up and down in celebration, chanting and screeching for hours. At dawn, the black sky gave way to gray and Evelyn could see everything clearly; she had been brought back to the Renfrew. Scynn presented her to Kavan, who took her and carried her across the river, walking on the surface of the red water. As he carried her along he dunked her head in the river several times. "Care for another drink?" he asked.

As he reached the center of the river he halted and knelt down to take up his chain. He placed one of Evelyn's feet into a link, jamming her ankle through an opening. "We need to talk, my dear," said Kavan, "but first my colleagues desire to see how well you can swim." Kavan released the chain and Evelyn plunged into the water, the heavy metal taking her down fast.

"Not very good, is she!" exclaimed Elzib. The horde cheered as she sank helplessly.

"No, not at all, I had expected more from someone who lived her whole life on an island," said Kavan playfully. "Feloniche, go and get her!" A tall gaunt figure, though quick and agile, dove into the river.

Evelyn was about to lose consciousness when she felt a hand grab her hair and pull her upward. The chain tugged heavily at her foot and leg as she ascended. She was relieved when air finally entered her lungs. She bobbed up and down on top of the river, lying at Kavan's feet; his power kept her afloat. Kavan removed her leg from the chain, pulling it free of the links as rough as he had placed it inside.

Some of Evelyn's courage returned. "What do you want from me?" she asked timidly, getting to her feet, standing on the river.

"Let us have a proper introduction before we discuss business. I am Kavan, the guardian of this river." Evelyn was not surprised to learn for certain Kavan's identity, but realizing that she was before the legendary captain of the Hypatia, she felt as insignificant and powerless as a butterfly before a dragon. "And this is my colleague, whom you have seen before in the water of Corliss Lake when you were only a young girl; I present to you Scynn." The creature smiled to reveal many sharp teeth.

"To business," said Kavan, "in answer to your question, only two things can you do to please me." The horde became silent to observe what would be done with the woman. "One is to die, which you shall tonight, and the other is to kneel before me and renounce the one you call 'Caretaker'. Do so and I shall make your death easy, and others you care about may be spared."

Thoughts of the Caretaker's giant smile, even in her dire situation, brought her a moment of hope. "What do you mean 'others I care about may be spared'?"

"You will be the first of our victims, and you should feel honored. I'm sure the others will remember you with monuments and stories. But you are not the last islander that we will claim," gloated Kavan. "Your Caretaker is powerless to stop us, why would you cling to hope of aid from him?"

"I don't believe you!" exclaimed Evelyn, her eyes welling up with tears.

"Do you think we would have been able to bring you here if he could stop us? Or is it that he doesn't care for you as much as you thought?" retorted Kavan. "Observe my stature, my power, my knowledge; is it not more than you can comprehend? I am worthy of admiration!" At this, all present, except Scynn and Evelyn, bowed low. Kavan delighted in their worship, but saw that Evelyn still stood erect. "Do I not deserve your submission?" Kavan shouted so forcefully that water sprayed up and branches of distant trees were blown back.

Evelyn was so distraught that her mind could no longer focus on conversing with the mighty Kavan. All of her thoughts went to the Caretaker, and she resolved to keep any binds that still existed between him and her intact; she would not give Kavan the pleasure that he desired.

Kavan grabbed Evelyn and carried her a few steps up the river. The square pillar emerged from the water. With one hand he held her against one of the pillar's sides, while he extended his other hand to catch the chain as it came flying into his waiting grasp. He wrapped the chain around Evelyn and the pillar.

"I'm sorry! I'm so sorry!" Evelyn sobbed as she spoke sincerely, thinking of the Caretaker. It seemed so long since she had enjoyed the pleasant island, though it was only yesterday when she was there, happy. Now she was bound before a mighty creature that wanted only to destroy her. Her husband, friends, and family were nowhere to be seen. She closed her eyes, not wanting to view the hideous monsters all around her, wanting instead to picture Justin and the Caretaker in her mind. She longed now more than ever to see the happy face of the Caretaker smile approvingly at her.

Suddenly, a new sensation overcame Evelyn; sharp pains seized her wrists and throat, followed by warm ticklish trickles that ran down her fingers and chest. She opened her eyes to see red blood leaking from her body; its dark color matched that of the Renfrew exactly. She could hear the plasma splashing into the river in spite of the cheers and shouts from the horde. She became faint and dizzy and passed out. Her body went limp and the red blood, corrupted though it was, was necessary for her to live, and when it was emptied from her body she died.

In her new form, Evelyn looked upon her limp and lifeless body chained to the stone pillar. She saw her abductor and murderer before her, and they also saw her. Kavan became confused and angry.

"What treachery is this!" he shouted. His twin swords dripped of blood that had been stolen from Evelyn's body. He raised one of his blades and hurled it at Evelyn.

Clang! A bright light flashed and the blade was knocked down just before it reached Evelyn's face. Kavan's sword was driven through the depth of the river and stuck into the rocky bottom. "This one's mine," said a deep voice of authority, not in exclamation, but in a matter-of-fact tone. Immediately, Scynn dove below the surface of the Renfrew and swam away.

"She must die!" shouted Kavan.

"She has died," answered her king.

"She must die til she is no more! She must surrender her life again!" said Kavan angrily. He summoned his fallen sword from the river bottom and paced around Evelyn with his blades. The king stood beside her.

"She has already surrendered her life; *to me*, and her body has been forfeit," answered King Iman. "You can see that is true." He pointed to Evelyn's vacant body.

"She is not able to escape her fate! She is unable to pay her debt!"

"Her dept will be paid in full," answered the king. "Enough of this debate; be gone from this place!" At once, Kavan turned and flew away, carrying his long chain with him. His horde followed behind him in the air, through the trees, and under the water. After a few moments, only Evelyn and King Iman remained; both of them stood on the river.

Evelyn did not understand what was happening, but she became filled with peaceful joy when she looked at the Caretaker and saw him smiling the smile she longed to see. She didn't know what question to ask first, so she started with what seemed most pressing, "What is to happen to my body?"

"It will return to the earth for now," answered King Iman. "You will be fine without it for awhile, but it will not be lost forever."

The Caretaker looked at the stone pillar and it began to descend. He escorted Evelyn to the western shore and stood with her at the edge of the water. Evelyn's body remained on the river's surface, bouncing gently up and down with the waves at the spot where the pillar had been.

"The other rivers have returned to the places from which they came; it is time for this one to return to the deep as well to join other great internal springs," said King Iman. He turned to the Renfrew and commanded, "Sink to whence you were brought forth."

The velocity of the Renfrew increased and Evelyn's body bounced vigorously with the new frequency of the waves. The level of the red water dropped, and soon Evelyn saw the last bit of the finite river flow past; a small clear stream flowed behind, attempting to fill the void in the large riverbed.

*   *   *   *   *   *   *   *   *   *   *

Justin awoke in the dim light of morning to the chirping of woodland songbirds. For a brief moment he enjoyed their tune, but then remembered his situation. It had been hours since he had last seen Evelyn. He did not know where she had been taken, but he stumbled to his feet and began to run in the direction he thought he was last headed before crashing into the tree. His head pounded in searing pain with every step but he was determined to not let anything slow him down; he could not be delayed, for Evelyn needed him. He ran through the dense underbrush, enduring the scratching and cutting of branches and thorns on his arms, legs, and face, yet he advanced with abandon. Whatever price he must pay to see his wife again he would pay.

At last he recognized where he was; he was not far from the ledge that hid the Renfrew. "The Renfrew! She must be there!" he exclaimed, and ran toward where he thought the red river lay.

Pressing on despite his suffering, he came to the place where the Renfrew had flowed, then he stopped, amazed. What he saw before him was not the red River of Power, but a vacant bed of rock with a small, clear stream trickling down its belly. But downstream, just within sight, he saw her.

Evelyn stood beside King Iman and watched Justin approach, stumbling over slippery rocks in the riverbed. He walked slowly to the body.

"Justin! I'm here!" she cried. "I'm with the Caretaker!" Justin did not respond to her calls and she saw that he was hurt. "Why doesn't he answer? Can't he see us?"

"He cannot," replied King Iman. "He must remain in that realm for a time, but your time there is done."

"But look how distraught he is, can't I let him know that I am all right?" she pleaded.

"No."

Justin lifted Evelyn's limp body from the cold stream and pressed his cheek to hers, nuzzling her with his nose. He sat down on a rock and held her in his arms, sobbing and wailing as the stream ran over his sore feet. After a long time, he stood up and pulled her body aside and prepared a shallow trough beside the stream. He placed her delicately within and piled rocks to cover her. At least she seemed to be at peace, he thought.

But he was not. He told himself that it wasn't true, that it hadn't really happened, but the next moment his senses reminded him that it had. With all his might he desired to change what had happened, but there was nothing that he could do to bring back his beloved. He walked to the woods, taking a rock with him. Driven by madness and rage he beat the first tree that he came near. Again and again, harder and harder he hit with the stone, even though it caused the wound on his hand to open again. He had put a large gash in the helpless tree but the rock became slippery in his grasp from the blood that flowed from his cut, and his hand slipped and he fell forward into the tree, reopening the wound on his forehead. He dropped to his knees and wept.

"Is there anything that can be done for him?" asked Evelyn.

"It grieves me to see him in such condition, just as much as it does you, but it is necessary for him to endure this," answered King Iman. "He must learn about the pain that others will experience because of the choice that he made."

They watched as Justin stood up, washed his hands and face in the stream, giving special attention to cleaning the wounds on his hand and head. Then he departed to the north.

Evelyn wanted to follow him, but she knew she shouldn't; she sensed the Caretaker wanted her to stay beside him, so she did.

King Iman knelt down and picked up an unusually round stone amid the rocks of the riverbed. It was light in color, as big as his fist, and smooth. He rubbed it in his hands for a moment and a thin layer of brown crust fell away to reveal a polished white gem - it was a pearl. He presented it to Evelyn. "This belongs to you."

"I don't understand."

"There are many things you do not yet understand, and it is time now for you to learn. But let the lessons begin away from here; it is time to go. You do not belong here in this corrupted land. There is a better place for you now. Come with me to my home. It is a beautiful city called Casilda. I have prepared a place for you there." Evelyn took the king's hand and the two of them departed from Marland.

*   *   *   *   *   *   *   *   *   *   *

Back at the sea the islanders had been paralyzed with fear, uncertain what action to take. The island was gone; the top of Mount Manor had disappeared below the surface of the water. Unwilling to return to the Marland shore for fear of Kavan and his army, and having no island to return to, the people spent the night on the waves. Some reclined on the bridge, and some remained in the boats that they tied to the bridge or to other boats. Most of the children had fallen asleep. Only a few adults were fortunate to also fall asleep, but most of them stayed awake and discussed what to do when the sun rose. The moonlight faded as the night passed, aiding those who were trying to sleep, but causing dismay for those who desired to look upon the Marland shore to keep watch for any activity there.

Among them, only Elson and Warrick had any knowledge of the reason why these things were happening. They kept their knowledge concealed; they didn't think that sharing what they knew could be productive. Besides, analyzing the past was not a task that any of them felt like performing: they were all occupied with surviving the night and planning what to do when the sun came up, if it even did. Given their circumstance, it wouldn't have surprised them if the sun never shone again.

Finally, the people decided to use the boats to drag the bridge across the sea to the southern mainland. This seemed the most sensible thing they could do.

The sun did rise that morning, bright and warm, as the people had always known it. Warrick volunteered to cut the ropes that secured the bridge to Marland. He dove from his boat, leaving his wife and his young daughter, Lucy, and swam ashore. Tears ran down their faces as they watched him climb up the beach; they knew that he would not be rejoining them soon. He cut the lines with his knife and the bridge came loose. Once the others saw that it was free, they began to paddle.

"Elson!" cried Warrick. "I am going to look for Justin and Evelyn!"

"Wait, I'll go with you!" Elson shouted in reply and started heading for the beach.

"No, stay here in case they come back!" called Warrick. "Look, everyone is leaving. No one will be here to meet them if you don't stay. I'll be back by nightfall."

"But what if you don't come back by then?" Warrick didn't answer; he had already run into the forest. Elson would want to join the others on Tilden if Warrick didn't come back, but that would mean there would be no boat left for Warrick to use when he finally did return. He looked at the departing people and observed that all of the boats were full of men struggling to tow the heavy bridge across the sea. He couldn't bring himself to ask them to leave one of their precious vessels behind. He would simply have to wait for Warrick to return, even if he didn't return by nightfall. From the distance, he could see Conroy and his father waving to him.

*　　*　　*　　*　　*　　*　　*　　*　　*　　*　　*

"Mother, mother! What about Ginger?" cried Megan. Megan and her two little brothers sat on the bridge beside her parents. Her father had just finished his turn at rowing and joined his family on the bridge. Megan was the first to note the absence of Ginger, a large cougar that had befriended the Prendt family, Megan in particular. Ginger, named for her habit of digging among the aromatic plant, had spent many nights inside their home curled up on the floor at the foot of Megan's bed, filling the house with her fragrance.

"I haven't seen her since yesterday," answered Megan's mother. "But I'm sure she is all right. She is a very good swimmer, remember?"

"Do you think we'll be able to find her?" asked Megan.

"I think it's more likely that she'll find us," replied Megan's father. "Cats always find their way home."

Megan relaxed about finding Ginger and looked at the men in the boats. Crossing the sea was proving to be a lengthy chore. The pace was very slow, as the weight of the bridge resisted the work of the many little oars. It was fortunate for the people that the current remained gentle, as it had been before the falling away of the island.

Many hands were blistered, and many backs and shoulders were cramped and sore, but the resilient islanders pressed on.

It was the morning of the second day after their departure from the island when at last they landed on the shore of Tilden. Those who had been rowing climbed up onto the land to recline in some shade and closed their eyes for some well deserved rest. Others who were not so worn out from the journey went inland to find food. Tilden was not without its own natural produce, though it was not as nutritious or delicious as the fruits that had grown on the island.

Members of the Island Council took charge and organized the people, gathering them together to discuss what should be done. Most of them held onto the hope that whatever force had taken the island away would restore it, floating it up from the deep and placing it once more into the empty expanse that now existed between them and Marland. But such hope was unfounded and they knew this. Yet, wanting to remain close by, they decided to find a suitable location for constructing a new village near the water. It was natural for them to build and they were not intimidated to construct new homes. Teams of six were sent out to find suitable locations.

Megan, Conroy, Keelan, and Allison found one another and sat together just far enough away from the other islanders so that they would not be heard. It wasn't long before their conversation involved their expedition to the Renfrew.

"Do you think we had anything to do with what is happening?" asked Keelan.

"How could we? We didn't do anything wrong," said Conroy.

"What is going to happen to Evelyn?" Allison asked, her voice cracked and tears formed in her eyes. Megan put her arm around her.

Emotions flooded Conroy as well as he remembered the last time he saw Elson, standing alone on the Marland shore.

*   *   *   *   *   *   *   *   *   *   *

The restlessness was unbearable. For a day and a half Elson had waited on the beach. He tried to sleep occasionally, though he feared missing Evelyn or Justin or Warrick calling for him if he dozed off. And all the while a fear lingered in his mind, that of Kavan and his horde returning to abduct him. He was tempted to go and look for them in the woods, but knew that remaining where he was, at the seashore, provided the best chance for them to be reunited, so he did not abandon his post.

* * * * * * * * * * *

Several large bonfires had been lit as evening came to Tilden. The fires were positioned in a semicircle of about one hundred feet in diameter. Within the ring of fires were gathered the elders of the island and the members of the Island Council. Behind the council and elders was the sea, now totally blackened by the night. It seemed that the moon had spent its store of light the night before and had none left to give now. Among the gathering, several torches placed on long staffs had been lit to provide light for the people, just as they had been placed at the telling of the legend of the Island Caretaker. It was the first opportunity for the islanders to gather and discuss past, current, and future events. Wendel Wright, the person selected by the council members to lead the proceedings, stood to speak.

"Please listen now," began Wendel, "it was intended that this meeting should have been held yesterday, but for obvious reasons it was delayed. I know at the front of everyone's mind is the desire to understand what has happened. But first we must discuss what steps to take to ensure our survival, for we may now be vulnerable to death."

"Why was my daughter stolen from me?" the sad voice of a woman cried out from the crowd behind the rim of the bonfires. "Why was my daughter stolen from me?" Evelyn's mother asked again.

"Why is my home gone?" demanded an angry man. Other petitions and questions came rushing from the crowd toward the incapable council.

"Everyone, stay calm!" shouted a tall, black man, standing up beside Wendel. He spoke as loud as he could with a scratchy voice. "Order must be maintained; anyone causing disorder shall be removed from the meeting for the sake of the majority."

"Thank you, Linus," said Wendel. "Now, first things first. We have all observed that, over the last two days, a drastic change has occurred within all of us. I know that many of you suspect this is a result of the disobedience to the Caretaker's command, but there is no proof of that at this point. What is most pressing is the fact that we need new homes. Today, several teams were sent out to find desirable locations to build a new community. Two sites close to here were found. Tomorrow we will move to the first site and begin building. It is imperative that we do not delay construction, for we know that the winters here are cold and merciless. Hopefully, we will find food enough to gather so that we may endure the long months until spring. When spring comes, we will, for the first time, need to work for our survival. We must learn to grow our own crops and tend livestock. We have no promise that the island will return, and there have been no signs of the servants who used to care for us and for the island. Tomorrow, whoever is able to help will be called upon to serve in whatever capacity they can."

"Now," Wendel continued, "to address the reason why our island is gone: the Council has no explanation for the events of last two days." Wendel said nothing else. The council members were totally helpless to explain why their homes now lay at the bottom of the sea. Evelyn's mother became a wreck of tears and screams, and those close to her tried to comfort her, or at least to keep her wailing to a minimum so that she wouldn't be removed from the assembly.

"There is only one logical explanation to this," declared Ansen Verrill. "The only thing that would cause such destruction is the violation of the command that was written on the stone pillar."

"Does anyone have evidence that the Caretaker's command was broken?" shouted Wendel, so that even those far away from him could hear the question clearly. The islanders answered him with silence.

"I know why the island is gone!" shouted a voice from the blackness of the sea. "The law written in the stone *was* violated!" The crowd gasped and looked hard at the water, squinting to glimpse who had spoken. At last a small boat came into sight; it was Elson Verrill. With Elson, curled up and in a wretched state was one other passenger.

Elson's arrival at Tilden initiated intense discussion and debate that endured late into the night. After answering the question that Wendel had posed to the people, Elson brought the boat into shore and helped his weary passenger to his feet and led him to a place where he could receive care and rest. Then Elson was escorted to the center of the assembly and asked to give further explanation of what he knew in regard to the breaking of the Caretaker's command. He spoke at length, telling the whole assembly, slowly and sorrowfully, everything that had happened concerning the red river, Renfrew. He began at the beginning, recounting the journey of the eight to the river before the island games. He told them what he had seen there, and how they had left with uncertainty about what to do with the knowledge of their discovery. Then he told them about the second trip to the river made by Justin and Evelyn, revealing everything that Justin had shared with him. Finally Elson finished speaking and sat down beside a fire to eat some food that had been prepared and brought for him.

Conroy and Keelan sat to the side of the crowd, hidden from the light of the fires. When Elson began his story, naming all eight of the islanders who had trailed the twins to the Renfrew, the boys were glad that they were out of sight, fearing that the attention they would have received then would have had a different flavor than the adulation they had received for creating the signs of the island games.

Many different reactions came from the people when they learned all that had happened. Motivated by anger, fear, regret, or despair, they voiced the thoughts of their various perspectives to the others and to the night. Russel Minns stood up, his red hair and beard glowing even redder in the firelight, and declared that what Evelyn and Justin had done could not be the true cause for the disappearance of their island. It did not make sense to him that all of the people would be made to suffer for the actions of these two. Many agreed with Russel, and they murmured softly to each other and nodded sharply to indicate their concurrence.

Lachlan declared that whether or not Justin and Evelyn had violated the command, the Caretaker was no longer worthy of their friendship, if he was even alive. "Where was he when our island was sinking and we struggled to cross the lake in the darkness of night only to face the army of monsters on Marland?" he demanded. "Where were he and all of his servants when we needed aid most?" The anger in Lachlan's heart came out sharply in his voice and worked to grow the anger in the hearts of others as dry kindling works to fuel embers to raging flames.

A few, like Ansen Verrill and his sons, were quietly downcast, wishing that Justin and Evelyn had acted more wisely and not given into selfish desires.

When the discussion grew dysfunctional, as several people shouted at once, Linus Darring and Wendel Wright stood and commanded the people to collect themselves. It took several minutes, but their effort was successful, and afterwards the people were so quiet that for a few moments only the waves could be heard. The repeating sound of the breaking surf brought a sense of peace to those who would welcome it, or a relentless attack on the hearts of the people who held a bitter frame of mind.

Linus' scratchy voice overcame the sound of the sea and he expressed his observation that many various opinions had been presented. Being very practical, he stated that no matter what the truth was, knowing it would not restore the island to them that night, nor aid them in beginning to build new homes in the morning. Soon after, everyone sought a soft place to spend the night, unwilling to waste the little time that remained to sleep until the sun would rise and a long day of labor would begin.

*   *   *   *   *   *   *   *   *   *   *

Allison and Megan had not been awake when Elson arrived. They had fallen asleep on the sandy shore, exhausted from the day's events. However, it did not take long the next morning for Conroy and Keelan to inform them about Justin and Evelyn's second trip to the Renfrew and what they had done. The four youngsters did not have much time to discuss the significance of this before the boys were called out to help gather lumber with the men, and Allison and Megan were informed that they had been given the task of collecting food for the evening meal. This news annoyed Allison, but she realized that her help was needed and consented to do as her father asked.

She had not walked more than twenty steps through the wet grass of the field when her sandals became totally soaked, making her feet cold and further decaying her sour attitude. At least Megan was with her, though Megan's habit of chewing on a long piece of grass, dangling it from her mouth, was irritating.

"Why do you do that?" she asked Megan sharply. "You look like a silly cow with that grass hanging out of your mouth."

Megan was taken aback by Allison's snappy criticism. "You've never complained about me doing this before," she answered, spitting the grass out of her mouth. "Is that better?"

Allison nodded that it was and the two girls proceeded through the field to a large patch of raspberry bushes. Megan took her bow from around her shoulder, placing it aside on the ground so that she could pick berries more easily. She had not wanted to bring the bow with her; it was quite cumbersome for her to carry along with all of the other packs that were needed for gathering food. But her parents had been persistent that she should take it; "*Things are different now,*" her dad had said, "*Don't go too far from here, stay close to the others, and make sure you take your bow.*"

Megan turned and looked behind her to see the people bustling about on the beach about a half mile to the north. The view of the shore was below her, through some clusters of small trees, but she could plainly see the little children running about, testing the boundaries of the area in which a group of women attempted to contain them. To her right, further from the shore were several men working in the woods, cutting down trees for lumber. That evening it was planned that the islanders would move away from the shore, about a mile south to a gentle meadow that had been selected as the place to build the first Tilden village. Until then, she and Allison had a lot of berries to pick.

*　　*　　*　　*　　*　　*　　*　　*　　*　　*　　*

Elson opened his eyes and rejoiced in the view of white sand and sparkling blue water. For an instant he forgot what had happened and believed he had awakened on the shore of the island as he had often done. But then he remembered and the sand didn't seem so bright and the water didn't seem so blue. He looked around at his surroundings and recalled the previous night. Warrick lay on the opposite side of the tent, still sleeping. Elson heard a slight shuffle behind him and turned to see that someone else was there.

"Kira, is that you?"

"Of course it's me." Kira was mildly offended that he hadn't recognized her.

Warrick stirred and Kira brought a cup of water to him and helped him sit up. "Here, drink this."

Warrick consumed it in a couple of gulps; the water felt tremendously refreshing on his parched throat. He sucked the last drops from the cup and handed it back to Kira. "More," he begged, his feeble voice barley audible.

Kira filled the cup again. "When you were brought here last night it was too dark to get a good look at you to see if you were injured. Now that I can see you, I don't detect that you're hurt. Do you feel alright?" Kira took the cup and filled it yet again.

"I was just tired," said Warrick, his voice sounding more like normal.

"Tired!" exclaimed Elson. "That's making light of it! I can't imagine how you managed to get back to shore in the condition you were in. It wasn't until we were halfway across the sea before you even tried to speak. Even then, all I could make of your moaning was something about Evelyn and some rocks, and I couldn't tell if you were awake or talking in your sleep."

Warrick recovered suddenly and surged with a new desperation; "I have to go back, Elson! Come with me! We have to go back and find Justin! He's still alive, I know he is!"

"What about Evelyn?" cried Elson, "shouldn't we look for her too?"

Warrick slumped. "I found her. She's gone."

"What do you mean?"

"She's dead. I found her body under a pile of rocks where the Renfrew had been. That was gone too. I don't know what happened to her - I was too late for everything!" Tears began to stream and he threw his head down, angry with himself for not running after Evelyn with Justin. "Why did I wait so long to look for them? I'm such a coward!"

Elson sighed. "No more than I."

"You both acted heroically for the sake of your friends," said Kira. "Besides, you would have been helpless to find them in the dark. Even if you did, what could you have done? Do you think you could have rescued her from them?"

"Probably not," admitted Warrick, "but I have to go back."

"I'm going with you," said Elson.

"Please don't leave," said Kira, staring at Elson all the while. Elson returned her gaze and she began to flush. "Here, have something to eat." She gave them both some fruit.

"Thanks," said Elson.

Warrick stood up and asked; "Where are Tanya and Lucy?"

"They spent the night here with you," answered Kira, "they left a few minutes ago to help watch the younger children."

Without another word, Warrick dashed out of the tent to find his wife and daughter. Never before had he so strongly desired to see them.

Alone in the tent with Kira, Elson felt suddenly awkward. "Why don't you want me to go?" he asked. "And why are you looking at me like that?"

"Like what?"

"It's a look that I've observed you giving to Idris before."

Kira winced. "Idris has changed. I don't want to be with him anymore."

"We've all changed."

Kira went to the entrance of the tent to make sure no one else was around and pulled the curtain across the opening. "I know, but he frightens me. My feelings for him are gone." Her tone softened and she approached Elson and took his hands. "The feelings that I used to have for him I have for you now."

Elson's uneasiness grew. Kira was exceedingly beautiful and her affection was delicious, but she wasn't meant for him, and he dared not oppose the islanders' ancient tradition of betrothal.

"I have to go," said Kira, backing away from Elson, "there are others that need my attention."

*   *   *   *   *   *   *   *   *   *   *

Megan's fingers were sore. She had filled about half of the many containers with raspberries and thought she had earned a rest. "Want to stop for a while?"

Allison nodded. "Let's get out of the sun," she suggested, pointing to the south end of the clearing where a thick forest began. Except for a small container of berries that Allison carried, they left the rest of them in the field by the bushes. Megan picked up her bow, thinking she might take this opportunity to shoot a few arrows. As they entered the woods, they welcomed the cool shade of the trees.

"I can't believe Evelyn's gone," said Allison.

"Some people say she and Justin deserve whatever happens to them on Marland."

"Who said that?" Allison asked angrily, "That's cruel!"

"Elleron and Brant," answered Megan.

"Do you think Evelyn deserved to be carried off by that...that... thing?"

"No, not really," said Megan, "but I also don't think its fair that our island is gone."

The girls were both tired. Neither spoke for a few moments. Allison munched on some berries and Megan fitted an arrow to her bow.

"I wonder whose house will be built first?" asked Megan, changing the subject.

"Probably Wendel Wright's. He seems to be in charge of everything," answered Allison, criticizing the councilman. She remained annoyed at having to gather food. "Why did you bring that?" she said, watching Megan pull back the bowstring.

"My parents wanted me to."

"We probably won't even have any more island games," said Allison. "How can we without the island or any of the Fruits of Ability?"

"I think people are more concerned about surviving until next summer, not whether or not there will be any games to play," said Megan, a bit disgusted. "I think you need a new perspective – and a new attitude as well." She shot a couple of arrows at a thick ash tree about twenty yards away, hitting it with both, then went to retrieve them, leaving Allison to think about what she just said. Allison sat quietly on the ground, eating berries.

Megan had to work the arrows back and forth a number of times to get them to wiggle enough so that she could pull them free. As she turned back to Allison, she saw something move quickly but quietly across the ground. Then, suddenly it sprang up and collided with Allison, knocking her over and cutting her arm. About five feet away from Allison, between her and Megan, a mountain lion crouched, growling, ready to pounce on Allison again.

"Ginger!" exclaimed Megan, happy to see that her large cougar was safe. "Ginger!" Megan called to the familiar cat. Ginger didn't acknowledge Megan's call. Megan glanced at Allison and noticed that she was tense with fear.

"Don't be scared, Allison. She just wants to play!" Megan didn't see that Allison had been cut by some of Ginger's playing.

Megan became confused when Ginger didn't respond to her. "Allison, she wants your berries. She's hungry! Give her the berries!"

Allison pointed to the where she had been sitting; there the container lay toppled over and the berries had spilled onto the ground: Ginger did not want the berries.

Though neither girl had ever observed the death of anything due to the influence of the Icyandic, they knew what it was and knew they were now vulnerable to its effect. This knowledge drove their minds and hearts to race as never before.

Allison got to her feet, picking up a stone as she did. She flung it at Ginger, then spun around and dashed to the nearest tree and began to climb. The stone distracted the cat long enough to allow her to climb about six feet up the tree, but a moment later the cat began to ascend the tree in pursuit of its prey.

"Ginger, stop!" shouted Megan. Allison couldn't climb fast enough to get away and the cat's front paws reached out and snagged and cut her foot.

"Megan, help!" shouted Allison.

Nothing made sense. Even as Megan fitted the arrow to her bow and pulled back the string, her mind couldn't believe what her eyes were seeing. Allison fell and Ginger turned on the trunk of the tree and prepared to pounce.

A shrill cry came from the cougar as the arrow pierced it and pinned it to the tree. A trickle of blood ran down the bark below the limp cat. Megan dropped her bow as conflicting emotions came over her: sorrow from the death of her beloved Ginger, and joy that Allison was alive.

With eyes shedding tears, the two girls embraced for a long time. Then Allison went and picked up Megan's bow and put it over her own shoulder. Megan gathered up the spilled raspberries, then they returned to the shore to tell their families what had happened, collecting the other containers of berries as they passed. And all the while Megan asking, "What kind of a world has this become that I must kill one that I love in order to save another?"

*   *   *   *   *   *   *   *   *   *   *

For those working in the Tilden forests, it seemed that the amount of time in a day had increased. Satisfaction of their work remained as they had known it, but now it was mingled with pain and sweat. Time dragged slowly by, but eventually the first day of wearisome labor came to an end as the sun began to drop and they made their way back toward the sea.

The islanders had barely finished eating their evening meal when the darkness of night came. The fires on the beach were relit and the people reclined next to them, hoping to enjoy a short period of relaxation before falling asleep for the night, having to rise the next morning only to repeat another day's toil.

Though the leaders of the Island Council had no intention of holding another public assembly that evening, there were some who wanted to present new ideas to the rest of the people. Idris Wincrest had contemplated many things throughout the long day while laboring. His quick mind considered numerous strategies that might remove him from his current situation; all he could see before him was an unending series of days of drudgery. One strategy appealed to him above the others and he nurtured it into a plan. At first, he was uncertain that his plan would gain the popularity that it would need in order to work, but after talking with some of his close friends his confidence grew. Lachlan, the first one Idris spoke with, gave him a pat on the back and a nod of encouragement as he stood to speak.

"May I have your attention for a few moments?" said Idris firmly, his tone lively for one who should be weary from a long day of labor.

It did not take long for the crowd to quiet; most of them were already silent due to exhaustion. A few people had begun to leave the gathering, planning to retire early to get some much needed rest, but when they heard Idris' request, returned to listen to what he had to say.

"I know that you are all tired, as I am, so I will be right to the point." Idris paused for a moment, then declared; "If we are to restore our island, we must return to Marland."

Fear flicked at the hearts of the surprised people as they recalled the last time they visited the shores of the northern mainland. "Have you forgotten what happened there only two nights ago? I thought you were gifted with intelligence," snapped Russel Minns, impatiently.

Idris was quick to reply before others reacted like Russel and dismissed his proposal; "Marland is the place where mysteries are found, not here, not Tilden; Marland is the place where the red Renfrew flows; Marland is the place of buried gems and treasures; Marland is the place of adventure! Perhaps, hidden there, just waiting for us to come and find it, is a secret that will restore the isle!" Idris spoke with energy and clarity, and what he said carried weight with most of the people. In all their years of adventuring, never was anything precious found in Tilden, while it was rare for anyone to visit Marland without making a new discovery or uncovering a sparkling jewel in its rich soil.

Wendel Wright, however, was not swayed by Idris' smooth words. All he could envision of Marland was the awful horde standing on its shore, not shiny gemstones. He threw off drowsiness and challenged Idris; "You speak of what that land used to be! What it was is not what it is now! Marland has become a place of monsters! It has become a place of death!" exclaimed Wendel. "No! We cannot go back there! We must stay here, rebuild our community, and call on the aid of the Caretaker."

"The Caretaker is most likely dead!" said Idris. And it wasn't only him, the thought lingered in everyone's mind. "The island is gone; if the Caretaker existed to guard it and to tend it, then it is easy to consider that the Caretaker is no longer alive."

"That is nonsense!" shouted Ansen Verrill, angrily. He stood and pointed at Idris, "The island is gone because of Justin and Evelyn." Ansen lowered his arm and turned to address the crowd, "Have you already forgotten the Legend, or is it that you've chosen to ignore it? Remember how Kavan's rebellion resulted in the Caretaker's wrath against him? It is the same for us now - we are corrupt, like Kavan. The Icyandic is gone and we will all die!"

Russel Minns, infuriated by Ansen's words, replied angrily; "I've done nothing, but now I am corrupt and have to die? I've been corrupted because of the actions of others - that cannot be true!"

"It is true, whether you're able to accept it or not!" retorted Ansen. "Does blood flow red from your body now? Not one of us has the white lifeblood left in our veins. The white blood, which was sustained by the Icyandic, was tainted when Justin and Evelyn returned to our island, carrying the red river's effect with them and exposing it to the power of the other island rivers."

Russel had enough. Lacking energy to debate both Idris and Ansen, he picked himself up, threw his empty mug to the sand, and trounced off into the darkness. There was work to do tomorrow and he wasn't about to sacrifice precious sleep to argue. As he left, he gazed up to see stars shining in the sky and heard Wendel Wright's voice crying out to the people.

"It was only last night when we all agreed to the plan proposed by the Island Council to..."

Idris cut off Wendel; "There is no more island! There is no need for the Island Council! I will be leaving for Marland tomorrow with any who share my desire to seek a solution rather than remain here and toil endlessly on Tilden. We shall take our share of the boats, tools, and food supplies with us."

On one side of the gathering, two people hung their heads sadly, knowing that their daughter would have to go with Idris. Kira's parents did not speak to challenge the premarital obligation between their daughter and Idris, but they hoped that Wendel and the other Council members would persuade Idris not to go.

"That's outrageous!" exclaimed Wendel. "You can't take our supplies?"

The crowd became boisterous in spite of their exhaustion. To the dismay of Wendel and Ansen, many people voiced their opinion in agreement with Idris. A chant of "Marland! Marland!" even began.

The raspy voice of Linus Darring called to calm the crowd, as it had the previous night, "It shall be as you say!" he said to Idris. "It is fair that you should take the supplies in proportion to the people that are departing with you. Go in peace. We will miss you, and we wish you success."

"They cannot go!" Wendel pulled Linus aside and spoke desperately but quietly to him. "Our homes will not be finished before winter comes without their help and without all of the supplies."

"Can't you see that they will leave, with or without our approval?" came Linus' rebuttal. "We'll find a way to be prepared for winter."

"Let them leave then, without our approval and without our supplies," answered Wendel.

"It would be wise not to give them reason to despise us," said Linus, remaining calm.

Idris eyed Wendel and Linus as they conversed, but did not approach them; instead he waited patiently for their answer.

"Let us quit this debate and get to rest," said Linus at last. "We all need sleep. Tomorrow we will finalize the details of your departure."

"Shall I have my share of the supplies?" challenged Idris.

"Yes," said Linus.

Idris instructed those that had gathered around him to heed Linus' request. And everyone else got up to leave as well, and soon the area was vacant, save for Wendel, Linus, and Ansen.

"How can they do this?" asked Wendel. "How can they abandon us?"

"They have no regard for the Caretaker now," said Ansen. "They have a skewed perspective of the truth, they think that the Caretaker has allowed this to happen to us, and that he has been overpowered and killed, but they don't see that it is not the Caretaker who has changed, but us. It is not he who has left us, but we have been exiled from his island."

"The others have retired and so should we," said Linus. "There will be time to talk about this later, but let us show an equal attempt to break discussions for the night. We also need rest."

*   *   *   *   *   *   *   *   *   *   *

Wendel had hoped that next morning there would be further negotiating to keep Idris and his followers from leaving. It was not to be, however, for when both parties gathered again beside the sea, no further pleas were made to keep the islanders together on Tilden. The Council had agreed with Linus that it would be best not to hinder their departure. Even Wendel, in the end, put aside his concerns and wished Idris well. After all, he thought, they will have enough challenges to face in that cursed land before winter.

Idris was given ships, tools, and food in proportion to the number of people departing. He bid farewell to the members of the Council, though he no longer saw them as a body of authority, then left to collect those who were to depart for Marland. He instructed Lachlan and Valena to load the vessels and then went to find Kira.

"I don't want to go to Marland with you," pleaded Kira.

"You have no choice," responded Idris, "you are my betrothed. Have you forgotten that?"

"Of course I haven't!" she replied bitterly. "You've changed, Idris."

"We've all changed, but the traditions of our people have not." Idris gathered some of her clothes and stuffed them in his pack, then looked at her. Kira had turned away, and he stared at the pleasant shape of her profile and her tangled brown hair and noticed that his desire for her had increased. "It's time to leave."

Kira's heart sank. She despaired going back to the *place of monsters,* as Wendel had called Marland, but to disregard the traditional commitment that existed between her and Idris could not be done – it would result in dreadful consequences for both her and her family. Idris took hold of her hand and led her out of the tent toward the place on the shore where his loaded vessels awaited him.

Kira was startled when she saw her parents and Amara among Lachlan's crew. She ran ahead to speak with them, her hand coming free from Idris'. "What are you doing?" she demanded of them after she pulled them aside.

"We're going to Marland with you," answered her father.

"Returning to Marland is dreadful enough for me, but I'll not have you, the people I care for most, going back there. I couldn't bear it!" Kira's emotions overwhelmed her. "No! You are not going to Marland! No!"

"We're not letting you leave us," her father replied. "We would rather go to Marland with you than stay here and worry about you."

"Please, please, don't come with me! I am obligated to go with Idris, and when I do the only joy that will remain in my heart is knowing that you are safe here. Please don't take this last bit of happiness from me."

Kira's mother grabbed her husband's arm to keep him from answering. "If that is what you wish, we will remain here," she said, tears forming in her eyes. "It will be harder for us, but better for you." She resolved to be strong and her voice did not crack and the tears did not stream down her cheeks.

Kira's father embraced her and then went to inform Idris and Lachlan that they would not be making the journey to Marland after all. Idris was pleased that the parents of his bride would not be making the journey, closely watching his every interaction with Kira.

After they gave Kira a final embrace, Idris came and took her away, escorting her to his ship. Kira's parents and Amara stood aside to watch her leave, and Elson came to talk with them.

"I know you are afraid for Kira," he said. "I am returning to Marland to search for my friend, not to join in Idris' quest. I will bring back word to you of her condition." Then he went to join Warrick, pleased that he had brought a slight smile to the faces of Kira's mother and Amara.

The journey from Tilden to Marland across the South Sea that morning was the most difficult that the islanders had ever experienced. The sun shone down hot on them, burning exposed skin while the wind blew stiffly against them. The sails were low and the oars were out, stroking the sea to maintain a slow, but steady, pace northward. Only a few of the vessels were large enough to have enclosed quarters below deck. Many of them were small rowboats or canoes with seating for no more than four people, like the battered canoe Warrick and Elson paddled along. In front of them was the largest vessel, which carried about twenty passengers, including Idris, Lachlan, Valena, and Kira.

Conversation between people in different boats was challenging, given the noise of the wind and waves. Such conditions were to the benefit of Warrick and Elson; they had no desire for any of the others to overhear their discussion. Like most of the people who stayed behind on Tilden, the two men felt that Idris' plan was reckless.

Elson glanced frequently at the stern of the large boat to observe Kira. She stood at the rear of the deck, leaning over the hull with her head bowed, gazing into the water while holding on to the rail of the ship with both hands, her brown, tangled hair whipping in the wind. She avoided looking at Elson, fearing that Idris might take notice. Instead, she kept her eyes focused on the rough waves beneath her. To Kira, the blue sea seemed an endless space of peace; she wished she could sink into it and escape her destiny. She imagined life below the surface, where fish swam at ease, darting back and forth, while everything above was jostled about by billows and whipped by wind and scorched by sunshine. If only she had an ample supply of island meer she would slip off the ship and disappear forever into the mysterious deep. But she did not have any, and there was no place for her to go but below deck where the others were. But she disliked them, and would not join them if she had any other option. For her, the best place she could be was on the deck of the ship, so there she stayed, looking at the creatures of the sea and envying their freedom.

*   *   *   *   *   *   *   *   *   *   *

Back on Tilden, the others spent the day moving their camp to the site where their new homes were to be built. Fortunately for them, many of the horses that had escaped from the island remained close by, grazing in the fields, and the islanders were able to corral them and use their strength to haul the lumber to the place that had been selected for their new town. In order to get to the place, a large open meadow, they had to traverse a mile long path through thick forest.

After the long day, Kira's mother and father ventured slightly away from the others to partake in private conversation.

"I don't think a relationship between Kira and Elson is something that we should welcome," warned Kira's father. "No matter what has happened these last few days, her betrothal to Idris has not been dissolved."

"Don't you care for your daughter's happiness as well as her safety?" his wife replied. "You were willing to rush back to Marland to guard her against physical harm, but you have no desire to protect her heart and mind? Do you really place a greater value on obeying our ancient ritual than on her being happy?"

"Happiness may return to her in time. Remember how fond she was of Idris for so many years on the island? I doubt that she has lost all of those feelings."

"You have always been clueless of such things," snapped Kira's mother. "She is strong, but the traditions of our people place a load on her that she is unwilling and maybe unable to carry. If she attempts to carry it for too long, it will break her. Something will give way: either her spirit will be broken, or this old tradition must be put down. I will welcome anything that brings Kira happiness!"

"I cannot encourage her to leave him. That would only result in isolation and exile for all three of us."

That night, the frightened, tired, sad people gathered around fires in the center of the meadow. Exhausted, they quickly fell asleep under the stars of a clear sky, save for a half dozen men who had been assigned first watch over the camp.

Where the forest met the meadow, all around its perimeter, stood twelve tall, strong statues of living stone. At twenty feet above the ground, their heads were as high as the tops of some of the smaller trees. Their limbs seemed thin, but only because of their colossal height, for their legs and arms were as thick as any man. They were spaced equally apart, some facing in toward the sleeping people, and every other one facing out into the Tilden forest. In the darkness, and with unblinking eyes, they saw everything clearly as if the brightness of the midday sun shone. They stood guard over the islanders, keeping as still as the cool, smooth stones that they were. Their minds were joined, each knowing the thoughts of the other eleven. The leader was a figure of solid black, smooth and polished.

There was no need for the people to keep watch for enemies that night, but the islanders were unaware of the presence of the twelve living Gemstones. Had they known who they were and what their task was, the people would have been able to sleep peacefully.

Day after day for the next several weeks the people worked on building the town that they had named Bentleigh. And every evening, fires were lit and the people gathered together before sleep overcame them. And all the while the Gemstones stood guard around them.

Though the days seemed long, the summer ended quickly for the Tildenians. By summer's end, the majority of their new homes had been built, but they began to wonder whether or not they had stored enough provisions to last through the winter and whether or not their clothing would prove sufficient to endure the months of bitter cold.

Ansen Verrill pleaded with the people to remain hopeful that the Island Caretaker would yet aid them. In spite of everything that had happened, his attitude toward the Caretaker remained one of a loyal friend and he reminded the others daily of the times that the Caretaker had visited them while on the island. Although many of the Tildenians thought differently than Ansen, none opposed his efforts, or even tried to discourage him. Some believed, like Idris, that the Caretaker had been overthrown and killed, but they understood how beneficial it was for Ansen to hold on to the hope that the Caretaker yet lived. Besides, nobody knew for certain what had become of the Caretaker; it was possible that he was alive and capable of giving them aid.

Meanwhile on Marland, Idris became more and more frustrated by the fact that neither he nor his fellow Marlanders had discovered any of the secrets of which the bird, Shanahan, had spoken. Even the red river, the Renfrew, which had supposedly been found by eight islanders, and even drank by Justin and Evelyn Nickols, eluded them. The only woodland river that they found was a small clear stream that flowed within a disproportionately large riverbed located to the northwest of their new village, which they named Seton, on the opposite side of a rocky ridge. One thing at least brought him pleasure - Kira.

The fog of early morning disappeared to expose a cloudless sky over the two countries and the water between them. Idris awoke feeling convinced that the search parties had passed by numerous treasures buried beneath Marland's precious soil, or hidden behind one of the many trees of its dense woods. They had lunged blindly into Marland at random directions, advanced into it by various distances, and none had kept record of where they had gone. With regret, he clenched his fists and pounded the solid planks of his dining table, angry that he had not taken care to thoroughly organize the searches.

Not willing to withstand further days and weeks of aimless searching, he resolved to do what he realized he should have done when he first arrived: create a map of the land and use it in directing the search efforts. He retrieved a spotting scope that hung by its strap from the rafters of his cabin and headed outside. The scope, a series of telescoping hollowed out tubes, each containing a magnifying lens, was one of only three that the islanders possessed. Linus Darring, on the morning of their departure from Tilden, had presented it to Idris as a gift in spite of Wendel Wright's desire for the Tildenians to maintain possession of all three. Linus openly rebuked Wendell, handed Idris the scope, and wished him and his companions good fortune on Marland. Idris savored the memory of seeing Wendell put down in front of the other council members. Once outside he became filled with energy, uncertain whether it was from the crisp, cool autumn air or the excitement of the task of making a map, something that would surely bring him success in discovering the land's secrets, or perhaps both.

"What instructions shall I give the teams today, sir?" asked a tall, blonde boy coming toward Idris. Brant had been waiting for Idris to emerge from his cabin, for he had become Idris' apprentice of a sort and his responsibilities included conveying Idris' commands to the search parties.

"You're in charge today," answered Idris. "I've got a map to make."

"What should I have them do?" asked Brant, "What if they won't listen to me?"

"Have they ever not listened to you before?"

"No, but they always knew that I was giving them orders from you."

"How will they know that today you are not?" With that, Idris departed the village briskly, hoping to avoid anyone else who might hinder him.

Brant turned and walked slowly away, trying desperately to think of a clever assignment for the search groups, but in the end he just sent them into the woods to discover whatever they may, just as he had every other day.

Idris walked southeast toward the highest peak in southern Marland, Great Falls. A spectacular waterfall decorated the lower half of the mountain on its western side, the reason for the mountain's name. He proceeded up the narrow trail toward the peak clumsily, his feet slipping frequently on the rough terrain. With the grade so steep, he often fell forward and had to catch himself with one hand while holding the scope in his other, trying his best not to smash the precious device. At a plateau on the mountainside where the river ran over, he paused to look out and observe the falls emptying into a clear pool far below. He had already reached a tremendous height and returned to the ascent, pleased at how far he'd climbed. But then he lost his footing again, and this time the scope slipped from his grasp. It ricocheted off a stone, tumbled off the trail, and fell for several seconds before splashing into the pool. He cursed loudly at his misfortune, then began to head back down the trail.

Descending was even more treacherous than climbing. Some sections were too steep to proceed forward; one slip and Idris would tumble to the bottom, so he had to climb down these backward. He ground his teeth and cursed sporadically as he proceeded slowly downward.

Finally, he reached the base of the mountain and made his way over to the pool, expecting to see the scope smashed and scattered across the bottom. Instead, he found that someone was there, waiting for him. Like Warrick, Justin, and Elson, Idris had been quite young the last time he had seen the Island Caretaker, but he recognized him at once. King Iman stood at the southernmost edge of the pool, away from the crashing of the waterfall, and in his hand, fully intact, was the spotting scope.

"I know the desires of your heart," said the king, "I know the schemes that are turning round your mind."

Idris approached the Caretaker. "I would understand recent events more clearly if you were dead," replied Idris, "for then some sense may be made of the fact that the island that you cared for was destroyed without your defense of it. You are, or were rather, the Caretaker, the one responsible for its care. And if you had been killed, then there may be some plausible explanation for why you did not rush to aid us in our time of peril."

"I come to offer you aid now," answered the king, "but I offer it to you on condition that you declare my enemy your own."

"Your enemy?"

"A great and terrible beast has been unleashed on the lands, a creature that tirelessly opposes all that I endorse. Its endeavors have caused the island to fall away along with the Rivers of Power and the Fruits of Ability. This is the beast that Kavan and his horde serve, and they desire nothing more than to hand you over to the creature. The poison of the beast is already within you working its evil, but you have the power to reduce its effect. I urge you to do so, that you and I may be friends again."

"Again?" said Idris, "What have I done that you stand so rigidly against me? I've never seen this creature, how can I have been poisoned by it?"

"It's not a matter of the past – it's a matter of your current condition. You have been infected by creature's poison; that is why your blood now flows red."

"So Ansen was right? Everything that has happened is because of Justin and Evelyn?"

"Yes." The king paused, knowing this was difficult for Idris to accept. "Consider what has happened to you; realize and understand that you have gained knowledge that you were not ready to wield, but you must do what you can to master it."

"And what will happen if I don't?"

"There is no middle ground between the beast and I. All who remain in its hungry clutches, those who refuse to be free from its grasp, will eventually become one with it and will be victims of my wrath when I annihilate the beast."

"And what of the people on Tilden?" asked Idris. "Have they been infected by this same poison?"

"All things have been spoiled," answered the king. "If you want me to be on your side, then you must side with me. Resist the creature; put away the plans that you have to do wrong, and I will come to your aid at once, as I have done for my friends on Tilden."

"What aid have you given them?" Idris became immediately envious of whatever they had received.

"Go and see for yourself." King Iman handed Idris the scope.

Idris took the scope and pivoted to return to the mountain trail. After walking only a few steps to the edge of the clearing, however, he turned to look back at the Caretaker, but he was nowhere to be seen. He dashed to the trail and climbed furiously, moving up the mountain swifter than he had earlier, his pace quickened by impatience to learn what the Caretaker had done for the Tildenians. A sudden thought occurred to him; "Perhaps they have been returned to the island!"

He reached the pinnacle of Great Falls, turned to look across the South Sea and Corliss Lake at Tilden, paused for a moment to catch his breath and steady his hands, then lifted the spotting scope to his eye. Through the lenses of the scope he saw the Tilden shore clearly. He was disappointed to observe that the island had not resurfaced to divide the South Sea and Corliss Lake, but what he did see was impressive. Anchored off the coast was a vessel of magnificent size and splendor. At its rear, the name of the ship was boldly engraved, Thalassa's Crown, and at the bow, standing tall and dressed in white and gold was a spectacular individual. A large shield was slung over his shoulder, and on the shield Idris could see the emblem of an eagle. He deduced at once that this was Gavril, the captain of the legendary ship. As he watched, Gavril was lowered to the water and some of his crew delivered him in a small boat to the shore where several smiling Tildenians met him.

All along the beach were stacks and stacks of chests, wooden boxes, books, and strange machines. People were dancing and cheering and laughing amidst the bounty that surrounded them. Teams of wagons and horses had been brought to collect the gifts.

Idris boiled with envy, "Such things should burden the shores of Marland!" Gavril produced two large books from within his garments and handed them to someone. Idris squirmed and squinted to see who had received them, but Idris' view of the person was blocked.

"What are these?" Wendel Wright asked Gavril as he received the first of two heavy books.

"This is a history of the great city of Casilda, the city of the king," answered Gavril. "Read and study it well and tell the others what is written within so that you all will obtain important knowledge." Gavril handed Wendel the second book; "And this is an empty volume which you are to fill with the history of your people as it unfolds."

Wendel, honored to have been given such significant responsibilities, bowed low and then scurried up the sandy beach to a fully loaded horse drawn cart that was preparing to depart for the village. Wendel held onto the precious books firmly as he hopped up to sit beside Russel Minns, anxious to return to his home and begin reading and writing.

Idris never had an opportunity to see that Wendel had been the recipient of the mysterious books. His attention had been drawn to another gathering. To his dismay, the Caretaker had somehow returned to Tilden and was now speaking with Ansen Verrill. Idris watched as the king reached out and placed his hand on Ansen's shoulder. Ansen began to speak, but as he did, the king glanced slightly away from him and looked toward Marland. Idris felt the powerful gaze and winced and lowered the scope.

After a few minutes his nerves calmed and he raised the scope again to his eye. The king and Gavril had boarded Thalassa's Crown and the anchor was raised in preparation for their departure. Steadily, the ship slipped out to sea, sailing east, never swerving toward Marland, and then was gone.

Idris continued to spy on the Tildenians until the last chest had been carried off, then he put away the scope and began the difficult descent down the mountain as daylight faded. For the second time that day, he proceeded carefully and slowly down the trail, cursing under his breath and grinding his teeth.

As he went, he replayed events of the day in his mind. Of all the things the king said to him, the words which he recited most were '...my friends on Tilden.' Envy swelled within him, producing hatred toward the Tildenians and bitterness toward the Caretaker. He couldn't wait to talk to Valena and Lachlan and tell them how the Marlanders had been slighted.

* * * * * * * * * * *

A solitary figure walked swiftly along the stone paved road that led to the gates of Casilda. He wasn't afraid, yet neither was he at ease. Slung on his back was a pair of sheathed short swords, their blades crossing each other. As he approached, he observed that there was no evidence to suggest a mighty battle had taken place there not long ago. Upon reaching the entrance he noticed that the doors of the gateway, which his companion had ripped from its hinges, had been fully repaired. He removed his swords from his back and knocked on one of the large wooden doors. Immediately, the door swung open to reveal the main street of the city behind a pair of guards.

"I come in peace," declared Kavan, "I have need to meet with Iman."

One of the two gatekeepers took Kavan's swords while the other looked up to the sky where a swarm of Casildan soldiers were soaring. One of them departed from the group, descended toward the gate, and landed softly before Kavan and glared at him.

"Kavan states that he has come in peace to see the king," said one of the guards.

"I doubt that you can still comprehend the concept of peace," replied Sandor, moving closer to Kavan to stand eye to eye with him. Not intimidated by Casilda's captain, Kavan did not reply, but returned Sandor's intense gaze. "Even so, King Iman has granted you audience. Come."

Kavan followed Sandor down the central street of the immaculate city to the king's palace and climbed the stairs to a gigantic door where they were met by one of the four guardians of the palace and were granted permission to enter. King Iman was waiting for them in the outer court.

"You have visited the Tildenians and given them aid," said Kavan bitterly.

"I have," confessed the king.

"Then you agree that you have violated your own decree?"

"My decree was placed upon you and your kind, not on myself."

"Gavril was with you," replied Kavan.

"What do you want?" asked the king, driving his former captain to present his petition forthright.

"I want an equal opportunity to present myself to those who are not inclined to seek your friendship. I want to reveal myself to the Marlanders without resistance from you. I have as much right as you to seek their allegiance."

"You and one other may reveal yourselves to the Marlanders, but only for one evening. Sandor will be watching to ensure that my will is enforced." Kavan and Sandor locked eyes again.

Satisfied, Kavan turned abruptly and marched out of the palace, through the large doorway and past the guard, giving him a devious smile as he left. Sandor followed him to the gateway, reminding him that he needed an escort at all times while inside the city. Kavan received his twin blades from the doorkeepers and flew out of sight. So quickly did he depart that a thunderclap sounded as air came violently together to fill the void of his wake, and startled, the citizens of Casilda turned to see what had caused the sound.

Back in the palace, two others emerged from the inner court to join the king. The first was his son, the prince, and the other was the living fire, called Elyon. Both knew all that had transpired between King Iman and Kavan.

"It is not likely to go well for those on Tilden," said the prince.

"Nor for those on Marland," crackled Elyon, "not if Kavan is successful in breeding jealousy in their hearts and hatred in their minds."

King Iman shook his head. "It will begin with Idris," he said. "Scynn has hold of him and has begun to fuel his wicked desires."

*   *   *   *   *   *   *   *   *   *   *

"What did he give the Tildenians? Did he say when he would bring such things here to us, to Marland?" demanded Lachlan.

"I saw a multitude of chests being loaded onto wagons and carted away," replied Idris. "I'm not sure what was in all of them, but I did see some of them opened and saw that they contained clothing and food. As to whether the Caretaker will do the same for us..." Idris paused, "he said that he would not, ...unless we swore to make his enemy ours." Idris proceeded to recite the king's words, telling them about the creature that had been 'unleashed on the lands'. "He considers us to be against him and even stated that we would become 'victims of his wrath' if we refuse to do as he asks."

Lachlan was clearly upset; Valena remained calm with a pensive look on her face. Her eyes shifted from the floor of the cabin to the walls as her mind wrestled with thoughts. Idris didn't speak further, but waited to observe their responses. At last, Valena's eyes stopped shifting and rested on Idris.

"Let's not be too quick to side with the old Caretaker," she said. "Other options may better suit us."

"What options?" replied Lachlan. "Join Kavan? That's what you're thinking, isn't it? He cannot stand against the Caretaker."

"According to legend, one that the Caretaker himself passed on to his dull servants to deceive us." Valena's eyes were alight with ideas and a smile began to curve her lips.

"You think the legend was a lie?" asked Idris.

"I think parts of it may be true, but some of it may have been manufactured," answered Valena. "It is conceivable that this...*creature*, has powers to rival the Caretaker's, otherwise he surely would have destroyed it by now."

"Without the island to protect us, nothing guarantees our survival. That is why I am driven to seek its restoration at any cost," stated Idris. "An alliance with the Caretaker seems necessary to recover the island and regain our immortality."

"If he has the power to raise the island back up to its place between the South Sea and Corliss Lake, then why hasn't he done so? And why did he let it fall in the first place?" demanded Lachlan, remaining skeptical of the Caretaker's strength.

"You're forgetting a critical fact, Idris," said Valena, ignoring Lachlan. "It wasn't the island that protected us, it was the Icyandic."

"What are you suggesting?" replied Idris.

"Have you considered that the white river could be summoned to flow somewhere besides the island? Kavan possesses knowledge of the Rivers of Power! According to the legend, and I believe this part of the legend to be true, the Renfrew, when it was removed from the island, was brought here by the banished captain. He may be able to bring the Icyandic to Marland just as he did the Renfrew!"

Valena rose and grabbed a walking stick from beside the door. She paced around the cabin, swinging the stick gently back and forth. Ringlets of her raven hair bounced slightly as she encircled her friends. Idris wondered why he had never before noticed her pleasant shape. Lachlan was about to speak, but Valena was not yet finished; "There are other reasons why I desire to remain apart from the Caretaker."

"Such as?" replied Idris curiously.

"Let's consider what we've gained since leaving the island. Knowledge, pleasures, and power that we never had before are now available to us. It was as if we were under a spell while on the island, a spell that kept us safe and pleasant, but also kept us dull and docile, a spell that kept us from experiencing things that we now can."

"Such as?" Idris asked, again.

"Look at how the others have been submitting to us and doing everything we bid them," she replied. "Lachlan, I've never seen you so excited as you've been these last few weeks, developing fighting skills and making weapons. And Idris, look what you've gained - authority over all these Marlanders and a new bride to serve you and delight your appetites." A slight jealousy altered Valena's tone as she spoke of Kira.

"She would have been my bride even if we remained on the island," replied Idris.

"Yes, but I think you'll both agree that your hunger for a woman's..." Valena searched for a tactful word, "*companionship* has grown more intense."

"What about you," asked Lachlan, mildly embarrassed by Valena's perception of his lust. "What have you gained that you want to turn away from the Caretaker?"

"Since we departed the island I have become aware of a mysterious and intriguing, but unseen, power. I cannot say for sure that what I have sensed is this creature, but I know it is not of the Caretaker. If we are returned to the island and are placed once more under his spell, I fear that I will not have an opportunity to learn more about this force that I have felt. And I very much want to."

Idris had heard all that he needed; they each had reason enough to pursue a path other than the one that led them to side with the Caretaker. "Valena," said Idris, his decision made, "will you seek out Kavan and make arrangements for us to meet with him?"

*   *   *   *   *   *   *   *   *   *   *

No one had been as happy as Ansen Verrill to see the mighty and ancient Thalassa's Crown arrive at the Tilden shore. His friendship toward the Caretaker remained constant in spite of the plight of the islanders, and although he wasn't necessarily glad to hear the king affirm that the disappearance of the island was a direct consequence of the actions of Justin and Evelyn, it provided him with some satisfaction that his understanding of events had been accurate. Although this news weighed them with sorrow, the Tildenians were relieved to learn that the king promised to restore to them, in due time, all that they had lost. Until then, he would provide them with aid, contingent upon their pledging allegiance to him. Without hesitation, the Tildenians unanimously agreed to the conditions set before them and the shipment from Casilda was unloaded from Thalassa's Crown; a bounty of food, clothing, and machinery for growing and harvesting their own crops.

Several weeks had passed since Thalassa's Crown visited. Ansen sat on the front steps of his newly constructed cabin and observed many of his friends and neighbors at work or at play around their new homes. He was pleased to see them smiling and laughing again, and it suggested that their worries of the upcoming winter had faded due to the provisions they had received.

But on the faces of Ansen and Monica Verrill there were no smiles, for Elson had not yet returned from Marland. For the rest of the afternoon, Ansen wandered around the village, visiting with Russel Minns and Wendel Wright before going down to Corliss Lake to work on a stone statue that he had begun carving in tribute to King Iman's visit.

He found he could not keep focused on his work for very long and stopped frequently to glance across the water toward Marland, hoping each time to see a vessel carrying his son back to him. He pondered going to search for Elson, but deduced that his chances of finding him were slim, and their paths might cross without him knowing it; Elson might return and he'd be in Marland looking for him where he wouldn't be found. As the day wore on, his reasoning gave way to his desire for his son, and he could no longer wait for Elson to return. He bundled his tools and took them home, having hardly made any progress on the statue.

Against his wife's wishes, he resolved to go to Marland and look for Elson. The next morning he gathered his essentials and bid Conroy farewell with a fatherly embrace and gave Monica a gentle kiss and tender squeeze, then set out to cross the sea alone.

*   *   *   *   *   *   *   *   *   *   *

"Excuse me, sir, but someone is coming." Brant came running up to Idris. "Someone is coming from Tilden." The guards at the docks had seen a single small boat coming toward Marland and requested that the news be delivered to Idris at once. Brant had been nearby and knew that it was his place to keep Idris informed.

Curious, Idris went down to the water and saw who it was that had come; he met Ansen and greeted him cheerfully, though his heart was pricked by envy. "Good day, my friend," said Idris. "What purpose drove you across the sea by yourself in such a vessel?"

"I have come to look for Elson," Ansen answered. "Have you seen him recently?"

"I am sorry I have not," said Idris truthfully. "I have not seen him since the day we arrived, weeks ago. He and Warrick went straight into the woods in search of Justin, and nothing has been seen or heard of them since. I was wondering if perhaps they had given up their search and returned to Tilden without my knowing."

Ansen shook his head sadly.

"Why don't you stay with us tonight," said Idris. "The day is getting old and it will soon be dark; the sun sinks earlier in this new season, and you must be tired from making the crossing."

"I think it might be better if I went on without delay," replied Ansen.

"We have plenty of food and drink and fire and shelter," said Idris. "Besides, much has happened since we left Tilden and it would be good for us to discuss all that has transpired in both countries."

Ansen *was* tired and hungry and he could feel the coldness of night coming. As he considered Idris' invitation, his eyes wandered toward the darkening woods and he couldn't help but think of the beasts that had emerged from them the last time he had been there. He stared at the trees for several moments, watching to see if any creature moved behind them and thought about Elson being somewhere within that awful darkness.

"Ansen?" said Idris.

Joining his hunger and fear, the knowledge that he would not get far before he would have to stop and build a camp, and curiosity to learn about the activities on Marland persuaded him to stay. "I would be grateful for something to eat and a soft bed in a warm cabin."

Idris helped Ansen pull his small boat up the beach and secure it to one of the hitching posts that were used for smaller vessels which were not kept at the docks. Then he proudly led Ansen to his new village, Seton.

The first thing Ansen spotted among the many little cabins, which were similar to those that had been built on Tilden, was a large fire pit in the village center. An animal had been slaughtered and was suspended over the open flame. The scent of roasting meet was pleasant and his mouth began to water. He followed Idris to the table nearest the fire and both men sat down.

Soon others gathered round, for it was time for the evening meal. A number of women came to serve them; Kira was among them. Her hair was pulled back from her face, which made her large eyes seem even larger. Ansen was pleased to see her again and he rose and greeted her with a kind embrace. Kira wanted desperately to question him about her family and to speak of Elson, but she was not about to do that in front of Idris. She offered only a kind greeting to him in return, but planned to seek him out later and speak with him in private. She caught Idris staring at her with impatient eyes, so she departed abruptly so that she could begin serving their meal.

"I am aware that the Caretaker visited Tilden not too long ago," said Idris. "I myself saw Thalassa's Crown anchored in the bay."

"Yes," replied Ansen excitedly, "Gavril and the Caretaker came to us, bringing provisions to help us prepare for winter. Though I shouldn't refer to him anymore as the Caretaker; he revealed his identity to us, *King Iman*." Ansen sensed some uneasiness with Idris. "Didn't they come here and deliver similar gifts?" Just then, Valena and Lachlan joined them and greeted Ansen coolly.

"The Caretaker did come here and speak with me," admitted Idris, "but he did not have any kind words to say, in fact he threatened us and..."

Lachlan couldn't restrain himself from interrupting; "There were no gifts bestowed on us! The Caretaker gave us nothing!" he said bitterly, "it seems he does not look on us with favor."

"What was his attitude toward you and the other Tildenians?" asked Idris, doubting that they had received harsh words from the Caretaker.

"Tildenians?" asked Ansen, "Have we become so separated that we are called different peoples?"

"The differentiation seems appropriate to us," replied Valena.

Ansen didn't agree but answered, "He expressed great concern for us, speaking of a creature that now prowls throughout our land looking to infect us with its poison. He warned us how, while standing before his throne, he swore to destroy this beast and all who aligned with it. Believing the king, and realizing that we had become, somehow, associated with this terrible creature, we all pledged to serve the king and do as he commanded so that the poison may be drawn out from us."

"Did the king extract the venom, then?" asked Valena.

"No, he said that he would return to Casilda and make arrangements for a remedy."

"He gave you nothing: no incantation; no magic river; no special fruit; no potion?" Ansen shook his head at each of these and Valena continued to pose questions; "What evidence is there of this poison? And, presuming it is real, why do you believe that King Iman is able to overthrow his enemy and heal you from its invisible venom?"

"The evidence for the poison is clear enough; it is present in us all," answered Ansen, "it is what make our blood flow red. And I..."

"That could have happened for any number of reasons," contested Idris. "But, I'm sorry for interrupting, please continue."

"I know the king well, and am convinced that he is able to do what he claims he will. Consider what we know about his power from the legend."

"Oh yes, of course," said Valena, rolling her eyes, "the mighty *legend*." She made no attempt to conceal her sarcasm, and Idris and Lachlan glanced at each other and grinned. Ansen continued to look down at his plate. "Lastly, my island friend, if the Caretaker has such powers as you say, then why hasn't he defeated this beast already? Why did he allow you to become poisoned by it in the first place?"

Ansen began to get uncomfortable with Valena's questions and turned his attention toward his meal, stuffing his mouth with food, and besides, his hunger had not yet been suppressed. He waited until he had cleared the food from his mouth to speak, using the time to prepare his response carefully; "A system had been established that was built upon a fundamental foundation of freedom. This system is still in place, but such a system does not prevent suffering and consequences as a result of poor choices, choices we are allowed to make. And I trust the king because I believe that he intends to help me, not harm me."

"You've offered only opinions and beliefs," said Valena, "you have not presented any evidence to convince me that I should submit to the Caretaker and pledge myself to him. Contrary to this, I have observed a number of recent events which suggest that this creature is greater than the Caretaker and that there is no poison as he would have you believe."

"We *have* been infected by it," replied Ansen, his tone firm, "whether we like it or not; whether we understand it or not; and whether we think it's fair or not. Deception is not a strategy of King Iman."

Lachlan lashed out at Ansen, "How can you so easily accept that the Caretaker considers us enemies as a result of choices and actions that we did not commit!"

For Ansen's sake, Idris attempted to shift the discussion, "Too bad Russel Minns isn't here," he said to Lachlan, "the two of you might actually have something to agree upon; remember that this was his opinion also? Does Russel's attitude toward the Caretaker remain unchanged, Ansen?"

"Russel has sworn allegiance to the king and stated his intent to play whatever part he must in order to recover what he lost," answered Ansen. "If you are not seeking aid from the king, then what do you plan to do? Aren't you afraid of the beast?"

"We are not sure that the beast is something that should be feared," said Idris. "It may have more to offer us than the Caretaker."

Ansen was stunned; he did not even know how to continue the conversation. No one spoke for several moments, then, finally, Ansen introduced a new topic, "Tell me, Idris, what has been going on here these last several weeks. I see that you have had success in constructing new homes and have made a nice village, Seton, but have you found any of the *secrets of Marland*?"

"Nothing to speak of yet. But something may happen soon." Idris looked knowingly at Valena.

Ansen returned again to his meal; the food was delicious and he was glad that he had decided to stay. He was distraught that the king had not given provisions to the Marlanders, and he made up his mind to bring back some of the gifts from Tilden as soon as he returned there with his son. Conversations eventually died off, as did the large fire in the pit, and Ansen was shown to his quarters, a small empty cabin that had been constructed with leftover building materials. He lay down on the soft bed of cotton covered over straw, anxious to plan how to begin his search the next morning. Instead, tired from the day's events, he fell quickly asleep.

Late that night in a nearby cabin a single candle glowed to give light for a single person. It was evident that it had been burning for some time, for there were numerous columns of wax around the shaft where the molten fluid had cascaded down the sides and solidified. Idris sat wide awake, spinning the spotting scope by its strap until it became completely entangled and gripped his fingers. He released the scope to let the strap unwind itself. The air was heavy and stale, and it was so silent that the thoughts in his mind seemed to be shouting to him. Unbeknownst to the frustrated islander, Scynn stood beside him. Twenty-four fingers of the creature's four hands caressed Idris' mind, manipulating the thoughts within. There was no physical contact between the two and Idris did not detect Scynn's groping of him.

He spoke softy to himself in broken fragments as ideas emerged. "They have what I need... I must ask for it. No, no, they would never part with it – I must take it." He quickly stood up, as if to shake off the notion, for it disgusted him. Scynn had lost its grip for a moment and different thoughts came forward, thoughts that pleased him: Kira smiling, the island, winning the Launtrining. Scynn wrapped the fingers of one of its hands around Idris' heart and squeezed; bitterness returned. He looked out a window toward the cabin where Ansen slept. "Look at him! Even here, where he is among his enemies, he sleeps calmly while I fret about our future and the recovery of the island. I am the same as he, yet the Caretaker gives him aid while I am given warning."

Idris sat down at the table and tossed the spotting scope aside. It landed on a cushion and rolled along the planks of the wooden floor. He leaned forward and propped up his head on his hands.

Suddenly Scynn twitched excitedly; the creature had finally elicited the thought he had been searching for. It delicately positioned two of its hands to block all other thoughts from interfering with this special one that his fourth hand grasped firmly – his other hand remained holding Idris' heart.

Idris' eyes widened and his head lifted slowly from his hands, which he let fall to the table. He spoke out loud to himself; "They would be without their leader...the king might not give them further aid...no one would know...it would be so easy to do." The candle burned out and Idris sat in darkness, plotting.

When he was finished, he rose and went to his bed, which was separate from where Kira slept - she was in the next room and her door was shut. He was so immersed in his plan that he didn't go to wake her for some attention, as had become his habit.

Satisfied, Scynn slithered silently from Seton.

Ansen woke to find his fire out and the cabin full of cold autumn air. He wondered if Warrick and Elson were warm, wherever they were. Although cold, he was well rested and ready to begin the search for his son. He arose and gathered his gear, then departed the cabin to seek out and bid farewell to Idris and the others, as well as to thank them for their kindness.

Ansen returned to the village center and found Idris, Lachlan, and Valena gathered near the pit, which was caked in black soot all around. He noticed that Idris appeared very tired; "Did you get any sleep, Idris? You look exhausted."

"I'll be fine," replied Idris. "It looks like you're ready to be on your way."

"I am. Thanks for your hospitality; I shall not forget your generosity. Farewell." Valena, Lachlan, and Idris offered no further conversation, but only nodded to Ansen as he turned to leave.

When Ansen had gone, Idris said to Valena and Lachlan, "I need to go and speak with Brant. Search parties are not to be sent out today, and not again until I have finished the map. It should be done soon." Then he also left.

Ansen began his quest by going directly north, following one of the trails from the village and walking swiftly to keep warm. He had not been walking for long when he heard a familiar voice calling to him from behind, "Ansen! Ansen!" He stopped as Idris came running up the trail to meet him; the spotting scope was slung over his shoulder.

"Did I forget something?" asked Ansen.

"No," Idris panted, attempting to catch his breath.

"Did you see Elson?"

"No, and you didn't forget anything. I remembered that I had this and thought it might help you." Idris pointed to the scope. "We should go to the top of the Falls and see if we can find any sign of them, maybe smoke from a fire; surely they would have built one last night."

Ansen recognized the scope at once and saw the merit in the idea, so he agreed to do as Idris suggested. He followed Idris to the base of Great Falls and they began the ascent up the steep path beside the waterfall.

As he climbed, Idris envisioned the fulfillment of his plan, but as he did, some force inside him struggled to dissuade him from his intended course. But the work of Scynn was effective and Idris' desire overcame all other influences.

Meanwhile, Ansen thought only about finding Elson and hoped that he would soon see some sign of him and Warrick through the scope. The trek to the top took a long time, but eventually he crested the peak and gazed across the South Sea and Corliss Lake to Tilden. A stiff breeze blew against him as he stood exposed on the cliff. The water was beautifully blue as always, but was tossed about by the wind in a manner that he was not yet used to seeing.

"Here," said Idris, handing Ansen the scope, fully extended and ready to use. "I don't think you'll find them out there."

"No, I don't suppose so," said Ansen. He turned around to face north and lifted the scope to his eye and began to pan the large, dense forest of Marland.

"What's that?" asked Idris, "Do you see it?" He stepped to the edge of the cliff and pointed straight ahead. Below him was the pool that caught the falls. "Is that smoke?"

Ansen stepped forward so that he stood beside Idris and, with the scope lifted to his eye, looked toward where Idris pointed. He was excited to see a thin wisp of white extend from the treetops to the sky, where it dispersed and disappeared. "That's got to be them!"

* * * * * * * * * * *

That morning Kira had gone down to the seashore to be by herself, as had become her custom. Although she had spent her whole life among the people that now inhabited Seton, they had become different from her since their departure from the island; they had new desires for things never before pursued, and she was uncomfortable to be with them. She observed the change most in Idris, and she had grown to despise and fear him, but others were quite capable of making her uneasy to the point that she would tremble. She observed the thrill Lachlan had as he developed fighting techniques to harm others efficiently, and, to go along with his learning to inflict pain, he had begun to craft weapons, a task for which he was readily prepared, given his knowledge and experience of metalworking. And strangest and most unpleasant of all to her was Valena, who sought to convince the Marlanders to seek an allegiance with Kavan and his horde. Each of these self-imposed rulers of Marland had gathered followers to assist them in their endeavors, and the people of Marland spent most of their time serving these three.

With no intent to participate willingly in these activities, Kira kept away from Seton whenever her duties, which were placed upon her by Idris and Valena, allowed for her to have a respite. Venturing into the forest was not an option; she feared that Kavan and his horde were there, and that they would pounce on her if she went there. So it was that she went to the sea. Her favorite spot was a calm cove of fresh water near the shore just to the west of Great Falls. Looking across the sea, she felt the same feeling of escape that she had experienced on the boat when she came to Marland, and it was comforting for her to look upon the land where her loved ones were.

Often she would bathe in the cove to cleanse away the grime of her toilsome chores. But she also bathed in an attempt to rid herself of the feelings of guilt and shame that weighed upon her; Kira had accepted the duties of her new position as Idris' wife and she withheld nothing from him to which he was entitled. The wedding had been performed the second night after their arrival on Marland. It was a ceremony unlike any that Kira had ever seen before. Valena had worn a long black gown and her pale skin was decorated with symbols of animals drawn from her own blood. There was no petition of Kira as to whether or not she wished to become Idris' wife; but rather she was informed of the stipulations to which she would be required to uphold from that time forward.

On this day she did not go into the water to wash herself. Her husband, it seemed, had been preoccupied the night before and did not come to her in the night. Instead, she sat quietly beside the cove and basked in the warmth of the sunshine.

Suddenly she heard a cracking noise behind her. Being continually fearful, she jumped sharply to her feet and looked back at the trees. She saw a lone blue jay fly out from the forest and she calmed herself, realizing that the bird had caused the noise. As she watched the jay fly away something else caught her eye. From where she stood, she could see clearly the exposed peak of Great Falls. She recognized Ansen Verrill and saw him holding the long spotting scope to his eye, looking northward into the heart of Marland.

Ansen continued to look through the scope and tried to find a path that would lead him to the base of the smoke stream. Idris did not hesitate; it was the moment for which his plan required him to act. He smoothly positioned himself behind Ansen and then lunged at him, driving his shoulders into Ansen's back and launching him helplessly off the edge. Idris leaned cautiously forward and bent down to view the death of the Caretaker's favorite Tildenian.

Ansen realized that his life was about to end. He struggled to focus on the ground as he raced toward it and saw the pool by the base of the waterfall. He tried unsuccessfully to direct himself toward it. Thoughts raced through his mind all at once: he thought about the unlawful act that Idris had just committed and longed for justice to be done to him; he thought of Conroy being left behind, fatherless, on Tilden; he thought of his wife, Monica, and felt sad that he wouldn't be able to be with her again; he thought of Elson and hoped that he was well wherever he was, and that he would hurry back to Tilden to be with Conroy and Monica; and he thought of King Iman and desired to see him again. Then Ansen Verrill crashed into the hard earth beside the pool. Blood spilled from his broken body and seeped into the ground and ran into the water, leaving trails of red all about him.

Kira was struck with the same kind of horror that she had known when she saw Kavan standing on the Marland shore in the night. She watched in panicked silence as Ansen fell and disappeared from her view behind the trees. She attempted to convince herself that what she had just seen was an accident, but she could not. She had seen everything clearly: she had seen her husband charge at Ansen and force him, unsuspecting and defenseless, off the cliff.

This was too much for her to bear. She had to get away from Idris, away from Seton and all the others. Her best path lay across the water and back toward Tilden. She had traversed the water many times in her life without the aid of boat or bridge, but she knew she could not swim across it now. She thought about taking a boat from the harbor, but they were always carefully guarded.

She decided to go into the woods, figuring that she would rather face the unknown things of Marland than to remain with her viscous husband among the twisted Marlanders. She dashed into the forest and ran as fast as she could into the shadows of the trees. She had little hope of escaping; the numerous troops that foraged through the forest every day at Idris' command would be sure to see her. But she couldn't stop: fear and panic drove her swiftly onward.

Steering away from the trail that led back to the village, she tried to pass between Seton and Great Falls. She only hoped that her path would not intersect Idris', should he already be down from the mountain on his way back to the village. As she ran she tried to listen carefully for anyone or anything else in the woods, but the sound of her footsteps on leaves and branches, and her loud breathing prevented her from hearing anything around her. About every hundred yards or so she stopped and held her breath as best she could to hear clearly. Only when she was certain that she had passed the village did she allow herself to slow to a jog.

All around her, massive trees seemed alive, like slender soldiers of Marland; oak, maple, pine, beech, and ash servants of the evil land, Kira imagined them bending down and snaring her with their long limbs. Fear was still with her; fear that Idris pursued her from behind, and fear that Kavan lie in wait for her ahead. The sound of a branch breaking pierced the air and Kira froze to listen for more sounds. She heard the rustling of footsteps - something was running toward her but she couldn't discern from which direction it was coming.

She sprinted forward as fast as she could, looking for a place to hide. Before she could find cover, she was grabbed from behind and tackled to the ground and whatever pursued her fell on top of her. She screamed and kicked and swung her arms wildly to break free. She was surprised to find that she was released and got to her feet, searching frantically for what had caught her. A familiar figure stood nearby. Her fear faded and she flung herself into his arms.

chapter ten: ·glimmerstone·

After a long embrace, Elson pushed Kira away gently, holding her shoulders so that he could look into her teary eyes. "What's wrong?"

"I can't go back," she sobbed, "there's nothing good in Seton."

"*Seton*?"

"It's what Idris has named the new village," explained Kira.

"Where will you go?"

"Far away, I don't care." Then a thought occurred to her, one that presented a possible future, one of a life worth living. "Come with me!" She removed his hands from her shoulders and squeezed them in her own.

Retreating north into Marland as winter approached did not appeal to Elson. Having spent the last several weeks in the forest, he knew the specifications of the climate and landscape and the difficulties they would present. He was certain she would not succeed by herself. "Come, let's talk for moment. Warrick's there, over that hill waiting for me."

They began to walk in silence; Elson hoped the quiet would allow her time to calm.

"What took you so long?" asked Warrick when he saw Elson coming down the slope.

"She's fast," answered Elson. He stepped to the side and Warrick saw Kira. He rushed to her and embraced her and sensed her trembling.

"Why are you shaking?" he asked.

Kira explained to them how she had grown to fear the Marlanders, especially Idris. She did not tell them about her marriage to him, nor was she ready to reveal that she had just witnessed the death of Elson's father, worried that if Elson found out what happened he would return to Tilden at once. That would quickly thwart her plan to run away with him, and she couldn't return to Tilden with him; the fact that she abandoned her betrothed wouldn't be accepted by anyone, not even her family.

Elson resumed their discussion; "You can't go into the Marland woods by yourself. How could you survive?"

Kira thought about shrugging her shoulders and pretending she believed she couldn't make it on her own in an attempt to play on their sympathy, but that wasn't who she was. "You did – so will I. And besides, I can't go back to Tilden, and I won't go back to Seton."

It became obvious to Elson that she would not be persuaded.

"There's no time! I have to leave before anyone discovers I'm gone."

"I'll go with you," declared Elson. His recent thoughts had been much about Kira, and a longing to be with her swelled within him. But his imagination always played scenes of happiness and laughter, not the cloud of desperation that surrounded the present circumstance. If he went with her now he might be forever viewed as a violator of sacred tradition. In that moment he decided - he would not let Kira venture into the Marland wild alone. "Warrick, hand me the flasks."

Warrick consented and Elson took them and went to find water and fill them.

When Kira was satisfied that Elson was out of earshot, she told Warrick that Elson's father was dead.

"What happened?"

"It was Idris, he pushed Ansen off the peak of Great Falls just minutes ago."

"Does Elson know yet?"

Kira shook her head.

"We have to tell him!"

"No, he must not find out!" countered Kira immediately. "If he finds out, he won't come with me. Please don't tell him, I need him! Nothing good can come from him learning about this."

After a few moments of considering Kira's plea, he agreed not to tell Elson.

"I only told you so that you can go back to Tilden and look after Elson's mother and Conroy. Tell them what happened. Tell them that Elson and I are together. And tell everyone on Tilden that the Marlanders are not to be trusted. And don't go near the Marland village."

Elson returned with full flasks. "Warrick, go back to the others and tell them that we didn't find Justin. Tell my family that I'm fine and that I'm with Kira. Above all, tell my father what we saw, he might be able to explain what everything means."

Kira cast a worried glance at Warrick, but it was for naught, for Warrick only nodded to do as Elson requested. Then Elson and Kira departed, going north and taking all of the supplies. Warrick continued south to make his way back to Tilden, wondering how he would cross the sea without passing through Seton to retrieve a boat.

*   *   *   *   *   *   *   *   *   *   *

Valena knelt quietly in her cabin, alone, facing out her southern window, which she had flung open wide. With hands on knees and eyes closed, she focused her mind on the voice of the world, taking in all the sounds. She sought the master of the land. After hours of submitting her mind to the unseen powers of Marland, she heard a faint scratching on the windowsill and opened her eyes.

Stunned by the sudden influx of daylight, she held up her hands to shield her eyes until they adjusted to the brightness. Then she lowered them to see a spectrum of living color. Shanahan, the large parrot, was perched in her window, filling almost the entire opening. He stretched his long wings and gave a loud squawk.

Valena was frightened. Shanahan *was* unusually large for a parrot, and she had never noticed before the sharp talons that these birds possess. "What do you want?" she demanded, and not expecting a response, she stood up, collected her walking staff, and prepared to shoo the bird from her home. "Here, I've got something for you," she threatened.

"Something for you, something for you," repeated the parrot. With one of his large, spiked feet, he tossed a shiny object on the floor near Valena's feet. She looked down to see a round, gold pendant. She retrieved it and examined it. On the back was engraved a single name, *Evelyn*.

Remembering that Elson had spoken of a parrot on the night he came ashore on Tilden, she asked, "You're the parrot that helped free us from the Caretaker's spell, aren't you? You're the one that spoke with Evelyn at the pillar, and again with her and Justin at the Renfrew?"

Shanahan only issued a dumb caw in response.

"Kavan is your master, isn't he?" The tone of her voice rose as she became excited. "Do you know where he is?"

"Know where he is," repeated Shanahan as he jerked his head up and down.

"Will you take me to him?"

"Take to him, take to him, *squawk*," replied Shanahan, nodding several more times before flying off the windowsill to a nearby tree. Even the backdrop of the autumn foliage paled beside Shanahan's dazzling feathers.

Valena, with walking staff in hand, extended her long, pale legs over the sill and dropped gracefully to the ground to follow. As she approached the bird, he flew away to perch on another distant tree, to where Valena once more followed. In this manner, Shanahan led Valena across Marland until a time came, at last, when Valena approached him and he did not fly away. She found herself standing near the pool at the base of Great Falls. Unbeknownst to her, Ansen's body lay out of sight not more than one hundred feet away.

"Where should I go now?" she asked her guide.

"Go now, *squawk*, go now," answered Shanahan, lifting a wing toward the falls.

Valena looked perplexingly at the bird.

"Go now, *squawk*, go now," he called out again.

"There? Into the falls?"

"Into the falls, into the falls," repeated Shanahan.

Valena stared at the massive stream of water descending before her. She had no idea how to proceed; there was no place to walk behind the falls, the cliffs offered no ledge for footing, but she trusted the bird and resolved to get behind the falls somehow. She removed her sandals and cloak and placed them along with her staff down beside the pool and dove into the cold water. After her body relaxed from the shock of the chill, she swam toward the place at the north end of the pool where the water crashed down. She went as far as she could until the strong currents began to push her back, then, with the deepest breath she could hold, dove down and swam along the bottom of the pool to the wall behind the falls. She surfaced, out of air and hoping that she was far enough away from the descending water that she wouldn't be driven back under.

Behind her the noise was tremendous and the spray of water constantly dowsed her head, but she was clear of the cascading falls. In front of her was an opening, round and black, and large enough for her to pass through easily. Inside, she found herself in an unexpectedly large passageway. Streams of oil and wax burned in random, twisting stripes along the rock walls, offering light for her to see a steep staircase of white stone leading down. A foul odor saturated the air, but she moved forward and descended the stairs, for she was sure that was where Shanahan intended her to go. As she went on the smell grew stronger and it became uncomfortably hot so that she had to constantly wipe perspiration from her brow with her forearm.

At the bottom of the stairs she entered a large chamber with a high, vaulted ceiling. Here the trickling fires provided light still, but there were also a few openings in the high walls where sunlight entered and hot air escaped. In spite of the hot draft, Shanahan was perched in one of these openings, waiting for her to arrive. When he finally saw her enter, he left his perch and alighted on a boulder beside her.

Valena glanced around to see that the place was empty except for shadows, the rock, and a small pool of dark fluid on the other side of the room.

"Is Kavan here?" she whispered.

"Kavan here, *squawk*," answered the bird, but shook his head. His loud response echoed through the cave.

"Will Kavan come here?"

"Kavan come here, *squawk*, come here!" Shanahan nodded his sharp beak up and down purposefully.

"When? Will he come today?"

The parrot tossed his head from side to side.

"Will Kavan come tonight?" she asked.

"Come tonight, *squawk*. Kavan come tonight." Then, having delivered his master's message, Shanahan shot upward in flight through one of the wall openings, retracting his long wings tight to his body in order to pass, and disappeared.

Delighted with her new knowledge, Valena climbed back up the marble staircase and dove once more into the pool, swam ashore, collected her gear, and returned to Seton. Ignoring the need to change from her wet clothes and get warm, she went straight to Lachlan and Idris to inform them of the very important meeting that would take place that evening.

* * * * * * * * * * *

Justin stared at the vast wasteland. The cliffs were now far behind, but the image, that of the two lands separated by the great chasm, burned in his mind still. He walked alone through an endless and barren country in search of anything that might help him across. Loneliness and futility became more intense the further he went, and he told himself that it was foolish to walk in the opposite direction of the expanse, but something within him made him press on into the nothingness.

Morning sunlight shone on Justin's closed eyelids, unhindered by the few dead, brittle leaves that clung to tree branches above. He awoke to realize that his current circumstance was not so different from that of his dream. He was alone. Loneliness and futility overwhelmed him. In some aspects, the desolate world of his vision was preferable - at least there he was warm and had a goal, and he wasn't hungry. Without motivation to rise, he remained lying amidst the clump of birch trees on the hardening ground.

For weeks he'd been trying to form a plan of action, but with every idea came an avalanche of reasons persuading him that his efforts would result in failure. Seeking out Kavan and his horde to avenge his lost love had been his first plan. In spite of his fear, and in spite of not having a weapon that would likely inflict injury upon them, his desire for vengeance drove him recklessly to search for Evelyn's killers. After the first week his rage subsided to sorrow for a time, then an intense sense of guilt set in from the fact that he was the reason that despair now plagued the whole world. It was this conviction that pushed him northward into the deep wild of Marland to get far away from everyone - he could never return to his island friends. He couldn't bear the thought of having to look into the eyes of even one innocent person whose life he had ruined.

Hunger and cold finally gave him adequate reason to abandon his rough bed and continue his trek north. It mattered not the time of year on the island, food could always be found. But here on Marland, where the winters were cold and full of snow, food had to be gotten before the harvest time expired. Justin knew that time was almost passed because the fruit and berries on which he had been surviving were becoming impossibly difficult to find. Soon, after a few minutes of walking, his heart was pumping hard and, except for his ears and nose, he was no longer cold. The sudden movement of a large animal startled him. He glanced to the spot, about fifty feet away, and saw the tall white tail and spiked antlers of an enormous deer, a buck. Justin felt that he should try to pursue it; in his journey to that point he had not seen many animals and the next opportunity for him to hunt such a creature might not come soon. But the deer was quick, hurdling brush and rocks with deft grace, moving through the forest with utmost efficiency. Still, he did his best to follow.

He was beginning to wonder whether he had lost the deer when a loud crash came from up ahead. The sound of a struggle followed: branches broke, dry foliage was trampled, and several treetops shook, creating a flurry of falling leaves. Justin didn't proceed forward, yet neither did he turn back.

At last he moved ahead slowly and cautiously. When he came to the place of the struggle he saw that a fire had been made and above it, roasting on wooden spits, were pieces of meat that had been cut from the deer. Beside the fire were garments, freshly fashioned from the skin of the great buck, and all that remained of the animal was a crumpled skeleton. Only the skull, with the rack of horns, remained whole - everything else was already turning to dust and ash, for the rest of the animal had been used as fuel for the fire.

Justin looked to see who had done this, but saw no one. He knelt by the fire and examined the garments. They were clean and warm, having been taken from a living animal only a few minutes before. He put them on and sat down to eat.

*   *   *   *   *   *   *   *   *   *   *

"Do you think it wise to heed the instructions of a dumb bird?" Lachlan was put out at having to dive into the cold pool and swim under the falls to the cave in the dark. As he descended the long marble staircase, he slipped and fell into the next lower stair, twisting his ankle, not enough to cause a sprain, but enough to make him curse loudly.

"Shanahan is not dumb," answered Valena, disbelieving that Lachlan spoke so foolishly about a servant of Kavan. "You'll know when you see him. He's very clever."

"How is it that this place was never discovered?" Idris was clearly irritated by this fact. "Brant, have you ever heard anyone talk about this cave?"

"No, never, sir," Brant promptly replied. Idris had requested that Brant accompany them. He was exceedingly pleased at having been invited and followed closely behind Valena and in front of Idris, warning him of every potential danger on the path.

Fearing the unknown, Brant, Lachlan, and Idris had each brought a sword with them. As they descended, the heat of the place warmed them and soon they began to perspire.

"What is this horrid place?" muttered Lachlan. Though they were all covered with sweat and detested the odor, he was the only one to express any displeasure.

"We're almost there," said Valena, continuing to ignore Lachlan's complaining.

Sure enough, they reached the bottom of the stairs and gathered around the large stone. Lachlan was the first to wander over to the black pool, drawing his sword as he approached. He crouched down to examine the curious liquid and lowered his sword so as to dip the tip of the blade into the pool, but before he could, a voice called out; "Good evening, my friends!"

A giant figure stood at the bottom of the stairs. They were certain that he had not descended from above, but seemed to have appeared from thin air. His appearance was magnificent, with features handsome and strong. Another tall, spindly figure stood behind him, not as tall as the giant and his appearance ghastly. Lachlan stood up and tightened his grip on his sword. Idris and Brant also drew theirs.

Upon seeing them, Valena dropped to her knees and bowed her face to the warm earth. The foul odor of the soil filled her nostrils, but she remained prone before them. "Rise, daughter," said Kavan, "you have done well." As soon as he said this, Shanahan came soaring through one of the openings in the wall and glided down to perch on Kavan's shoulder. In spite of the bird's size, sitting upon Kavan's broad frame one would not guess that he was large at all. "Please put down your swords, you'll not need them, not yet," directed Kavan.

The men reluctantly put their swords on top of the stone, but positioned them such that they could retrieve them quickly.

"As you are likely to know already, I am Kavan. With me are Shanahan, a worthy and clever bird, and Feloniche, my most loyal servant." Feloniche stepped forward. His lanky, emaciated shape was unpleasant to behold. "No introductions are necessary on your part - you're all known by us."

*   *   *   *   *   *   *   *   *   *   *

Warrick waited until sundown to attempt to cross the sea and return to Tilden, hoping to recover a boat from the docks and float away quietly in the dark unnoticed, fearing Kira's description of the Marlanders' ruthlessness. Now was the time to move, he decided, and he began to make his way through the dimming woods on the outskirts of Seton, and down to the water.

By the time he arrived at the shore of the South Sea, all daylight had disappeared, but the moon shone bright enough to allow him to see guards pacing the docks – a sight that confirmed that he could not depart from there. He glanced around and saw, right in front of him, not more than ten feet away, the small boat that Ansen had brought from Tilden. It lay on the edge of the sandy beach, tied to the small post just as Idris had left it the day before.

Taking advantage of a shadow cast by a passing cloud, Warrick crawled out into the open, slipped the tether over the top of the hitching post, and quietly pulled the boat back into the cover of the trees. He lifted the front end of the vessel and positioned himself underneath, then he stood up and, using his shoulders, raised the boat off the ground. It was heavier than he expected and he found himself back on his knees while the back end of the boat crashed silently to the ground.

He knew he wouldn't have to go far, and that this vessel was his best, if not only, chance to escape. He had to get back; back to his family, back to Conroy and Mrs. Verrill, and back to tell the others what he and Elson had seen. He stood again and hoisted the craft off the ground. This time he remained standing and attempted to take a step – it was difficult but he managed. He took another, then another, wondering if his muscles would sustain his advance, until he came to a section of shore that was out of sight from the docks. Exhausted, he collapsed and let the boat tumble off his weary body. He lay face down, unmoving except for the swelling and shrinking of his chest cavity with every breath and exhalation, beside the boat for several minutes to rest, not caring that his elbow was bruised, nor that his right cheek and brow had been scraped and were now covered with damp sand. Once he felt recovered, he rolled the boat over and dragged it down the beach and into the sea. He climbed inside, found the oar, and began to paddle.

* * * * * * * * * * *

"Why have you come here?" Kavan remained standing at the bottom of the staircase; he sensed that if he moved he would frighten the four humans in the same manner that a hunter frightens his prey. "You were there the night I took Evelyn away. Aren't you afraid?"

Idris boldly responded; "We understand that she violated something that was part of this land, and we believe that was why she, and only she, was taken."

"Indeed, you have a clear understanding in that matter!" exclaimed Kavan. "As lord of this land, and guardian of the red river, it was my duty to discipline her. But judgment is not to be limited to only her." The four humans grew even more uncomfortable, and Kavan, perceiving this spoke swiftly to put them at ease; "But you need not fear me, for I don't intend any harm to come to you, in fact it is my desire to see you prosper."

But Kavan's actions confused them - he stepped forward and took up Lachlan's sword. The men were too afraid to react and the two remaining swords lay unclaimed upon the stone. Shanahan flew from his master's shoulder to one of the high openings and perched there while Kavan lifted the blade and swung it easily, slicing the air noisily. The sword was but a small dagger in Kavan's massive hand.

"I *am* glad that you brought your sword, Lachlan, for if you hadn't it would have been difficult for me to show you this." Kavan crossed the cave, knelt down, and dipped the whole blade into the dark pool. When he withdrew it, streams of black spread across the sword, hardening in a random pattern to contrast with the silver steel. Kavan returned to his guests and handed the sword to Brant. "Lachlan, if you wouldn't mind taking up one of the other swords."

Without delay, Lachlan retrieved the sword nearest him.

"Now, try to disarm him," Kavan turned from Lachlan to Brant. "Don't be intimidated, son, just hold on firmly like I know you can."

Brant gripped the handle of the sword with both hands and held it up in front of him, determined to obey.

Lachlan saw that Brant was ready, so he struck fast with a series of quick moves that he was sure would remove the blade from the boy's grasp. Brant's arms twisted and contorted, but he kept hold of the sword. Lachlan came in again, more ferocious this time, repeating his tactic. Brant was barely able to keep the sword in front of him, but it remained firmly in his hands.

Brant looked at his fingers wrapped tightly around the handle. He liked the image and knew he'd do whatever he could to keep the blade within his grasp.

Worried to seem a weakling before mighty Kavan, Lachlan came in at Brant swinging furiously, dealing blow after blow until Brant was forced to his knees, his arms lay across the stone and the blade dangled from his closed hands. Lachlan hammered again and again on the sword, but it would not come free.

"Enough!" declared Kavan, delighted. Lachlan ceased striking. Brant released the sword and stood up, exhausted, and rubbed his sore arms. "That satisfactorily demonstrates one of the qualities of glimmerstone."

"*Glimmerstone*?" asked Idris.

"The black stone," answered Kavan. "You'll find it nowhere else in all the world except for in this cave." He picked up the silver and black sword that Brant had dropped and swung it at the large stone. *Crack*! The rock split in half, sliced through the center by Kavan's stroke. He lifted the sword to reveal that it was not damaged. "Another quality of glimmerstone is that it is indestructible. But more importantly, as was demonstrated a few moments ago, glimmerstone becomes one with, and serves the imagination of, its possessor. The reason Brant could not be disarmed is because he wanted to hold onto the sword. The glimmerstone perceived his desire and obeyed. It is my gift to you."

"Try it yourself," Kavan flipped the sword to Lachlan, spinning it half a revolution so that its handle fell into Lachlan's awaiting grasp. Lachlan swung it slowly in a couple of side-to-side then up-and-down maneuvers - it felt as if it were part of his own flesh. Then he followed Kavan's example and swung it downward at one of the stones, creating three pieces of broken rock instead of two.

Lachlan raised the blade and stared at its edges, squinting to detect any blemish using the faint light of the fires, but as before, it had split stone without obtaining even a scratch. Impressed to the point of being speechless, he knelt before Kavan and bowed his head in an expression of deep thanks for showing him such a precious thing.

"I'm glad that you're pleased, Lachlan," said Kavan, "but there's more to discuss tonight than glimmerstone. Idris, why are you here? What do you desire?"

Idris replied at once, and spoke boldly; "Can you bring me to the Icyandic?"

"The Icyandic? The most powerful of the four Rivers of Power?" replied Kavan.

Idris nodded.

"Do you know what the white water will do to you?"

"It will return that which was taken from me: immortality."

A scratchy voice spoke from the darkness behind Kavan; "What do you have to offer us in return for taking you to the white river?" Feloniche, who had been silently standing aside up until this point, came forward. "Have you asked this of your beloved Island Caretaker?"

"Calm yourself, Feloniche," said Kavan, "Perhaps Idris is worthy of the Icyandic. Besides, why should he be kept from it now that he's free from the king's spell?"

"The Caretaker considers me his enemy, though I don't know why, but I'll play my part as such if it pleases you," answered Idris. "I'll do whatever you command if you promise to lead me there. Tell me what I must do."

"You'll learn soon enough what is required from you, my friend," answered Kavan, "it's not much, certainly nothing worth considering now."

"Please don't be offended, but what proof is there that you have access to the Icyandic?" Idris watched Kavan's expression carefully - it remained unchanged, but Feloniche was aroused.

"Fool!" shouted Kavan's thin servant, "how dare you question my master! You must learn your place!"

"It's a fair question, Feloniche," said Kavan, grabbing hold of his servant's arm to restrain him. "I told you to be calm!" Kavan stepped toward Lachlan and reached out a hand. "May I?"

Lachlan obediently handed him the sword.

Kavan took the weapon and carried it back to Feloniche, silently instructing him to remain still. "Observe," he called out, then ran one of the edges across Feloniche's outstretched arm. A sudden flood of white shot from the wound, illuminating the entire cave. Kavan continued to cut, passing the blade over Feloniche's chest to open a new gash. Feloniche winced in terrible pain but did not cry out. Light flowing from both openings merged and intensified so that the humans had to shield their eyes. Then, quickly, Feloniche's split flesh came together and healed without leaving a scar.

"So it is with all who have drunk from the Icyandic; so it is with all of my servants; so shall it be with you." Kavan saw that his demonstration satisfied Idris and returned the sword to Lachlan.

"Daughter, what about you? Why have you come?" Kavan turned to Valena. "Glimmerstone for Lachlan, the Icyandic for Idris, what is it that you desire?"

Valena approached Kavan with her utmost grace and, in a fluid motion, knelt low on the ground before him. "It has been said that a great creature, an enemy to King Iman, dwells within this land. I wish to know if this is true, and if so, is it the creature that you formed an alliance with when you brought forth the Renfrew long ago?"

"It is, and it is," answered Kavan, "but know that it is not contained within the borders of Marland and Tilden; its domain is the whole world."

Valena's eyes widened as she raised her head just high enough to lift her black hair off the ground. "I wish to serve you and this creature, to be your priestess so that I might lead others to serve you and rejoice in your magnificence, even as I now rejoice in my heart for having the privilege to speak with you."

"I can sense your loyalty to me. You would be an effective priestess, worthy to deliver messages from my higher realm to your people."

"Nothing would bring me more joy, my lord," Valena bowed low again and her hair swept the ground. "One more thing, my lord," she pleaded; "We desire to see the creature from the Renfrew. We have heard its legend told for ages but have never beheld it. Would you bring us to it?"

"There's no need to take you anywhere," replied Kavan, "and you *have* seen it before! The creature, Scynn, is already here!"

"Already here, *squawk*!" repeated Shanahan from high above.

Through an opening beside the one in which Shanahan perched crawled a small reptilian creature, delightful to look upon at first sight, and not much larger than a cat. It had smooth, dark scales that reflected the dim and flickering firelight, and they couldn't discern its true appearance. It moved with unmatched efficiency and grace, crawling forward on six nimble limbs down toward the floor of the cave without concern that gravity would pull it free and dash it to the floor. As it descended it grew, as if feeding on the attention the Marlanders offered. When it reached the floor it stood up straight, like a man, on its two lowest limbs and met the mortals in the center of the cave. It had grown so much that it now towered over them with its middle limbs folded behind its back and its upper limbs crossed over its large, firm, plated chest.

They recognized it as the creature that had taken Evelyn away, and now the four of them were amazed at the magnificent creature, though for different reasons. Idris noticed most the superior intelligence, a type more cunning than intellectual, like the kind a squirrel possesses which it uses to reach even the most well-placed bird feeders. Clearly, Idris perceived that Scynn was not a dumb animal that wandered about with concern only for filling its belly. Its face, its posture, even its long tail, which danced gently back and forth, convinced Idris that it was the cleverest creature in the world.

Lachlan took notice of Scynn's powerful appearance, and his eyes shifted over the pleasing images of taut, massive muscles in its arms, legs, back, shoulders, and tail. He saw the creature as being supreme, with no weakness to be exploited.

Valena was captivated by the shifting colors of its scales: emerald, topaz, ruby; she saw all the colors of precious gems in the flawless coverings of its body. And its face, which she first considered to be like that of an animal, but when she looked more closely upon it realized that it was more beautiful than a human face, gave her a rush of mingled pleasure and contentment.

After it had purposefully indulged the humans' long stares, the creature spoke; "I am Scynn, born of the ancient Renfrew, friend to Kavan." Its voice was not the sound of a hiss, but was clear and gentle and concise. "Tell me, are you pleased with all that Kavan has revealed to you?"

The four eagerly expressed that they were.

"Good! I knew you would be, after all it was I who instructed Kavan to show them to you, for I know the desires of your hearts." Scynn looked from one to the other until it met each of their gazes with its own. "I can lead you to more of such things if you are willing to follow me."

"What more do you have to offer? And what do you ask from us in return?" questioned Idris.

"If you are to be the recipients of further objects of my grace, you must separate yourselves from King Iman. He and I are enemies; no one who loves him can follow me to where I desire to lead them."

"The king has threatened to destroy us along with you," offered Lachlan, watching Scynn's expression closely to see if his words caused any despair.

"Lachlan speaks the truth," added Idris. "The Caretaker himself warned me that he pledged to destroy you and all who befriend you."

"Truth! The truth is that that king's threats are empty! Don't heed them!" Kavan, obviously angered, joined the group and stood beside Scynn. Feloniche followed. "He's proclaimed our doom for ages. The truth is that no harm has come to us. The truth is that we've grown stronger while his strength has diminished." Scynn remained silent, motionless, while Kavan spoke; Feloniche nodded enthusiastically at every point his master drove home. "You shall be safe enough if you join us. I promise that we are able to guard you against the king's weakened wrath."

"Surely, my lord, it is as you say," cried Valena, falling to her knees again, hoping that the gesture would appease Kavan.

"I came here seeking the Icyandic by means other than King Iman, and your words my ears receive with joy," said Idris. "We have no love for the king — as far as we're concerned he has proven himself incompetent. We'll follow you."

Kavan instructed Brant to apply glimmerstone to the other blades. The boy readily obeyed, taking the remaining swords timidly toward the mysterious black pool, while Kavan, Scynn and Feloniche met privately with Idris, Valena, and Lachlan, respectively, withdrawing them to separate parts of the cave.

Feloniche stood over Lachlan, one long, thin limb of an arm slung around Lachlan's shorter, but thicker frame. "Prove yourself worthy of my lords by learning to use the glimmerstone," he hissed. "Slay one who serves King Iman and earn what has been given to you. By so doing, you'll show the Marlanders, as well as those Tildenian fools, that the king is incapable of defending those who call themselves his friend. Afterward, when there's still no sign of him, it will be known that the king is just as powerless to avenge."

Lachlan agreed to the mission set before him, recognizing its multiple good purposes.

In another section of the cave, Kavan spoke intimately with Valena. She constantly fell to kneel before him, but Kavan preferred her to stand so that he could look into her eyes. Finally she accepted his will and stood, staring up into Kavan's simultaneously fearsome and handsome face.

"The other Marlanders may not be as wise as you," he began, "I worry that some of them cling deludedly to hope of being reconciled with the Caretaker, and even believe that he will restore the island. Others may be too frightened of me to follow your guidance, though it be for their own good. But with the truth that I will now reveal, you may be able to persuade them to follow me."

Valena listened attentively to her new master as he looked with unwavering eyes into hers and continued to speak compassionately. "You must understand that when the king's spell was broken, due to the violation of the Renfrew, he became furious at *all* the islanders; his anger should have been focused on only Justin and Evelyn, the two violators, but it was not. In his impatient and uncontrolled rage he sought to destroy all of you. That's why he sent his servants to collapse the foundations of the isle and send it sinking into the sea, and why they herded you mercilessly into the water."

"His servants?" asked Valena.

"The giant brutes with whips and swords and all sorts of gear for destruction, those were his servants," explained Kavan. "Because the spell was broken, you were able to see them as they truly are, brainless oafs, but stronger than your kind, incapable of thinking for themselves, able only to do as they are told. Knowing the peril you and your people faced, I gathered a number of my own servants and went to speak with him. For your sake I risked battle, pleading with him to restrain from taking so many precious lives."

Valena's heart filled with love toward Kavan and tears welled up in her eyes. "Thank you." She cleared the wetness from her face.

"Don't be too pleased," warned Kavan, "for the king agreed to spare your people on the condition that one of you, every season, be killed as punishment for breaking the spell that he held over you. With sorrow, I declared that I would be the one to carry out this decree for fear that if anyone else was responsible to do it they would not refrain from slaughtering more than one of you."

"Evelyn was the first?"

"She was," replied Kavan gently, "it seemed appropriate that she should be first, for this sentence was brought about by what she did."

"Has there been another?"

"Not yet," answered Kavan, "but the second season is almost past and the king grows impatient for more blood."

"My lord, who will be chosen?" Valena tensed.

"It's my decision to make, I can select whoever I want."

"If I convince the Marlanders to serve you, surely you would not make your selection from among them?"

"I would not!" he exclaimed. "It's difficult enough to select a victim, but I could never put one who served me in line of the king's careless judgment."

"I'll work to bring my people into an alliance with you. Surely, they'll consent," promised Valena.

"That would be best, my daughter," said Kavan, "If I delay much longer the king may change his mind and send his servants to destroy you all. I swear to protect all who submit to me."

Meanwhile, in yet another corner of the cave, Scynn spoke privately with Idris; "How have you come to be the leader of these people?"

"I chose to pursue a life other than what the Tildenians were ready to accept," answered Idris. "Having similar desires, and being inspired by my initiative, these people followed me here. Valena has become my eyes and ears, and Lachlan, my right hand. The people obey us without question and..."

"Your people are not prepared for the coming winter," Scynn scolded, unimpressed, putting a halt to Idris' boasting. "How long do you think they will submit to you if you fail to give them what they need to survive."

Idris nodded, admitting there was truth in Scynn's words.

"Can you help us? Do you have any provisions for us?"

"All you need is within your own reach!" said Scynn, "you need only to act!"

After a moment, Idris began to understand, "Are you referring to the provisions that the Caretaker brought to Tilden?"

Scynn replied with a wide, toothy grin. "What better way to declare your independence from the king than to take what he gave to his subjects? What better way to prove yourself worthy of Kavan's promise? What better way to solidify yourself as ruler over the Marlanders?"

"My people may not be willing to steal from their old friends and families."

"Let them endure the cold of winter for awhile and let them hunger, then see what they're willing to do," advised Scynn, "but take care to remain master over them."

Idris was silent as he pondered the creature's proposal, thinking how he could subject his followers to discomfort and yet prevent rebellion.

"Killing the Tildenian was very satisfying, I know, but you need to have greater vision."

Idris was not surprised that Scynn knew of his murderous deed; he believed it impossible for any knowledge to be hidden from it.

"Allow me to show you what might be." Scynn reached its middle arms toward Idris and placed two hands on his head, not intending to inflict pain, but to manipulate thoughts. Instantly, Idris found himself on a balcony high on a stone tower looking down on Seton. He was ruler of Marland and all northern lands as far as he could see. Dozens of beautiful women waited on him to meet his every need and desire. He had enslaved the Tildenians and forced them to perform all the labor of his kingdom, including building the tower in which he stood. All around the tower's base was an army, impressive in stature, armed with glimmerstone, fearless and invincible. Best of all, Idris no longer feared death, for he had tasted the water of the Icyandic.

Scynn removed its fingertips from Idris' head, certain the images freshly conjured would not soon fade. "I can lead you to this future if you are willing."

"I'll do anything you ask." There was nothing Idris desired which had been absent from the vision, so he saw no reason to withhold anything he had to offer.

"Do as I suggested," answered Scynn, while spinning Idris around with its two upper right hands and nudging him back toward the center of the cave, "It's time to rejoin the others."

Kavan and Valena, and Lachlan and Feloniche had gathered around the broken fragments of stone and were speaking with Brant, admiring the newly glimmerstoned swords.

"It has been a pleasure to speak with you," said Kavan, "but we must go now. You go also, and do as you've been bidden." Even as his last words echoed within the cave, the three immortals vanished.

"Go now! Go now! *Squawk*," repeated Shanahan, still a spectator from the window above. "Do as bidden, do as bidden." Then the large bird turned and leapt into the darkness, the sound of his wings beating the night air served as an epilogue.

chapter eleven: ·the grip of fear·

Conroy had gone down to the shore to work on the monument that his father had begun. He had promised to work on it while Ansen journeyed to Marland to search for Elson, and he was making noticeable progress, beginning early in the morning and working on it for the better portion of the day. It beat laboring in the fields and forests, and he worked hard so that he wouldn't be considered one who avoided work. He finished carving a fold of the Caretaker's robe and then took a moment to inspect his work; he was pleased at the angles and curves he had made in the hard, white stone. Not yet ready to resume work, he glanced out at the water to see a small boat with a single passenger gliding toward him. His heart pounded when he recognized Warrick, and he quickly lowered his gaze to the statue, hoping this would deter Warrick from approaching.

As anxious as he was to return, seeing Conroy made Warrick wish to delay his arrival. But when Conroy looked up and spotted him, he knew he couldn't hesitate and pulled on the oar to traverse the last bit of sea that remained between him and the fatherless boy. Warrick loved Conroy, and telling him that his father was gone wasn't going to be easy. He fitted the oar into the holding slot and got out, waded through the shallow water and pulled the boat onto the beach. He breathed in and out deeply and turned to approach Conroy. He attempted a smile, but it didn't feel right.

Warrick placed his hand on Conroy's shoulder. "I have sad news that I must share." Conroy held his carving tools tightly as he shifted his eyes up to Warrick's somber face. "Your father has fallen and won't be returning. He...he's dead." Warrick felt the weight of his words as he spoke them; was he sure of this? What if Kira was mistaken? Maybe Ansen was alive?

Conroy lowered his head again. Several moments passed and he did not sob or curse or speak. Warrick began to wonder whether he even breathed. Finally, he raised his wet eyes and, with great effort to keep his emotions in check, spoke; "I have sad news I must share. Lucy had an accident...she's dead."

"What do you mean?" exclaimed Warrick. "What happened to my daughter?"

Conroy's composure then departed as news of his father's death overwhelmed him. He collapsed into the statue and folded his arms around his face and wept.

Realizing that he wouldn't be able to get any more information about Lucy from Conroy, Warrick found the path that led to the village and began to run. He tried to shake off feelings of despair, which were more intense than anything he had ever known, by telling himself that it wasn't true, that Conroy only said it to be cruel, hurt at the loss of his father.

Suddenly his pain disappeared. Lucy, his darling daughter, stood smiling on the path before him! He ran to her and caught her up in his arms. She seemed more alive than ever before! What a cruel hoax for Conroy to pull! "Lucy! Lucy! I was so worried, but you're all right! I'm so happy to see you!"

"I'm happy to see you too, Daddy." Her voice sounded so beautiful to Warrick.

"Conroy told me that you had an accident. What an awful thing for him to lie like that."

"I did have an accident; Conroy didn't lie."

"But you're all right now; Conroy told me that you were..." Warrick couldn't bring himself to say the word, even the thought of it recalled the intense pain.

"I can't see you again," said Lucy. Warrick was confused, for she had such a pleasant tone as she made the statement. "King Iman says that you're only allowed to see me this one last time."

"King Iman? Who is King Iman? What sort of delusion is this?"

"The Island Caretaker," Lucy explained, her smile never fading. "He brought me here so you could see me and so he could talk with you."

Warrick was sure he was dreaming and began to think of ways to wake himself.

"The Tildenians need you, Warrick, son of Spenser."

Warrick turned to find the owner of the deep voice. The man was large and wore garments which seemed impossibly white, yet his hair and flesh were even brighter, glowing like the sun from some internal power. "Caretaker?"

"Lucy is to accompany me now. But you must remain on Tilden and help those who live here."

Warrick's inner aching returned. "Who are you to take my daughter from me? I'll not let her go!"

"Open your mind to acknowledge truth! You have an improper perspective." The king's firmness established himself as one having authority, and Warrick submitted. "I'm the one who brought her to you so you could say goodbye. It's not by my shortcoming that she has to leave: that was Scynn's doing." The king's tone softened; "be comforted to know that I love her as much as you, and that I'll take her to a place where she'll be happy and safe."

The king had convinced Warrick to believe him, but he held Lucy in his arms still. "What can I do for the Tildenians?"

"Stay with them and be their leader," replied King Iman. "I plan to bring aid to them through you."

If all this was only his imagination, Lucy's weight on his tired arms seemed real enough. He put her down. "Why me?"

"Because you led Justin to the Renfrew. Had you not done so, things might not be as they are now. It will be good for you to find a sense of redemption – serve them."

"What about Justin and Elson?"

"They aren't here, only you are." King Iman walked past Lucy and reached out and placed his hand on the trunk of a thin tree that stood a few feet from the trail. He stepped backward without releasing it from his grasp; roots squirmed beneath the ground as the entire tree was brought closer to the path. Lucy danced happily over the roots as the ground shifted under her feet. Then the king let go of the tree, crossed the path, and took hold of a similar one. Likewise, he brought this tree close to that side of the path.

"Where should I lead them?" asked Warrick.

"You don't have to take them anywhere to lead them. I want you to encourage them and keep them full of hope."

"How?"

"By reminding them that aid will come. But remember," warned the king, raising a finger, "*I* will aid them, not you."

Warrick retrieved Lucy – his arms had rested sufficiently.

"It's time for you to say goodbye," said King Iman.

Warrick drew Lucy close and felt the smooth skin of her cheek with his own, and smelled her neck. Then he pushed her away slightly so that he could look upon her clearly, studying, memorizing every line and curve of her face. Finally, when his arms ached so he couldn't hold her anymore, he put her down. Lucy went directly to King Iman and took his hand, then the two of them turned and walked away, heading up the path toward the village. They rounded a bend and disappeared from sight. Warrick raced ahead in hope of seeing Lucy again, but when he passed the corner, she was nowhere to be seen. Instead, running down the path toward him was his wife, Tanya.

"I heard of your return and came to see you at once," she said. "Lucy's gone!" She wiped a tear away with the back of her hand, then rolled it over to collect one from her other eye with her thumb.

"I just saw Lucy," Warrick said. "I spoke with her! She was alive!"

"But I buried her," replied Tanya. "I went to wake her one morning and found her dead. She had stopped breathing some time during the night."

"The Caretaker was with her. He spoke to me, then took her away."

"What did he say?"

"That he'd help us."

*   *   *   *   *   *   *   *   *   *   *

Warrick passed on the information that Kira had revealed to him, beginning by speaking with Linus Darring and Wendel Wright, and soon afterward the news spread throughout Tilden. The Tildenians were very disappointed and angry when they learned about the new endeavors of the Marlanders. Russel Minns' anger was extraordinary, and he attempted to rally others to go to Marland and avenge Ansen Verrill. Although justice was desired, the Tildenians were not willing to send a few men to Marland for fear that the Marlanders would resist the seizing of their leader and deal harshly with those that had been sent. Sending more than a few men would likely result in war between the two lands, which was something they were not prepared to wage. But, fearing future hostility from their friends on the north side of the South Sea, the Tildenians planned to form a military force to defend themselves.

The other significant news Warrick passed on, that of Kira abandoning Idris and running away with Elson, drew mixed reactions from the people; even Kira's parents felt differently on the matter. Kira's mother was pleased to know that her daughter had escaped the desperate situation that she had been in, while her father was ashamed of having a daughter who tossed aside the island tradition of betrothal. Kira's friend, Amara, drilled Warrick with questions, but since he had only seen Kira for a few minutes, he was unable to reveal further details of her ordeals. Given the more pressing matter of protecting themselves, however, debate about the morality of the relationship between Elson and Kira was not given priority within discussions of most social circles.

The first thing they did was to establish a means by which to keep watch for enemies advancing across the sea. A large bell that hung in the center of Bentleigh, which had been used, up til then, to summon workers to midday and evening meals, would now be used for this more serious purpose. Two platforms were erected in the treetops near the coast and camouflaged so as to not be easily noticed from the water. Within these, two large reels were placed, around which wound the ends of long cables that reached back to the bell, running aboveground, threaded through eyes of long spikes that had been driven deep into the soil. The bell was loud enough so that its ringing could be heard by those operating the reels, allowing them to be confident that their warning signal had been satisfactorily issued, but not so loud that one miles out on the water would hear. It was this feature which made the bell the best strategy, for any kind of visual signal would allow for the oncoming assailants to know they've been spotted. Another benefit was that it allowed the watchers, as they were to be called, to act without giving away their position. The two spotting scopes that remained in possession of the Tildenians would be used by the watchers to perform their duties.

The assignments for watchers went mostly to the younger men, but also to some of the women who were not content with the usual responsibilities designated them, that of preparing meals and watching children. Conroy and Bethany Krunser, Allison's older sister, were partnered to be one of many teams. This suited both of them well: for Bethany, it was a responsibility similar to what she had on the island, that of an island messenger; and Conroy was eager to participate in anything intended to oppose the Marlanders. Amara and Keelan formed another team, and when the day came that all work on the alarms was complete, these four were the first to be sent out. They arrived at their stations at sunrise to initiate the rather boring, but critically important, work of staring out at the empty South Sea.

Back in the village, Wendel walked proudly around the bell, a large metal disc about twelve feet in diameter, pleased that the Tildenians had been able to construct their signal in so short a time. He grasped each of the strong cables in his hands and felt their tension. In his mind he pictured the reel turning to wind the cable to raise the sounding arm, then releasing to let it fall back down into the bell. Surely this would thwart Idris from coming to Tilden with malicious intent, he thought. He would not have been so smug had he known that a Marlander had already come with evil purpose, arriving only moments before the watchers reached their posts.

*   *   *   *   *   *   *   *   *   *   *

No offensive was to be launched against Marland. He heard the words from Linus himself, the spokesman of the Council. With such a verdict, Russel Minns' rage would not subside. Discontent swelled within him from the moment he learned what had been done to Ansen. Throughout the following weeks he released his frustration on the metal spikes that held the bell's cables, pounding down one after another with his mallet. But now the cables were run and there were no more spikes to pound, and his anger was as consuming as ever.

Russel found himself often glancing at Conroy to observe the boy's condition, and sometimes noticed his head hung low and saw wetness in his eyes. It was good that he had close friends around him, but still he was sure that Conroy appreciated his desire for vengeance. It wasn't fair! It wasn't right that this young boy should suffer great loss, while the one who caused the loss suffered no consequence.

Monica Verrill observed Russel's enthusiasm and went to speak with him one morning. She thanked him for his attitude, but expressed her desire for Russel to not act against the Council's decision; two good men dead would be worse than one, she said.

Russel had no intention of leaving his people while they needed him, and though his burden seemed greater than that of any other man in the community, he felt it was deservedly so; no one else was as strong or could work as hard. Besides, he truly loved the people in spite of his gruff demeanor. But now his work was done, at least for awhile, and the day after the cables were installed, on the last day of the ninth month, he took his pack and mallet and made his way for the coast, riding in his cart pulled by his beloved horse, Mudlick. He did not inform anyone of his plan, not even those he knew who supported his effort.

Sunlight began to shine through the barren autumn branches as he went north. A sudden blur of silver and black startled him, and Mudlick continued to advance along the path, but the cart slowed. When the distance between horse and master became sufficient, Russel saw that the harness straps were broken. "Stop, you dumb beast!" Russel called out. But Mudlick, unusually strong and rough among horses as Russel was among men, continued several yards before stopping. The cart proceeded slowly, without control, off the trail and came to a rough stop. Confused, Russel looked around to see what had caused the separation. Behind him, standing beside the trail was Lachlan, holding a shiny, silver sword with streaks of black across the whole blade. He held out the sword, as if to show it off.

Russel completed his circumferential survey, decided Lachlan was alone, then acknowledged the unusual weapon; "What sort of malformed metal is that?"

"I'm certain you've never seen a blade like this," replied Lachlan proudly. "I'll show you its secrets, but then you must die."

"So, you wish to take my life? How have I wronged you that you want me to die?"

"A new alliance requires it."

Russel retrieved his mallet and stepped down from the cart.

Lachlan laughed at Russel's meager weapon. Many words came to mind that he could use to declare the superiority of his sword over the dumb, oversized hammer, but he decided a demonstration would be most effective. He swung at a nearby oak tree nearly two feet thick. The dense hardwood did not slow the circling sword, and after its motion was complete Lachlan held it out once more. The tree began to lean forward, slowly at first, but accelerated until it toppled over with great speed toward Russel.

Russel leapt aside to avoid the falling tree, realizing that his strength and skill would be no match for Lachlan's mysterious weapon. But he resolved not to let Lachlan decide the manner in which the fight would proceed. He sprinted up the trail and drew back his mallet. He stopped suddenly and let momentum carry the mallet over his shoulder; adding all of his own force, he hurled it at Lachlan.

Lachlan was surprised by the move, but lifted the glimmerstone blade confidently to meet the spinning head of the heavy mallet. The blade sliced through it so easily that it did not slow the oncoming mass, but succeeded only in dividing it in two. Both pieces landed firmly on Lachlan's chest, knocking him backward into another tree, slamming his head against the trunk. Lachlan released his sword as he fell unconscious to the ground. Russel rushed and quickly took up the black and silver blade.

"That's not for you," hissed a voice.

Russel looked around but didn't see anyone. He sensed a presence, however, and tightened his grip on the handle.

"Russel Minns," said the voice, "many believe that you're the strongest of all the islanders."

"It is true," declared Russel, his adrenaline still flowing, ready for another fight.

"Then I'll test myself against the mightiest of men!" Feloniche cast off his invisibility.

"Who are you?" asked Russel, now able to view the slender and ghastly figure. Though he held no weapon, Russel saw that he possessed long claws that he could use to slash and stab. "You know my name, it's fair that I know yours."

"I'm Feloniche, servant of Kavan. It will be impossible for you to defeat me - I'm an immortal."

"If you attack, I'll fight."

Feloniche charged at Russel with amazing speed, lifting both sets of claws to pierce him. Russel raised the sword and swung, surprised at how quickly it moved, as if its motion depended more on his thoughts than his muscles. The sword struck the outstretched arms of Feloniche and pushed him aside. Light spewed from where the sword struck and Feloniche gave a loud cry. Russel kept attentive to his opponent and noticed as the creature turned to face him again that the wounds were healed.

Feloniche desired to pounce again, but was afraid of the blade. He encircled Russel angrily, looking for a way to penetrate his defense. It annoyed him that he couldn't rush in and easily take the life of one so inferior. He rubbed his claws together and kept out of reach of the sword.

Russel's senses were heightened. The smell of the forest filled his nostrils, his eyes fixed on his taller foe, and his ears took in the awful sound of the rubbing claws. Having seen that he could inflict damage to Feloniche, his confidence grew, and he waved the sword back and forth slightly, always keeping it between himself and Feloniche.

"Don't think you can last against me!" snarled Feloniche, responding to Russel's growing confidence. "Aren't you aware how fragile you've become? You have only a few breaths left to take."

Feloniche could hold back no longer – he rushed at Russel again, and just as before, Russel swung the sword to divert the sharp claws and produced more flashes of light and another loud cry. Feloniche's rage grew as he recovered and resumed circling Russel. It became evident that he would not be able to defeat Russel without incurring more significant damage. But such damage would be temporary, and he accepted this. If he used invisibility to gain victory over a human, the resulting mockery from his colleagues would be endless.

Russel watched Feloniche come at him again and prepared to slice him with the sword once more. This time Feloniche swung only one arm at him, which Russel easily met - the clawed hand sailed past, severed from its body. Light was everywhere, blinding him. Feloniche expected this, and while Russel reacted, he kicked and knocked Russel's legs out from under him. Russel landed hard on his back and was unable to see the path of Feloniche's remaining arm until five claws sank into his chest. Feloniche watched with glee as life left Russel. He felt the twitching of muscles, the breaking of bones, the warmth of blood, and the escaping of air one last time until Russel's face became blank.

When it was done, he rose and retrieved his lost hand and held it up to his open forearm so that the two sources of light merged. In a moment he was whole again and went and removed the glimmerstone blade from Russel's clenched grasp.

"What have you done?" Feloniche was startled to hear his master's voice. "Why have you killed the human?" Kavan was angry.

"Master, I came to oversee Lachlan fulfill his pledge to you," whimpered Feloniche. "He intended to kill this man to show his loyalty to you, as I instructed, but he was defeated and Russel took up the glimmerstone blade. I couldn't let him have it." Feloniche gripped the blade of the sword and offered the handle to his master. Kavan received the weapon.

"But in doing this you've claimed the victim of the second season. And the Tildenians have no idea what has happened." Kavan paused to allow Feloniche a moment to process what he said. "If none of them know that *we* killed Russel, they have no reason to fear us; they think that we will have claimed only Evelyn and have gone. I intended to plant fear in them; I intended to claim someone different, in a different fashion, and inform them that this will continue. Now I must wait until next season to fill them with terror!"

"Forget the rule of the seasons, Master, do as you intended!"

Kavan glared at Feloniche. "Perhaps I should send you to do it! Would you like to fight against Iman himself? Or cause him to send the Riders?"

"No." Feloniche quickly replied. "I'm sorry master, I only did what I thought was necessary."

"You're a fool!" Kavan stepped toward his failed servant and lifted the blade. Feloniche stood still, awaiting his punishment. The sword unmercifully cut through Feloniche's waist, separating upper and lower body.

The forest filled with light and cries of pain as Feloniche lay disassembled on its floor. With his arms, he dragged his upper body and aligned it with the rest of himself. After he was reassembled, he stood silently before Kavan with his head hung.

"I don't want to see you again until you've done something to redeem yourself," warned Kavan.

Feloniche bowed low, then ran off into the forest.

*　　*　　*　　*　　*　　*　　*　　*　　*　　*　　*

Conroy and Bethany stood in their elevated post among the treetops and glanced north across the beautiful blue sea. The cool wind of a cloudless sky breathed gently into their faces. Their senses delighted in the day, and inwardly they rejoiced that life sometimes dealt such pleasantries similar to what they had known on the island. Conroy lifted the spotting scope and viewed the Marland coast. He saw a few people at the docks, as expected, and things there appeared calm.

He lowered the scope and observed the large reel around which wound the thick, metal cable. He touched the locking mechanism that prevented the reel from spinning freely with the weight and tension of the cable, and grabbed the handle, imagining how swiftly he could act to ring the distant iron bell if circumstances demanded. He looked to the other treetop post to see Amara waving at him, smiling. She disappeared below the camouflaged side for a moment, then reappeared with Keelan, who offered an additional wave and smile. When the fit of greetings passed, he returned his focus to his own station and partner.

Conroy enjoyed being with Bethany; not only did the partnership provide him with plentiful opportunities to discuss Allison, but she was continually cheerful, and this attitude helped Conroy as he struggled to get on with his life after the untimely passing of his father and the absence of his brother. He glanced to see what Bethany was doing, and silently confessed that her beauty easily matched Allison's. Her curled, yellow locks dangled against her smooth, tanned cheek and almost into her eye. She had arranged the various things that had been assigned them on the floor and seemed to be searching for something that wasn't there.

"I forgot the journal," she declared, mildly frustrated. "Linus wanted us to keep a record of everything we see. I'll run back and get it." Without delay, she threw up the hinged floor hatch and exited the post, leaving it open for Conroy to close, and descended quickly, using the rungs that had been installed on the south side of the tree. She took care not to touch the wet spots of sticky pitch as she climbed down - there was no way to get it off but to wait for hours until it seemingly disappeared on its own. She leapt from the rungs when she reached a height at which she was comfortable to do so, and began to jog toward Bentleigh, but stopped suddenly when a man emerged from the woods onto the path in front of her.

When Lachlan had regained consciousness, he quickly recovered his glimmerstone blade, which, to his delight, he found stuck in the ground only a few yards away. He prepared to seek out Russel to continue the fight, but then saw Russel's limp body near the fallen tree. Though he couldn't explain how, he was certain that he had killed Russel, or more precisely that his sword had acted on his intent and killed Russel. However it had happened didn't matter; he proceeded to the northern shore confident that his duty had been fulfilled. He was startled to see Bethany, who seemed to come from nowhere, running toward him.

She waited for Lachlan to speak, and strained herself to detect his attitude toward her.

Lachlan said nothing and watched to see how Bethany would react at seeing him; would she still consider him a friend? He offered her half a smile to lighten the moment while taking in her appearance – she had such fine shape and color.

Bethany felt Lachlan's stare and tensed. She did not let herself look back to the tree post to see whether or not Conroy was aware of her situation, for she would give away his location and put him in danger. Instead, she looked for a way to get past Lachlan.

High above, Conroy had begun to close the hatch when he saw Bethany stop short. Curious to know why, he peered through the opening and saw Lachlan blocking her way. He could tell that she was afraid, and he knew that he should release the reel and ring the bell, ... but he did not.

Bethany made a dash for an opening to her right. Lachlan, in spite of his size, moved unexpectedly quick and was upon her in an instant. She screamed for help and struggled to get free of Lachlan's grasp.

Finally, Bethany's screaming jolted him. Conroy went to the reel and placed his hand on the locking mechanism. He was about to release it when several thoughts rushed into his mind: *'What if there's something wrong with the cable and the bell doesn't ring? What if I make too much noise and Lachlan hears me? No one would be able to get here before he reached me! Maybe Keelan and*

Amara will hear Bethany and give warning!' Conroy removed his hand from the reel and shrank into the corner.

Bethany's screams grew fainter as Lachlan dragged her toward the sea. When he reached his vessel, which he had hidden haphazardly beneath a pile of sticks and leaves, he found some rope to bind her hands and feet, and a cloth which he wrapped around her mouth to quiet her.

When Conroy could no longer hear Bethany's screams, he climbed down the tree as fast as he could. He was careless and nearly fell twice, and by the time he reached the ground his arms and legs were badly scratched and covered in pitch. He sprinted up the path to Bentleigh as blood began to leak through his abrasions.

Warrick and Linus were the first people Conroy saw. "Help!" he cried to the two men, "Bethany needs help!" As he spoke, the bell tolled – Amara and Keelan had seen Lachlan departing.

"What happened? Where is she?" asked Warrick.

Conroy explained what happened, and as he did he realized with every word how selfishly and cowardly he had been. He tried to emphasize the danger that he was in, that if he had issued the signal, it surely would have cost him his life. But he now saw how unlikely it was that he would have been harmed. Linus and Warrick understood the truth of the matter quickly. Warrick raced off toward the sea, even though he knew he would be too late to help Bethany. Linus was upset at himself for assigning Conroy the responsibility of a being a watcher; he had thought it an important task that should be assigned to one not so distressed. But at the heeding of Wendel, who said it would be good for Conroy, that it would ease the loss of his father, he had agreed to pair Conroy with Bethany.

Just when Conroy felt as full of shame and regret and guilt as he thought possible, Allison came running up. She had heard the news and came straight at him. All of her feelings toward him seemed to have dissolved in the heat of the crisis, and she spoke roughly to him; "Why didn't you help my sister?" she screamed, inches from Conroy's gloomy face. She wasn't about to let him answer; "Now she's gone! All you had to do was ring the bell! Why? Why didn't you?" Now she stopped, really wanting to know why Conroy hadn't done what he was supposed to.

"I was afraid." It was the best reply he could offer, and it was the truth.

"If you weren't such a coward, my sister would still be here!"
Allison was sobbing now, but managed to lunge at Conroy and push
him backward. He couldn't keep his feet under him and fell. Megan
caught up to them, wrapped her arm around Allison and escorted her
away. Linus extended his hand to help Conroy to his feet, but
Conroy didn't accept his assistance. His face was flushed red, and
tears filled his eyes. He didn't speak to anyone as he headed home.

*   *   *   *   *   *   *   *   *   *   *

The Tildenians had gone to great lengths to ready themselves
to defend their new homeland, but crossing the sea to confront the
Marlanders remained something for which they were not prepared.
And, for the same reasons that no one went to Marland on behalf of
Ansen Verrill, no one would be sent there on behalf of Bethany
Krunser.

Bethany's father was determined to set off to rescue his
daughter. His wife, however, persuaded him that he had no chance
of success, and that if he left he would only cause her more grief.
Besides, she reasoned, Lachlan's intentions were unknown.

*   *   *   *   *   *   *   *   *   *   *

Like his island home, Lachlan's cabin was removed from the
village, as he preferred to spend his evenings in quiet seclusion,
rather than be disturbed by the noise of Seton. It was here that
Bethany found herself, brought across the sea by boat, and carried
on the large shoulders of her captor. Their arrival had been after
dark to a shore away from the main docks. They reached the cabin
without meeting anyone else, and her bindings and gag remained in
place until she was safely locked within a back room. There were no
windows in the room, but a skylight in the vaulted ceiling allowed the
light of a new morning inside.

Bethany was surprised by Lachlan's demeanor; he carried her
to a chair and afterward removed the ropes from her hands and feet,
and gently took off the cloth that covered her mouth. He offered her
all that she desired to eat and drink and spoke calmly to her. She
had to keep glancing at the solid door behind her host, barred shut

and locked, and the key attached to a chain around Lachlan's neck to remind herself that she was being held captive.

"This'll do," said Lachlan. "Tell me anything you lack and I'll get it for you if it can be gotten."

"What do you want from me, Lachlan?" asked Bethany plainly. "Why'd you bring me here?"

"I've always like you," admitted Lachlan. "And when I saw you,… This wasn't planned."

"If this wasn't your plan, what were you doing on Tilden?"

"It was necessary for me to go there," replied Lachlan, not wanting to reveal his true purpose. "I hope the manner in which I brought you here won't hinder our relationship. I hope you know I mean you no harm."

"Then why is the door locked while the key hangs from your neck?"

"Because I want you," replied Lachlan simply, as if she was a gem he had found. "A new order has been established here. I'm like a king, and I get what I want."

"I don't know what's been going on over here, but I doubt the other Marlanders will allow you to keep me a prisoner in your home."

"Perhaps," agreed Lachlan, "that's why they won't learn of it." He stood up quickly and turned to leave. "I have to go now, but I'll be back soon."

Lachlan removed the chain from his neck, opened the door, then closed it behind him. Bethany heard the sound of the iron key turn and engage the lock. She banged on the wall and screamed, but no one heard her cries.

chapter twelve: ·wintry wanderings·

In spite of the sullen burden Justin bore, he found a bit of satisfaction in how quickly he had adjusted to the new ways of the world. His first success had been quenching his hunger; having become efficient at plucking fish out of the numerous streams he happened upon, and stumbling into several berry patches and fruit trees each day, he discovered he could eat pretty much any time he wanted. Dry kindling was easy enough to find, which lit easily and quickly shrunk to coals on which he could cook his catch. He also learned to snare small woodland animals and prepare them in the same fashion as the deer that he had come across that had been slain, butchered, and placed on spits over the flame. The garments he had found beside the roasting deer had kept him warm through the coldest nights he had endured so far.

Journeying ever northward, his only companion a walking stick he found near where he buried Evelyn, the landscape of the country became more severe the further he went. Although this slowed his progress, he was glad it was so, believing that others would not pursue the same path to search for him. He hoped he'd never have to see any of the islanders again, but every day he struggled for words that might form an explanation that they would find acceptable should his hopes be dashed. None ever came which seemed fitting, at least in his opinion. Sure, he missed them, but being apart from them was best, he thought, even if it meant being alone.

When he had walked for almost four months, he put a stop to his advance, settling in a place reminiscent of the sloped side of Mount Manor; what better place to live than one like where he spent his last day on the island with Evelyn. As there, a clear stream flowed down the incline, bubbling and churning to offer a continuously soothing sound. By fastening a sharp rock to the end of his staff, which was surprisingly strong, yet light, he managed to hew some timbers and construct a modest shelter. Within his new home he had what was essential; a stone fire pit with a chimney, hollowed out pieces of wood for storing water, and a bed of evergreen branches covered with a thick layer of animal skins.

To his chagrin, the very day after he finished building his cabin, he went for a leisurely jaunt, cresting a nearby ridge, to discover that a family lived in a clearing on the other side!

When he saw them, he realized how lonely he was. Two children came running out the front door of the solitary house, laughing loudly. His ears tingled from sounds not heard in a long while, and he smiled for the first time since leaving the island. He crouched behind a boulder to hide and watch. The children seemed familiar, and when their mother leaned outside to call to them, he knew them immediately: Emily was about five years older than he, and she married a large, stocky man named MaGowan. Even as he recalled their names, they stepped outside to collect the youngsters to clean them off for the evening meal.

Justin was dumbfounded as to how MaGowan and Emily had arrived here before him, but was content to be ignorant of that matter for now, and he was surprised at the happiness that swelled inside him in learning that they were his neighbors. He moved to a new spot so that he could look into the house and watch them for awhile more. The winter's early darkness allowed him to move about more freely, without worry of being seen. After the meal was finished and the children had been put to bed, Justin retreated to his cabin, but looked forward to the next time he would visit; he saw no reason why he shouldn't return the next day.

Loneliness leapt upon him again surprisingly quick, striking him even before he reached his cabin. He ate a meager meal then fell into bed, hoping thoughts of Emily and MaGowan would fill his sleeping mind and replace the loneliness. It was not to be – as had become a frequent occurrence, he was plagued by an awful dream. The sense of dread was terrible as always, but the content of his dreams had been transformed over the last few weeks: no longer was he wandering through a barren wasteland, instead, he found himself standing back at the edge of the chasm. Suspended before him, in the space above the nothingness, were all his island friends, looks of terror twisted their faces as they floated. It seemed that time had frozen, but would begin to move forward at any moment, sending them falling into the chasm. Then came laughter, a slow, deep laugh that made Justin cringe in disgust, for what foul being would laugh at their inevitable demise? As feared, time starts to creep forward slowly. The laughter grows louder and faster as the people begin to struggle in vain to reach the ground where Justin stands. They keep falling, but only a few feet, until stopped by an unseen force. Some get up and try again, unsuccessfully, to advance to Justin; some remain on all fours, fearful that any attempt to rise will result in plummeting further. The laughter grows to an unbearable volume...

Justin woke covered in sweat, he was hot and his heart was pounding. He stepped outside into the cold air, hoping that breathing it in would chase away the burning images echoing in his mind. He emerged to find a thick layer of snow covering everything, and that the silence of the snowfall reigned over the forest. Large flakes fell on his head; he looked up and they filled his eyes. He stood outside his door for several minutes, enjoying the beauty of the scene before him and the utter calm, watching the snow slowly and silently piling up. The air was cold in his lungs, even more so blowing against his wet body; the burning in his mind was still hot, but fading slowly. With a gentle kick, he brushed off the rock that had become his front step to see how quickly snow would cover it again. The cascading crystals soothed his spirit until he realized dawn was quickly coming, and he went back inside.

He poked at the last logs burning on the fire to expose the bed of coals, then doused it with water. It was likely that Emily and MaGowan would awaken soon and venture outside. He feared that the smoke plume would be visible to them, and decided he'd only have a fire while the darkness of night hid the smoke, and he was grateful the days were short, for without a fire he would be cold and hungry.

*   *   *   *   *   *   *   *   *   *   *

"Do you know where we are?" asked Kira, more out of a desire for conversation than of concern.

"Yes," snapped Elson, insulted. He was pretty sure that he'd passed through the area before, but now it was covered in snow and he failed to spot anything he remembered from his previous wanderings with Warrick. The intended destination, a low valley beside a small lake, Elson knew would be found by passing between two distant parallel mountain ranges, then turning east. In spite of not recognizing anything, the mountains on both sides convinced him that they were heading in the right direction. Besides, he was the leader, the one who had accompanied Kira to be her guide, her protector and provider. This was why he agreed to come, but not the only reason, he was beginning to admit to himself. Even if he didn't know where they were, there would have been no reason to confess such a thing; it was his duty to help her survive, after all, he had stated that he was qualified to do so.

"My feet are cold," said Kira, shivering.

Feeling that he could use some time to contemplate his route, Elson put down his pack and set out to find some wood. "It's a good time to stop. I'll get a fire going."

Elson and Kira were better prepared to face the harsh climate than Justin had been due to the fact that they carried the supplies that Elson and Warrick had collected from Tilden before setting out in search of their lost friend. Kira wore garments that had been intended for Warrick, folded over and tied up in an attempt to make them more fitting to her feminine form, and his boots, which she had stuffed with cloth to make them snug against her smaller feet. She wiped snow off of a rock and sat down while Elson gathered firewood. Heat from her backside began to escape rapidly into the frozen rock, giving her a quick chill. But her toes demanded attention, and she remained seated and pulled her left foot out of her boot and cupped her hands around it, all the while hoping it wouldn't be long before the fire was burning.

Kira's attitude was one of constrained joy. She was far away from Seton, free from the nasty chores that had been forced upon her, and most importantly, free from Idris. No more would she have to receive him in the night. All of these things gave her a sense of relief, but she longed to pour her affections on Elson. So far, however, he had resisted sharing the idea of them being together. She looked at him; he was crouching on the ground, working to grow a few flickering flames so that they would ignite the pile of kindling. He did this for her sake alone, she knew; he wasn't cold, only she was in need of warmth. She loved Elson. She wanted to tell him, but was afraid her proclamation would not be received with the joy she thought it deserved. No, she would wait to share this with him only when she was sure he would respond likewise. For now, she was content to just be with him. Wherever they were going, she really didn't care.

Flames rose to engulf the wood, and Elson placed their gear so that Kira could sit elevated off the cold ground. Kira put her boot on loosely, shuffled over to sit down on one of the packs that Elson had prepared for her, and lifted her foot to the fire. Elson sat beside her and removed her boot, placed it beside the fire, and held her bare foot in the radiating heat and rubbed it gently with his warm hands.

Kira enjoyed his touch and was glad that she had another cold foot that he could warm. She wondered whether her mother felt this way toward her father, and whether Elson's mother felt this way toward his. As soon as the image of Ansen came she banished it. Her foot was warm now, and she pulled it away from Elson, who quickly put her boot, now also warm, back on. Kira lifted her other foot and gave it to him.

"You know, you never told me what you and Warrick saw; what was he supposed to tell your father?" Her curiosity compelled her to ask, not realizing until her words were audible that the question would recall the topic of Ansen Verrill. She scolded herself for her carelessness, and inwardly cringed at her deception.

Elson hadn't meant to keep it from her, he had simply been consumed with his responsibilities. He saw that it was a good time to recite his tale, and began to tell her what had happened; "Warrick and I were so determined to find Justin that we went for days without sleeping. One morning, we were so exhausted we had no choice but to stop and rest. We found a soft, grassy spot on the edge of a field beside a large beech tree. I don't think it took more than five minutes before we were asleep. While we slept, we each had the same powerful dream, which we knew was not of our own minds. We woke at the same time to find ourselves sitting with our backs against the smooth bark of the large beech. At first we thought the forest was on fire, for all we could see were flames. Then we realized that what we were seeing were the extended arms of some creature, its hands gripped our foreheads. We felt hot, but it wasn't the same sensation as feeling heat from a fire, not like this," he moved Kira's foot closer to the fire just long enough so that it began to make her uncomfortable. Her foot was quite warm now, but she wanted him to keep holding it and didn't pull away. "Our bodies were cool, but inside, in our minds and hearts, we felt a burning, and we were afraid. Finally, it released us and stepped back, allowing us a clear view of it; it was a man ablaze."

Kira continued to listen intently, her eyes wide, and her foot still in Elson's caressing hands.

"Then we heard it speak. With a quiet, but penetrating, voice, like crackling embers on wind, it said; 'Iman knows your troubles.

Trust in his purpose, he'll rescue all who accept his help. He's able to restore all things lost'." Elson finally released Kira's foot, feeling that it was warm, and slid on her boot. "Then it disappeared with a loud hiss, like the sound of dry pine needles burning up. We weren't sure if it had been destroyed, or whether this was normal for the creature."

Elson stood and kicked snow on the fire in preparation to resume the journey, and then helped Kira stand. "I wish he stayed to speak with us further, then I might have learned who Iman is. I thought my father might know, that's why I urged Warrick to return to Tilden and speak with him."

"He did know!" exclaimed Kira, again speaking before realizing where her response would lead the conversation.

"What?" said Elson. He forgot about gathering up the gear and stood, empty handed, facing Kira, waiting for further explanation.

She positioned her words quickly to cleverly reveal only a portion of the truth; "Iman is the name of the Island Caretaker! King Iman is his title, I heard your father speak of him once in Seton."

"King Iman is the Caretaker." Elson said it aloud as if doing so would help him solve some kind of riddle. "So the Caretaker will offer us aid...yes, that fits!" It was obvious to Kira that he was thinking hard to connect the words of the man of fire with the Island Caretaker. Then, to her dismay, she heard; "Why was my father in Marland? Didn't he stay in Tilden with my mother and Conroy? He didn't come here to join with Idris in search of Marland's secrets, did he?" Elson winced at the possibility.

"No! No, he didn't come here to help Idris, he was just passing through," Kira quickly replied, "before everything in Seton had gone too rotten. He *did* stay in Tilden and built a new home there, but afterward he came here to look for you." She felt she was losing her grasp on the conversation, and she was desperate to change its course and make the questions about Ansen stop.

"Where is he now?" Elson seemed relentless.

Kira had not been able to think swiftly enough to keep up with the questions; she felt uncomfortably exposed as she stood with nothing between her and Elson. She became tense, curling her fingers and toes into tight balls, though this went unnoticed by Elson due to her oversized mittens and boots. "The morning after he arrived, he journeyed north into the Marland woods." She was pleased that everything she said was true, yet her secret was still hidden.

"If you knew that my father was here, why didn't you protest when I told Warrick to return to Tilden to find him there?"

Kira's heart was heavy with truth, and she suddenly felt hot, but resolved not to reveal her full knowledge. She remained tense, but pushed back feelings that were about to conceive tears. "It had been a long time since I'd last seen your father, he may well have returned to Tilden by then," she lied.

"I hope so," said Elson, "Warrick and the others will need him, especially Conroy and my mother. But, if he *is* still here, I hope he's warm and well - perhaps our paths will cross."

Kira finally sensed an opportune moment had arrived to pass to a new subject; "Do you remember the dream?" She felt the rush of heat fade and began to relax.

"Vividly," answered Elson. "A tall tower of white stone loomed high over the sea. It had three equal sides, and was broader and taller than the familiar tower of the Island Council, but it was of similar construction. At first I gazed upon it from afar, then suddenly I was outside its very top level, standing on a balcony, looking down at masses of people. They were smiling and cheering, and in my heart I knew they were full love and respect for me. I waved to them and then stepped inside the tower, where I joined Justin and Warrick; the three of us were the only ones there. Something was in the center of the round room, an enormous diamond, as large as a man, floating above our heads. We approached it slowly and gazed at it from below. In one of its many sides I saw my reflection, but the image only partially resembled me: it was an image of a hideously disfigured version of myself, but the image faded as the diamond filled with smoke. Then the smoke transformed to fire, and the flames grew brighter until it glowed with such intensity that we were blinded. Then I awoke in the creature's grasp."

"Do you think it means something?"

"I think it means that the Caretaker, or King Iman rather, is going to help us." Hope filled his heart for the first time, now that he was finally able to associate the creature's words with someone he knew and trusted. "I think it means that Justin is all right and that he and Warrick and I will be together again, and that we'll all be saved from the monsters that took Evelyn!" he exclaimed. "I didn't allow myself to believe in the vision because I didn't know who Iman was, but now I know and it all makes sense. I believe that King Iman will help us!" he exclaimed again.

Kira's heart rejoiced, believing as Elson that King Iman would help them, but more so at seeing Elson smile. He knelt down to pick up his heavy pack, which held most of their gear. Kira couldn't restrain her emotions - she lunged forward and tackled Elson before he could rise, both of her feet slipping out of her oversized boots. The pack dropped and flopped open, while Elson fell sideways in the snow and Kira landed softly on top of him. Elson rolled onto his back and looked up to see the expanse of blue sky disappearing from his view as Kira lowered her face to his. Her hair tickled his cheeks and forehead, and her large eyes pierced his for a moment, then closed as she pressed her lips gently to his. She felt the cold air and snow on her exposed feet, but didn't care; she could ask Elson to warm them again.

"We could return to Tilden," suggested Elson when his lips were free to speak. "Maybe King Iman has already made things good again."

"But what if he hasn't? Besides, they would never accept our being together," replied Kira. "I'm not ready to return."

"Things might change with time. One day they may welcome us back, both of us, together."

"It's too much to hope for."

*   *   *   *   *   *   *   *   *   *   *

As darkness fell upon Bentleigh, the twelve statues of living stone, the Gemstones, stood guard around its perimeter as always. Onyx, the leader of the twelve, comprised of solid black rock, smooth and shiny, stood at the northern point of their circle, facing away from the town, toward the forest and beyond that the South Sea. Something startled him and he turned his head sharply to the left.

"What is it, Jasper?" he questioned his companion silently, only with thought.

"Someone approaches from the west," came Jasper's telepathic response.

"Amethyst, Sardius, I'm going to join Jasper; shift round to fill the void." When he perceived that the two Gemstones nearest him on either side acknowledged the command, Onyx strode across the field toward the westernmost side of the circumference. With sight unhindered by darkness, he saw Jasper's red and white striped form facing the forest in a pose that suggested he was ready to fight: his knees were bent slightly, and his stony hands were balled up into dense fists.

"Relax, Jasper, it's me." Jasper recognized the familiar, deep voice at once, stood up straight and let his fingers unravel. From within the forest, soaring about twenty feet above the ground, came Sandor, his sword sheathed and his shield slung across his back. He landed beside Jasper as Onyx arrived. "It's good to see you again."

"We're honored by your presence," said Onyx, speaking out loud, his voice like wind through a cave. He nodded to greet the captain. "What brings you here?"

"I've come to warn you that Kavan may come soon, I'm sure he's anxious to act, now that a new season has come."

"It's fortunate that the people aren't aware of the truth of Russel's death" said Jasper, his voice similar to, but distinguishable from Onyx's.

"Yes," agreed Sandor, "their ignorance has allowed them to live without fear, but I expect Kavan will act soon to change that. Tell me, who was it that found Russel's body?"

"Warrick Spencer," answered Onyx. "When he heard of Bethany's capture he ran straightaway to the coast, only to discover that Lachlan's boat was too far out to pursue. As he returned to Bentleigh, he found Russel lying beside the large tree that had been freshly felled. It looked to him as if Russel had been trying to cut down the tree for firewood, but that something had gone wrong and the tree fell on him."

"He was fond of Russel," added Jasper, "I watched him weep beside his body for a long time, for I had been sent to collect Russel's spirit and wait for his escort to Casilda to arrive."

Sandor seemed stricken by a fit of sorrow as he gave a long sigh and dropped his head. "It's unfortunate that things have become as they are." He sighed again.

"What of the girl?" asked Jasper, "What's become of Bethany?"

"Carollan has been sent to watch over her. Lachlan cares for her, and he likely won't hurt her. Nevertheless, I'm on my way to Marland to see Carollan."

"I would prefer you stay," said Onyx, a hint of worry detectable in his breezy voice.

"I have full confidence in you and the other Gemstones," said Sandor encouragingly. "Remember how you fought Kavan before?"

"But he defeated me!" Onyx's voice grew quicker and his words whistled. "He threw me down and stole from me!"

"But it was your purpose that succeeded, not his. Your efforts thwarted his assault and caused him and his horde to flee. Has he ever dared to come against you in the same manner?"

"No," replied Onyx, conceding the point to Sandor.

Sandor lifted up from the ground so he could place a hand on Onyx's shoulder and spoke gently to his friend; "You must raise your confidence to match your strength, only then will you be as great as you can be. King Iman himself assigned you to guard the island, and now Tilden. He wouldn't ask you to do anything that you cannot do."

"Very well, I trust his wisdom. We'll face whatever enemy may come," said Onyx. Jasper nodded in agreement.

"If Kavan is accompanied by his horde, and likely he will be, only he should be allowed to go to Bentleigh," cautioned Sandor. "Letting too many of them pass may result in disaster. I'll return immediately after I meet with Carollan. Don't worry, just know that you're capable of fulfilling this purpose." With that, Sandor soared quickly away to the north, passing over the twenty-mile span of sea in only a few seconds.

Onyx turned to Jasper and spoke audibly to him, and silently to the other ten Gemstones; "Let's hope Sandor returns in time."

*   *   *   *   *   *   *   *   *   *   *

The clouds, having been emptied throughout the night of the snow they carried, had departed by morning. After returning to bed, Justin enjoyed a calm and deep sleep for the remainder of the night, but now rays of the sun invaded his cabin to lay upon his closed eyelids, waking him. He rose from his warm bed and crossed the cold space to open his door; he had to lean firmly into it to push back the snow. He gazed at the white landscape, now several times brighter than it had been when he'd seen it in the night, and with the sun shining unobstructed, was so bright that it hurt his eyes, and he squinted to shield them from the brilliance. The sun felt warm on his face and he was sure that his neighbors would be outside on such a glorious day. Anxious to visit them, he went back inside, packed a few things, and set out toward Emily and MaGowan's cabin.

It was difficult walking in the snow, which was at least a foot deep, even deeper in areas where it had been blown into drifts, but the slow going didn't hamper Justin's pleasant mood; he wasn't in a hurry, besides, he certainly had nothing more important to do. As he ascended the hill, he stopped for a second to rest and glanced back toward his cabin; all his hopes to visit his neighbors that day were dashed. The snow, the very thing that had been the cause of his good mood, was also the reason that he could not visit his neighbors, at least not if he wanted to keep his presence unknown to them - his footprints would give him away.

Having prepared for a day out, however, he decided not to return home. He altered his course, choosing a direction that would take him away from where MaGowan and Emily might be likely to venture, and began making tracks toward a place that he had not yet explored.

After wandering through the snow-filled forest for about an hour, Justin came to a small river in which were scattered randomly mounds of snow piled upon rocks, whose tops peeked just above the flowing water. Ice crystals clinging to the sides of the riverbanks and rocks enhanced this spectacle of beauty. He stood in silence and gazed at the sight.

Then, to add to his delight, a large deer, a doe, approached the river from the opposite side. Very slowly, it took delicate, silent steps toward the water, cocked its ears a few times in different positions to scan the area for sounds of anything potentially dangerous, then lowered its head to drink once it determined that it was safe to do so.

But the deer was wrong: another creature *had* been nearby, waiting for an opportune moment to attack. Justin, startled, nearly fell backward when a large lion leapt from nowhere to spring on the unsuspecting deer. The doe had only enough time to lift its head, presenting an easy target for the bounding predator, which sank its teeth and claws into the exposed neck. Both animals tumbled to the ground in a balled mass of flailing legs and tails and hair, appearing as a single creature. The doe struggled for only a moment, expending what strength it had against the power of the big cat, which held it securely with its sharp claws and unyielding jaws.

Justin watched the snow around the pair become red. It was the first time that he'd seen the effect of the world's new nature among animals. He observed that the lion didn't seem angry, it didn't appear to hate the deer; it was only that it needed to eat it to survive. Justin felt sick as he perceived that his actions were the reason for the new order of things.

He felt faint as blood rushed from his head; he bent over, placing his hands on his knees and lowering his head to recover from the lightheadedness. As he did, he glimpsed a dark form shifting among some small trees nearby. While still hunched over, he turned his head to further examine the movement. His eyes focused on a lion, a different one, this time on the same side of the river. Unlike the other, this one had a majestic mane of long, brown hair. It began to walk slowly toward Justin on its large padded feet, no longer attempting to approach in secrecy, its huge muscles flexing beneath its furry coat, displaying awesome power. Justin jerked upright, his heart pumping rapidly as the image of the attack on the deer played fresh in his mind. He gripped his staff and held it out, wondering whether or not he could use it to successfully fend off the beast.

The lion saw two figures. The one further away was weak and scared; the lion's desire was to pounce on this one, which would be a good-sized meal, easy to catch. But it didn't advance: the second figure stood directly between it and Justin. He was small, but there was no fear in him; he calmly held out his hand in gesture for the cat to stay away. He carried a blade, but it was sheathed and he did not reach for it.

Justin turned to keep his staff pointed at the lion, which continued to stride while eyeing him, but kept a safe distance from the small one, who decided to intensify his warning – he glared into the eyes of the lion and it surrendered its desire to attack. It trotted away, moving along the riverbank in search of a place to cross so it could go and participate in the feeding on the other side.

"Have you had to do that often, Carollan?"

"No, that was the first time."

"It won't be the last," said Sandor, "for Scynn takes pleasure in destroying in an instant that which took ages to construct; particularly enjoying the death of an islander. And among the animals, it demands that creatures must kill to eat, or starve; either way Scynn collects its earnings."

Justin's nerves calmed after the lion departed. He decided he had enough adventures for one day and retraced his footprints back to his cabin.

Carollan and Sandor remained beside the river.

"I passed through Seton on my way here," said Sandor. "I observed Lachlan's treatment of Bethany; he hopes that she'll return his feelings."

"As demented as he's become, he'll not harm her," replied Carollan. "I'm glad you've come - I have some news concerning the twins, disturbing news, I'm afraid."

"Oh?" Sandor replied, raising his eyebrows.

"They've joined Kavan."

"That's not true! Who told you this?" Sandor quickly dismissed the claim.

"Justin Nickols," answered Carollan. "I looked into his mind and confirmed it was true."

"Could Kavan have finally persuaded them to join him?" gasped Sandor, feeling that he had underestimated the power of Kavan's manipulation, or overestimated the twins' loyalty to the king.

"I've struggled with this knowledge for weeks and searched for another explanation, but..."

"Who knows?"

"Only you and I."

"If they believe their treason remains secret, perhaps we can better thwart them from completing whatever dastardly role Kavan has for them to play."

*   *   *   *   *   *   *   *   *   *   *

"Let us pass without a fight, for we have business in Bentleigh tonight!" Onyx tensed at the ridiculous rhyme. Kavan arrived from the north and faced the leader of the Gemstones, a number of his unholy horde following. "It's our right, our duty, to go into this town you guard so intently and claim the life of one of these foul people. Wages are due!"

Onyx complied with a slow, sad nod as he made himself as tall as he could. "You only may pass." He knew Kavan's demeanor was volatile, and though he had approached with warning and seemed calm, Onyx knew too well how quickly his attitude could change, and prepared for blows.

Elzib was the first to protest, bellowing loudly and snorting. Unwilling to be denied, the rest of Kavan's companions followed Elzib's lead; they moved as one toward the black statue of living stone. Three other Gemstones - Jasper, Emerald, and Topaz, ran from their stations to support Onyx. The horde paused and reconsidered engaging the stalwart guardians.

"I'll honor your request ... tonight," consented Kavan, his demeanor still calm. "But next time, be ready to fight if you want my friends to stay behind."

Kavan stepped past the black guardian and noticed the moonlight reflecting from Onyx's glossy surface. "I see that you still glimmer after all these years, though your stature is still not what it used to be, is it?" Kavan smirked, turned his back on Onyx and the other Gemstones, and began pacing purposefully toward Bentleigh.

Onyx didn't reply. Instead, he kept focused on the villains before him, knowing that the other eight Gemstones would supervise Kavan. He was satisfied that it seemed the encounter would not come to blows, but still wished Sandor was there.

*   *   *   *   *   *   *   *   *   *   *

Kira was as happy as she could have imagined herself to ever be again. Elson had finally given in to the idea that they could be together, and gradually began to return her affections. Though he desired to descend gently into love, rather than fall into it as Kira wished to do, she accepted his pace and didn't attempt to accelerate the blossoming of their emotions.

Elson courted Kira slowly with gifts and thoughtful gestures, such as preparing the fire and cooking meals; always serving her first when the meals were ready; asking to make sure she was warm, offering her his coat if she was not. He continually looked for wildflowers to present to her, but the winter landscape was barren of such things; he was anxious for spring to come.

Like Justin, Elson had found a suitable spot and built a home. Kira delighted in watching him work, talking to him constantly as he hacked and hewed and stacked and secured. She praised him for the clever way that he built, using techniques taught by his father. He often mentioned his father to Kira, sending a sting into her heart, but she had become skilled at quenching these pangs, making them brief, and continued to suppress all thoughts of revealing to Elson what had happened to his father.

chapter thirteen: ·the anointing of the overlords·

"I can't bear this any longer!" A weary man sat among a few of his friends, expressing his frustration. He was pale-skinned and had red hair covering a head that was slightly small for his body. His clothes hung loosely from his bony shoulders and thinning arms and waist. "I won't sit here for another day, waiting for them to find things that aren't to be found while we all starve. I've no confidence left in those three!" He slammed his fist down hard on the wooden table. The other three winced at the blow, but not as much as they would have had they not been malnourished. Still, they had a lot of respect for Prevor, and each one knew that, had he had his strength, his blow would have sundered the table to pieces.

The same frustration was found throughout Seton, where hunger plagued every home. It had been several weeks since the Marlanders slaughtered the last of their animals, and all of their other provisions had been depleted before that. Hunting and fishing parties usually returned to the village with some catch, but not enough to feed the large number of people in desperate need of food.

"What're you gonna do, Prevor?" asked one of his companions, young and stretched extremely thin, whose straight brown hair hung nearly to his waist.

"Whatever it takes, Treytoni," replied Prevor plainly.

"Are you suggesting that you'll challenge the authority of Idris?" questioned another, bald, but with a thick, unkempt beard.

"If that's what it takes, Dug, then yes!"

"But to go against the three that Kavan selected to..."

Prevor interrupted Dug; "We've no proof that Kavan spoke with them. We don't know if they even saw Kavan and this other creature, Scynn. They could've made up the whole business to keep power over us."

"But Idris – he's a sharp one," warned Treytoni.

"Smarts come in many types," countered Prevor. "Idris may be clever in many ways, but he has yet to demonstrate he's worthy to be our leader. We've trusted him long enough - if we don't challenge him soon, we won't survive the winter!"

"That's right! He's had his chance!" Fineggle, the fourth member of the group, the oldest among them, with thick, gray hair and eyes to match, spoke for the first time. "For weeks, and months, and half a year we've done everything he's commanded, searching for secrets, but none have been found. Had we spent our efforts hunting and gathering, we'd have enough provisions to last, but time was wasted and now our food is gone. Idris, Valena, Lachlan; none of their endeavors has done us any good!"

Fineggle and Prevor spoke further with Treytoni and Dug, gradually persuading them that what they were proposing was best for everyone, and that most Marlanders, if they knew about an uprising, would join them. Dug and Treytoni finally embraced the roles that they were needed to fill: they would spread the word around Seton to those whose involvement would be critical for success. Stronger leaders, ones capable of meeting the needs of the people, were going to take over, leaders not obsessed with searching for nonexistent secrets. This was the message that they'd carry. Complaining turned to planning and, fueled by ideas rather than food, the four men grew excited for the next day to come, a day they would take hold of and bring change to Marland.

*   *   *   *   *   *   *   *   *   *   *

Conroy had nothing to do. He had spent nearly every hour of daylight down by the sea working on the statue, enduring the cold and sometimes snowy days of winter, which seemed to be finally growing milder. From the giant slab of white rock, he had completed the work his father began, and now instead of a misshapen stone, a beautiful, intricately carved image of King Iman decorated the Tilden shore. Conroy wished that he hadn't finished so soon; he had no other tasks to occupy his time, and it would have been more enjoyable to work on the statue now that the days were getting longer and warmer. He paced without purpose around the cabin, which now only he and his mother inhabited.

Monica Verrill noticed the moping of her son and paused from her work. "There must be something more productive for you to do than sulk around here all day."

"Keelan's on watcher duty, the statue is finished, and Allison..." Conroy stopped, not wanting to speak with his mother about Allison, and definitely not wanting to bring up the subject of his cowardice again.

It was too late, her response came right away, as if the words were rehearsed and she'd been waiting to release them; "It was a decision made in a moment of extreme pressure, a thoughtless reaction. You can't punish yourself forever. I know how awful you feel about what happened to Bethany, but it wasn't your fault. You're not the one who took her away!"

"I know," replied Conroy. He didn't offer any further response in hope that the conversation would end. He knew how much his mother cared for him, and if she was ashamed for how he had acted, she never expressed it, instead, she constantly reminded him how it wasn't his fault and how he needed to let go of the guilty feelings that oppressed him.

"If you *know* these things, why are you still suffering so?"

Conroy had never been offered this challenge before, and the fact that it was issued to him now by his own mother made him feel even more of a failure. "I don't know," he admitted dully.

Monica suddenly felt that she was being harsh toward her son. She hadn't intended to be; she only wanted to advise him so that he might find joy in life again. But maybe this approach is needed, she thought, after all, all of her other words previously offered to him in kindness seemed to have had little effect, if any. She decided to continue speaking firmly; "I'm not implying that it'll be easy, but a change must occur within you, a change that only you can bring about. If you know in your mind that it's not your fault, then you must force your heart to accept this and healing will begin. But if you can't rid yourself of these feelings of guilt, then this will stay with you forever and consume you all of your days. Perhaps Bethany might return here safely and unharmed, but she might not - you have no control over it. You have to move past this!"

The words kept erupting from within; they hadn't been prepared, but they continued to spew from someplace within her, shooting right into Conroy's mind; "You have no power to change the actions of your past, but you have a choice on what you'll do today. The past can't ever be totally surrendered, for you'll never be able to be separated from it, but you can put it out of the way and move ahead. Make good choices today and your mistakes of yesterday will fade."

Conroy was emotionally struck down by his mother's words; he felt very small and wanted to get away. "I'm going to see Wendell." He feared to say anything more, knowing that if he attempted to his voice would fail and tears would flow. He threw on his heavy coat and boots and left.

Monica attempted to return to her work, that of mending a pile of clothes that had been delivered to her, but it was no use, she put down her needles. "Can't I at least keep Conroy?" she pleaded out loud. "Ansen is gone! Elson is gone! Conroy might as well be gone, why did this have to happen to *him*?" She cast the ripped garments to the floor and buried her head in her hands and wept. The people of Bentleigh would have to wait a little longer for reparation to their clothes.

*　*　*　*　*　*　*　*　*　*　*

"They're not going to submit to us much longer!" declared Lachlan. At his request, Valena and Idris had gathered to meet with him in Idris' cabin. "The rumors of rebellion have become more intense."

"There's no need to worry," Idris answered, remaining calm, a faint smile on his thin lips suggested he was pleased to learn of the severity of the Marlanders' malcontent. "Don't doubt now, not when our plans are coming to fruition; this is the destination to which we have steered, just as Scynn instructed."

"We won't make it to our *destination* if we're overthrown and killed! I've heard the grumbling; whispers of an uprising soon to occur, most likely lead by Prevor Marristor and Finnegle Dravenes!"

"Prevor and Finnegle," repeated Idris softly, but becoming more serious as he considered the significant clout these two men had over the older Marlanders. "Will others follow their lead?"

"Yes, I believe so."

"To what end?"

Lachlan stood directly before Idris, who remained sitting, and spoke clearly and slowly so that Idris could sense the gravity of his words; "I believe they're willing to risk their lives to remove us from power: if we refuse to surrender our authority, they'll kill us."

"Good!" Idris sprang to his feet and Lachlan had to step back to get out of the way. "The time has come!" Excitement filled him with a renewed energy. "How many weapons have been made?"

"Enough for a thousand men. They're hidden in the cave behind the falls."

"Perfect! Retrieve them and make ready to distribute them, they'll be needed soon."

"You can't hand out glimmerstone to anyone who wants it," warned Valena. "If even one of these weapons escaped our control and was used against us it could ruin us."

"What do you suggest?" asked Lachlan.

Valena rose and paced around the two men. "Those who wish to wield the precious black stone must pledge the life of a loved one in return for a lost or stolen weapon."

"Who would carry them at such a price?" asked Idris, skeptical of her proposal.

"One who carries glimmerstone is nearly invincible: who would want their husband, or father, or son to go into battle without it? Besides, the power of the black stone is appealing, and many men will want to be made strong by it."

"I see you've given this some thought," admitted Idris.

Lachlan was still worried; "But how are we going to quell the revolt?"

"I'll handle that," replied Idris. "You be concerned with getting the glimmerstone."

"Very well, I'll have Brant assist me." Lachlan departed, his step lightened by Idris' confidence, though the stares he received as he walked through Seton burned intensely as ever. He was glad that things would be changing soon, though he had no idea what Idris was going to do to satisfy the hungry and unhappy Marlanders. He kept his face down to avoid eye contact with anyone, hoping to exit the village without being delayed, anxious to get home and talk to Bethany.

Back in Idris' cabin, Valena lingered. She was pleasantly surprised when Idris turned toward her, threw his arms around her tall frame and pulled her close to him so quickly that her raven black hair swept forward into his cheeks and neck. He stared into her eyes for a moment before pressing his mouth to hers.

"Why did you wait so long to embrace me?" she said when the kiss was finished and her breath recovered. "You knew I desired to be with you all this time, ever since we first arrived."

"Some Marlanders still cling to the island traditions. No one yet knows the reason behind Kira's disappearance, and I feared that becoming intimate with you might lead to rebellion prematurely. I couldn't risk it." Idris kept holding Valena tight. "Men like Prevor and Finnegle, for example, might have exploited my pursuit of you as being of poor taste, and might have stirred up the rest of Marland in an untimely mutiny."

"You have no fear of them now?"

"No, it doesn't matter what they might try to do now. I've recently discovered something that allowed me to shake off all such fears." Idris stroked Valena's back, and looked past the side of her head to stare into an elegant mirror behind them. Feelings of satisfaction coursed through him. The graceful curves of Valena's body; the way her long hair moved as he caressed her; all of these images delighted him, but he took most pleasure from viewing his arms; his two healthy, strong arms. He realized he had even come to revere the faint rings of scars, encircling each arm just above the elbow.

*   *   *   *   *   *   *   *   *   *   *

Wendel opened the door, greeted Conroy warmly and welcomed him inside. Conroy observed that the bottom of Wendel's left hand was smeared with black, as was his white shirt on the side of his pudgy belly. Wendel's figure was proof that he wasn't suffering from lack of food; in fact, none of the Tildenians were.

"You've got something on your shirt," said Conroy immediately. He and Wendel had spent a significant amount of time together over the last few months, and their relationship had grown to the point where they spoke openly to each other. "And on your hand too."

"Ahh," moaned Wendel, looking first at his shirt and then at his left hand. "I can't write a sentence without making a mess of myself. Maybe I should learn to use my other hand."

"What're you writing about?"

"Something I've put off for a while – the night that Kavan came to Bentleigh."

"Oh." Conroy paused, then asked, "Can I read it?"

Wendel nodded and led Conroy to a desk where a large leather-bound book lay open. Conroy glanced at the open entry:

<u>Winter's First Night, year 272:</u>

Our worst nightmare is real: Kavan is not gone - he came to Bentleigh as we gathered to celebrate the end of the harvest. He acted so quickly that none of us had a chance to flee.

Standing before us with hate in his eyes, just as he had on the night of our island's disappearance, he declared...

   "I've come to collect payment that's owed!"

Without offering any further explanation, he drew a three-pronged sword from his back and cast it through Cornelius Ditlancey. Everyone watched with horror as the blade passed through Cornelius' chest without slowing, then swirled through the air to return to the hand of its owner.

In the background, Conroy heard Wendel speak, but didn't really listen, as he was trying to finish reading the entry.

"I'll return soon!" Kavan shouted, then vanished, just before Cornelius dropped to the ground.

Cornelius was a leading member of the Council, his loss was felt at once by the entire village. When morning came, his body was buried and kind words were said of his life.

"Do you know the last thing Cornelius said to me? .... Don't forget to read what you write."

Life goes on for the rest of us, though it's a life filled with the fear that any day could be the one when Kavan comes again.

Conroy continued to read, and Wendel continued to talk about Cornelius, though mostly to himself. For some reason, Conroy flipped the pages back and read an earlier entry:

<u>Last Day of the Tenth Month, year 272:</u>
The watch posts were implemented today. But, in spite of our efforts, Lachlan Amwahr managed to come here unnoticed. He captured Bethany Krunser and took her, against her will, back to Marland.

Also today, Russel Minns was found dead in the forest. Warrick Spencer found his body. It appears that Russel had gone to gather firewood, even though the winter stores were full, but was killed accidentally when the tree he was cutting fell on him. His chest was pierced in multiple locations, presumable by the limbs of the tree.

"I'm glad you stopped by, but I've got to go in few minutes. I'm meeting with Linus and Warrick to take inventory of our provisions."

Conroy looked up from the book at Wendel, who was attempting to clean his shirt, but his efforts only smeared the stain. "How come you've never asked me about the time Bethany was captured?"

"I didn't see any point to it; you've endured enough hardship from something that wasn't your fault. Besides, I figured that if you needed to talk about it that you'd bring it up…. Now that you have, would you like to?"

Conroy tucked his bottom lip in, bit on it gently, and nodded. "My mother is always telling me that what happened wasn't my fault, and you just said so yourself, but it *was* my fault. If I acted differently, Lachlan could've been stopped and Bethany never would've been taken away! I'd give anything to go back to that moment and toll the bell."

"We've no power over time. The best we can do is take advantage of the opportunities available to us, keeping our minds open to future possibilities, remembering lessons of the past, all the while accepting the fact that any day may be our last. No one can change what's been done, I wish that wasn't so, then we could all go back to the island. But it is, and all you can do is make good choices for today." Wendel watched Conroy to see how he would receive the advice.

"I'm *choosing* now to do something, Wendel, whatever I can to make things right! It's better for me to try to redeem myself and fail then to remain a coward and survive; this place where I'm at is not truly living."

"What will you do?" Wendel folded the book closed and picked it up to take it with him – he carried it with him always.

Conroy had made up his mind; "I'm going to Marland."

Wendel's eyes widened. "You cannot be serious! There's a difference between trying to make amends for past mistakes and casting yourself into a desperate situation that will likely cost you your life."

"I'm already destroyed! Didn't you hear what I just said? Don't you understand?"

"I can't stop you; you have the freedom to do what you want, and that's a significant power, but there's something you should know." Wendel drew closer to Conroy and said, "When Warrick last returned from Marland, he told the Council that he'd met a strange creature, made of living fire, which he believed to be an ally to King Iman. This has been kept a secret among only the Council members that were present at the time. I'm only telling you now so that if you come across this thing, you might consider it a friend, rather than flee from it."

"Why has this been kept secret?"

"Remember the first time Warrick returned from Marland, when Elson brought him across the sea? He wasn't in good condition, mentally or physically - apparently whatever adventure he had had a lasting effect on him. So it was that when he came back the second time, the Council listened to his account with uncertainty, disbelief for some. For yet again, he came to us with outrageous tales, this time about Idris, meeting a man of fire, and proclaiming that he had seen King Iman. According to Warrick, the king spoke with him as he made his way from the sea to Bentleigh, yet no one else saw him. To make matters worse for his cause was the fact that he had just learned of daughter's death, as you well know. Lucy had been buried several days before, yet he insisted that he had seen her and spoken with her at the same time that he spoke with King Iman. The Council decided that Warrick's tale should be kept quiet – we made him pledge not to mention the creature of fire to anyone else."

"But what if it's true? Wouldn't it be good to give the people hope that a creature like that might exist, and that it might be able to help us?"

"You are your father's son, Conroy. Indeed, the Council was somewhat relieved that they didn't have to argue him on this decision, for surely he would have pressed to make the existence of the creature known. But more harm than good would be done if Warrick's stories aren't true; it's better to be cautious than to plant hope carelessly. Nothing would be more devastating, and foolish, than waiting for help from someone that wasn't coming."

Conroy sucked his lower lip in again and pondered the information. He remembered the dreadful conversation he had with Warrick on that day: how sad Warrick had been to bring him the news of his father's murder. But Conroy had no reason to think Warrick was deranged - even when he learned about Lucy, Warrick still seemed to act rationally.

"Please keep this information to yourself," pleaded Wendel. "I swore that I wouldn't speak of this outside the Council - if it was to become known that I told you, I would suffer expulsion from the Council, and perhaps additional reprisal as well."

"I don't agree with the Council's decision," replied Conroy. "Warrick is truthful and reliable; he's like a brother to me."

"You're certainly becoming an honorable young man," beamed Wendel. "It pleases me to hear you speak with the wisdom of your father. You may find yourself on the Council one day."

*   *   *   *   *   *   *   *   *   *   *

Dusk fell on Seton as the Marlanders gathered, just as Valena and Idris had instructed. They were told that there would be a message shared that evening, one that would enlighten them concerning their current circumstance and unveil new opportunities. Though few had any confidence left in the three self-proclaimed leaders, all of Marland had come to witness what would unfold.

Behind the fire pit, a thick and high wall of stone had been built to serve as a platform on which Idris, Valena, and Lachlan could stand above the masses. Already on the wall, Idris took in the sight of the Marlanders in the fading daylight. They were gaunt, pale, and weak: they seemed barley alive, but they had enough life to grumble to one another, and Idris saw firsthand that Lachlan's estimate of their discontent had been accurate. Glares shot from the eyes of men and women alike and made him glad that he stood high above his unhappy subjects, and that there was a roaring fire between them. For a moment he wondered if he had waited too long to act, but then he remembered the surprise that Lachlan had in store for them, as well as the advice that Scynn had given him – to let them suffer and grow hungry and desperate. No, the timing was good; everything had fallen into place as planned. He banished all doubt from his mind, then raised his arms to prepare the crowd to receive his message.

Before Idris could begin, Brant, who had been wandering through the crowd, cried out; "Master, behind you!"

The entire assembly saw two men approaching Idris, but only Brant called to warn him. Idris dropped his arms and turned quickly to meet the oncoming men, while Lachlan and Valena leapt from the wall in obedience to Idris' gesture for them to leave. Idris wasn't surprised by the confrontation, in fact he was glad that it was now happening, certain he could handle the situation – he even found it difficult to suppress a smile.

There were no grins on the bony visages of Prevor and Finnegle, however. Finnegle halted, his sword at the ready, and allowed Prevor to advance by himself to stand beside Idris. "It's time for a change!" shouted Prevor as he punched his fist into the air. His voice was strong, but fluttered slightly as the flow of adrenaline rushed through his body. "For too long have we accepted the guidance of these three." Although Lachlan and Valena had removed themselves from the wall, Prevor made it clear that the mutiny would be against them as well.

The crowd erupted, proclaiming affirmation of the revolt. Prevor drew his sword and turned to face Idris squarely. "Renounce your authority and you'll live. Otherwise, you'll die, you and your accomplices."

Finnegle cast a curious eye to see Lachlan standing calmly at the base of the platform's stone stairs. He hadn't drawn his weapon and seemed content not to flee.

"What do you propose to do with these people if I am removed as their leader?" asked Idris. "Do you know better than I where to find food for them? Do you have the ability to restore their immortality?"

"I'll lead them to better lives than this," exclaimed Prevor, angrily. "Your cunning may have been renown on the island, but you've done nothing here to earn your position! Your wits sank with the island."

"What makes you think the people will accept your leadership in place of mine? Why not let them decide who's the better one to lead them?" said Idris, still standing on the wall, showing no intention of leaving.

"Isn't it obvious that we're all ready to be rid of you?" Prevor grew impatient; "Submit or die! Choose now!"

"Let there be a challenge to show which of you is most suited to lead!" cried Finnegle, stepping forward and giving a sly wink to Prevor. The idea of a contest wasn't something he and Prevor had discussed, but Finnegle was certain Prevor would prevail. The crowd shouted their approval, and Finnegle continued; "In this new..." he searched for a word, "world, this new era, strength and courage are superior to cunning. I propose a contest to weigh these men's strength and courage - the victor earns the right to lead!" Again, the crowd consented with applause.

The two challengers were now powerless to influence the manner in which a leader would be selected. Neither had expected this, but neither was worried of defeat, for they both had extreme confidence in their measure of strength and courage.

"It shall be done!" exclaimed Finnegle. "Lachlan, give me a sword!"

Idris gave a nod of approval, and Lachlan handed a blade, which was not covered in streaks of black, up to Finnegle. Concealed beneath his garments, Lachlan wore another sword, one that had been dipped in the pool of glimmerstone.

Finnegle received the sword and secured it to his own, handle to handle so that the blades pointed away from each other, then carefully presented them to Idris and Prevor. "Take hold! When one of you possesses both swords, the contest is over and that person will be declared rightful ruler of Marland!" The crowd shouted and cheered yet again.

Idris and Prevor obeyed and grasped the blades. At first, they squeezed only the center portion of the blades, using their fingertips in an attempt to avoid contact with the sharp edges. But when Prevor's efforts began to prevail, Idris was forced to squeeze the blade with his whole hand, abandoning care for the edges; he strengthened his grip until the sword stopped sliding from his grasp.

Then Idris pulled hard. The sharp steel pressed against the flesh of his hands, but didn't cut him. The swords began to slide out of Prevor's grasp, forcing him to squeeze harder, to the detriment of his hands - blood spurted from where the sword sliced him, running down and around his fingers and along the blade, before dripping off and puddling on the stone wall. For the first time, Prevor considered that he might not prevail. Soon, the sword cut through the flesh of his fingers to the bones. Prevor's blood could no longer be contained by the puddle and began trickling down the side of the wall into the fire.

Idris pulled harder still, mercilessly inflicting pain on his adversary. He didn't want it to end too quickly, though. The crowd needed time to accept that he was the one who would win, to realize that he was meant to be their leader. He saw defeat on Prevor's face, and suspected that Prevor was considering letting go. But Idris was not about to let it end with a simple surrender. He squeezed even harder, his skin still impervious to the razor sharp sword, and pulled back quickly.

Prevor couldn't release the blade in time to save his hands. Both of his index fingers and thumbs were sliced off as he cried out in pain and fell to his knees in the puddle of his blood. Idris took both swords, removed the binding, and held them out wide, spread apart, ready to bring them together and deal a deathblow to the loser.

"Renounce your mutiny and you'll live, oppose me and you'll die, you and your accomplices!" He delighted in using Prevor's threats against him now. "Submit or die! Choose now!"

Prevor stared in disbelief at Idris. *How could he not be cut? What magic gave him power?* "I surrender! I submit!" cried Prevor, glancing back and forth between Idris' stern face and his disfigured hands.

Idris lowered the swords, touched their tips to the floor, and leaned on them gently. Two of Prevor's companions, Dug and Treytoni, came around the fire and took him away to bandage his hands.

"Consider what you just saw a demonstration of the power that can be ours again!" proclaimed Idris. He held out his hands to show they were unharmed. Follow me to power: join me and recover our lost immortality! The time has come for the quest to advance. Scynn has counseled me and shown me visions of a glorious future. All we need to do is heed the instruction of this magnificent creature. Don't doubt what we have proclaimed about Kavan: he has ever been an ancient guardian here, and will lead us to the mighty Icyandic! For proof of his benevolent intentions, I present the first secret of Marland, a secret that will ensure our success, a secret revealed to us by Kavan himself!" Idris leapt from the wall and landed beside Lachlan.

He spoke privately to his friend; "It's time to show them the glimmerstone – use this opportunity to secure your position over the people, as I've just done."

Lachlan quickly ascended to the top of the wall, efficiently drawing a sword from beneath his coat, one smeared all over with black streaks. He spotted Finnegle still standing on the platform; he glared at him and commanded; "Come here!"

Perched on a branch of a tree behind the mob, Carollan watched Finnegle pick up one of the swords that Idris had left on the wall and approach Lachlan. Carollan had been passing through Seton on his way to Tilden when he came across the gathering and decided to delay his journey south to observe the Marlanders.

When Lachlan drew his black and silver sword, Carollan recognized the glimmerstone at once. He dropped from the tree and prepared to confront Lachlan...

A sudden jolt sent Carollan spinning sideways violently. When he finally stopped tumbling, he saw a large dark object coming at him fast. Before he could get up and move out of its way, the thing was on top of him, pressing him down with its great weight.

"Delightful to bump into you today," said Elzib, playfully. "What was it you were planning to do just then?"

"I *was* going to stop these people from making a terrible mistake," replied Carollan with noticeable effort.

"I can't have you meddling here today." Then, not wanting to risk that Carollan might escape his grasp, and because he wanted to, Elzib repositioned himself and drove one of his long shoulder spikes through Carollan's chest, pinning him to the ground. Carollan refused to scream as light shot from his pierced chest, but he was in tremendous pain and was helpless to escape.

Oblivious to Carollan and Elzib, both of whom remained invisible to them, the Marlanders remained focused on the continuing battle between Finnegle and Lachlan. Finnegle reached for the remaining sword that Idris had left behind, for the one he had been using was destroyed a moment earlier by a stroke of the glimmerstone blade. But the second sword proved just as useless, for Lachlan lashed out and easily cut it in half, leaving Finnegle holding a short stub of a broken blade. Finnegle cast it into the fire and fearfully awaited Lachlan's next blow. He was relieved when Lachlan, instead of striking him down, turned to the crowd.

"A secret of Marland, bestowed upon us by Kavan himself!" shouted Lachlan. "I reveal to you, glimmerstone! Indestructible and ..."

Thew! ... Thew! The people recognized the sound of two loosened arrows and saw Lachlan lift the sword to meet them, one after the other, smashing the first to dust and catching the second at its tip; the blade kicked back slightly as it absorbed the full momentum of the arrow... "able to obey my thoughts." Lachlan removed the arrow and held it up. The people looked back to see who had shot the arrows and saw Brant holding an empty bow and smiling.

"With glimmerstone, we'll be a force none can stop! With glimmerstone, we'll never lack anything ever again!" Everyone was amazed; Idris was pleased that the demonstration had had the effect that he hoped it would.

Then, before the awe of the crowd wore off, Valena rose into the air, encapsulated in a flaming sphere. Silence overcame the crowd and all eyes went to her as she hovered above them. The ball of fire began to dissolve from around her, fading first from the top of her head, then progressing slowly downward so that her shapely figure was revealed, and at last exposing her long legs. But a patch of fire remained beneath her feet, upon which she stood. It stretched forward to form a winding ribbon, and she began to walk on it, following the leading edge as it elongated before her. As she walked, she issued a soft chant, barely audible to the crowd:

> "*dl'a sevo dn'a zhivi,*
> *i t'agoteniam serdtsa sleduy,*
> *tsena tomu ne velika.*
> *i vs'o v por'adke budet.*"

Over and over she repeated the words, never raising her voice; she spoke as if to place them under a spell that they need not know about, only obey.

> "*dl'a sevo dn'a zhivi,*
> *i t'agoteniam serdtsa sleduy,*
> *tsena tomu ne velika.*
> *i vs'o v por'adke budet.*"

Though none of them knew the meaning of what she was uttering, the sound of the chant was like a melody to them and they became entranced.

As if this wasn't enough to overwhelm their senses, two new enchanting figures emerged from the fire pit. They recognized both Kavan and Scynn, for they had all seen them before, on the night the island was lost, however, this time they were not afraid, but comforted and pleased by their presence.

The people stared at Scynn, and just as when Valena, Lachlan, and Idris had gawked at it in the cave, they were all captivated by the creature's appearance: some struck by its beauty; some by its strength; and others by the intelligence they perceived it to possess.

Scynn moved from the pit to follow behind Valena, flicking its tail repeatedly in the flaming ribbon. The crowd gazed reverently as glowing embers fell on them, burning them not physically, but inwardly to their delight, for the embers mingled with Valena's chanting to form a sweet cerebral flavor.

The ribbon beneath Valena continued to advance until it had led her in a large circle around the Marlanders. When she had completely encircled the crowd, she stopped beside Kavan, and reiterated the chant one final time:

> "*dl'a sevo dn'a zhivi,*
> *i t'agoteniam serdtsa sleduy,*
> *tsena tomu ne velika.*
> *i vs'o v por'adke budet.*"

Kavan grasped Valena in his large hands as the ring of fire disappeared, and placed her gently on the ground beside Idris and Lachlan, then stepped forward into the very center of the gathering, and turned to face the three. "These are my faithful servants, in whom I am well pleased! They shall rule over you, Marlanders! Lachlan shall be the mighty steward of glimmerstone; Valena shall be my voice – through her I will speak to you; and Idris is to be the wise leader of you all. These are your Overlords!"

Carollan continued to struggle against Elzib, but the weight of the large brute, coupled with his strength, which he used by grasping some ledge embedded in the earth, and pulling himself toward the ground, made it impossible for the Casildan soldier to break free.

Kavan said nothing more, his declaration complete, his purpose fulfilled: none would challenge the authority of his three servants again. He and Scynn disappeared from the mortals' sight simultaneously; but as they vanished, around each of the Overlords' head appeared a blazing band, which, after several moments, transformed into a gold crown embedded with glossy black stones. And in Valena' hands there was a dark staff, all along its length were inscribed strange symbols - the markings of her chant. In Lachlan's crown were three gems, each the size of an olive; in Valena's were two of the same, but these were slightly larger; and Idris' crown contained only a single black stone, the largest gem of them all, about the size of a plum.

Elzib released his grip on the ledge and withdrew his horn from Carollan's chest. The light that had been pouring from Carollan's body ceased, and he threw Elzib aside, smashing him into the tree in which he had been perched.

Carollan glanced toward the fire pit, where he saw Scynn contorting and writhing in a wild dance among the flames. In front of the beast, he observed the Marlanders, also moving their bodies in celebration, and shouting, *"Overlords! Overlords! Overlords!"*

"There's no need for you to stay," Kavan said to Carollan as he smiled a triumphant smile. "They're not calling for your king - they no longer desire his aid."

Carollan looked from the frenzied congregation to Kavan's beaming face, then back to the crowd. Valena, Lachlan, and Idris had returned to the top of the stone wall where they could peer down on their loyal subjects. The dancing and cheering continued, *"Overlords! Overlords! Overlords!"* Disgusted, Carollan flew away.

Elson thought they were perfect. He bundled the freshly picked daffodils, two dozen of the first flowers of spring, and tied a string around their stems; obtaining the bouquet meant that all his preparations were complete. Today was the day, now was the time; he was finally ready to consent to the feelings that had grown within him, and soon he'd release the floodgates of his heart that held his emotions back. He was certain that Kira would comply, but he couldn't help feeling nervous as he carried the bright yellow flowers back to the cabin where she slept.

Even as he walked he felt different, renewed even, perhaps partly because Kira had cut his hair the night before. Without his shaggy hair, which remained as straight as ever, he could now feel the air breezing across the back of his neck, and he no longer felt the weight of it when he turned his head. He had wanted it to remain long throughout the winter, believing that it would help keep him warm. If so, there were many frozen nights when his hair was not nearly long enough. During the coldest weather he was often awoken by an icy draft coming through the cracks in the cabin wall, and through miniscule openings at the seams where the walls met the floor. He would rise, patch the suspect hole, and return to bed for whatever portion of the night remained, plagued by having been awakened. This process was repeated for about a week, until Elson seemed to have found and filled all the holes, or perhaps he grew more accustomed to the cold, his body adjusting to function under the circumstances. But now the warmth of spring was here. No need for long, unkempt hair any longer, besides, he wanted to look his best for Kira today.

He arrived at the cabin and opened the door as silently as he could, but it had a tendency to creak no matter how gently it was moved. When the door swung wide enough for him to enter, he went inside, but left the door open, fearful that closing it might wake Kira. He was anxious to present her with her favorite flowers, but there were other things he had to get before he did. He walked over to the corner, delicately placed the bouquet on the floor, and retrieved a number of long, yellow cloths from beneath a pile of clutter, which he had created intentionally for the purpose of hiding them. With the ribbons and flowers in hand, he went to Kira.

Before reaching to wake her, he observed how peaceful she was in sleep. As with anyone whose eyes are closed, her expression was plain, empty, lifeless. In a moment he knew that her calm face would come to life with the opening of her big, beautiful eyes, one of Elson's favorites of her features. Hopefully a wide-spreading smile would follow, once she learned what he had in store for her. He extended his left arm and held the flowers near her nose for a minute, allowing her to unconsciously delight in their fragrance. Then he lowered them further so that the petals tickled one of her soft, smooth cheeks.

Kira woke slowly, raising her arms while arching her back in a long morning stretch. She released a breath and opened her eyes to see the dazzling yellow flowers. She smiled immediately. "Where did you find these?"

Elson smiled in return. "Not too far from here, I knew they were your favorite."

"What a delightful start to the day."

"But today will be better than any other," replied Elson, hoping his words would prove true. He presented her the yellow cloths, lifting them up from down low, where he was holding them out of sight. "Will you wear these today?"

Kira didn't recognize the garments for what they were at first, for they were all crumpled up together, and the room was still somewhat dark, but she didn't dare offend Elson by asking what they were.

Elson allowed the silence to remain for only a second; "Isn't it tradition for the bride to carry flowers and wear ribbons?"

Kira became overwhelmed with joy. Tears streamed down her face as she snatched up the ribbons and unraveled them.

Later that morning, the bride and groom departed the cabin together, looking as elegant and polished as could be expected. Both wore sandals of leather, the material that they had learned to use most for making garments and sacks and such. Elson, with nothing special to wear, had simply picked out some clothes that were clean, and not ripped anywhere, and shaved his face. Then he waited patiently for Kira to finish preparing herself.

Kira, for lack of a gown, wore a short brown skirt, a garment that she had fashioned from a pair of Warrick's trousers. A matching top, made from the same material as the skirt, with thin leather straps lacing up each side to hold the front and back together, not tightly, but leaving a gap of about three inches between them, covered her upper body. More straps, like the others, ran from her midriff to below her neck. It was her favorite shirt, and she could wear it in every season, adjusting the laces to allow for additional clothing to be worn underneath when it was cold. Matching her flowers, which she carried gracefully, she wore the seven yellow ribbons: the smallest four she tied around her ankles and wrists; the largest she wrapped around her waist; one she wore as a scarf; and the last she wore in her hair, tied up neatly in a bow. The excess lengths of ribbon hung down from where they were tied to her, flowing in the wind as she moved, for Elson led her through the forest, all the while clinging to her hand.

After walking for about twenty minutes, traveling from the field where their cabin was, through a patch of thick forest, then into another open field, they stopped. "This is it," he declared. Kira looked around and wondered why Elson had brought her to the top of a knoll, on which grew a large, solitary tree.

"Do you know what kind of tree this is?" Kira shook her head. "This is an ash tree." Elson allowed her to observe it before continuing... "It's said that the ash is the strongest tree - that it can bend more than any other kind of tree before breaking."

Kira was impressed by this information, but didn't understand how that applied to her current circumstance.

Elson read her puzzled expression and spoke quickly to explain the significance. "We're living in a new world now, where trouble comes against us in the same manner that the wind blows against this tree. He placed his hand on the solid trunk. I want our marriage to be strong enough to withstand the gusts of this world; I want this to be the symbol of our love and commitment to each other."

Kira let go of Elson and shifted the daffodils to her right hand so that she could place her left hand on the tree while facing him. As she did, she couldn't help but recall one particular example of the ways of the new world, but she worked quickly to suppress the image of Ansen Verrill, making it fade fast.

Then, with their hands on the ash, and overflowing with feelings, they pledged lifelong love and devotion to each other. Nature played the part of witness, especially the large ash, while the two bound themselves together as husband and wife.

When no more words needed to be said, Elson took Kira in his arms and drew her close to him, reveling in her body. Everywhere he touched her was soft: her face, the small of her back, her neck, her sides above her hips, and especially her lips. He withdrew from the kiss to look down at her breasts, viewable through the openings in the laces of her shirt. Slowly, he began to untie the ribbons, starting at her feet and working his way upward, as though unwrapping a present for which he had waited so long to open. When the last one was removed, he proceeded to loosen the leather straps at her sides, then those at her neck, until her shirt fell away.

Kira felt the warmth of security rush through her as Elson held her tight. Her heart drank in the joy of being married to the man she loved. She let the flowers slip from her grasp to land beside the ribbons. They lowered themselves slowly to the ground, never losing hold of each other, then shed what clothes remained and consummated their vows at the foot of the giant ash.

*　　*　　*　　*　　*　　*　　*　　*　　*　　*　　*

The tolling of the iron bell pierced the quiet of morning in Bentleigh, waking Wendel Wright, the sound sending shivers through him. Was it only an exercise to demonstrate that the alarm was functional? He hoped so, though he wasn't aware of any such order from the Council. The bell and all of the associated signaling mechanisms had been inspected the previous week; surely it wasn't time to perform another test. He dressed quickly and departed his home, heading for the bell, which rang a couple more times, for the watchers were required to sound it three times to warn of trouble; this confirmed that it was no drill.

As he drew near the village square, he saw that a number of other Council members were already there, including Linus and Ruth. "What's going on?" shouted Wendel, after the vibration of the bell calmed so that he could be heard.

"You know as much as any of us!" declared Ruth, obviously panicked.

"Have any of the watchers brought news?" Wendel asked. The others shook their heads. Just then, Keelan came running toward them.

"Boats... many... at least thirty... from Marland," Keelan attempted to inform the Council what he had seen from his watch post, sputtering words in between his drawing of breaths. "They were about five miles away when I... left Amara in the post to come here... now they are probably about only... a couple of miles out."

"How could they come more than half way across the water before being spotted?" demanded Linus, angrily.

"It was dark," answered Keelan, "We couldn't see them until just a little while ago."

"There's no time for this!" scolded Wendel, "Send the archers to the trees! Arm the swordsmen and send them down to the sea! Hurry!"

Most of the people had emerged from their homes by this point, alarmed at the sound of the bell, wondering what was happening. Wendel dashed back to his home. He would join the fight, but he would not leave the books unprotected, sitting open on his table. They had been entrusted to him, and he intended to keep them safe.

"Overlord Lachlan, surely they've seen us by now," advised the first mate of Lachlan's vessel.

"No matter." The Overlord's tone was indifferent. And it didn't matter, not even if every Tildenian came to fight against them, victory was certain. His troops were strong and capable; he had trained them all himself, and trained them well. They each wielded a weapon coated in glimmerstone, one that he taught them how to use with their hands and with their minds, and that made them far superior, even bordering on invincible. And they had strength again, for it had been restored to them through a secret stash of food that Idris had kept hidden until the Marlanders accepted his lordship and subscribed to his plans. Now they were coming fiercely across the waves of Corliss Lake and the South Sea to take what they desired.

Standing tall on the Tilden coast, invisible to the islanders, as always, the twelve Gemstones watched two distinctly different groups of assailants. Bobbing across the water was the Marland fleet, visible to the Tildenian foot soldiers, who had taken their positions within the forest behind the cover of newly formed spring foliage, and the archers stationed high up in the treetops. But unseen to the Tildenians was another group, one that concerned the Gemstones more than the advancing ships; hovering over the vessels was a swarm of Kavan's horde.

When the Gemstones first learned of the assault, they abandoned their sentinel stations around Bentleigh and marched together to the sea, where they formed a line along the coast, in front of the large stone statue of King Iman, all at Onyx's command. They arrived just as Amara signaled the initial bell stroke and Keelan began his sprint to the village, and held their positions until now, when the Tildenian warriors reached their battle stations, and the Marlander fleet drew to within range of arrow shot.

The Gemstones were identical in shape and size, save for Onyx, who was slightly smaller than the others, but this was noticeable only when he stood beside one of them. They varied only in color, each unique, each with a brilliant appearance. Onyx was positioned toward the middle of the line, with four Gemstones to his right and seven to his left. To his right was the bright green Emerald, then Chalcedony, who was mostly a sky-blue color, but striped by a multitude of other colors, followed by the deep-blue Sapphire, and lastly the red and white Jasper. On Onyx's left was a fiery-red figure, Sardius, then the yellowish-green Chrysolyte, followed by the sea-green Beryl, the golden-yellow Topaz, the blue-green Chrysoprase, the reddish-orange Jacinth, and finally, a flashy purple figure, Amethyst. As they always did when preparing to fight, they had their elbows and knees bent slightly, crouched for action, and held their fists clenched tight.

Being of one mind, they thought to each other; "Remember, our duty is confined to this realm, to guard the Tildenians against Kavan and his minions only," declared Onyx. "It's not our place to hinder the fleet and interfere in the battle between the mortals."

"I don't see Kavan, but I detect his presence," said Amethyst.

Indeed, Kavan was not hovering in the air with the horde. Elzib was there, as was the well known Drimelen, Kavan's second in command, beside a few other high ranking generals of Kavan's legions.

"He's walking behind the fleet," a new voice informed the Gemstones of Kavan's whereabouts. It was Gavril. The king's captain had soared in from the west and landed at the end of the line beside Amethyst. "Scynn is also there; see it moving amongst the ships."

The unique shape of the multi-limbed creature could be seen clearly, silhouetted against the pale haze of a gloomy sky. In a jubilant jumping dance, the webbed Scynn launched itself from ship to ship to ship. To Gavril and the Gemstones, it seemed that it did this either to perform some sort of task on each vessel, which had only a temporary effect, and therefore had to be repeated often, or else because the creature was so excited that it couldn't remain still, or perhaps both suspicions were correct.

"Have any other servants come from Casilda?" Onyx asked Gavril, hoping they had.

"Sandor and Carollan have come." This made Onyx glad, and his confidence grew at knowing that mighty Sandor was near, not to mention that Carollan and Gavril were also present, their skills were also very welcome.

Arrows began to fly from the treetops toward the Marlanders. None struck their mark, though most had been well aimed. Some landed in the wooden timbers of the vessels, while those that had been on target were easily deflected or destroyed by the glimmerstone weapons. The archers continued to let their arrows fly, though it seemed that their efforts were not hindering the attack.

The larger vessels hit the sandy bottom first, while the smaller ones advanced nearer to the coast before grounding in more shallow water. When they came to a stop, the Marlanders leapt from their boats and stormed onto the shore, still using the glimmerstone to guard against the showers of arrows coming from high above. The vanguard of the attacking force advanced directly up the beach to the forest's edge to cut down the trees in which the archers were perched, doing so easily. As the trees toppled over, the archers were forced to flee their posts, leaping to the safety of nearby branches of other trees, but losing most of their bows and arrows in the process.

At the same time, the Tildenian warriors emerged from the woods to meet the Marlanders to battle against them in swordplay. By now, they knew that the Marlanders possessed some mysterious power, one that enabled them to reach Tilden without a single warrior injured, and did they really just see large trees sliced clean through by only a single stroke? Whatever the source of their power, it didn't matter, the archers had been nullified and they were all that was left between the Marlanders and the path to Bentleigh. They rushed forward to fight; they had to try.

The defensive stand was brief. When they lifted their swords to meet the black and silver steel of their opponents, their weapons were rendered useless by the magical black material, which obeyed the images conjured in the minds of Marlanders. Most of the Tildenian blades were shattered to pieces, some became soft and drooped impotently limp after contacting the glimmerstone, and some were simply sliced off, leaving the Tildenian warriors holding hardly more than a handle. With no weapons left, the Tildenians were utterly and immediately defeated; the battle was over in less than ten minutes. Now they would begin to learn just how demented their former neighbors, friends, and family had become.

"What do you want from us?" cried Linus, his raspy voice making audible the question that all of Tilden was desperate to ask. At first they worried that no answer would be given, for none came from any of the triumphant Marlanders standing near. "What do you want?" shouted Linus again.

"We want much, old friend!" At last a voice called out, a voice that everyone recognized, a voice they used to delight in hearing, but one that now caused them to be afraid. Idris made his way forward to face Linus. "The first thing we want is for you, all of you, to accept positions of servitude under our authority. There's no need to kill any of you, but that is the alternative."

"What is this black magic that you've used against us?" demanded Wendel. He had been late in arriving at the scene, but not too late to avoid having his weapon annihilated by glimmerstone.

"A secret of Marland," replied Lachlan, approaching Wendel and holding out his blade so that Wendel could examine it closely. "All you need know is that it has made us stronger than you!"

Idris snapped at Wendel, "Don't interrupt me again or you'll get an intimate lesson about the powers of the black stone!"

He paced up and down the shore while shouting out to the Tildenians, "All who wisely choose to live, drop to the ground and kneel, extend your arms and lean forward so that your face is to the ground. Any who do not will be slain at once!"

"Is that how you've spent your winter, honing your skills for killing?" retorted Wendel. Idris glared angrily at the councilman, the fact that Wendel had dropped to his knees and was bowing forward with his hands out saved him from experiencing Idris' wrath.

None of the Tildenians dared defy Idris; all bowed low with their faces to the ground and their arms outstretched.

"Good!" declared Idris.

The Gemstones hadn't moved, not even when the Marland invaders strode onto the shore, unknowingly passing by them, even walking between their long, stony legs. Their focus remained on the couple dozen of Kavan's horde hanging in the air over the water, watching the action from aloof, not making any attempt to partake in the battle, only to relish in the spectacle of victory. Though they did call out obscenities at the Gemstones every so often, particularly Drimelen, who seemed to despise the fiery-red Sardius more than any of the other Gemstones. The twelve defenders remained poised with knees and elbows bent slightly, fists still balled up.

Kavan had joined his friends in the air when the Marlanders went onto the shore, taking a position between Drimelen and Elzib, while Scynn continued forward, keeping pace with the attackers to make sure their hearts did not grow faint and forget their desire. Just as Drimelen aimed most of his curses at Sardius, Kavan's mockery focused mostly on Onyx, but he also cast a few choice words at Gavril. He took special joy in ridiculing Onyx for being the smallest of the Gemstones, and he asked the other eleven why they allowed him to remain their leader.

Kavan and Drimelen's obscenities drew loud lowing from Elzib. But in between his fits of laughter, he feigned attacks on the Gemstones, making them flinch; they'd bend their knees and elbows further, and then relax slightly when they saw that Elzib wasn't really going to carry out an attack. This drew hoots and howls from those surrounding him, so Elzib continued repeatedly, until he finally grew bored with it, then settled back to enjoy more of the ridicules that spewed forth from Kavan and Drimelen.

Finally convinced that Kavan and his followers did not intend to fight, the Gemstones took notice of what was happening behind them. A large number of Tildenian warriors had been bound by chains and herded into some of the boats. Once on board, their chains were secured to the vessel to keep them from leaping over the sides and attempting to swim away. These boats, about half of the Marland fleet, then set off from shore and headed back to Marland under Lachlan's command.

As they watched the ships depart, the Gemstones questioned whether they were to follow. "We remain here," declared Onyx, sensing the inquiry. "We've not been excused from our duty to guard the king's friends from Kavan here on Tilden. If help is to come to those being taken to Marland, it will need to come from someone else."

Kavan and his horde departed as the ships sailed away, and the Gemstones followed the people back to Bentleigh, for Idris had ordered everyone that remained back to the town so that they could be given their new 'assignments'.

$$* \quad * \quad * \quad * \quad * \quad * \quad * \quad * \quad * \quad * \quad *$$

Conroy landed on Marland just as the hazy dawn arrived. He managed to reach the spot he wanted, far enough east to keep out of sight from anyone at the docks. He was somewhat familiar with the dock area, having been a watcher, though it was a post he held for too short a time. His journey across the sea had gone smoothly, though he heard quite a commotion at one point in the night. He couldn't tell what caused the noises, and he stopped rowing to drift silently until the ruckus dissipated. He didn't know how lucky he had been – it was the entire Marland fleet sailing past, not more than fifty yards to the west of him!

He dragged his small vessel from the water and hid it in the woods, covering it with branches and leaves. Then he snuck closer to the docks and spied to see what was happening. He was surprised to see only a few people lingering lazily about, and even fewer boats.

All through the night, he had thought hard to determine what he would do when he arrived. His plan was this: to find Bethany, he was certain that he first had to locate Lachlan. He hoped that he might be at the docks, but now discovered that he was not. Conroy knew Lachlan well enough to suspect that he would likely build his new home outside of the village, Seton, as Warrick had called it, just as his cabin on the island had been outside of Epidomon. Conroy further suspected that Lachlan would want to live fairly close to the water, so all he had to do was discover which side of Seton his cabin was on. Since he had landed on the east side, that would be where he searched first.

He had questions to answer before he proceeded: if he were seen would anyone know who he was? Would they know he was from Tilden? Could he pass as a Marlander? ... No, he decided against that, since the entire island had celebrated his signs of the Island Games, not to mention that he was a member of the victorious rookie team for those same games. No, they would surely recognize him - he couldn't be seen.

He considered waiting until dark to move about, but decided that was not a wise strategy, and given that there were few people around, wouldn't it be best if he took advantage of the opportunity? If he delayed, the place might be crawling with people later, after all, the ships that were absent might return soon. He thought of Allison and resolved not to delay exploring for her sister. He passed by his boat, making sure it was concealed from all normal vantages of any passersby, then walked quietly northeastward into the woods.

It wasn't long before he came upon a solitary cabin that looked similar to Lachlan's old island cabin. One unique feature, in particular, indicated this was likely Lachlan's home - a brown banner decorated with a three-tongued flame of red and yellow was flying on a wooden pole beside the structure.

Conroy stepped carefully through the forest as he circumvented the cabin, always ending the short stretches of his advance crouched low behind a rock or hiding behind a thick tree. When he rounded the north side he saw a familiar figure standing outside an entryway. Beside the door, which was swung fully inward to leave the passageway open wide, stood Brant, brandishing a black and silver blade in the air. Conroy watched Brant lunge forward and swing at some invisible enemy, seemingly some character of his imagination with which he was engaged in a mighty battle.

For a split second, Conroy relaxed and almost stepped into the open to reveal himself to his old friend and teammate. But then he recovered caution and surmised that it would be careless for him to assume that Brant would respond benevolently to his presence. But what should he do? Brant had been his friend, might be still, and certainly didn't deserve to die. Conroy was not about to hurt Brant, though he could have, for he came prepared to fight, carrying a sword, daggers, bow, and all the arrows he could fit into the sack slung across his back. But Brant couldn't be trusted either, at least not yet.

Conroy watched the imaginary duel continue for a few more minutes, uncertain what to do. He was surprised when Brant stepped toward a boulder in the yard, lifted the sword, and brought it down violently into the rock. What a way to dull your blade, if not bust it, thought Conroy. But then, he always knew Brant to be reckless. Brant turned to walk back to the cabin and Conroy saw that two pieces of rock remained where one had been!

Brant was getting bored with his assignment. He would've much rather gone with his friends to Tilden and shown all those patsies who lived on the southern mainland how great he had become. He pictured himself fending off one Tildenian warrior, then another, and then taking his place in victory beside Valena, Lachlan, and Idris as they looked over the defeated weaklings. But Lachlan needed him to stay back for this special task, a secret task. No one else even knew she was here; Brant felt privileged in the fact that Lachlan had confided in him, and that gave him some consolation for not being able to go. But the day was barely more than half over and he didn't know when his appointment would end – it could be several more days. He was restless.

He had given her morning and midday meals as instructed, opening the low slot in the wall and sliding them into her room, watching her through another slot at eye level to observe that she was all right and confirm that she knew that food had been delivered. He noticed right away that she remained exceedingly beautiful.

When he opened the hatch to view her the second time, his gaze lingered upon her and a new thought came to him. They were alone; no one would try to stop him. He was sure he could overpower her, if it came to that, but perhaps she would be willing.

He recalled a sour memory of a past attempt at love, his first attempt. The girl, a red-haired beauty named Shiren, who had been brought to Marland by her parents, had laughed at his less than competent performance. Suddenly he viewed the circumstance as one with more to offer than only a few moments of pleasure with Bethany - it could also be a chance to practice and gain experience. Then he could prove himself to Shiren, and he desperately desired to, for she was popular among many of the Marland girls. He knew well enough that information passed freely between them, especially anything pertaining to acts of intimacy.

Then something in him made him dismiss the idea; besides, Lachlan would not be pleased with him when he returned. The next few minutes passed slowly, however, and he found it difficult to keep his desire suppressed - the thought grew stronger, larger, as if it had roots that spread to draw energy from new places. Lachlan wouldn't have to know; he could let her go afterward and tell him that she escaped. Surely she'd run away and never see any of the Marlanders again. But she might, and if that happened she could tell on him. He could kill her and say that she escaped. There would certainly be other women for Lachlan to choose from after they brought back the slaves.

He swung the blade down at the stone, breaking it in half, just as he envisioned, using rage from his experience with Shiren and for having to stay there and play the guard dog. Since he had to be there, he might as well make the most of the circumstance. He walked back to the cabin with an image of Bethany Krunser beneath him filling his mind - he would have her!

Conroy watched Brant pass through the doorway with quick strides, seemingly driven by a new, immediate purpose. Conroy was frustrated and angry - here he was, having come so far on his journey, only to be dumfounded as to what should be his next move. Had he encountered Lachlan or Idris, he would have let loose an arrow at their heart without hesitation, but not at Brant. He thought hard, so hard that his head hurt - he needed desperately to decide his course of action. He stepped out from behind the tree. If Brant was no longer a friend, then it would be a fair fight, both were armed, and no one else was around to assist the Marlander. He took two steps forward then halted; *what is that?*

A new figure emerged from the west. Conroy waited expectantly to hear wails of pain, for the person was ablaze, completely engulfed in red and yellow flames. Surely whoever it is must be in tremendous agony! But silence surprised him, for no cries were issued. Then he remembered: it wasn't a man, but a creature of living fire. The thing stepped calmly, but briskly, past the broken rock, moving with determined pace inside the wooden structure.

Conroy wondered how long it would be before the cabin burst into a burning inferno, given the quality of the being now present within. Sure enough, a stream of black smoke started to pass back through the open doorway and rise upward. Conroy's thoughts turned quickly to Bethany, for he presumed she was inside, and wondered if he could get her out to safety before the fire grew too hot. He proceeded forward, but stopped abruptly again, this time as the burning figure withdrew from the cabin. It stopped, turned to Conroy, and gave him an omniscient nod.

"Well done, Conroy Verrill," it said.

Conroy got a good look at it. There was a face; solid ovals of orange with bright yellow rings for irises around black pupils were its eyes, dark holes of black voids indicated its nostrils, red lips parted to reveal a flaming tongue surrounded by the white interior of its mouth. It resumed walking and strode off in the direction from which it had come.

Conroy moved toward the doorway, quickening his pace to a jog, ready to act quickly to free Bethany, though there was no indication that the fire was growing, in fact the stream of smoke that escaped into the atmosphere seemed to dwindle.

Inside, Conroy found himself in a small hallway. To his right, the hall lead to the main area of the cabin, to his left was a thick wooden door, locked and barred. A single key hung from a chain on a hook beside the door. Next to the key was a metal panel with a handle at the far side. On the floor, right in front of the door was a pile of smoldering ash beside the sword with a black and silver blade.

She heard the familiar sound of the panel sliding open and hoped that it would be Lachlan who looked inside. This new individual, the first person other than Lachlan she had seen since her abduction, made her uncomfortable. Lachlan may be holding her captive, but she knew that he cared for her, in a demented, possessive way, but he never gave her reason to be afraid for her life, and she knew that he would not force himself upon her. But the eyes of the newcomer were hungry, younger yes, but not innocent, not warm. Bethany knew where Lachlan had gone, and what his mission had been - she knew it was unlikely that he would have returned so soon.

She nervously lifted her gaze to see who had opened the panel, and was surprised to see a new pair of eyes staring at her. These eyes she knew! They were the bright, blue eyes of a friend and partner! They were the last friendly eyes she'd seen before being taken from Tilden - she leapt to her feet! The person disappeared from the viewing window, moved to the door, and turned the key. The groan of the iron lock never sounded so good!

"Conroy!" she called out excitedly, but also quietly. "Be careful, there's someone else here," she whispered. "I'm not sure who it is, but I don't think he…"

"It was Brant."

Bethany was surprised. "Where is he… what's that smell?"

Conroy stepped into the room and gestured behind him, pointing at the smoldering pile of ash, "I think that's him." He quickly explained to her about the creature of fire.

Bethany stared at the ashes in amazement. She saw the blade and snatched it up immediately, knowing that it would be more than useful for whatever adventure lay ahead. "We need to get away from here!" she declared. "Lachlan might not be back for a long time. We have a good chance to get far, far away before he returns. I'm pretty sure he's the only Marlander who knows I'm here."

Conroy stated that he had seen Brant slice a large stone in two with the sword and asked her how he was able to do that. Bethany replied that she knew how, "It was the glimmerstone," she said, though now was not the time for explaining. She forced herself to return inside the room one final time, overcoming all the unpleasant memories of the place, which urged her to run away at once, and grabbed a bundle of clothes that she always kept ready in case an opportunity to escape arose. She promised to tell Conroy about glimmerstone later, for he kept inquiring of her as to what it was. After a quick pass through the main part of the cabin to scavenge what food and supplies they could find, they went cautiously outside.

"Follow me," said Conroy, "I have a boat hidden in the woods just off the beach. We can wait there until dark and then return to Tilden."

"No," replied Bethany firmly, "we can't go to Tilden; it's not safe there."

"What do you mean?"

"That's where Lachlan went. He led a raid against Tilden this morning! We have to go north."

Conroy consented hesitantly, realizing that Bethany was likely to have been privy to information about any planned raids, being as she was Lachlan's ... roommate and all.

Relief and anxiety mixed within Bethany. She was free again, but could she stay free? If no one else knew about her being on Marland, no one would be searching for her. Conroy seemed to have reached her without being seen, and that was certainly a good stroke of luck. But the actions of the fiery creature concerned her. Did the thing really mean to help her by turning Brant to dust and ash? The timing of its appearance seemed more than favorable coincidence. Why did it come and kill Brant at the very moment that Conroy was there? But, if it meant to help her, why hadn't it come before and killed Lachlan? To her, the creature seemed another dangerous obstacle to encounter as they fled. She squeezed the handle of the blade and was confident that she would not return to Lachlan's prison. She might have to fight everyone on Marland, but she would if that's what it took for her to keep her freedom. She knew about the mysterious black material that coated the blade she carried; she knew what it could do and knew how to make it work, for Lachlan had boasted to her about it for hours upon hours.

The two pressed on to the north, well armed and well supplied, but saddened that their destiny was in the opposite direction of where their hearts wanted to go - south to Tilden and their families. Like an ever-hungry beast, the Marland woods swallowed them, another pair of lost islanders running away in an attempt to escape despair. So far, of Conroy's loved ones who ventured there, only Warrick had returned, not in good shape, but he had returned, and Conroy held onto this fact to bolster hope that he and Bethany would do so as well.

*   *   *   *   *   *   *   *   *   *   *

The Marland assailants that did not accompany Lachlan back to Seton spent the day dividing up the defeated Tildenians into various groups, and pillaging Bentleigh to relieve it of many of King Iman's gifts. They did not take everything, however, for it was planned that a large garrison of Marlander soldiers would remain on Tilden to oversee the slaves as they worked the land and raised livestock. Specifically, the machines that were used for the crops were left behind to be put to good use, after all, the Tilden slaves would now have to harvest enough food to feed all of Marland as well as Tilden. Any shortage and their children would be the first to be deprived of food. All of this was, of course, as Idris and Valena directed.

Wendel was pleased when Idris asked for the Council to be assembled, believing that in the midst of all his corruption, Idris at least recognized the wisdom of the Council and wished to hear their opinion on some matter. Without hesitation, he led a few of the Marlanders around the village to summon the members of the Council before Idris.

Wendel was disappointed when he heard the tone in which Idris spoke to them, however; "Members of the Island Council," he snapped. "There is no island, there is no Island Council! If I ever hear mention of the 'Council' from this point forward, the one who makes the reference will regret it severely. Am I clear?" The council members, even Wendel, nodded.

Idris did, in fact, recognize the capabilities of the group before him, and was fearful that if they were left together on Tilden, instead of crops, they would grow a rebellion against the Marlanders that ruled over them. Therefore, he declared that they would accompany him back to Marland, where he would make sure they were kept busy enough to not have energy left for any mutinous activity.

One thing comforted Wendel; he had successfully concealed the books from the Marlanders, tucking them inside a pouch on the inside of his shirt. The chill of spring remained and nobody thought his bulky garments were unusual. At least he could continue to perform the task assigned to him: that of keeping a history of his people, and this day certainly provided him with much to write.

$*$ $*$ $*$ $*$ $*$ $*$ $*$ $*$ $*$ $*$ $*$

Nearly a month had passed since that blissful morning when Elson led Kira to the large ash tree where they vowed their love for each other, and every day since had been filled with frolic and delight for the couple. Another sunny day began and Kira went down to the lake to wash clothes; it was one of the few times as of late that she and Elson were more than twenty yards apart. She deposited the baskets in the water, tied tight so that the clothes wouldn't escape, bathed, and then decided to venture off to her new favorite spot while the clothes soaked for awhile.

The solitary ash on the knoll was as grand as ever, a beautiful sight every time she beheld it. She went straight to it, sat down, and placed her back against the thick trunk, drinking in the soft sounds of nature and breathing in the clean spring air. She loosened the straps of her sandals and kicked them aside so that she could rub her feet against the soft grass. Life was good!

She quickly found herself caught in a moment of reflection. She could hardly believe that recent events had actually happened! Yet, here she was, married to the man she loved, sharing a peaceful life with him in a splendid lake valley, a place that she was beginning to consider her home. She remembered how, not long ago, she wondered whether she would ever smile again, yet alone find joy in everyday life. She could vividly remember the feelings that she had on the boat when Idris forced her to leave her family on Tilden and accompany him to Marland, as well as how she had felt during the times spent by herself at the cove at the base of Great Falls. The cove had been the place where she tried to find escape, to think pleasant thoughts about her family and her friend, Amara. But these thoughts always led her to question whether she would ever again see these people she loved so dearly. Then her thoughts would grow darker still, as she would dwell on her unpleasant marriage to Idris, not to mention the terrible burden of labor that had been placed on her by her husband and Valena. No, during these times she thought it impossible that happiness would find her again. But it had found her!

There was work to do, she knew, and the clothes had soaked plenty long enough by now. She rose and wrapped her arms as far around the trunk of the tree as she could to give it an affectionate hug. Then she put her sandals on and went back to the lake.

She found the submerged baskets and pulled them up. As Kira knelt by the water, she turned to look at Elson. He was working to till the soil for planting a garden beside their cabin. He was hers, and she was his. No longer did he ward off her attempts for affection; in fact, she was somewhat surprised that Elson had become the one to initiate intimacy more often than not. She rejoiced in the freedom of their relationship, knowing that she could expose herself to him without shame, physically and emotionally, and that she could do so any time she pleased. Perhaps now would be a good time. She returned the few garments that she had washed back to the baskets, cinched them shut, and dropped them into the water once more - soaking a little longer wouldn't hurt. She loosened the ties of her shirt and shorts and slipped them off, wondering how close she could get to Elson before he looked up to see her approaching wearing only sandals.

But a glimmer of light reflected off the surface of the water, catching her eye. She looked up and saw two people coming down from the wooded hill on the opposite side of the lake. She retrieved her clothes and put them back on as fast as she could, then stared to get a better look at the newcomers. When Kira saw the blonde curls of the woman, she recognized Bethany at once. Trailing a short distance behind was Conroy.

Kira turned to look at Elson again. He was still working hard in the garden and was not aware of them. Suddenly, Kira grew fearful of the possibility that either Conroy or Bethany, or perhaps both, knew the truth about Ansen Verrill. It seemed that there was a part of her that she might feel ashamed to reveal to Elson after all.

Bethany and Conroy were making their way around the lake, and it would be only a few minutes until they arrived. Kira knew things were about to change for the worse, and that the *winds of trouble* might soon be blowing on her new marriage. She planned to go and inspect the ash at the next appropriate opportunity.

chapter fifteen: ·feloniche's Redemption·

"Will you do as I have asked?" King Iman spoke with the twins in his giant throne room. The sound of his voice echoed off the majestic stone walls of the vacant space. It wasn't often that the king spoke privately to any of his servants in this most special place, and Durwin and Baldwin felt esteemed to have been summoned there.

"Of course," answered Durwin and Baldwin together.

"Even though what I command seems to contradict certain aspects of my character?"

"Whose ways are above yours?" answered Baldwin.

"We're wise enough to know that you're able to turn all things good," added Durwin.

The king smiled as he returned to take a seat on his throne. The twins bowed low and departed.

Sandor looked disapprovingly at the twins when he saw them come out of the throne room. They didn't notice him glaring at them, and for that he was thankful, for they would have easily observed his sour expression. Sandor knew them to be traitors, and talented ones at that, for no one had ever successfully deceived the king. Sandor arose from a small table in the corner of the large common room, a place reserved for the leaders of Casilda's army, and a place that the high captain frequented. He slung his shield in its proper place on his back and moved from the table, where a group of his comrades remained sitting, and proceeded to follow the twins.

"Sandor!" The door to the throne room was open wide and Sandor saw the king standing in the void – he was the one who had called out. "I have a task for you."

Sandor wanted very much to continue following the twins, but duty forced him to submit to the king. He adjusted his course and went to meet King Iman. "What is it, my Lord?"

King Iman stepped into the corridor to meet Sandor. "I want you to go and speak to Carollan."

"Very well."

"You'll find him in Bentleigh, he's been assisting Onyx and the other Gemstones. Go at once and tell him to bring Justin back from his exile."

Sandor demonstrated compliance by bowing, then turned to leave the palace.

But the king sensed trouble within him; "Is something bothering you? You're agitated."

Sandor knew he could not hide anything from King Iman and revealed his concern about the twins, knowing that it was always best to be open with him. "I believe that the twins have turned against us and now support Kavan."

"It would be tragic if Durwin and Baldwin were lost to us," replied King Iman. His expression was serious, but did not display any sign of surprise.

"I intend to watch them to see if they do anything that will confirm my suspicion, after I see Carollan, of course."

"Follow them if you feel it necessary, but don't hinder them, no matter what they do. Report back to me of their actions."

Sandor bowed again and left. By the time he passed the large palace guard at the exit, the twins were nowhere to be seen. It didn't matter, he supposed, since he was obligated to go to Bentleigh anyway. But as soon as he imparted the king's will to Carollan, he would be free to find them; he only hoped he could before they caused significant devastation.

*   *   *   *   *   *   *   *   *   *   *

Not again! Justin awoke almost as angry as he was afraid. The dreams would not cease; instead, it seemed that they were becoming relentlessly more intense. Almost every night he woke, covered in sweat, after experiencing the dread of seeing his friends struggling for their lives over a large chasm, and hearing the booming, wicked laughter ring out from someone who seemed to take delight in their despair.

Justin felt cold, most of his covers having been pushed off of him while he flailed against the nightmare, and the moisture of his sweat allowed the chilly air to suck the heat from his body. He reached down and grabbed the edge of the covers and pulled them up over his shoulders and held them tucked tightly under his chin. Even still, he couldn't stop shivering for several minutes due to the cold, but also due to the terror that lingered in his mind. He closed his eyes and tried to conjure images that would usher the unpleasant ones away.

He exhaled a deep breath and saw the stream of warm air condense into a faint mist. It was really cold! Justin hadn't bothered to start a fire; the weather had gotten warm enough so that he hadn't needed one for warmth for some time. But it was freezing now, and he was sure that he'd not been this cold all winter. Since it would be hours until the sun came up, and because he was extremely uncomfortable, Justin decided to build a fire.

Feloniche rubbed his claws together and chuckled as he watched Justin, trembling with cold and fear, attempt to light the kindling. Justin was unaware of the fact that Feloniche had been visiting him often, usually at night shortly after he had fallen asleep. He had discovered the dream in Justin's mind and frequently summoned it to fill him with terror. Although he enjoyed watching Justin struggle, Feloniche had additional mischief planned for the night, and he slipped off into the darkness, howling with laughter inaudible to the human.

He found MaGowan asleep beside Emily and went and crouched down to lean in close to him. "It's cold," he whispered in his ear, "It's so cold."

MaGowan shifted and breathed slightly deeper.

"Emily is cold. The children are cold."

MaGowan shivered and pulled the blankets tighter.

"The fire is out. You need to rekindle it. You need to get wood."

MaGowan's sleep grew shallow as his mind created images consistent with Feloniche's words.

"She needs you to get more wood."

MaGowan cracked open his eyes and saw that the fire was out, for he had not made a large one that evening. Similar to Justin, he hadn't expected to need a fire for warmth throughout the night – the weather had become quite warm the last few weeks. He drew in another long breath through his nostrils, surprised at how much the icy air cooled his insides, all the way to his lungs, and consented that a fire was needed.

"There's wood on the other side of the stream," continued Feloniche, speaking once more to MaGowan's awakening mind.

MaGowan, though barely conscious, got up and went outside to retrieve the wood. He stumbled across the yard and turned down a path to where his last reserves were stacked. He had not expected to need to burn this wood yet; had he known otherwise, he would have brought it closer to the cabin. "Lazy fool," he mumbled to himself. During the winter, he had cut the tree from which the wood came, a tall, dead poplar that leaned toward the cabin. Worried that a heavy snowfall would bring it down, he cut it. But the tree, to his surprise, fell in a direction opposite his home, the bulk of it landing on the far side of the stream. He chopped the tree where it fell and piled it there.

Across the stream he went, too much in a daze to realize that it wasn't safe, that the ice had become thin. All he thought about was making a fire and getting back into bed. Nevertheless, he made it across and selected a few logs that would burn quickly, then turned to make his way back.

The ice beneath his feet gave way this time, his weight having been increased by his burden. Ice cold water sent jolts of pain through his body. Now he was wide awake! The stream wasn't very deep in most places, but it was over six feet in one particular spot, which provided a nice swimming hole in the summertime. Unfortunately for MaGowan, this is the very spot into which he had fallen. Completely submerged, and blocked from the surface by the ice, he struggled to get back to the opening. But it was dark, and there was a current pushing against him, and his limbs were becoming numb.

Feloniche danced on top of the frozen stream, shouting gleefully at the man. "What are you doing? There's no air down there! Perhaps some island meer would help!" Feloniche pulled some meer from his tattered garments and cast them down at the spot where he could see MaGowan pressing his hands in an attempt to break the ice. "Here!" Feloniche stepped on the meer, squishing them above the terrified man, the layer of ice making the meer useless to him.

Feloniche wanted a closer look. He slid through the ice and moved beside MaGowan. Just as he delighted in watching Russel Minns die, so he enjoyed viewing MaGowan's death. Kavan would be pleased, he knew, but not so pleased as to consider his debt paid. No, he would have to accomplish something more substantial before approaching his master and requesting reinstatement. He returned to the surface as the pleasure of MaGowan's death quickly faded and an appetite for destruction began to reform within him.

"That was a foul act," a voice called out.

"And cruel, very cruel," added another.

Out of the cold, quiet night, Baldwin and Durwin emerged, stepping from the woods to the stream. They strode across the slippery surface to stand over Feloniche, who sat at the open hole with his legs dangling in the water while he etched obscene runes into the ice with his claws. He had been immersed in thought of how he might make amends to his master, envisioning standing beside him once again, and the twins' arrival caught him by surprise. Immediately, he pulled his lean and lanky form up to stand with his claws out in front of him. "What do you want?" he hissed angrily.

"We haven't come to fight," replied Durwin. He held up his hands in a gesture of peace to calm Feloniche.

"We have pertinent information for your master," stated Baldwin.

"Information that he would like to have," offered Durwin.

"Why have you come to me?" snapped Feloniche, doubting that they really intended to offer anything to Kavan that would truly please him.

"Even if we knew where Kavan was, we could not get to him safely," answered Baldwin.

"But we knew where you were, and knew that you'd be able to take us to him," said Durwin.

"Why should I? My lord is displeased with me enough. What would he think if I led two of the king's lackeys to his lair?" Feloniche kept his claws ready, just in case the twins moved too suddenly.

"Exactly for that reason, don't you see?" replied Baldwin.

"Take us to him and when he sees what we have for him, he'll restore you to your rightful place," suggested Durwin.

"I have a better idea, why don't you give me the information and I'll take it to him myself, if I think it's worthy of him." Feloniche could tell right away that they were not going to consider his offer.

"We must see that our message is delivered to Kavan ourselves," answered Baldwin.

"Will you tell me what the message is then, so that I may consider this task?" Feloniche relaxed a bit, hoping that this would demonstrate a show of trust that might be returned by the revealing of their message.

The twins looked at one another for a second. "Very well," they answered.

Nearby, Sandor spied on the threesome, disgusted that two of the king's trusted servants had sought out Kavan's vile aid. He had completed his assignment of delivering the king's request to Carollan, who readily accepted the charge of retrieving Justin from exile. Sandor had accompanied Carollan north and figured that he might as well investigate what Feloniche has been doing, for rumor had it that he was wandering around these parts, sharing his own exile with that of the guilt-ridden islander.

It never occurred to him that the twins would be there. Though he suspected they were up to some kind of treachery, he didn't think that their depravity had yet descended to such a level as to associate with the likes of Feloniche. He exercised tremendous self-control in not barreling into their huddle and giving them each a good thrashing; if the king hadn't told him to not interfere he surely would have.

It had been awhile since Sandor had seen any of those that had fallen away from the king's favor. He took the opportunity to examine Feloniche closely, studying his bent, emaciated frame, which his splotchy, pale skin stretched thinly over so that the contour of his skeleton was easily seen; his long, wild claws; his shifty, yellowed eyes; his tattered garments, shredded remnants of a once splendid uniform worn in service to Casilda. Sandor glanced at his own clothes in comparison. They were as white as they had ever been, and the gold embroidering emanated a steady glow as if from its own source of power.

Nothing within him envied Feloniche. Granted, not all of Kavan's horde were as hideous, for they all had control over the alterations to their form. Some of the more powerful, so it was said, possessed the ability to change their appearance at will. Sandor did not perceive anything appealing about Feloniche to justify why he had allowed, or perhaps caused, such a transformation. Even more unfathomable, what did any of them ever gain in disregard of their service to the king? What had enticed them to act in such a manner that they would be ripped of their rank and cast out of Casilda?

Sandor knew the answer – it was Scynn. He had always been wise enough to not let the creature get a hold on him - some of his companions had not been so, and they were now counted among his enemies. They had hoped to frolic with the scaly monster for only a short time, but found that the creature had not meant for them to leave, and found that it was strong enough to prevent their escape. Even after Kavan's falling away, in spite of the warnings, Sandor watched too many of his friends become slaves to Scynn. Hubris was used to snare Kavan and the crew of the Hypatia, but Sandor had seen a number of others lured away by different vices of the beast. Often a brief romp affording pleasure to its prey was the bait; all too brief the pleasure passed and the consequences were revealed. They all had known there would be consequences, and knew they would arrive on time afterward, but the consequences never seemed to be as manageable as initially thought: always they were more severe than the offender anticipated. And when regret came it was too late; Scynn had asserted itself as their new master, one incapable of letting any of its prizes ever find freedom again.

As he gazed upon one of his lost friends of old, Sandor worried that the number of companions-turned-enemy had increased by two, for Durwin and Baldwin conversed at length with Feloniche.

Finally, the three finished speaking and started moving south, walking swiftly through the woods. Sandor wondered whether he should inform Carollan what he had seen, or report back to King Iman; he would do both, he decided, but only after he learned exactly what they were up to. As he took to the air and gave silent pursuit, he strengthened his resolve to never let his guard down against Scynn's tactics – even he was not invulnerable to the wiles of the beast.

Feloniche walked with renewed energy, anxious to lead the twins to his master. He wondered what reward might be given him –

perhaps he would be allowed to contend for a new and higher rank. "Wait!" he demanded of himself, for his thoughts were racing ahead too quickly; was it too risky? Would he bring more shame upon himself? With the images of a glorious return subdued, he wondered whether there was anything that he had overlooked that might foil his plan. What if the twins lied? It didn't matter - if they didn't deliver the prize they promised, he would still have the privilege to present these two long sought after servants of the king to Kavan. If they spoke truthfully, Kavan should be pleased as well.

But there was still risk. Though he saw no reason for Kavan to be displeased, it wouldn't be the first time the two of them held differing perspectives. But what other chance did he have to redeem himself?

"Is this the fastest way to Kavan?" Baldwin asked.

"Why aren't we flying?" added Durwin.

"We'll be there soon enough," snapped Feloniche. He didn't feel obligated to explain that he desired to approach his master with as much humility as possible, and being contrite while flying is something that cannot be done.

The twins didn't press their guide for an explanation, fearful that he might change his mind and abandon them. Instead, they pondered what might happen when they met Kavan, and what he'd do with what was delivered to him. They walked south for a great distance in silence.

When Corliss Lake and the South Sea came into view, Feloniche grew nervous; they were very near their destination. They continued directly south, passing east of Seton, and soon Great Falls loomed over them.

"Kavan's lair is here?" asked Baldwin.

"One of his strongholds," replied Feloniche.

Suddenly, Drimelen, Kavan's second in command, and two other of Kavan's personal guards appeared before them, blocking their way. Drimelen was not nearly as gruesomely disfigured as Feloniche, yet, every feature suggested he was built for battle. His chest, back, and middle were covered with an armor of a dark gray metal; brown and black plates covered his thick arms and legs, similar to the scales of a great dragon, extending down the length of his limbs and even covering the exposed upper sides of his hands and feet. His face was unpleasant to behold, not because his features weren't fair, but because bitterness seemed to have taken a permanent hold and given him an ever-enraged expression. The other guards wore armor made of the same gray metal, but their physiques were inferior to Drimelen, for they were smaller and did not have the scaled limbs and extremities. Surely, if either of them were met alone, they would prove intimidating, but beside Drimelen they were unimpressive.

"What're you doing here with them?" demanded Drimelen. All three were armed; Drimelen carried a long spear, and the guards each held a spiked club, but none brandished their weapon at the intruders – because Feloniche guided them, a chance for explanation would be permitted before force would be imposed.

"They have something for our master," answered Feloniche.

"They serve the king and cannot pass," retorted Drimelen.

"I know what it is they bring – Kavan won't be pleased if they're delayed." Feloniche relished being able to issue a warning to Drimelen, rarely had he been able to do so. Perhaps, he hoped with all his might, that things were about to change and that would become a common event.

"You dare return from exile with two of the king's servants, demanding that I let you bring them to Kavan?" But if Feloniche wanted to rush into ruin, so be it, thought Drimelen, he didn't care if Feloniche earned further penalty, and besides, the twins were unarmed. "It's your doom!" Drimelen turned and beckoned them to follow.

Feloniche remained smugly silent, glad of the escort, for with Drimelen leading he'd not have to explain what he was doing to anyone else - such an imposing figure would ensure that the right to deliver the prize to Kavan remained his. It was the best thing that could've happened.

When Drimelen and the guards appeared, Sandor realized he was close to one of Kavan's lairs, and even he, the head of Casilda's forces, dared not proceed alone. He recalled the time Gavril had gone, a solitary soldier, to deliver the king's decrees to Kavan and his horde at the Renfrew immediately after the islanders had been corrupted. How brave he had been to do that!

Gavril had been sent there by the king, Sandor was on his own mission, and that made all the difference. He turned aside for the time being, but suspected the purpose for the twins' visit might soon be revealed, so he decided to remain nearby for awhile. Perhaps he would observe the activities in Seton and see if what Carollan had said about the people was true.

Drimelen led the way to the base of Great Falls, Feloniche and the twins followed, and the two guards trailed last, keeping a close watch on their guests. None of them slowed at the pool where the falls collected; instead, they strolled right atop it and headed into the crashing, massive stream of falling water. They entered the mouth of the cave, unaffected by the waterfalls, descended down the wide marble staircase into the putrid room below, where they were met by Kavan. The master of the place sat on a makeshift throne comprised of a pile of large stones beside the black pool. A few others were scattered about the area, and most of them drew near the throne when they caught sight of the newcomers.

Laughter erupted from Kavan the instant he recognized King Iman's servants. "Welcome, Durwin and Baldwin, the Twilight Twins!"

Feloniche rushed ahead of Drimelen and threw himself down, prostrate at Kavan's feet. "Master, master! I've brought them here so they can give you news!" he proclaimed, doing all that he could to make sure that Kavan recognized him for his part. "You'll be pleased! You'll be so pleased!"

"That's to be seen," Kavan's expression of gleeful anticipation dropped away just long enough to give Feloniche a scowl.

Suddenly, a large number of Kavan's followers entered, and the cavernous room became filled with the horde. Not restricted to standing on the floor, some hovered overhead, and others climbed up the sides of the cave wall, all the way to the high ceiling.

"Don't tease me," demanded Kavan, growing impatient, "why are you here?"

"To reveal a secret," answered Durwin.

"A secret of the land," added Baldwin.

"I'm master here, what could you possibly know about the land that I don't?"

"Information that you might find useful," answered Durwin.

"For the tower that is being built for your Overlords," said Baldwin.

Kavan looked at them with hungry eyes that instructed them to continue.

"We know the location of a quarry of white stone," answered Durwin.

"The same that was used in constructing Casilda's castles," added Baldwin.

"Swear by King Iman that what you say is true!"

"By King Iman, we swear it's true," said Durwin.

"Swear by my name that what you say is true!"

"By Kavan, we swear it's true," obeyed Baldwin.

A smile spread across Kavan's face. "Whether you serve King Iman or me, you're bound - one of us will hold you accountable for your words. Tell me, where is the stone?"

"Closer than you might think," hinted Durwin.

"You might hit it with your head and never know it," added Baldwin.

Feloniche's impatience forced him to snap at the twins – how dare they play games with Kavan! "Enough riddles!" he shouted, "tell us where the quarry is! Now!"

Before Feloniche could react, the twins reached for him; Durwin grabbed his wrists and Baldwin ducked down and took him by the ankles. In one fluid movement they swung him about in a circle in the same manner as two children playfully swinging a rope. On the second revolution, they released Feloniche, sending him soaring into the ceiling of the high cave. Some of the onlookers darted out of the way, and all of them watched, amused, as Feloniche crashed into the roof, loosening a large chunk of rock, then soared angrily down to meet the twins. This was not how he wanted to return! He would not be humiliated! Especially not by these two!

Feloniche landed prepared to lash out. The section of roof that had come loose fell between him and the twins, and cracked into a pile of rubble. He moved to strike them both at once, but was stopped by the hand of his master.

"Well done, Feloniche!" boomed Kavan.

Feloniche, completely taken off guard by Kavan's praise, rescinded his attack. He looked to Kavan in hope to discover why he was pleased.

"You found the quarry!" explained Kavan, gesturing to the rocks at his feet.

Feloniche looked down and saw that the rocks weren't as he expected - they were white. He looked up at the spot where he slammed into the roof to see a light colored patch where the dark shell of the cave had been peeled off to reveal the essence of the mountain – pure, white marble.

Kavan wasted no time giving orders; "Split the mountain! Open its belly for Marland mortals! But don't destroy the cave!"

His horde was eager to obey; they flew from the place and started ripping a giant gash up the middle of Great Falls. They broke apart, and tore, and dug at the mountain until water no longer flowed from high up on the mountainside, but fell over the top of the cave into a newly formed gorge to empty into the pool, same as always. It took only a few minutes until their work was complete - the mountain had been split, a wide trench had been cut, its open gash glowed bright as sunlight reflected off the walls of white marble.

In Seton, the people trembled with fear. They had not felt the earth shake beneath their feet since the night the island fell into the sea - it was a sore omen indeed! Crashes and rumblings echoed as ground and rock and water sprayed high into the air above Great Falls. Then it was over as soon as it had started, and the people went, tentatively, to investigate what had happened.

*   *   *   *   *   *   *   *   *   *   *

The day that followed the frigid night was surprisingly mild. The sun shone strong and made the temperature rise back to that normal for the season, melting what snow and ice remained at the higher elevation. It seemed as if winter had made one last lunge to assert itself during the moon's reign, exerting what strength it still held, only to be supplanted by the gentle and fresh power of spring the next morning.

Despite the pleasant weather, the day was one of the more stressful days Justin had known for a long time. The first crisis came when he opened his eyes to find that the fire, which he had lit because he was painfully cold, was still burning vigorously, emitting smoke into the clear morning sky. Surely Emily and MaGowan would see it! He threw off his covers, jumped out of bed and doused the fire, then removed himself from the cabin at once so he would not be found in case his neighbors came to investigate. After a few hours passed and no one came, he began to relax, believing that his carelessness had gone unnoticed.

Then came the tremors! Images of the quaking island rushed to his memory, and familiar sensations of that night presented themselves. The shaking was not as violent as before, but there was no mistake, it was trembling beneath him! Was Marland going to sink into Corliss Lake too? Would the distant waters reach up to the great height where he was and overtake him? Were the monsters with whips going to come back and send him away? He didn't know what to do. He didn't know where to go. Should he look for higher ground?

The tremors stopped. The land did not sink. No monsters came.

That night, Justin slept peacefully. Feloniche was no longer there to torment him with awful dreams, but he wasn't alone - Carollan had accepted the request of his king, and had come to seek out the exiled islander. He arrived just after Feloniche had gone, but knew that Kavan's outcast attendant had been there before him, plaguing Justin. He watched Justin slumber, and could see the cords of thoughts that were exposed and raw, the work of Feloniche. They could be used for the task at hand, he thought, but not tonight; tonight Justin needed rest.

The next day was as pleasant as the day before, at least with regard to the weather, and Justin decided to pay a visit to Emily and MaGowan. It had been a long time since he'd seen them, and now that the snow was gone, he could visit without fear of being discovered. He didn't pack much, for he didn't plan to be away for long, and set off early.

An unusual sound caught his ear as he passed through the woods. It wasn't the normal crying of birds or other such noises. As he came nearer to the place where he could view MaGowan and Emily's cabin, the noise became clear; it was the sad wailing of a woman. Justin peered over the bank to see what was happening.

He could see well enough into the interior of the cabin to see the calm faces of the two children as they slept. Emily was outside, off to his right, near a stream, kneeling on the ground and crying loudly. He didn't see MaGowan.

All of sudden, something tugged hard at Justin's heart. He had to see what was the matter. Enough pain and suffering had he caused! Here may be an opportunity to help someone that he hurt. In spite of his previous actions, working for months to guard his solitude, Emily's cries made him forget about his own sorrow for a moment. He stood up straight and stepped quietly down the incline, surprised that he was acting so quickly, and without considering what he would say.

Carollan wouldn't allow him to consider turning back. He knew what had happened; he knew that Emily needed Justin, and he would make sure that Justin went to her. He held his hand on Justin's back, as high as he could reach, urging him on gently, and walking with him every step.

Justin wished that he could approach her from the other direction. Her back was to him, and he couldn't walk to her front side because of the stream. He noticed that her brown hair hung down slightly below her shoulders, tangled and matted with dirt. She was sobbing with her head hung low, her chin pressed against her chest. He really didn't want to startle her. The best he could do would be to walk a few paces to her side and come in at her from there, walking along the edge of the water, and hope that she would see him and not be scared.

Emily didn't know Justin was there. He stood beside her and waited patiently for several seconds for her to notice him, unsure what to do next, but she didn't seem to perceive his presence. He tried to look at her face but couldn't see her eyes, only the profile of her nose, straight and high and joining her brow at a perfect, clean angle. Without thinking too much about whether or not he should, he placed his hand on the upper part of her arm.

Carollan released Justin's hand, having successfully moved it to touch Emily, and stepped back.

Justin knew what the look on Emily's face meant. Though he hadn't seen his own face, he knew the expression that convulsed her mouth and eyes matched his own when he had found Evelyn's broken body. She was too distraught to be scared.

"Emily, it's me, Justin," he said it loud enough to be heard over her continuing sobs. Justin's beard had grown long and thick over the winter, and though they knew each other well while on the island, he didn't know if she recognized him. "Where is MaGowan?"

She continued to cry, but pointed to the ground under her bent legs. Justin noticed that the soil looked as if it had been dug up and filled back, smooth and without vegetation, and a small spade lay on the other side of her. Emily's front was covered in dirt and mud - her arms were brown, and dark arcs filled the space under her fingernails where dirt had been packed. She raised her hand to wipe the streams of tears away and smudged her face.

"Mag is ... dead!" she wailed.

Justin sat down beside her. There was no use trying to talk to her, but he at least wanted her to know that she wasn't alone. He remained quiet, his hand still on her arm until the wave of overwhelming sorrow had been put out of her.

"I don't know what to tell the children," she said. "They don't know their father is gone." No sooner had she said this than the two kids came running out of the cabin.

Justin spent the rest of the day doing his best to console Emily, and together they tried to comfort the young children. Both Bernal, Emily's five year old son, and Elana, her four year old daughter, were of course saddened to learn that they wouldn't be able to see their father again. Without knowing for sure whether he spoke the truth, Justin explained that it had been time for MaGowan to leave and go to a better place. Though uncertain, this is what he hoped. In the case with Evelyn, he had thought incessantly about her death, and something within him believed that she lived on elsewhere in spirit. He shared his experience of losing Evelyn with them, and they all seemed to appreciate that he knew what it felt like to lose someone close.

Justin didn't return to his cabin at the end of the day; instead he decided to stay with them and do the chores that MaGowan would have normally done. In between the spurts of sorrow that came upon Emily, he learned the events that led to MaGowan's passing, or at least what Emily suspected had happened. For one whole day she did not know where her husband had gone. She felt no cause for alarm during the first few hours of that morning, as he would often rise early and go into the forest to hunt or cut wood, or just enjoy a quiet sunrise. When nightfall came, however, and there was still no sign of him, she became filled with worry. Unable to sleep that night, she prepared to go and search for him at the first light of day.

She was not at all comfortable leaving Bernal and Elana by themselves, but she felt that she had no choice. She carried her pack to the stream to fill up her canteen with fresh water for her journey; the ice had melted and the cold water would taste good. Then she would make sure there was enough food and water for the children, and instruct them to stay at home, that she would come back as soon as she could. Then she would be off. But as she knelt beside the water, she saw MaGowan's body floating face down, washed into a shallow part of the stream on the far side. The children weren't awake yet, and she used the opportunity to bury him before they could see him. It wasn't until he was interred that she allowed herself to cry. Shortly afterward was when Justin arrived.

Emily correctly suspected that MaGowan had attempted to cross the frozen stream, assuming it still strong enough to support his weight, not considering the weather had been warm for a number of days prior. He was not a dumb man, she explained, and he knew better. What could have possessed him to go onto the thinning ice? She was sure she would wonder about it the rest of her life.

The four of them were enjoying an evening meal of steak and potatoes. Elson and Kira sat on a makeshift bench, for Elson had only made two chairs, one for himself and one for Kira; he never imagined they would have a need to seat dinner guests. He believed that he'd done a good job in crafting the table, yet Conroy offered some gentle criticism; "The seams could be a little smoother," he said, running his fingertips along an opening that had formed at a mitered joint.

"Huh?" said Elson, disappointed, "it was perfect before. The wood must've shrunk," he threw out the explanation in defense of his work. "The chairs are nice, right?"

"Not bad. They feel sturdy enough," admitted Conroy, after shifting back and forth in the seat in an attempt make it flex and wobble.

"They are strong, they're made of ash," offered Kira. She gave a smile and a wink to Elson.

The serious conversations, recollections of the crises of each party, had already been shared throughout the day. When Conroy and Elson came together, and they were the first to greet each other since Conroy sprinted ahead of Bethany when he saw his brother, the recounting of adventures began. Like a quartet of volcanoes spewing smoke and ash, the four islanders told their tales. Of course, most urgent had been Conroy informing Elson of their father's tragic passing. Tears were shed, fists were pounded, curses issued, and, in spite of sad news, an occasional smile surfaced at the fact that they were together again. They spoke of Marland and Tilden, and the two towns, Seton and Bentleigh, Bethany's abduction, and the Overlords, the encounters with the living fire-man, and Elson's vision of the white tower. Bethany passed around the sword and gave a demonstration of the power of glimmerstone, making short work of a heap of firewood that needed to be cut.

Then it was as if the volcanoes had emptied themselves of everything bitter within that needed to be purged, for the urgent talk ceased. But when the expulsion of light matter had concluded, then began the steady, unstoppable flow of the heavy, hot lava - an intense irritation, a searing streak of discontent, lingered in their consciences and demanded vengeance. This was especially so for

Elson, in who was piled the greatest amount of bitter residue from knowledge gained.

But life went on, and the four of them sat for supper and did the best they could to make things seem normal.

"This is delicious, thank you," said Bethany.

In their good fortune, the valley where Elson and Kira had settled was abundant with free ranging cattle, a number of which Elson penned in and used for a source of milk and meat. The potatoes were from last fall, remnants from the previous season, kept cool throughout the winter.

"You're very welcome," answered Kira. She took a drink and straightened up, for she'd been sitting slouched on the backless bench; "We have something else to tell you."

"Oh?" said Bethany. She and Conroy paused from eating and braced for more terrible revelations.

Kira was silent - she had introduced the subject, but desired its substance to be delivered by Elson. News of their marriage had not been shared yet; other things had been more pressing, and they weren't anxious to tell how they'd discarded the ancient tradition of their people, one that had never before been forsaken.

Elson understood his wife's intent; "Kira and I have married." It was as simple as that, nothing else needed to be said, at least that's what he thought.

But Kira felt more words were warranted, especially if they were to convince Conroy and Bethany that what they had done was acceptable, and she took it upon herself to deliver the details of their story. Elson sat by quietly and nodded to support Kira as she recounted events.

Bethany and Conroy were delighted. Recent times had not afforded much good news, but the marriage of Kira and Elson seemed a dim light glowing in a world covered in shadow. They stood and embraced the couple.

After the meal was finished (all of the food had been consumed, for Conroy and Bethany were famished), Elson took pride in showing his younger brother around his home and pointing out all the things he built, the most significant being the cabin itself. Conroy recognized attempts to use carpentry techniques taught by his father, and though he noticed a number of errors, he didn't speak of them, for he could tell that Elson was pleased with his work.

Talk lasted well past the time when the sun disappeared, but they finally retired and fell asleep quickly, all except Elson. When morning came, he wasn't certain that he'd slept at all. But he was sure of one thing: he had to return to Tilden at once to do what he could to help his mother and Warrick.

Following his announcement, the others promptly decided to return as well: in spite of her fear of Idris and Valena, Kira refused to be separated from her husband; Conroy refused to be parted from his brother, who he had only just found the day before; despite her hatred of Lachlan, Bethany refused to be left there alone – she had quite enough of being by herself for countless days locked in Lachlan's cabin.

They gathered what things they thought best and prepared to journey south before a week passed. Elson opened the pen to let out the livestock, and left the gardens as they were – perhaps the wildlife could eat the fruit when it ripened, or maybe someone would wander through who needed food. Kira was disappointed to be leaving her new home, and to her it seemed that the winds of trouble that Elson spoke of had come, and much too soon. She wished that she had time to visit the ash one last time. At least she was spared from the shame of Elson learning that she had known about his father's death all this time, for neither Conroy nor Bethany knew that she witnessed Ansen Verrill's fall, how could they? And given that there was nothing good that could come from revealing this to Elson now, she kept it secret still.

*   *   *   *   *   *   *   *   *   *   *

Valena knelt as she always did when seeking an audience with her master. Her golden crown sat upon her bowed brow above closed eyes, squeezing her head tight enough so that it didn't slip off, but not too tight to cause her discomfort. But the crown had its own two eyes that never closed, nor ever did they even blink, so thought the slaves, and these eyes, the dual dark gems embedded in the inanimate ring, were believed to give her a power of perception beyond human ability; it seemed that she always found out about secret things. Even now, when she was alone and busy with her routine, the people wondered if she was watching them. The Overlord sought Kavan's council on a daily basis. She found that his willingness to speak with her varied, but he always gave a sign to show he acknowledged her and that her worship was received.

On this occasion no mere sign was issued; instead, Kavan came to her and gave her a vision. Four people, old friends, were making their way through the forest. Elson led the group, Conroy came second, followed by Bethany carrying a black and silver sword, and Kira was last. There was nothing obvious about the scene to reveal where they were or what their intent was, but Valena knew, somehow, that they were coming to Seton. Lachlan would be glad to learn what had become of the missing glimmerstone blade, and she looked forward to speaking with the Verrill brothers and giving them their reward, but she did not want Kira to return.

The vision faded and Valena opened her eyes. Though she couldn't see Kavan, she could feel his presence. She grabbed her staff, which she had placed nearby, and used it to help her stand. "What is this I've seen?"

"You know who they are," Kavan answered, "They'll be here soon."

"I saw that one of them possesses a glimmerstone blade. I presume Brant is dead, most likely slain by the one with his sword."

"Do with them as you wish."

"My lord, I..." she paused. Her relationship with Idris wasn't something with which she was content, for she always sensed that he still desired Kira more than her, and this embarrassed her. It was awkward for her to discuss her jealousy, even with Kavan, but she needed his help. "I don't want Kira to return - Idris will want her back as his wife, a role that I desire to fill alone. I can't kill her; Idris might find out and despise me."

Her request came as no surprise; "Bring her here and call for me."

"What will you do?"

"I'll solve your problem."

She didn't dare press him to learn how he intended to this, and humbly replied, "Thank you, Master."

"The tower is going well. Keep the workers motivated and strong."

"I'm glad you're pleased. The stones are being easily retrieved from Great Falls, and the glimmerstone allows for our masons to make quick work of shaping the blocks."

Valena felt Kavan's presence leave the place. She went to the edge of the room and flung open a window to observe the activity around the newly formed base of the tower. Progress was noticeable; already, after only a few weeks of labor, the foundation of the tower had been laid, and on top of the wide footings, a triangular structure was being built.

Along the path that led from the village to the mountain, recently widened to facilitate the work, slaves treaded wearily, moving marble from the quarry to the tower, two long lines of laborers pushed wheeled carts, filled ones coming down, empty ones going back. Irritating grains of sand filled the voids between their toes and between the skin of their feet and sandals, dust clung to sweating bodies, perspiration ran into their eyes as the sun beat upon them; they were hot, thirsty, and miserable. A span of at least ten paces separated them, so had Lachlan ordered, and so far the Overlord's tactics to keep the slaves submissive seemed effective. No quarrels had broken out, and there had not been even a need to use glimmerstone to discipline anyone; they knew and feared the capabilities of the guards' utilities. Lachlan was pleased that they knew their place, but wouldn't have been upset if a few of them gave him an excuse to use one of the glimmerstone whips on their flesh.

The idea to build the tower had been the Marlanders'; a work intended to honor the Overlords by giving them a magnificent palace from which to rule, and also to symbolize their ability and strength. Idris took it upon himself to design the structure, but for the first few days he struggled to decide what the tower should look like. Then, as if the answer was delivered to him as he slept, he awoke with a clarity in his mind, knowing what its shape was meant to be - three equal sides would it have, one for each Overlord, and thirty levels, ten for each again, and at the peak of the high tower would be a three-sided pyramid, its top pointing sharply at the sky and beyond to the heavens. This uppermost section would be a sacred place for the Overlords' thrones and a sanctuary where Kavan would come to meet with Valena.

Idris was at the tower, and from the open window Valena watched him supervising construction among a number of armed guards, directing the placement of a row of new blocks. She looked longingly at him and dreaded Kira's return.

*   *   *   *   *   *   *   *   *   *   *

It took a few days for Justin to dismantle his cabin, drag it in pieces across the forest floor, eight trips back and forth were required, and reassemble it beside Emily's. Bernal and Elana insisted on helping, and Justin entertained their desire to help, though the children succeeded more in misplacing tools and materials than helping rebuild the structure.

So it is with children, always wanting to help, thinking they know what to do, but not capable of accomplishing the task on their own, but needing close direction and assistance from someone greater. And so he was patient with them, to Emily's amusement, subtly correcting their mistakes when they weren't watching. Evelyn had wanted to have seven children; he recalled her wish for three girls and four boys. It was unfortunate - he would loved to have seen her as a mother. At least MaGowan had the opportunity to watch his wife experience motherhood, he thought.

Justin and Emily needed each other, and they both knew it, though neither expressed it in words. Having been alone for so long, Justin had a solid appreciation for the company of other people, and he knew that whatever troubles came his way, and whatever burden he had to bear, it would be better for him to not try to deal with them on his own. Likewise, Emily knew she needed Justin's assistance and made every effort to make him feel welcome, and she treated him almost as if he were a new member of her family. In fact, feelings deeper than those of friendship had quickly formed between them; neither were comfortable with this, what with Evelyn's death less than a year ago, and MaGowan's less than a month. The memories of both warranted a respite from intimacy to properly satisfy periods of mourning. But the feelings were there, seeds had already sprouted roots and were anxious to bloom, but neither allowed them to – it just wasn't right for them to feel this way so soon.

Unlike the lower region where Kira and Elson settled, though only about twenty five miles northwest, the area was mountainous, steep with giant rocks, and there were no cattle wandering about - food had to be hunted or caught. MaGowan had been a good hunter, Emily declared, and kept his family well fed. Justin assumed the role of provider, taking it upon himself to bring home meat from the forest and streams. He had succeeded in providing for himself without much difficulty, so he knew what to do, but it took him a little while to learn how much food was required to feed all four of them; it seemed like Bernal and Elana were always wanting to eat. But, with the arrival of spring, crops could be planted, and he felt he could easily provide all that they needed. He went to sleep each night pleased that he'd been able to help, but fighting the desire to leave his bed and go to Emily's.

Carollan saw the images in Justin's mind, the ones Feloniche had manipulated into the nightmare. "That dumb fool!" he said, and shook his head at what Feloniche had done; "He probably didn't even know what they were." But *he* did; he knew what the images were, and where they came from. The tangled strands that were left in Justin's head could be used, but not as they were, no, there was no need for fear. Something else would be more effective.

But the next morning Justin went to Emily, and Carollan felt that he should wait to begin his work – it wouldn't be good to overwhelm him. A few weeks passed and Carollan decided that it was time to start. He had already visited Emily and made sure she was awake; he recognized her as an another instrument that could be used to accelerate his plan. Justin was fast asleep, lying on his front with one arm and one leg sticking out from the covers, his mouth open to ease his breathing, and the images in his head sitting dormant. Carollan walked to him and grabbed hold of the thoughts, untangled them, rearranged them a bit, then started to massage them. Gradually becoming more firm, he stroked the chords of the vision and the familiar images went to the forefront of Justin's untroubled mind.

It had been awhile since Justin suffered the dream - the last time had been before he visited Emily, he was sure, and he was beginning to believe that it was gone for good. But here it was again; in fact it was more intense than ever, coming to him refreshed, with renewed potency. His body couldn't endure the vision and forced his mind to wake. He rolled over quickly, tossing what covers remained on him aside, and sat up. The dim light was sufficient for him to see the inside of his cabin, and he tried to focus on the fact that he'd only been dreaming. He expected the intensity to fade as it always did, but this time the images of loved ones in despair lingered, and the bellowing laughter seemed to echo in his ears still. He coughed and sniffed to create noise so that the awful sound would be drowned.

Three quick knocks on the door jolted his attention to the entrance. The door swung slowly open and Emily entered.

"Justin? Is everything alright? I heard you cry out."

Her feminine tone was soothing, and Justin wanted her to keep talking. He never considered that he might express the dread of his night dreams audibly; no one else had ever been around to hear, ... until now. "It was a bad dream." As he spoke, he realized something was different – he wasn't afraid, like he usually was when he awoke from the nightmare, instead he felt sorry. But more than that - his feelings went beyond sorrow, beyond regret, beyond remorse, even to the point of surrender. He'd made a mess of everything and was powerless to mend what was broken, and he let go of believing that he could.

"Do you want to talk about it?" Emily sensed his pain and suspected he had more to say.

"It's my fault! All of it! It's all mine!" Justin didn't know why he said it, but he was glad he did.

"What?"

"Everything!" he couldn't hold it inside any longer. "The destruction of the island! Death! Evelyn's death, the death of the animals, ... even MaGowan's death."

"What do you mean?"

"I did it! I did what shouldn't have been done – I drank from the Renfrew!" Suddenly it was if an icy stream flowed over his burning conscience, and he knew he'd been forgiven.

"I know."

Justin stared at her. There was no surprise in her face, no startle in her reply. She couldn't know - how could she? "You know?"

She nodded calmly. "We came here that day, all four of us, to look for some of Marland's treasures, and the Caretaker came and told us what you and Evelyn had done. He warned that the island would be destroyed and that we should leave at once; he instructed us to go north, deep into Marland. We did."

"Then you know that I'm the cause for all the wicked things that have come into the world."

"That's not true, you're not."

Justin looked dumfounded at her. How could she say that? She must not understand.

"You may have allowed the world to become corrupt, but you're not the cause."

"Yes, I am! It's because of me that your home was destroyed, that your husband is dead, and that we're all going to die!"

Emily's emotions began to swell and her voice fluttered as she spoke; "You didn't kill MaGowan! Was it your hand that took his life away? Did you come here in the night and lead him across the ice, knowing he would break through?"

Justin was wise enough to keep quiet; her point had been made.

"When we first came here I despised you both and considered you weak fools. I struggled to comprehend why you'd done it, but then, as time passed, I observed my own nature, and my harsh judgement of you subsided. I wondered whether I would have acted any differently if I'd been in your position, and I've come to realize that I'm no better than you, and I might have made the same choice. How many trips were made in search of the red river? I went on more than a few myself, and what did any of us intend to do if it was found - only look at it?"

Justin was very, very happy that Emily was there. "Why didn't you tell me you knew?"

"I could see your feeble attempts to hide the shame you felt - like every time you returned from hunting. MaGowan always came back proud of his kill, satisfied that he'd succeeded in providing for his family. Not you, you always come back with a bland expression, as if you should be the one dead and not your catch. And how angry you got one time when Bernal cut himself when he was trying to help you with your cabin. I could see the remorse on your face as you bandaged him, then I watched you beat the next board unnecessarily hard with the hammer, and a few more times than was required. It was obvious that you were sorry, but I wanted to let you confess in your own time."

Justin saw a strength in Emily that reminded him of Evelyn. Perhaps that was why he had developed feelings for her so quickly. He wanted to leap up and grab hold of her, but he didn't. "Thanks for being so gracious."

Emily sat down on the floor beside the foot of his bed. She reached up and put her hand on Justin's shin. Her touch made him feel alive again. "I only acted as I would want you to act toward me. I wonder though, when Bernal and Elana are older and I try to explain to them what happened, will they even remember the island? Will they understand what it was like to drink from the Rivers of Power and know what desire we had for the Renfrew?"

"Will they forgive me? That's what I wonder." Justin looked down, but not at Emily, at the floor. "Generation after generation, for all of time, will pass on the tale of my failure. Imagine the future, when our people have populated the empty spaces of the world, and in every nook and cranny they will be gathered around a table, or a fire, telling how Evelyn and I ruined everything; how we did the only thing we were asked not to do." He wished he could dissolve and sink through the cracks of the floor and disappear blissfully into the dust of the ground, never to think again about the inevitable formation of his legend. Would misery be his only legacy?

Emily wouldn't let him. She sensed he was stuck in sorrow and tried to shift his focus, "Tell me about your dream?"

"Alright." He began to reveal to her the vision, but as he began he realized something was different. He'd always believed the images were symbolic of the present darkness that oppressed his loved ones. But now he perceived the vision was of some future event, something specific that hadn't yet happened. And as he and Emily talked, he wondered, just maybe, this foreseen fate could be avoided if he were to return to them before it was too late.

*   *   *   *   *   *   *   *   *   *   *

For the most part, they traveled in silence; only when it was necessary to issue warning of a hole to go around, or a root to step over, or some other obstacle to avoid, did they speak to one another. But the voices of their fears were loud. Elson struggled to think what he could do to help his mother and Warrick when he arrived, if they were still alive. He tried to chase the possibility that they were not from his mind, but couldn't fully banish it, knowing of the transformation the Marlanders had undergone from what Kira and, more recently, Bethany had told him. Kira grew more and more uncomfortable as she drew nearer to a reunion with Valena and Idris. Would she be allowed to remain with Elson? Would she be punished? Would he? Bethany couldn't guess at how Lachlan would react to her return. Did he think she was dead? Did he think that she killed Brant? She wasn't dead, she didn't kill Brant, and she would not allow him to take her back to his cabin. She ran her fingers over the smooth handle of her sword and felt the comforting exchange of energy between her and the glimmerstone. Conroy's fear also centered around Lachlan - what would he do to him if he found out that he'd been the one that freed Bethany? They'd have all the answers soon enough, whether they wanted them or not, yet they pressed on despite despair.

But Conroy was also anxious. When he left Tilden, he'd been running from the reputation of a coward. Now he was returning redeemed, having ventured to Marland alone and freed Bethany. It wasn't his fault she was coming back and might be captured again, that was her choice, the fact that he did what he had couldn't be denied. Some might even call him a hero. But he had no control of what the people thought of him, he knew, and he felt at peace within himself now, that was more important. He did care deeply about someone's opinion, however, and longed for her forgiveness: Allison. Over and over he played the scene in his mind, imagining her rewarding him with a long embrace and perhaps a kiss for saving her sister. "No, no, it would never happen like that," he scolded himself. As much as he desired for it to happen, he doubted the situation into which they advanced would allow for any warm reunions.

Now, after having journeyed for over a week, walking as long as daylight allowed and resting otherwise, the familiar waters of Corliss Lake and the South Sea could be seen from higher elevations and they knew that they would reach Seton before day's end. This realization seemed to play on their nerves and loosened their tongues a bit.

"Kira, I need to speak with you," stated Elson. The fact that he said he needed to speak with her rather than simply saying what he wanted to say put Kira on edge. It was obvious to everyone that he was distressed, and Conroy and Bethany also became uncomfortable, feeling that they had no business hearing what was about to be shared. But their presence didn't hinder Elson, and he continued to speak with no regard for them. "When we arrive, it can't be found out that you and I are married."

"Why?" Tears came quickly to her.

"If Idris finds out that I'm your husband, he'll surely have me killed."

"But you *are* my husband!" The tears rolled freely over both cheeks and down her neck.

Bethany took hold of Conroy's arm and led him away.

Elson saw they were leaving and called out to them; "Neither of you can ever reveal that Kira is my wife. Our marriage must remain a secret." Conroy and Bethany continued to depart without responding.

It was happening again. All the good things in her life were going to be swept away, just as they had been when she was brought here the first time. She hated Seton.

Elson turned his attention back to Kira and spoke gently; "Perhaps in time things will change."

"Will you let him take me back? Don't you want me? What about us being like the ash?"

There was something about her words that pierced his self-imposed, and naïve, belief that she'd not had any intimate experience with anyone other than him. "What do you mean *take you back*?"

"Idris and I were married!" She didn't care if he learned now; it was over! Let him know everything! Let the ash burn!

"You were married? Did you let him..." Elson couldn't get the words out. He wasn't prepared for this now.

"I didn't have a choice!" Kira was angry. He had no idea what she'd been through! It was for his own sake that she hadn't told him about her marriage to Idris.

"So our vows were counterfeit?"

"No, our vows were real. My marriage to Idris was counterfeit!"

Elson's heart ripped as he pictured Kira and Idris tangled in a naked embrace. He had to get away.

"Where are you going?"

Elson stomped off without giving reply. Kira sank down and sat on the large root of a nearby tree.

Conroy and Bethany noticed immediately that Elson was severely distraught; apparently his talk with Kira hadn't gone well.

"Conroy, come with me," spat Elson. It wasn't a request, and Conroy obeyed.

Bethany watched the two of them leave, heading toward the mountain, so she returned to Kira, who still sat sobbing on the root. She took a seat beside Kira and was immediately embraced.

"We were so happy. We could've had a wonderful life together."

"Elson loves you very much, he hasn't abandoned you," encouraged Bethany.

"He might now," challenged Kira.

"What do you mean?"

"He just found out that Idris and I were married."

Bethany took Kira's hand in hers and squeezed. "I was wondering if he knew about that."

"You knew?"

Bethany nodded.

"How?" Kira figured out the answer herself; "Lachlan."

Bethany nodded again.

"I didn't tell him until just now. I thought nothing good could come from revealing it to him, so I didn't tell him. I guess I was hurt at how easily he seemed to want to pretend that we're not married. Maybe I wanted to hurt him back."

"You succeeded."

"Well, it's better that he learned the truth from me, rather than from someone else. And what good could have come from telling him before?"

"If you had told him at first, he would have had a choice to make: either to accept you with your past, or not to. Either way, it would have been less hurtful for him."

"But if he knew, he might not have loved me."

"I think he would have."

"I wasn't willing to risk it. And I was ashamed."

"Now his pain is deep."

Kira pondered Bethany's words. For a few moments neither spoke.

"I don't want to go back. I don't want to be with Idris again," said Kira.

"And I don't want to be with Lachlan again," replied Bethany.

Elson and Conroy stood high up looking over the gorge, the mountaintop having been split so that it was now comprised of two, twin peaks. The sun was sinking fast, creating a glorious orange ball of flame that no longer blinded their eyes. From their vantagepoint they could see people making their way down to the village, and stayed away from the edge of the cliff to avoid being spotted.

"Have you been here since father died?" asked Elson.

Conroy shook his head.

"What happened to the mountain?"

"It wasn't like this when I passed through," answered Conroy.

"Look at the white rock – have you ever seen stone like that?"

"Yes," answered Conroy, "it's what the statue of King Iman is made of."

"I've seen it before too," said Elson, remembering his vision of the white tower.

Conroy didn't care about the rock and he didn't ask where Elson had seen it. He picked up a stone and flung it into the void of the chasm, thinking of his father plummeting in the same manner.

"Curse this place!" snapped Elson. Then he began looking around furiously for something, anything that he could keep to remember the place where his father's last moments had been spent. He finally found something - a solid, straight piece of wood, maybe a section of a tree branch. Wherever it came from, it made a good walking staff and he decided that it would become a memento of his father's death.

"Are you sure it was Warrick who brought news of father's death to Tilden?"

"I'm sure." It wasn't something Conroy would ever forget.

"But he was with me the whole time... unless he saw it happen right after he left me and Kira. That's when it must've happened! I was so close – I could've stopped it!"

"You couldn't have saved him," said Conroy.

Elson sighed, "No, probably not."

"Would it be appropriate if we said kind words to honor his life?" suggested Conroy.

Elson nodded. "You go first."

The two brothers stood beside each other, their hands folded in front of them and their heads bowed slightly. They faced west and gazed into the dimming sun.

"Father, I miss you," began Conroy. "I finished the statue, just as you asked. I wish you could see it; you'd be pleased. Thanks for teaching me to carve, and for teaching me about the things of the island and the Island Caretaker. I'll remember you with love and respect. If I ever have my own children, I hope that I might be as good a father as you were."

"You were a good father, and a good man," said Elson. "Conroy and I will look after mother. King Iman has given me a vision of peace, and I'll hold fast to the hope that what I've seen will come to pass. I'm going to carry this staff in honor of you, and I promise your death will be avenged."

"Vengeance is mine."

The brothers turned around to find out who had spoken. Darkness had crept in behind them and covered the mountaintop and they couldn't make out anything, for their eyes hadn't adjusted yet, but a fire suddenly erupted, the flames taking the shape of a man -

the burning creature stood before them. Though they had both seen and heard him speak before, they stood in awe.

After several moments, Elson recalled his anger and asked, hesitantly, "Will you avenge our father?"

"All of Justice's needs shall be satisfied."

"Who are you?" asked Conroy bravely.

"I am Elyon from the great city of Casilda. I am a companion to King Iman."

"Have you come to offer us his help, like you said before, the last time we met?" asked Elson.

"Yes. I will end the oppression of the Tildenians and destroy the Overlords."

"But it's said that Kavan gives them power," said Elson.

"He does." Elyon didn't seem swayed by the fact. "Go to your friends and tell them what I'm planning to do. Bring them here and I will destroy Seton. Afterward, you will all be free to live peacefully. Encourage them to trust in my power and assure them that no one will be harmed. I will show them that King Iman is alive and strong, and that he treasures their friendship."

"What about the island?" asked Conroy. "Will you restore it?"

"All will be restored."

Images of the island rising up from the deep to again divide the South Sea from Corliss Lake filled Elson and Conroy's minds. They believed in this creature, Elyon, and trusted that he could restore the isle - but when? Now wouldn't be soon enough.

"What if our friends are afraid to leave?" asked Elson.

Answering only with a loud hiss as he departed, Elyon burned up, disappearing into nothing. The sun had spent all of its light for the day and darkness reigned again in Elyon's absence. Feeling better than they had since beginning the journey, the two of them made their way down Great Falls' steep slope to rejoin Kira and Bethany, anxious to tell them about their meeting with Elyon.

It took them awhile to find their way back to the place where the girls were, but eventually they saw them and Elson called out.

Neither Kira nor Bethany replied. He wondered if Kira was still angry with him and refused to answer. As he came nearer he saw that their hands were bound, tied behind their backs, and their mouths were gagged.

"What happened to..."

A blow to the back of his shoulders sent Elson toppling forward to the ground. A new voice spoke; "Welcome back, lost islanders."

Elson picked himself up and saw Valena, holding a staff, accompanied by three men he didn't recognize, each carrying a silver and black sword like Bethany's. He glanced at Bethany to see if she had her sword ready to use. He didn't see it. "What's going on here?"

"A lot has changed since you've been gone," Valena replied.

"So I've heard," said Elson. "What's changed you so that you'd bind them and strike me?"

"I'll take great pleasure in informing you of all that's happened, but not now." She spoke a word that no one understood and three torches that the soldiers held ignited, then she turned to the man nearest her, "Take them to the village and put them with the other slaves."

"Slaves! Have you made your own friends and family slaves?" Another blow to his back from the broad side of a sword made Elson refrain from speaking further. He and Conroy were promptly bound in the same fashion as Kira and Bethany, then the Marlanders began leading them away. The joy that Conroy and Elson brought back from the mountain was lost.

Just before they came into the village, Valena took Kira and separated from the rest of the group. Bethany, Conroy, and Elson were taken to the far side of the village, past the large fire pit and the base of the tower, to the place where a high metal fence ran around a large open area; a number of small shacks were erected within. They could see people gathered around bonfires, but the scene was eerily quiet. Around the fence, eight Marlander guards patrolled and eight others stood watch. Four of them circled the perimeter clockwise, the other four patrolled in the opposite rotation, their pace and spacing equal so that there were always two guards on each side. At each of the four corners stood a pair of guards, gazing constantly along their respective side of the perimeter, thus maintaining a continuous watch over the full length of the fence.

The guards opened a gate and pushed the three captives inside. "Here's your new home."

"If you were wise, you'd get some rest tonight," said one of the other guards as he slammed the gate closed behind them, and the third guard moved in and secured the lock.

*   *   *   *   *   *   *   *   *   *   *

Kira struggled to break free from the square wooden post to which she was tied, one of four columns that supported the roof in the central part of Valena's cabin. She was puzzled as to why Valena had brought her there, and why she had done so in secret. At first she suspected that she was being taken straightaway to Idris so that she could resume her marital responsibilities with him, but that didn't seem to be what Valena intended. Still gagged, she was unable to inquire what Valena was doing, or to question what had been done with her companions.

The Overlord knelt on the floor before Kira, doubled over so that her forehead pressed against the cold floor, her fingers wrapped around her decorated magical shaft that she held at arm's length in front of her. She was whispering something, but Kira couldn't hear the words clearly, or didn't understand. On each side of Valena was a small table with a large bowl. Something burned inside the bowls and faint wisps of smoke floated upward from them. A strong aroma filled Kira's nostrils. Had she been anywhere else, she would have found its sweet scent delightful, but given her circumstance she despised the scent at once and forevermore - she knew she would remember this moment if ever she smelled it again. Suddenly, Valena stood up, shifted the staff to her left hand, and began to walk around Kira. She spoke with more volume, and Kira heard clearly:

> "Izurodovannost', pobedivshaia formu;
> Priiatnoi byla forma, a urodlivoi stala;
> Sognutoi, byvshaia pr'am' iskrivilas';
> Gliadelas', a stala vygliadet' ploho."

> "Krasota uviadaiet. Krasota uviadaiet. Krasota uviadaiet."

Valena's master was there. Like before, she couldn't see Kavan, but could feel his presence. She had opened herself to him and he put the words on her tongue. She delighted in the sensation, feeling his strength pass through her. The words came faster, and Valena's walk sped to a jog. Faster still came the incantation, and faster Valena ran:

"Izurodovannost', pobedivshaia formu;
   Priiatnoi byla forma, a urodlivoi stala;
   Sognutoi, byvshaia pr'am' iskrivilas';
   Gliadelas', a stala vygliadet' ploho."

"Krasota uviadaiet. Krasota uviadaiet. Krasota uviadaiet."

Kavan's attention shifted from Valena to Kira. Seeing her bound to the post recalled thoughts of Evelyn at the Renfrew - what pleasure he'd had in cutting her. He drew one of his swords.

"No." The single word, more of a crackling sound than a spoken word, made Kavan sheath the blade. Elyon was there too.

Kavan would let the woman live, but he would make it so she would rather have died.

Kira was changing. She didn't feel any pain, but knew something strange was happening to her. The view from her right eye decreased as the bridge of her nose rose up and to the side. Her back pressed differently into the post as her spine bent, the ropes pulled at her from new angles as she shrunk. Other things happened too, things she wasn't aware of: the skin around her eyes pulled back; her toes became gnarled; hair fell from her head; her legs grew bowed; her knees went knobby. When the transformation was complete, a ghastly figure, a gruesome imitation of Kira, remained.

Valena finished the chant and saw that its purpose was complete. She faced Kira, now towering over her by a full ten inches. "You've no reason to worry about Idris, he'll not desire you any more," she said, panting. She cut Kira loose and removed her gag. The smoke went into Kira's mouth and she almost threw up when her taste buds received the flavor. "But if he ever learns that I did this to you, I'll return you to the way you were and you can go back to being his wife. The choice is yours."

The smile that spread across Valena's heat-flushed face made Kira shudder. She attempted to walk, but it felt strange, as if the ground was uneven. It took a significant amount of concentration not to fall, but she made it outside and found the village center mostly vacant. She wandered about for a few minutes and came to the slaves' quarters, at least she assumed that was what it was, given the ridiculously rugged fence and the patrolling guards. A small part of her wanted to go and call for Elson, but the rest of her needed to observe what had been done to her before she presented herself to anyone, especially Elson.

An adequate inspection couldn't be done in the dark; it would have to wait until morning. Preferring not to spend the night in Seton, she ventured to her old favorite spot, the cove beside the sea. The sound of the waves soothed her raw nerves and she fell asleep quickly.

When dawn came, Kira rose with the sun and looked at her reflection in the clear water of the pool. Her screams sounded through the morning air all the way back to the village.

Things were good, very good. He was master of the land, doing what he wanted, when he wanted, with whomever he wanted. Others scrambled to do his bidding, be they Tildenian slave or Marlander subject. His followers were finally content now that they were well fed and rich with the booty taken from Tilden. But he didn't have everything he wanted – Idris had yet to taste the Icyandic.

He spoke to Valena daily of this and urged her to ask Kavan when the white River of Power would be made available. Valena was always hesitant to press the matter with Kavan. Idris respected her position, for she was Kavan's priestess and knew him better than any mortal. But he was also impatient and didn't refrain from making his daily request, hoping that one day Valena would agree to do as he asked. Until then, he would have to accept her usual reply, reminding him that the things promised to her and Lachlan had been given, so would his request be granted in time, for so had Kavan promised. Perhaps when the tower is complete the time will be right, he thought, but that would mean he'd have to wait years, even decades.

He stepped outside to go and meet Valena, savoring the recollection of the night before as he walked along - a slumbering brunette was left behind in his cabin. Marland maidens often flung themselves anxiously into his bed, sometimes several at once. And occasionally he brought them there when they weren't willing, but not this time – she'd been very eager, Darienne was her name, he thought. Valena didn't seem to mind the lustful games he played with them; she took comfort in knowing that he felt no affection for any of these women, and that none of them had a permanent role in his life. The Overlord *was* special to him, and he made sure that he kept her satisfied.

Passing by a group of slaves working to make mortar for the tower bricks, he threw his leg out and gracefully toppled a jug of water. None of the slaves dared issue a curse or complaint at the Overlord. Instead, the youngest of the three grabbed the empty vessel and ran straightaway to fill it up again, knowing they'd be given no exemption from completing their usual quota. Idris smirked and continued on his way.

It had become a sort of morning ritual for the three Overlords to meet, and doing so served dual purposes. First, it gave them an opportunity to discuss the progress on the tower as well as any other pertinent current events. Secondly, the sight of the three Overlords sitting together on their thrones, united in purpose, wearing the crowns bestowed on them by Kavan himself, and Valena with her special staff, reminded everyone of their authority. Idris saw Lachlan and Valena already there and he took his place between them on a white marble throne. "What news today?" he asked.

"More lost islanders were found last night," replied Valena.

"Good," said Idris. "Who?"

"Elson and Conroy Verrill," replied Valena, "and Kira and..."

"Kira! Why wasn't she brought to me?" Idris' outburst was tempered by his relationship with Valena. He didn't want to scold her, he needed her, but she offered no looks as pleasing as Kira.

"I knew you had a guest and I didn't want to interrupt," she said, not caring that her reply carried an obvious sour tone. But the bitterness in her voice dissolved as she spoke of Kira, as if she was sorry to tell Idris sad news; "Besides, she's not well; something's happened to her."

Lachlan resolved to keep silent – there was no place for him in this.

"What do you mean?" inquired Idris.

"She's not the same; her beauty has faded."

"How?"

Valena shook her head and shrugged her shoulders to indicate that she wasn't sure, which was partly true, but offered a possible explanation; "It could be that she's been punished."

"For what?"

"They were trying to hide their marriage," she said, "Elson and Kira. But it was revealed to me that she had forsaken her vows to you and was living as Elson's wife. I think she's been punished for what she's done."

"Where is she now?"

"Down by the cove."

Idris was off at once to find her, but Valena wasn't afraid that he would want Kira back. No one would ever desire to be with her now.

"What about Elson and Conroy? Where are they?" Lachlan's silence broke, out of curiosity, and also out of intent to distract Valena from Idris.

"With the other slaves, for now."

"Time for me to go as well," said Lachlan, straightening up in preparation to stand.

"No, Lachlan, wait."

The Overlord relaxed in his throne, anxious to hear what Valena was going to say, for she was obviously excited.

"I have more news. The lost glimmerstone blade was recovered! Bethany Krunser was with them, carrying the weapon!"

"Are you sure?" Lachlan's eyes grew intense and he jumped to his feet.

"Yes, of course." Valena assumed his excitement had been over the recovery of the precious sword, for she didn't know about his abduction of Bethany — he'd managed to keep that secret.

"Where is she now?"

"With the slaves, until a more permanent arrangement can be made."

Then he was off, just like Idris, to pursue a woman of his past.

Bethany was in the middle of a long line of wretched men. They were physically healthy, even strong, but starving to find joy in any part of their lives. Many had been separated from their loved ones, their wives were made available to any desiring Marlander, and their children were destined to share their unfortunate fate. The only fulfillment they found was in their work, even though it was forced on them, for the project was a truly magnificent one. The only woman among them, she was easily observed as such; her curled, yellow locks bouncing as she walked, and her shapely figure moving softer, more graceful, and with an altogether different type of stride than the men. Together they formed the quarry block transport.

She still carried the sword. Valena had been mistaken in assuming that her companion guards had discovered the weapon and confiscated it from her. The Overlord had been so concerned with Kira that she forget to instruct the soldiers to search for it, and when she saw that none of the four prisoners carried it, she thought that one of the guards must have collected it. So talented at manipulating the glimmerstone had Bethany become that she had caused it to transform into an innocuous looking garment - a wide belt, solid black in color, wrapped around her waist, even the handle had been modified to resemble a typical silver buckle assembly. Only the most talented soldiers could manipulate glimmerstone in such a manner, altering the shape of the host object, and certainly none of the four would have been suspected of having the ability.

It was because of her belt that she wasn't afraid. She believed she could fight her way past any number of these Marlanders if she needed to; weaklings and fools she thought them all, but to do so now would be brash and pointless, and would help none but herself. She hoped by spending some time in slavery and observing the practices of the oppressors she would gain valuable insight as to how she could use her blade to benefit her fellow captives in the most significant manner.

Today she would gain an understanding of the life of one enlisted in the quarry block transport. It might be the only day she would be made to work beside them though, for she had overheard the discussions about her last night. It seemed that all of the Tildenian women that had been brought to Seton had each been given specialized tasks, mostly to become household servants for the Marland homes. If she had a choice, she'd rather work with the men on the tower; she'd never enjoyed performing routine domestic chores. There hadn't been enough time for the slave masters to make more appropriate arrangements for Bethany; it was easiest for them to toss her in with the male laborers for a short time. Tomorrow she expected she would be given a new assignment.

When she reached the base of the gorge, halfway up the mountainside, she took a cart and went to fill it with marble blocks, freshly hewn, for she saw that was what all of her companions were doing. She paused, though, when she caught a full view of the gorge walls; it was an amazing scene, one like she'd never beheld. She stood in silent awe for a few moments as her eyes drank in the picture of the white walls contrasting with the dark river bottom between them. They were relatively smooth, except for the areas where the workers had removed slivers of stone from base to top.

But even here it was beautiful, for the rock had been removed to expose only more white marble beneath, pure and strong.

Her apparent daze attracted the attention of nearby taskmaster, whose whip snapped against her lower back. It would have stung badly, but it hit mostly against the glimmerstone belt. Bethany turned to see who had struck her, placing her hand on her back and feigning more pain than she really felt, and was surprised to see a familiar face.

"Oren?" She asked, though she knew it *was* him. She had always been fond of him, and remembered wishing that she'd been betrothed to him. Instead, Oren had married Deryn, one of her good friends.

"Don't speak my name, it's forbidden. Just keep moving and don't say anything to anyone." His instruction was sincere, not an angry scolding. She could see in his eyes that he wasn't pleased with his position, and in that moment of interaction she understood that he was a man trapped.

She returned to work, using all of her strength to wrestle the heavy chunks of stone into her wagon, then lifting its handles and rolling it down to the village. It was difficult to make even the first trip, how she'd be able to do this for the whole day, she couldn't imagine.

Her full strength returned, however, when she arrived at the base of the tower and found him waiting there. Patience was put aside as her emotions roared – the feelings and memories swarmed too quickly for her to manage. She let go of the handles of the cart and it toppled over and the bricks crashed loudly to the ground. The blade unwrapped itself from her waist and went to her waiting hand, recovering its silver streaks to make its transformation complete. Everyone backed away from her, slaves and soldiers, everyone except him; Lachlan walked toward her.

"What are you..."

He was stunned that Bethany would attack him, but before he could ask her what she intended to do, she was upon him, her sword swung deftly in the air toward his royal head.

The blade didn't meet its intended target – a Marlander guard ran to help when he saw Bethany lunging at the Overlord and parried her strike. She regrouped and dealt a quick blow to the guard's head with the handle of her sword, dropping him to the ground unconscious. But this allowed Lachlan time, and when she next saw him he had drawn his own black and silver blade.

Again she launched herself at this man she despised, delivering stroke after stroke upon him with inhuman speed, intending to kill. She wanted him to die!

Lachlan defended himself, but no one else moved to interfere. Few, if any, of his trained men wielded the glimmerstone as well as she, he thought, and this made his desire for her stronger than ever.

He was good, Bethany realized, after every one of her attacks had been thwarted; she needed to try harder. She lifted the blade high over her head and brought it down toward Lachlan. His sword was easily brought into position to block the blow, but that's what she wanted. Focusing as intensely as she could, she imagined the black material of her sword pulling apart the steel where it would meet Lachlan's, and reforming it again when it passed the trailing edge, moving it unhindered through his defense. It had taken only the smallest of a fraction of a moment, and she should have been victorious, she knew, but she wasn't, for her blade landed on the three-studded crown, on the central black gem, and instead of ripping through it to reach the bone of his skull, the sword stopped as if there was a silent truce between it and the gem. In that moment that should have witnessed her triumph, she knew she had lost.

Surprise gave way to anger when he understood that she had intended to kill him, and had nearly succeeded. Lachlan took to the offensive.

Bethany did well to fend off his attacks, but he fought with new determination and she knew she couldn't last much longer. There was only one thing she could do that would give her even the slightest victory. She withdrew a few paces from her adversary, and Lachlan gave her time and space, for he was cautious, then she spun around in a half circle, her eyes closed but her mind focused, and let the sword fly. At least they won't recover the sword, she thought, as she saw it sailing over the trees to the east.

She collapsed to the ground, her hopes dashed, broken with the belief that there was no chance for her to help now; how could she without the sword? She stared at the ground, anticipating Lachlan to come and carry her off to be his prisoner once more.

A hand grasped her under her arm and lifted her up. "Back to work, slave!" It was the guard that she had knocked down.

She looked for Lachlan. He remained standing in the same spot as before, his sword hanging limply in a relaxed grip. Without a word, he turned and walked away, a perplexed look distorting his face.

Bethany righted her cart and put the fallen bricks back before the whip of the guard scourged her backside - she knew it would hurt now that her belt was gone.

*   *   *   *   *   *   *   *   *   *   *

Kira wished she could stay beside the cove by herself forever. But she knew it wouldn't be long before people came to collect water to take back to the village. The pool was the closest spot for them to obtain fresh water, easily drawing it from the calm cove, the last gathering place of the streams that flowed from northern Marland before entering the brackish South Sea. Whether those who would come would be Marlanders or Tildenian slaves she didn't know, not that it would matter - she'd likely feel the same amount of shame regardless of who saw her. To delay that event, she rounded the corner of the pool and went to the south end of the bay where the cove and sea merged, the point farthest from where the people would draw water. Perhaps they wouldn't see her, and even if they did, they probably wouldn't come and talk to her.

For a time she gazed out at the distant land across the water, drawing as much joy as she possibly could from memories of her family and friends there, then the first intruder arrived. She was surprised that he carried no vessel to fill with water, not even a small flask for his own use. He looked her way and spotted her. Kira's heart raced when he quickened his pace and advanced straight toward her calling out, "Kira! Kira!"

Her effort to flee was pathetic; her crooked legs and twisted feet couldn't obey her mind's commands to them to be swift.

"Kira!"

A hand grasped her shoulder and turned her around. Beside the sea, with waves crashing before them, Kira and Idris were reunited.

Idris winced in disgust and removed his hand from her when he caught the full sight of her disfigured face. Her big eyes, so beautiful before, now seemed too large, almost popping out of the sunken sockets of her gaunt face. He stared her down, his gaze dropping from her face to her feet and then climbing back up again to her eyes. "What happened to you?"

Idris' distaste for her appearance suddenly made Kira feel relieved and, for the moment at least, she was glad that she had been transformed.

"I..." Kira hesitated. "I'm not sure." It was the first time she spoke out loud since having been changed – even her speech had grown distorted, and she had to work hard to make the sounds intelligible.

"Did Elson do this?"

What did he mean by that? Did he know about her and Elson? Kira shook her head promptly.

"It *is* because of Elson, isn't it? You cast aside the vows you made to me. Now look what's happened - you've been punished!" The tone of Idris' voice changed, abandoning any sense of loss for her, or pity.

Kira turned away to face the cove. Others had arrived and they all were staring at her, so she turned back to Idris. "What will become of me?"

He looked at her and considered her limited dexterity and gestured to her knotted hands. "You can't work, not with those. You'll remain here in Seton and be a symbol of what happens to anyone who wrongs me."

"What about Elson?"

"Your husband? It will be most fitting for you two to be together, and I'll make sure all of Marland knows that you're his."

*   *   *   *   *   *   *   *   *   *   *

"Isn't our answer clear, young Verrill?" Linus was beginning to get angry at Conroy's refusal to accept their decision. A large group sat around a raging fire that was being used simultaneously for illumination and for cooking the meat that the guards had thrown them. Elson and Warrick sat beside Conroy, and Bethany was there too – the Marlanders had not yet removed her from the slave camp, but she was sure that she'd be taken away at any time for a special task that involved Lachlan in some way. All of the old Island Council members were there as well, but they sat in silence while Linus spoke on their behalf. His raspy voice was well suited for speaking quietly, and the guards pacing past didn't hear. "Since your return, you've plagued us every night with talk of this creature, Elyon. I used to think that the long days of work would wear down your hope in him, but it seems I was wrong, for you're not relenting. You *are* Ansen's boy."

"So I've been told. I'll consider it a compliment, though I don't think that's what you intended." Tonight Conroy wasn't going to let the subject be chewed over again, weighed again, and eventually dropped again, for that's what happened every night before. Time was up - this was their last chance, as far as he could see. "Why are you being so stubborn? Why won't you believe in Elyon?"

"Because we've never met him! We've never heard him speak or burn or crackle or whatever you say he does! We've no proof that he's even real, yet alone that he's strong enough to do what you say he can. We're not about to risk our lives because of rumors that someone is out there," he waved his hand at the darkness outside the camp, "who *might* be able to help us!" Linus recoiled for a moment, drew another breath and lashed out again; "For us to do what you want would be outright foolish." He turned to Keelan, who sat between Warrick and Bethany. "And you! You've never seen this Elyon thing either, how can you have such a blind faith as to risk your life trusting in him?"

"Elyon need not be seen to be known. Not all things that are real are visible - my faith might be blind, but it's not dumb!" answered Keelan. "Aside from that, I know Warrick and Elson and Conroy." He glanced at the three men across the fire. "I trust them. I believe them. I'm ready to leave with them."

Frustrated, Linus shook his head and looked to other members of the council to see if any of them had something to say. Wendel was sitting beside Linus and was writing feverishly. The days of toil had trimmed his chubby belly, though his round face and thick, bushy curls of hair allowed him to keep a seemingly robust appearance. "Why do you insist on writing everything in that book of yours?"

Wendel's reply was well rehearsed; "It's what I can do with what I've been given to serve my king for the benefit of others."

"How is your writing going to benefit others?" Linus asked curiously.

"I don't know yet, but I believe it will. Besides, the task was appointed to me by King Iman, remember?" Wendel put down his quill, folded his book closed, and looked to see where the guards were to make sure it was kept hidden from them.

"You may not have met Elyon, but he represents King Iman, the Island Caretaker," said Warrick. "Surely you remember him, and he wouldn't send someone to us who's powerless to help."

"That's right," added Elson, "remember the legend – how the king established the island in all of its magnificence; how he set his servants to watch over it; how he brought our kind to it. Remember all the wonderful things we saw him do there afterward during his visits; and most of all, remember how he overcame Kavan's rebellion and banished him from the island? Elyon's here with all the power of the king to do his will. He has no fear of Kavan, I saw that myself, and if we trust him with our lives we should have no reason to be afraid of Kavan either, nor those who serve him."

"But you've all been out there in the wilderness, exposed to something that's twisted your perceptions of reality," replied a tall, thin man called Blotcher. He waved his arms dramatically as he spoke. "You claim to have seen a man of living fire, fire!" he gestured to the flames between them, "and Warrick, you said you saw Lucy alive after she'd been buried! This is a strange new world, and we're still learning about its nature, but the things that you've said happened just don't happen! How can you expect us to go with you?"

"So it's not strange for Kavan, or one of his horde, to suddenly appear and kill one of us, but it's too far fetched for King Iman to have an ally such as Elyon, who might come and offer us aid?" retorted Warrick, now angry at Blotcher for speaking about his treasured memory of his last moments with Lucy.

"That's different," answered Linus.

"How?" challenged Elson.

"Kavan's been around ever since the island fell," explained Linus. "King Iman came to us once, and that was before we were assaulted. Where was he then? If he planned to keep us safe, that was the moment he should have come to help. If Elyon is real and able to offer us aid, then why hasn't he appeared to us? Why would he ask us to leave and risk our lives?"

"You don't know what they're capable of! You weren't here to see what their black blades can do!" said Blotcher as he pointed to Elson and Conroy and Bethany.

"We know well enough what they can do!" rebutted Bethany.

"There's been enough debating," said Conroy. "It's the same excuses all the time! You'll never believe!"

"All you need to do is leave!" pleaded Elson. "What's the worst thing that could happen if you try?"

"We could be killed! Our families could be killed!" said Linus.

"Elyon said that none of us would get hurt," said Elson.

"I may be younger than you all, but I'm wise enough to know that it's better to try and fail than to cower in fear and be paralyzed!" declared Conroy. "That's something I learned the hard way. Be brave enough to risk a better life, follow me!" Conroy leapt to his feet, trampling on his dinner meat.

"Now?" several asked in unison.

"Right now!" answered Conroy.

Warrick, Elson, Bethany, and Keelan all stood up with Conroy. Following his lead, they turned away from the fire to face east toward Great Falls and began pacing steadily for the fence. Linus, Wendel and the others remained sitting around the fire, watching their departure in disbelief and murmuring how brash they were and how they'd not live to see the morning once the guards caught them. Surely they'd soon feel glimmerstone whips tearing away their flesh, and maybe Valena's staff.

The advance of the renegades remained as steady as that of the two guards marching along the eastern side of the compound. They were heading directly to the center of the fence, right to the spot where the two guards would meet.

"They're mad!" declared Linus.

Conroy continued to lead them. None looked toward either of the two guards, nor did they look back at their faithless friends. When they had first arisen they were compelled by a desire to demonstrate their trust in Elyon. They didn't know what would happen; they only felt that it was time to act. But now, in a matter of a few seconds and a few steps, they were being driven by a power that did not fear death.

The rugged, formidable fence lay only a yard in front of Conroy. The approaching guards flanked them, only twenty feet away on either side. Suddenly, Conroy saw the fence rip open from top to bottom right before him. He walked through the sundered boundary without slowing, followed closely by his companions.

Sandor's sword cut so easily through the steel barrier that all he had to do was drag the blade down the fence, pressing it lightly and twisting it so that it spread wide for his master's friends to pass. When they had come through, he moved his hand back down the length of the ripped seam and glanced at his officers to make sure they had their tasks managed. They did – four other of the king's servants had covered the eyes of the Marland guards so that they could not see the Tildenians escape – they could see everything else, just not the five departing slaves.

Linus blinked hard several times and rubbed his eyes. He looked at his fellow council members to see if they'd also seen it – they had. Together, they stared at the guards in anticipation that they would cry out that some slaves were escaping. But no cries were issued and no pursuit was given. The two guards marched straight by the place where the fence had been severed. Wait! Now the fence was whole again!

Linus and Blotcher stood up and went to follow Conroy, now regretting that they hadn't done so initially. The others followed, but found that the fence was solid and they couldn't pass.

"What do you think you're doing? Get away from there!" The next pair of guards passing by saw the slaves easily enough and one of them poked a glimmerstone whip into Linus' thigh hard enough to draw blood. "Do I need to come inside?"

Linus shook his head to reassure the guard there was no need for that, then, limping, led his friends back to the fire.

Bethany and Keelan had never seen Elyon before and were anxious to behold him. The group reached the peak of Great Falls efficiently, in spite of the darkness, and rested for awhile in silent anticipation. When they had been still long enough for their hearts to slow to a calm rhythm, a crackling sound sent their pulses racing even faster than before.

"Well done, my faithful friends!" said Elyon, "Where are the rest?" His presence lit up the mountaintop.

"We've failed you!" cried Elson, tears welling in his eyes. "They haven't come! They were too afraid."

"Their fear is no failure on your account. You've done exactly as I asked, and some have come."

Bethany and Keelan shrunk backward to hide behind Elson and Warrick as Elyon's orange eyes shifted in their direction.

"I'm pleased with all who are here, and you shall rule over this land yourselves, once I've purged it from the corruption festering here." Elyon clenched his fists and the crackling of his flames became louder as he grew in stature twofold.

"No, wait!" begged Warrick. "Please don't destroy our friends."

Elyon stared at Warrick, who felt his legs beginning to fold beneath the powerful gaze.

"They haven't done anything deserving of death," added Elson, "please spare them."

Elyon's eyes passed from Warrick to Elson.

"They don't know you! They've never met you before – surely if they had, they would have fled Seton and come with us," said Conroy. "And imagine what the Marlanders will say about those who are friends with King Iman if you, his ally, destroy them!"

Again, Elyon's gaze shifted, this time to fall on Conroy. The violence of his crackling subsided as he shrunk to his former size. His fiery fingers unfurled from angry fists and at last he responded; "I would have destroyed all of Seton for your sake, and you would have lived prosperously there in peace. But you have perspective beyond yourselves, and that is honorable. I will spare Seton for your sake, so that others there may be freed to live with you in peace. But the time for that will not come soon, and you'll have to return there for awhile. Are you willing to do that?"

"If it means that our friends can be saved, then yes," answered Warrick.

"We'll endure the evils of Seton for their sake," added Elson.

"Very well." Elyon stepped in close to Elson and Warrick and raised his hands to rest them upon their heads. Just as they experienced once before, a vision of a tall white tower came into their minds, along with a burning sensation deep inside them. And as before, they found themselves transported into the topmost room of the tower where they were joined by Justin, and together the three of them encircled a giant sparkling diamond suspended in the air above them. Outside, far below, a vast assembly cheered for them. Oppression was no more – now there was peace!

Elyon lowered his hands and the vision dropped from the mens' minds. "Remember what I've shown you – it will come to pass." Then, in his usual manner, Elyon disappeared, bursting into a raging ball of embers and sizzling violently as he vanished.

         *   *   *   *   *   *   *   *   *   *   *

Linus stared at the fire. His belly was full, and the warmth of the blaze was comforting. It had come to be the most pleasant part of his toilsome life – the end of the day when his thoughts could be his own, no cursed glimmerstone-weapon-wielding Marlander barking orders at him.

The fire seemed to grow suddenly taller without any fuel having been added.

"Did you see that?" asked Wendel. Those that had watched Conroy and the others depart remained sitting around the fire. Many minutes had been spent discussing how dreadful it would be when the escaped prisoners were caught and brought before the Overlords. The initial feelings of regret, sharp at first, dulled as they repeatedly pronounced how foolish those that had left had been, even after they had seen them walk through the fence. *'Must've been a rip there that they weren't aware of,'* reasoned Blotcher. As time passed, this explanation took root in the minds of those who refused to leave, even in spite of the impression they first had immediately after observing the fence split apart before Conroy and close up behind Keelan.

Wendel had finally finished recording the events of the evening in his book and tucked it and his quill into the secret pouch in his shirt when he glanced up to observe the fire had grown strangely fierce. "Linus, did you see that?" he asked once more.

Linus, his expression of one lost deep in thought, looked at Wendel to see him gesture toward the fire. It was large – much larger than it should have been, and it began to crackle louder and louder, causing the Tildenians to back away. From within the center of the burning pillar a human figure emerged. From outside the compound, all that the marching guards could see was a bonfire, slightly larger than usual, but nothing gave them cause to be suspicious, for Elyon's back blended in with the other flames.

"Why were you afraid? Why didn't you believe that I'd come to help?" Elyon looked to Linus and Wendel for an answer.

"All we had was the testimony of two men and a boy. How can you expect us to wager our lives with only that?" replied Linus, his bold response fueled by fear and guilt and shame.

"If I had sent ten upright and worthy and truthful men who pleaded with you to trust me would you have come?"

Linus didn't know.

"If I had sent a hundred men would you have believed then?"

Linus still didn't know.

"We had reason to doubt the testimony of the three." Linus was exceedingly glad to hear Wendel speak up.

"Why would you doubt Elson and Warrick and Conroy? Do you not all know them to be upright and worthy and truthful?"

"We do, but – you see, they all journeyed into the Marland wilderness for days and days, and when they emerged they were full of talk of visions of strange things that seemed unlikely to have happened. Their perceptions of reality seemed skewed," explained Wendel.

"The testimony of the three was sufficient," declared Elyon. "I desire to destroy this place tonight, along with all who dwell here, so that this filth will be gone, but I will not – the five people who came to me on Great Falls, the five you did not trust, have begged for your lives to be spared."

No one dared speak.

"You've chosen to stay here, so here you shall stay." With a loud hissing sound, Elyon burned away. The guards paused from marching to observe the commotion, only to see the group of Tildenians somberly encircling a shrinking bonfire. It wasn't an uncommon sight and they resumed marching.

Suddenly, the shrill sound of shearing metal pierced the camp. Through a newly ripped seam in the fence, at the very spot where Conroy and the other four exited, a large, horned beast came bounding. It moved at full speed toward the campfire. The Tildenians barely had time to turn toward it before Elzib arrived. His attention focused on the man nearest him, Blotcher. Bellowing like an ox, he lowered his shoulders and drove one of his spikes through the helpless councilman.

Elzib straightened up and savored Blother's blood trickling out of his twitching body and down his ivory horn. When it was close enough to his face, he licked it with a long tongue and delighted in its flavor and warmth. When he was satisfied, he threw the corpse down, hard, so that it skidded along the ground and slammed into the shins of the horrified Tildenians. Then he issued a long bellow as he ran back through the broken fence, sealing it up again behind him, and disappeared.

Later that night, Conroy and his companions arrived to find the camp in disarray. No one saw them enter the grounds, and it wasn't clear how they had returned. They joined the others to bury Blotcher and offer kind words of farewell. Then they all went to sleep, for they knew the next day would be a long one.

His legs were heavy and each time he took a step it seemed he wouldn't be able to summon the strength to take another, but Justin continued even though his body resisted the decision to keep moving. The heat of the midsummer's day kept his muscles limber, but also drew perspiration down the sides of his face and neck, stinging his eyes and skin where he was freshly shaven. He led the way, carrying his staff – the familiar relic of Evelyn's gravesite, gripped tight by his right hand. Emily trailed behind, keeping distance enough to allow young Bernal and Elana to walk between her and Justin.

"What will happen to us when we get there?" Justin's tone revealed his nerves.

Emily shrugged her shoulders. "We'll have to wait and see," she said plainly.

She misunderstood – it was his fault, he hadn't been clear, but her stoic response to the question as she interpreted it irritated Justin. "I meant, what will happen to *us*?" He winced at his insecurity. "We've never acted on our feelings, we haven't even talked about it, but I know they're there, and so do you." He felt naked, exposed - maybe his perceptions had been wrong. "Or do you want to be rid of me?"

Emily stared at Justin, who had stopped walking and turned to look back at her. His face was contorted with anxiety. "Do you think I've encouraged you to come back here so that you'll be rightly punished? Do you think I hope you'll be taken away, while I rejoin old friends and live peacefully, apart from you?"

Bernal and Elana took advantage of the pause to find a place to sit and rest their tired little legs.

"Why'd you keep persuading me to return? You'll be a hero for bringing me back so the Council can execute judgement against me." He'd lost control of his emotions, and the words spewed from his fearful and desperate heart; "You've got no feelings for me at all, do you?"

"I've encouraged you to return for *you*, not me!" Emily was angry now too. "It's for your own good that I kept telling you to come back - so that you can get free of the guilt that's weighing you down!"

Suddenly, a wave of peace flowed over Justin and his reeling emotions calmed. He owed her an apology; "I'm sorry - I'm just scared."

Emily leaned into him and wrapped her arms around his neck. Her forehead pressed against his lips as she pulled her body close to his. "I'm not going to leave you. I don't want to be apart from you - you're my new partner in this world."

Justin felt a surge of strength. "If they all hate me, I won't care, as long as I know that you don't."

"It's not too late to turn back."

Justin thought about the pair of cabins, vacant and lifeless, and longed to be there, far away from the shame he was about to face.

Carollan grabbed hold of the cords in Justin's mind and squeezed. Intense images of the nightmare were projected into his thoughts. "Don't even think of turning around - I'll not permit it!"

The sight of his friends struggling and the sound of the accursed laughter pushed aside recollections of the cabins and reminded Justin of his purpose. "No, you're right. I have to do this if I want to find freedom."

    *   *   *   *   *   *   *   *   *   *   *

"You have a visitor!" A glimmerstone whip wrapped around Elson's waist and pulled him from the edge of the tower where he was perched to carefully lay a marble block in place. The whip cast him down on the newly completed ground floor of the tower, and the white brick that he'd been positioning fell beside him and split in two. "Your wife's here!" shouted the guard, amused that the slaves would have to replace the block.

The fall didn't hurt as much as the pain of discovering that his marriage to Kira had been found out - he gave no heed to the lost stone. She must've told them, he thought. A mix of fear and anger and desire took hold - he hadn't seen her for several weeks, not since the night they were captured by Valena and brought to Seton. He picked himself up and quickly glanced around to look for her.

Kerjem, the guard that had pulled Elson aside with his whip, playfully nudged one of his companions, "Watch this."

With their masters' focus temporarily elsewhere, the slaves stopped working so they could also observe.

Elson's eyes found the only woman around, but she wasn't his wife. The crippled figure limped awkwardly toward him. "Can I help you?" Elson addressed the woman, but found his eyes turning away from her detestable face. He hoped she wouldn't be offended by the sour expression that he sensed overtook him.

"It's me, Kira."

Kerjem's grin widened when he saw the expression on Elson's face change from bewilderment to shock to sorrow. Kerjem nodded to his companion, confirming that the reunion had been something special to witness, "Quite a beauty he's got there!"

The other guard laughed, then noticed the workers had ceased working. "Enough fun! Back to work! The tower isn't gonna build itself!"

The slaves obeyed quickly, returning to work before their backsides felt the sting of punishment.

Elson raised his gaze to study the woman's face, and after a long moment, which Kira bore with tolerant humility, recognized the once fine features of the woman he'd married. Only her lips remained unchanged – those soft, warm lips that he had so many times touched with his own.

"It happened the night we came back," Kira broke the awkward silence. Elson had to concentrate to understand her slurred speech. "I couldn't bear for you to see me like this. That's why I've stayed away."

He raised his hands to her face and caressed her cheeks. "How did this...?"

"I think it was because I abandoned my betrothed. At least he doesn't want me anymore. Do *you* still want me?" She couldn't believe she said it - she hadn't intended to, "No! Don't answer! I couldn't bear it if I knew you didn't."

"But why hasn't anything happened to me?" he asked, glad that Kira had revoked the question.

"You weren't betrothed to anyone."

Just then a young man ran up to Kerjem and whispered something in his ear.

"But today I *had* to come," she explained, grabbing his arm. "I've seen Justin! He's come back!"

"Are you sure?" He didn't wait for confirmation; "You've got to tell him to get away from here – as far away as he can!"

"It's too late. He's being taken to the Overlords."

"Elson!" snapped Kerjem, "Follow me! Now! Bring your wife!"

Elson took Kira's arm to help her walk swift enough to keep up with Kerjem and the boy that had brought the message, Norris, a red headed fifteen-year old who had taken Brant's place as Idris' personal servant. As they made their way back down to the village, Elson found himself contemplating Kira's transformation and Justin's return – combined, the events put his mind into a tumultuous swirl.

When they came into town, Elson saw that a crowd of Marlanders had gathered around the fire pit and the Overlords, and noticed that Warrick was being led toward them.

It was evident to Elson that Warrick had not yet heard of Justin's return, and when he saw his old friend his face lit up with joy and he dashed forward to greet him, ignoring threats from Marlanders he pushed aside.

Justin heard the commotion and started to turn around, but before he knew what was happening Warrick wrapped him in a strong embrace.

"Break it up!" called Lachlan as he rose from his throne to separate the two friends.

Norris kept Kira at the perimeter of the crowd beside Emily, Elana, and Bernal, while Kerjem led Elson through the crowd to Warrick and Justin. Elson's desire to greet Justin was put down by Lachlan's presence.

"Welcome to Seton!" Idris sat smugly on top of the wall behind the fire pit in the center, and tallest, of three stone chairs. He nodded subtly to Lachlan, a silent command for him to return to his seat. Valena sat on Idris' left, and Lachlan, understanding Idris, obediently resumed his place on Idris' right. "I've often wondered if you were still alive."

"I am," replied Justin.

"I'm not surprised, but I doubted I'd ever see you again. Why have you come back?"

Silence followed as Justin let the words he had so many time rehearsed form in his mind – they seemed hard to find now that the time for them had come. Finally he began; "It's my fault the island is gone. It's because of me that we're here. I'm very…"

"We all know about your visit to the Renfrew," Idris interrupted. "There's no reason for you to be sorry about that – in fact, we wish to thank you." The Overlords nodded in unison, a slight bow to show their gratitude.

"What?" Justin was taken aback. He looked to Elson.

"I told them everything."

Justin turned back to Idris, "Why are you happy about what has happened?"

"You freed us," answered Valena, "from the Caretaker's spell that kept us from knowing Scynn."

"Scynn?"

"You knew it as the Unknown Creature! It was the very symbol of your island team!" exclaimed Idris. "It is master of this land now, along with Kavan!"

"Those monsters that took Evelyn! You serve those beasts?"

"They gave us glimmerstone and empowered us as Overlords," replied Idris. "They showed me a vision of the tower that is now being built – a structure suited to become our home; a place that will bring glory to our masters."

"The tower is not for you," declared Warrick.

The Overlords, stunned by the brash claim, glared at Warrick.

"I've been given a different vision."

Valena retrieved her staff and pounced from the dais in a graceful leap to confront Warrick. Her height matched his and she stared evenly into his resolute eyes. "Tell me what you saw."

Warrick took a deep breath, then spoke without blinking; "On the highest level of the tower was a giant diamond, a raging flame contained within. Around the jewel were three who ruled over the land. There was peace, and the people loved and respected the three."

"That image is the same that Idris has seen!" Valena scoffed.

"In my vision, the three rulers weren't you – they were Elson, Justin, and I. We will dwell in the tower and rule the people!"

No sooner had Warrick finished speaking than Valena's staff struck his shins so hard that his legs were knocked out from beneath him and he collapsed to the ground.

"Blasphemer!" cried Valena. "By whose power will your vision come to pass? Who is stronger than Scynn and Kavan?"

Warrick stood up slowly, not allowing himself to reach for his legs and rub where they were sore.

But it was Elson that answered; "Elyon gave us the vision. I also saw this."

Valena moved toward Elson, her long staff at the ready. *"Elyon?"*

"He's a companion of King Iman." Elson watched Valena's staff and wondered if it would strike him.

Her anger became derision and she didn't lift the staff to hit him. "What you saw was only a dream – Iman has no power to make it real." She pivoted to return to the dais and Elson began to relax, but she extended the staff backward, jabbing at Elson without looking behind her, landing a blow solidly in his chest. "Don't speak of the dream again!"

"It's not our desire to harm you," said Idris. "You have freed us, as Valena said, and we wish to honor the three of you as our liberators."

"Their loyalty to Iman concerns me," warned Lachlan.

"Unfortunate," answered Idris, "but nothing to worry about. However, Seton is not the place for them - they'll have to be taken to Tilden."

Lachlan nodded.

"But they won't be made to work," added Idris. "They deserve to enjoy life free from Iman's curse; maybe in time they'll understand our perspective and we can be friends."

"No! Don't honor me," begged Justin, falling to his knees before the Overlords. "I want to work!"

Valena leaned in close to Idris and whispered, "They'll be too far away for me to watch closely, and they shouldn't be given too much freedom to stir up rebellion."

"The Tildenians have a tradition of building a bonfire at dusk, it seems they're afraid of the darkness of night," said Idris. "You three will be responsible for this fire from tomorrow forward."

"Kerjem!" Lachlan summoned the guard. "Take them, along with Justin's companions to Tilden," he gestured to Emily and her children.

"Take Kira as well," added Idris. "Let her be with her husband. Besides, she's making all of our women jealous of her beauty."

The laughter of the crowd didn't hurt too much; Kira was already growing accustom to such foul treatment. Elson came and took hold of her arm again, and as she turned to leave she looked at Valena - the Overlord had an air of satisfaction about her, but Kira detected a subtle warning in her eyes, cautioning her to remember her threat. Things could be worse, she thought. As it was, she was leaving Seton with Elson to go to Tilden, where Amara and her parents waited. Yes, things could be much worse.

Shortly afterward, a transport ship departed from the Marland docks and began the passage to Tilden. Other than Kerjem, the crew consisted of the usual men - Lachlan had ordered the senior officer to oversee the vessel's mission personally. He had obeyed, of course, but there was no need for him to watch over the cargo in the hold below - the restraints were adequate and there was nowhere for them to escape. He lingered among the crew for awhile, then, when he grew weary of their company, retired to a private room and went to sleep.

In the lowest level of the ship, seven slaves sat chained together, rocking up and down and back and forth with the constant movement of the sea. Besides them, the only things occupying the space were several rows of large, empty crop baskets. They had been joined together by a single chain encircling the large shaft of the mainsail, which penetrated each deck above and was fixed to the floor.

The trip would take several hours, and they saw their situation as one that afforded ample time to discuss all that had happened. Sad news flowed in every direction with talk of Lucy, Ansen, Evelyn, Russel, and MacGowan. Justin talked about his nightmares, and Warrick and Elson shared about their encounters with Elyon and the vision he'd given them.

After all the news had been shared, Warrick, Justin, and Emily reclined to join Elana and Bernal in getting some rest – the children had fallen asleep with the locking of the chain. Of the adults, only Warrick fell asleep quickly; Justin and Emily were both exhausted, but were having a difficult time relaxing.

Kira and Elson were wide awake with much to say still. They withdrew from the others as much as possible to speak privately; "Do you really believe this happened to you because of me?" he asked.

"That may be part of it," responded Kira, her words as misshapen as her face.

"Why else?"

She hesitated, then decided she could trust him with the truth, after all, he was her husband. "Valena did this so that Idris wouldn't want me."

"Does she really have such power?"

Kira nodded. "Sometimes I'm glad. I couldn't go on living if he took me again, not while my heart belongs to you." She looked at Elson and longed to ask him if he still loved her – she was discovering that it was impossible for her to keep this question caged.

Elson sensed her unspoken query, but wasn't sure if he was ready to answer. "I couldn't bear for you to be with him either, but I can't rejoice in what's been done to you."

"There's something I should tell you," Kira dropped her gaze to the wooden planks of the floor. "I've known about your father's death all along. I saw it happen." Tears, sized proportionately to her eyes, trickled down both of her cheeks. "It had just happened when you found me. I was scared and confused. I wanted you to come with me, and I knew that you wouldn't if you found out." She continued to stare at the floor. "I'm sorry."

Elson felt pity for her. In spite of her disfigurement he recognized her as the woman he married. There wasn't a physical attraction, no, that was gone, but he found that he loved her. "You're the one who told Warrick what happened?"

She nodded frantically and the streams of tears that clung to her face fell to add marks to her soiled blouse.

"I won't leave you." He drew her to him and put his arms around her twisted frame. "I'll take care of you."

"I guess you were right; the winds of trouble have started blowing against us."

"We're still standing."

She nuzzled in close to him, and neither of them said anything else for several minutes.

"I'm scared to see my parents," she said at last, after her tears had stopped. "You can't tell them what Valena did."

"Will you say that it's because of our marriage, and that you've been punished?"

"That wouldn't be fair to you," she answered, "and it's not true. I'll say simply that it happened to me the night I came back to Seton, but that I don't know how. That is the truth, mostly."

On the opposite side of the hold, Emily, not yet asleep, observed Kira and Elson embrace. A warmth swept over her and she turned aside and tugged at Elana to draw her up so that the girl's head rested on her lap. Remaining wrapped in slumber, Elana exhaled and shifted to obtain a more comfortable position under her mother's arms.

Then, without fully realizing what she was doing, Emily leaned back and her head pressed against Justin's chest. Suddenly she felt as if she'd overstepped a boundary. She put her hand down to reposition herself, but was surprised to see Justin's arm reach around and pull her in tighter to him. She didn't speak; instead she glanced toward Bernal to see if he was still asleep and was pleased to see that he was nuzzled into Justin's other side. She looked up at Justin and, with her eyes, told him she was ready to love him.

She treasured the moment; it feels like a complete family again, she thought. Then she looked at the metal clasps around their ankles and remembered that things could be better.

*   *   *   *   *   *   *   *   *   *   *

"Ow!" Allison jerked her hand back. She stood up to give her back and legs and knees a much needed change of position, then kicked at the spiked weed, driving at it with the heel of her foot to uproot it. Tending gardens had been the task assigned to her.

Planting and watering wasn't so bad, but weeding was dismal. "Where do they all come from? I never saw any of these in the island gardens!"

But weeds were plentiful on Tilden. Around nearly every stalk and stem of every row of planted crop they had intruded, stealing water and sunlight for themselves.

"Pay attention! Watch what you're doing!" scolded a nearby worker, but only after checking to make sure a guard wasn't around. The slaves weren't supposed to talk to each other, at least that was the Overlords' decree. But the soldiers stationed on Tilden weren't as strict as they were supposed to be - administering close supervision over the slaves was too much work, besides, the Overlords were miles away.

"Thanks for the tip, Megan!" replied Allison sarcastically. "I'm sure that'll never happen again, now that you told me to be careful." She stretched her back and legs again, then dropped to her knees and resumed plucking weeds and placing them in her basket. She looked up for a second and saw that a guard was watching her, so she lowered her face so he wouldn't see her lips move; "Sorry, I didn't mean to be snappy."

"I know."

"We'd better not talk for awhile – they're watching us."

As bad as things were, they could always be worse. As good as things were, they could always be better. This was her perception of the nature of the new world. Bethany was gone, but Megan was still there. Her body was sore, but she enjoyed the sights and sounds around her: the green field, white clouds, the blue sea, and the songs of birds. Some things were still good, like feeling the sun shine on her face; or a breeze that carried pleasant scents to her nose; and the feeling of cold water running down her parched throat. But there was always bad mixed with good, death mingled among life, foul entwined with fair – it was this way everywhere. Before her was evidence of this phenomena - weeds and crops; destructive nuisances and pleasant nourishment.

Both girls filled their baskets at the same time and went to empty them outside the garden. They passed by Amara, whose basket was also full, and she rose and followed them. They each dumped their basket in turn and were about to go back to work, but paused when they observed the arrival of the ship. They dared not delay too long for fear of being reprimanded, but there was something curious about the new arrivals that were being escorted off the vessel.

"Go and fill the baskets quickly," Amara instructed, sensing that Allison and Megan were equally intrigued to find out who'd been brought to Tilden. They returned to their work and began filling their baskets as fast as they could, giving no effort to avoid being pricked by the spiked plants.

"Think you can handle a few more?" cried Kerjem, the first to debark.

Elson helped Kira step down from the ramp to clear the way for the others behind them while two armed guards met with Kerjem; it was obvious that one was superior to the other and that he was annoyed that Kerjem's question suggested incompetence. He made no reply as he looked over the new arrivals, taking notice of the staffs that Justin and Elson carried.

"The Overlords said they could keep those, Prevor," said Kerjem. "Apparently they have sentimental value."

"Since when have they cared about the slaves' feelings?" countered Prevor. He reached his hand out to take Elson's staff, revealing his dismembered fingers.

"They're not to be slaves, exactly - don't you recognize any of them?" Prevor and his assistant looked closely at the men.

"Justin, Elson, and Warrick!" exclaimed Prevor, "Welcome back!" He returned the staff to Elson. "I guess there's no harm; there's no glimmerstone on it."

"They're not to be made to work like the rest of them," explained Kerjem. "Send them up to the village and let's discuss the details over some ale."

"Dug, see that they're taken care of," commanded Prevor. "Bring them to Finnegle and let him know that I'll be bringing special instructions concerning them."

Dug, with his sheathed black and silver blade hanging from a belt wrapped too loosely about his waist, beckoned two new guards to accompany him, and together they began to usher the group toward Bentleigh. Meanwhile, Prevor led Kerjem to a nearby shack, where they proceeded inside and opened a barrel of ale.

The girls succeeded in filling their baskets quickly, in fact they had to dawdle a few minutes before getting up to go empty them - the people were moving up the path slower than they'd anticipated. They each recognized Justin, Warrick, and Elson immediately.

"Amara!" A woman that Amara didn't recognize called to her. "Amara, it's me, Kira!" She let go of Elson's arm and started for the garden.

Amara stared at Kira as she wobbled toward her, and finally understood that she was looking at her friend. "Kira!" She ran to meet her, but was stopped abruptly when something entangled about her leg and jolted it backward, causing her to fall. She threw out her hands and caught herself before she slammed into the ground.

"What do you think you're doin'?" One of the guards had noticed the three girls emptying their baskets together for the second consecutive time and thought he should investigate. The glimmerstone whip tightened, and Amara felt not only the pressure of its squeeze, but also a burning where it touched her skin.

"There'll be time for reunions later," said Dug.

The guard looked suspiciously at Dug. It was the first time he'd heard anyone speak kindly to a slave.

Dug was uncertain how to treat the newcomers and thought it prudent to err on the side of kindness, yet neither did he want to cause any interruption in work. "Keep moving."

The guard flicked his wrist and the whip uncoiled from Amara's leg, leaving a spiraled bruise in its place. She stood up and looked at Kira; though neither spoke, they agreed to meet up as soon as they could. Then she returned to the garden, gently nudging Megan and Allison to do the same, both of whom had been speechless, for Allison, as much as she wanted to ask about Bethany and Conroy, kept quiet out of fear of the whip.

*   *   *   *   *   *   *   *   *   *   *

Days passed. The Tildenians tended the gardens; the Marlanders built the tower. Months passed. The Tildenians harvested the crops; the Marlanders built the tower. Years passed.

The Tildenians worked the land; the Marlanders built the tower. Six years passed and the tower grew tall...

*   *   *   *   *   *   *   *   *   *   *

The firelight became more noticeable, and when the sun at last dipped below the horizon completely the torches seemed brilliant, their power no longer lessened by rays of the mighty sun. The Overlords sat on their thrones in the center of the topmost level of the tower. Though only a fraction of what it would be when complete, the structure was already much higher than any other building in Seton, and taller than all but the oldest trees. It had become their custom to move their royal chairs to the uppermost level of the tower as soon as it was finished. Bathed, groomed, and adorned with regal garments, which included the black-jeweled crowns, they sat still and silent as Valena summoned their masters.

Scynn was already there, but none of the three were aware of its presence. The creature took on the small catlike shape, the same form that it had assumed when it appeared to them in the cave. It paced gracefully on its six limbs around the thrones and gently caressed them with brushes from its long, leathery tail.

It had been a long time, in Idris' opinion, since he talked with Kavan and Scynn – the last time being on the night he was appointed Overlord. Valena spoke often with Kavan, so she claimed, for that was her privilege and duty, she always said, but Idris needed to see him again for himself, for he had not yet been given the opportunity to sip from the Icyandic. As he sat there watching Valena, however, he wondered whether he'd made a wise choice. "I'm the only one of us who hasn't received what was promised to me!" His oft made plea to Valena echoed in his mind and restored his resolve. "How much longer?"

Valena remained silent, however, offering no indication of what was happening. In her mind she continued to call out for her masters to come, summoning them with words of the new, beautiful language.

"Does it usually take this long?" Idris asked Lachlan.

Lachlan had no reply but to raise his eyebrows and shrug.

Valena heard the question and, though she didn't open her eyes or speak, shook her head slowly.

Lachlan settled into his throne to make himself as comfortable as he could, leaned back and shut his eyes.

Idris stood up to leave and began to walk away. "Maybe Kavan's asleep," he said sourly.

He didn't get far – a tall, thin figure appeared and pushed him backward, lifting him off the floor and tossing him into his empty seat.

Lachlan started at the ruckus; his drowsiness fled.

Valena prepared to drop from her throne and bow to her lord, but when she opened her eyes to see that it wasn't Kavan who had come, she remained seated.

"My Master has no need of sleep!" spat Feloniche. "Nor do I! It's only your kind that need to rest." His tone implied weakness. "Ironic that only you mortals, whose days are brief, spend a third of your time in idle slumber. Truly, I wish it wasn't so, then this tower would be much taller."

Scynn paced around Feloniche's long legs, wiping his shins with its serpent tail. Then the creature grew in size until its back was as high as Feloniche's waist. Unlike the humans, Feloniche was aware of the creature and held out his claws to scratch it as it circled – a subtle movement that didn't elicit suspicion from the Overlords.

"I wish our condition was different as well," replied Idris, attempting to recover his confidence after being thrown down so easily. "That's why I wish to speak with Kavan."

"Don't use the name of my master recklessly, foolish human. I've been sent in his stead."

"All right," consented Idris, "after all, you were there when Kav..., your master promised to take me to the Icyandic. I've done as I was asked – conquered the Tildenians, plundered their treasures, and made them slaves; the Tower is growing taller every day - when will I receive what was promised to..."

"Don't doubt Kavan's promise!" Feloniche took the crown from Idris' head and gazed into the single large black gem. Anger surged through him and he cast the crown to the stone floor, then grabbed Idris. His long fingers wrapped easily around the full circumference of the Overlord's neck, and Idris heard the spine-chilling sound of claws rubbing together. "Finish the tower!"

Idris dared not reply.

Lachlan considered drawing his weapon, but wasn't confident in a favorable outcome of that battle.

Feloniche released Idris and stepped back. He held out his hand and the crown flew to his waiting grasp. He handed it back to Idris.

"Finish the tower," Feloniche repeated , "then you'll taste the white water."

The fear of dying presented itself in Idris' thoughts, for he was still vulnerable, and would be until he drank from the Icyandic.

Feloniche perceived the fear and grinned. "Finish the tower," he said again, then vanished.

Lachlan sighed.

Valena prayed.

Idris cursed.

Scynn smiled.

*   *   *   *   *   *   *   *   *   *   *

Idris spent the remainder of the day overseeing the tower work crews and devising new tactics to make the construction progress more rapidly. Late that night, unable to sleep, he returned to the tower alone and made his way up to the top. Lachlan and Valena had deserted him long before, retiring to their beds anxious to remove themselves from Idris and his impatience. He was glad he couldn't sleep, for he wanted to convince himself, and perhaps even Feloniche, that he wasn't weak.

His legs were burning as he reached the sixth floor where his throne sat. He paused on the exterior spiraling stairs to look down at his kingdom, lit up by the stars and moon and torches along pathways. He was about to enter the throne room when he heard faint whimpering coming from above. He grabbed for his glimmerstone dagger to make sure it was in its proper place – it was, then went onto the roof by ascending the remaining steps which led up to the unfinished seventh level.

The trespasser noticed him right away, and Idris was surprised that his presence didn't seem to evoke panic.

"What are you doing here, slave?" he demanded.

"My name is Ruth, Idris, and you know it!" She wiped her eyes. "I came up here to escape all that." She gestured to the slave compound.

"You were free to join me; you made the choice to stay behind." Since there was no one else around, and she'd been brave enough to venture there, Idris let the conversation continue. "Do you wish to join me now?"

"Do you think, even now, that I would choose to join you? Do you think I could turn against my friends and treat them like filth?" She gestured to the compound again. "How can you live with yourself?"

"I live very well - like a king! Behold my tower; my land - look at what I've gained!"

"You're too blinded by why you think you've gained to realize what you've lost! You think you're something that you're not!" Tears flooded her eyes again and her voice fluttered.

"I can see I won't be persuading you to change your mind tonight." He allowed her a moment to calm down, then asked; "Did you find your *escape* up here?"

"All I have to do is jump; an act that would take less than a second would take me away from this forever." She faded into a disassociated daze.

"What? You'd kill yourself? I don't believe it."

"Why shouldn't I? I have nothing to look forward to: I wake up in the morning and try to imagine something good in my life. I can't bear the thought of waking up even one more time to face that challenge. I'm helpless and hopeless - all I can see is endless toil until I die with nothing significant to leave behind, and no joy to experience along the way. If death is my inevitable destiny, why should it be delayed? It's got to be better than this."

Idris didn't want her to die. She was a good worker, besides she was delightful to look at. "Come away from there, you're talking nonsense."

Ruth stood up and walked toward the stairs, toward Idris.

Satisfied that she'd given up her desire to *escape*, Idris turned to descend the stairs. But he suddenly found himself knocked sideways off his feet, tumbling over the edge of the tower. He grabbed at the ledge with one of his strong hands, his fingers pressing supernaturally hard into the marble. With his other hand he grabbed Ruth's wrist and squeezed.

The bones in her hand shattered and she let out an ear-piercing cry. "At least I tried," she thought. She had already accepted that she was going to die that night; if she could have killed Idris as well, perhaps things would have been better for her friends.

"I won't delay your destiny, but I won't be joining you." Idris let go of Ruth and pulled himself up, then looked down in time to see her crash into the ground – her body broke instantly and then was still. He punched the block wall, angry for having been so careless to expose himself to death. Broken pieces of stone fell on Ruth and he realized that the wall would need to be repaired and a new slave would need to be brought over from Tilden to replace her.

Silence ruled the night again, but a breeze flowed over Idris and he could swear that he heard Feloniche laughing.

A clear and calm sea beneath him, a multitude of gold and white-outfitted soldiers above him in a brilliant canopy, Elyon hovered – he was the center of attention. The sea was small, fully contained within the city, and around the water's edge stood countless onlookers, citizens of Casilda all. Unlike most seas, this one did not flow in waves onto a gradual inclining shore. Instead, it lay within a giant reservoir – smooth, steep walls encircled it all around. Only on the northern side, the side facing the king's palace, were there any outlets, should its level rise high enough to overflow the banks. As it was, the level was several stories below the rim, and those gathered around the perimeter gazed down to see its surface in its entirety.

The king was there, standing on the northern side beside the overflow trench, as was the prince, both wearing royal robes and jeweled crowns. Flanking them were Sandor and Gavril, both adorned in splendid military garb, and beside Sandor was a group of figures sitting on large gray creatures that resembled horses. The horses and riders were extremely still, as if they were statues waiting to come to life, but they didn't seem out of place, for the whole assembly was silent. The only sound to be heard was the soft crackling of Elyon's flames.

"Hear me now, my friends," Elyon spoke at last, crisp and strong words. "I will show you glimpses of the lost islanders' lives since the island fell. Let my testimony show that there are some who value the king's friendship, and some who don't."

Nothing else was said for a long time. Then the king spoke, "What have you to show us concerning the three Overlords and their reign of nearly thirty years?"

Elyon reached to his chest as one might do to retrieve something from an interior coat pocket. His hand disappeared into his flaming torso for a moment before withdrawing a clenched fist. He opened his hand and turned it over so that a round, white gem fell into the sea. As the ripples generated by the pearl grew wider, an image appeared on the surface.

"An event of the year 283, eleven years after the falling away of the island, ten years into the Overlords' reign." All eyes gazed upon the scene displayed on the water...

Conroy had grown into manhood handsomely. His blue eyes retained their dazzling sparkle, while the toil that was forced upon him gave him a strong back and broad shoulders, though he was not bulky and musclebound like Lachlan. He walked across the open area of the slave compound toward his friends, all sitting around a fire as usual, and sat down beside Wendel.

"This is all she could get for now." Conroy slipped a small package under Wendel's leg.

"Is Bethany well?" asked Wendel.

"Physically she's fine, but I can see sorrow in her face. I don't think she ever imagined being here for ten years and never once having the chance to see her sister or parents."

"At least they know she's here and that she's all right," Linus joined the conversation. Even after a decade of labor, he looked the same as he did on the day he left the island. "Is she still a house servant?"

Conroy nodded.

Wendel felt that it was safe, and he subtly shifted the package between his folded legs and peeled back one flap of the wrapping to examine the contents. "Is this all? This won't last." He folded the wrapper back over and tucked the vessel safely in his shirt.

"Why do you spend so much time writing in that book? I've watched you spend night after night, year after year, recording every little event that transpires," said Linus. "Your burden is great enough, why add to it? You should stop and get rest every chance you can. What purpose is there in it?"

"I'm tired of you asking that! You know full well why I do this! And your name's in here more than a few times!" The oppression proved to do some good for Wendel as well, for his potbelly had disappeared, giving him even more room inside his garments to hide his secret books. Yet his face remained round and chubby. "Speaking of such, I need to retire to my cabin."

Linus shook his head.

Wendel rose and went straight for a small shelter; it was barely large enough to fit a bed. Each slave was allowed a cabin, not because the Overlords desired to improve their lives, but because it seemed to help them be more productive in building the tower.

Wendel sat on his bed and pulled out his book and began to write; the moon shone through a small window near his head to provide light. On nights when the moon wasn't out, Wendel heeded Linus' advice and put away the book and slept.

Tonight the moonlight was ample enough and he began writing furiously to record recent events. It had become his custom to write quickly to minimize his exposure for being discovered, though the quality of his text suffered. He had only been at it a few minutes when a shadow fell across the open book. He wasn't immediately concerned – any number of things could have passed by his window, but he knew he was in trouble when the door of his wooden shelter flew open and an imposing figure stood in the doorway holding a long staff.

"What type of mischief are you about, old councilman?" Valena's black hair mixed with the dark sky, but her pale skin glowed, and Wendel identified her at once.

The expression on Wendel's face was like that of a young boy caught doing something that had been forbidden by his parents. Speechless, with eyes wide and mouth gaping, he waited for the Overlord to act.

"Answer me! What is that book?"

"It's an account, a ... a history of what has transpired since we left the island."

Valena marched over to grab the book from Wendel, making her way through the narrow aisle that ran alongside his bed. Wendel hesitated to let it go, but consented when he saw her raise the staff. She returned to the open doorway and used the moonlight to peruse Wendel's writings. She leaned the staff into the crease of her arm so that she could hold the book with one hand and manipulate the pages with the other.

Wendel swallowed hard and waited.

She began at the front, reading a few entries pertaining to the islanders' departing from Tilden to come to Marland – how some chose to leave and search for secrets that might restore the island. Then she flipped a number of pages until she came to an entry about the Marlanders' raid against Tilden, and a feeble description of the power of glimmerstone.

Wendel continued to wait, hoping that she'd find no offense to the book and return it. A scowl appeared on her face, however, and diminished such hope.

Valena flipped a number of pages carelessly, nearly ripping them out, until she arrived at the entry about the night Kira returned...

Sixteenth Day of the Sixth Month, year 273:

Conroy and Elson Verrill, Bethany Krunser, and Kira Lita returned from the Marland forest. Conroy, Elson, and Bethany were immediately put into the slave camp and made to work on the tower for the Overlords. But Kira was taken to Valena's home, and when she was next seen, she was hideously disfigured, and ....

She stopped reading, stunned that Wendel knew of Kira's visit to her house that night. How had he found out? Who else knew? She desperately wanted to question Wendel, but to do so would reveal her anxiety and draw attention to where it wasn't wanted. She flipped toward the end of the recorded entries, noticing her name mentioned often, usually an account of a slave receiving a well-deserved beating.

For the most part, she was not offended by what was written, but she was bothered by the entry about Kira, and she feared that it could find its way to Idris. She considered ripping that page from the book, but decided that Wendel would know what had been removed and would rewrite the entry.

"May I have it back?" Wendel spoke so timidly that he felt embarrassed.

Valena slammed the book closed and tucked it between her arm and waist, then grabbed the staff in her other hand. She shook her head; "I cannot let you keep this."

Wendel got up and dashed to recover the book. Valena was ready with the staff – she delivered a blow square on his forehead, opening a sideways gash on his brow and knocking him backward on his bed. He didn't stay down, however, and without knowing what he was going to do, rushed outside in pursuit of Valena.

Though Wendel wasn't aware of the invisible being, all of Casilda saw Elyon within the image projected on the surface of the sea. As the scene of the memory played on, they watched him lift up Wendel and escort him out of the cabin.

Wendel saw Valena and tried to discern her plan for the book - would she take it and leave? Was she going to keep it for herself? The he saw what lay directly ahead of her, and knew what she was going to do: she was going to destroy it.

The slaves had all left; they must have scurried away when they saw the Overlord, thought Wendel, and nothing hindered Valena from walking directly to the raging fire and casting in the book.

She didn't throw it in at once, though, for she opened it to the page containing Kira's transformation - that page must be the first to go, she thought. When she found it, she tossed it into the center of the burning mound, and when the flames rose up to embrace the book, she turned around and cast Wendel a satisfied look, then departed.

Wendel felt as if his purpose for living was being destroyed. Recording the history of his people had been a charge given to him – to him! Only him!

Casilda observed Elyon melt into Wendel, and together they became a short, stout figure with curly brownish-orange hair and flaming yellow eyes. The living flame empowered Wendel and drove him fearlessly forward into the fire.

Wendel pushed aside red and orange logs, reaching down to glowing embers where he thought the book had fallen. He tried to block out all sensation of pain, but expected it to overcome him at any moment, and he moved as fast as he could to get the book before his flesh failed. Yet, he wasn't as quick as he needed to be, he knew, and he should have been in agony.

There it is! He finally saw it; it appeared to be whole and intact, and the sight seemed strange, for the edges of the pages weren't blackened and curled.

No time to delay! He grabbed the book and retreated to his cabin, amazed that he felt no pain. Once inside he examined the book: none of the pages had been burned, nor did it smell of smoke. He examined himself: his skin was cool, and not even the hair of his arms had been singed. He raised his hand to touch his brow and discovered that the gash on his forehead had closed.

The image of Elyon separating from Wendel dissolved on the surface of the sea. When it was gone, Elyon, still hovering in place, presented another pearl and let it drop. All eyes turned to the water again as a new image began to form:

"An event of the year 295, twenty three years after the falling away of the island, twenty two years into the Overlords' reign." ...

Gray clouds stuffed the sky over Seton, so thick that there were no perceptible shapes to them, only an expansive fog that covered the land like a dreary blanket. Raindrops, large and cold, splattered on a stone walkway as a massive man made his way to the front entrance of a house. He knocked hard on the door, then reached for the latch without waiting for someone to answer.

The door was locked.

Lachlan heard footsteps and knocked again, harder.

The door didn't open.

Already having a difficult day, Lachlan was not going to be denied. The Overlord raised his arm high and pounded on the wooden door, breaking the latch and sending the door swinging wide with one blow.

The only person inside was a servant. She dropped to floor in submission when she saw him.

Lachlan drank in the sight of her blonde curls and shapely figure. "Where is the woman of the house?" he asked, remembering his purpose.

"She's not here," Bethany's reply was soft and revealed her nervousness.

"Where is she?" His temper enflamed as he was reminded of his failure to win the affections of this woman, a mere house servant.

"At the tower, Overlord. Deryn's work there is very important."

Lachlan inhaled quickly to respond, drawing air partially through his nose and partially through his mouth, creating a snorting noise that he hadn't intended and causing him to be embarrassed. "I've brought her more ink."

"I'll see that she gets it." Bethany thought it odd for an Overlord to act as a courier, but hoped that was the case and that he'd leave next. "Is there anything else?"

"No," Lachlan lied. "Yes. I wanted to see you again."

"Why?"

"It's been a long time."

"A long time since?..."

"A long time for a lot of things; a long time since we fought; a long time since we talked." A long time since I've been with a woman half as beautiful as you, he thought.

Bethany became noticeably uncomfortable and didn't reply. She felt like she was facing him on the wooded trail on Tilden all over again. But this time was worse - even if she could outrun him there was no place for her to run. The pair of glimmerstone blades swinging from his belt fueled her despair.

He pushed the battered door back in place as best he could and lodged a broken shard underneath to keep it shut. "I want you. I've always wanted you. Why don't you want me?" His previously gruff voice turned gentle as he pleaded; "What can I do to make you love me?"

"Nothing," answered Bethany, incapable of hiding her disgust any longer. "I'll never love you."

Lachlan's response was to draw the swords and walk toward her.

She'd seen the look in his eyes before, only they hadn't been his eyes, but those of a younger man staring at her through a narrow opening in the wall of her prison. The same feelings that she had that day came rushing back. She knew what he could do with the blades, and in her mind she saw him manipulating the steel to do terrible things, against which she couldn't defend herself.

"I should have done this long ago!" He held up the blades and they each split apart to form long, two-pronged forks.

Like Wendel, Bethany had not been aware that Elyon was near, but all of Casilda saw him. When Lachlan backed her into a corner, Elyon merged with Bethany, his form blended with hers to produce a glowing silhouette with blonde locks.

Lachlan pushed one of the swords toward her ankles when he saw that she couldn't back up any further, his mouth began to water in anticipation. He successfully pinned her feet to the floor, then moved the other sword to pin her at the neck. The swords dug firmly into the floor, and he let go of them and loosened his wide belt.

Elyon took over. Bethany lifted up her legs and sent the first sword flying, barely missing Lachlan's shoulder as it flew past and stuck into the wooden ceiling above. She kicked to knock Lachlan back, then grabbed the other sword with her hands and easily pulled it free and simply cast it aside. She rose to her feet and stared at him without fear.

Lachlan circled to the side and retrieved the sword, already having dislodged the other one from the rafters. Bethany offered no challenge for possession, and he soon had them both held out toward her again. "You won't deny me any longer!" he shouted.

Bethany swatted the prodding prongs.

Lachlan came in faster, not caring if he cut her - he'd probably kill her afterward anyway.

Bethany kicked it away.

He came in at her, swinging both blades.

She moved like a cat, ducking, dodging, pulling away and moving to the center of the room, slipping his belt from his waist. She stood calm and presented the limp belt to him, dangling it so the large metal buckle was just above the floor.

Lachlan's pants were uncomfortably loose, making his movement awkward. He pulled them down and kicked them free – they wouldn't be needed in a minute anyway. He came at her again, feeling strong and fast, manipulating the glimmerstone with utmost precision.

Bethany was too swift - she stepped clear and swung the belt in a wide arching loop and struck him in the back of the head.

The blow drew blood and rage. He came in again. The intent to bed her was giving way to a stronger desire to overpower her, no matter what the effort might do to her.

Bethany dropped low and slid on the smooth planks of polished wood, passing beneath his gaping legs. This time she slammed the heavy buckle into his knee.

He dropped to the floor and crouched there, a mound of pain and anger. When the pain subsided, he stood up and turned around to see her standing eerily calm with the belt dangling again. A new tactic was needed – he threw one of the swords at her. The blade hit the mark and knocked her backward as it sunk into her.

Bethany glanced down to see the handle a couple of inches from her chest – she couldn't see the rest of it – it was buried within her and protruded out her back. She looked up at Lachlan; there was no pain in her expression and no panic in her movement. She lifted her free hand and pulled the sword out, drawing it out in a few attempts, all the while holding the belt delicately in her other hand. She threw the blade back to him – it landed harmlessly at his feet.

Lachlan couldn't believe what he saw - there was no blood. There had been no cries of pain. There was only Bethany, calm, patiently awaiting the next assault. Her silence mocked him. He didn't know what to do. She was a thin slave woman armed with only a strap of leather, yet his mighty glimmerstone seemed impotent against her.

He flinched when she moved, not toward him, but to the side of the room. She picked up his pants and went to the fireplace. Though it was summer, the damp day was cool and she had been preparing to make a fire. She casually tossed the belt and pants on top of the wood.

Lachlan didn't move – he just watched.

Bethany took a deep breath so that her chest expanded, then she leaned forward and exhaled.

Lachlan fell backward when he saw fire come out of her mouth and ignite the pile. As quickly as he could, he recovered his blades and dashed to the door. He struggled to open it, for he neglected to remove the shim that he had put down to brace it, but finally pulled it free and ran out into the rain.

He cast silent threats to all who looked at him as he made his way back to the tower, and the pair of glimmerstone blades that he carried ensured that no one dared to inquire about his missing garments.

Elyon stood beside Bethany, who knelt in front of the roaring fire, his hand placed gently on her back. She watched as Lachlan's pants and belt burned to ember and ash, almost disappointed by their disappearance, for they were evidence to convince her that what had happened was real.

The surface of the sea became blank again as the image dissolved. After he allowed the people of Casilda time to digest the recollection, Elyon pulled forth yet another pearl and let it drop.

"An event of the year 303, thirty years after the falling away of the island, twenty nine years into the Overlords' reign." The jewel splashed into the sea, bringing it to life with a new image...

The tower was impressive, even to those who inhabited the great city of the king. Similar to Casilda's magnificent structures, it was fashioned from the same unblemished white marble. Constructed of countless blocks, it was strong and tall; the topmost level sat upon twenty-nine others. Like the tower of the Island Council, this one contained a central spiraling staircase that wound round and round the full height of the tower until it reached the floor of the top level. Here it stopped to allow the level above to be void of the stairway shaft that would otherwise protrude up through its middle. But the stairs weren't for the Overlords (unless they felt like using them, which they rarely did); the Overlords generally rode one of two elevators that were moved by long chains pulled by a team of slaves.

Thirty stories high, and thirty years to build; the progress of the work averaged one level completed per year, but since the bottom was the widest part of the tapered tower, the levels were erected more rapidly as the years passed. Idris had been architect, engineer, and was now lord over the whole place.

He was pleased in Kavan's selection of seasonal victims – nearly all members of the old Island Council were dead. But they weren't all gone, not yet, and he swore that he heard the forbidden word *council* whispered among the slaves occasionally.

Women came to him frequently, and Valena let them, for she wasn't threatened by them – she knew that none of them meant anything to him, and they both knew that she couldn't be replaced. She had become a special, necessary, part of his life.

But Valena wasn't Kira, and Idris craved to be with the girl of his youth. At night he would dream of her in visions of pale smooth skin and fine feminine features. He attempted to satisfy the craving with other women, but even Valena, with her long legs and raven-black hair and thirst for power, couldn't quench his hunger.

An image of a ship on the South Sea and Corliss Lake appeared on the Casildan sea, the Sea of Pearls, pushing Idris and the tower away. When the vessel reached the Marland docks, a solitary woman staggered onto land and began to make her way slowly to the tower. Elyon walked patiently beside her.

The distance from the sea to the tower wasn't far, only about a hundred yards, but Kira's gait was awkward and delayed. Still, she reached the entrance sooner than she hoped. Inside, she made her way to the winding stairs and took comfort in knowing that she wouldn't have to face him until she climbed all the way to the top.

"You don't have to use those." Before she had even ascended the first step, someone grabbed her arm and pulled her aside into one of the lifts. "If I had to wait for you to climb the stairs I'm not sure I'd ever see you."

Kira knew the voice - she didn't need to see his face to know that it was Idris who grabbed her. He was handsome to be sure, but when he barked orders at the slaves beneath them to make their ascent short and kicked dirt into their faces, she remembered why she had run away. Through open slots in the floor she could see the slaves, a half dozen men in a sunken pit, black with dirt, begin to pull as hard as they could at a thick chain. As the elevator rose, she grew more uncomfortable as the memory of Ansen Verrill's fall filled her mind.

"On this level is the library; the shelves are rather bare, but I'm sure they'll fill up quickly." He spoke with an enthusiasm that he couldn't, and didn't try to hide. As the elevator climbed he explained what was contained on each floor, noting something significant about each, spinning around and waving his arms to point at whatever he happened to be referring to at the moment. "And this is where soldiers are trained in the use of glimmerstone."

As Idris revealed the various purposes for each level, Kira couldn't help but think of Elson, Warrick, and Justin and their long-held belief that they would rule there; a belief they hadn't been quiet about, and Kira had seen Warrick bear the images of Valena's shaft in his tender flesh on numerous occasions.

"And this floor houses a gallery, displaying special artwork of the Marlanders," Idris went on, "Lachlan felt that it should be kept on a lower level to minimize the number of people coming up here, but the view adds so much to the beauty of the art."

The elevator stopped at its pinnacle, which was short of the topmost level, and they had to climb one flight of stairs to reach the throne room above. Idris took Kira's arm and tugged her upward gently. Kira was stunned by his audacity to treat her so - did he actually think she would forget all that he'd done for the last thirty years in a few moments because he displayed a moment of chivalry? He led her to the middle of the room and offered her a padded stool while he took his place on the central of three thrones. He took up the crown that rested in the seat and placed it on his head, positioning it just the way he liked.

"Why have you summoned me?" she bowed as best she could before Idris in an attempt to conform to the expected etiquette, and hoped that by being direct she could get him to stop feigning kindness.

"My tower is complete, my army is invincible, my subjects are loyal, whether out of admiration or fear, it doesn't matter, and soon I"ll be immortal."

Kira was confused and disgusted all at once; "Immortal? Did you avoid the effect of the Renfrew?"

"No, my dear." As hard as he was trying to find semblance of her pleasant looks of long ago, her slurred and sloppy sounds made him wince and wonder whether her beauty could be recovered. "The blessing of the Renfrew runs in my veins as it does in everyone, but soon the power of another river will course through me as well when I taste the white water of the Icyandic!"

"Impossible!"

"No, no," he shook his head feverishly, eager to inform her that she was wrong. "It's been promised to me, and I've seen it in visions, just like I saw this." He raised his arms wide to gesture to the tower. "Unlike the visions of some, mine come to pass. It won't be long before I stand on the bank of the Icyandic and drink deep – this time there won't be a thick layer of glass to stop me! *Nor a short swordsman*," he mumbled this last phrase under his breath.

"I don't know if I believe you, but you didn't answer me - why have you summoned me?"

"I desire the wife of my youth." Idris rose and began to pace around Kira, "I want you."

In Casilda, the Sea of Pearls revealed that two others were in the room with Kira and Idris. Elyon stood behind Kira, his flames glowing on the waves. Scynn was there as well, assuming its smaller catlike form, crouched on Idris' back with its thirty-six claws dug into the Overlord. As Idris circled, Scynn continually repositioned itself; to the audience, the reason for this seemed twofold - to use Idris as a shield from Elyon, and to display to Elyon the Overlord as a sort of trophy that had been earned.

"Surely, you don't find me attractive."

"No," he admitted, "not as you are. But I believe Kavan can restore your beauty. Valena could summon him and we could petition him to change you back to the way you were!"

She couldn't believe what she was hearing! There were so many reasons why this couldn't happen. "What about Valena? She's your lover now, and you can have any woman you want anytime you like."

"Valena will do whatever I ask, and I don't want anyone else – I want you."

"You underestimate her desire for you."

Idris paid her no heed. "Come." He helped her to her feet. As she stood, she caught a glimpse of her reflection in the glossy stone of his crown - it had been a long time since she had seen herself. Idris led her out of the room onto a balcony.

The walk gave her time to consider the hideousness of her appearance. More than ever, she was thankful for Elson. He had always treated her kindly and considered her his wife. Their relationship was like any typical marriage, if there is such a thing.

"Look." Below them the sand of the Marland shore ran to Corliss Lake, which merged with the South Sea, which ran to Tilden. "I'm lord over all this, but I'm not satisfied. I want you to be by my side." He turned to her and took her hands. "Kavan can restore your beauty, then drink from the Icyandic and rule over all this with me forever!"

Kira imagined Valena's reaction to Idris' request and wondered if she'd refuse. Maybe she would and the two of them might fight, they might even kill each other. But maybe Valena wouldn't refuse, then she'd be in the same terrible situation she was in thirty years ago.

The citizens of Casilda saw Elyon grab Kira's shoulder.

With a sudden fearlessness, Kira pulled her hands free of Idris' and replied; "I prefer to stay the way I am. I don't want to be with you." She was surprised at her words, but couldn't stop more from coming; "I'd rather be dead than be with you again." She turned to look over the handrail toward Rigid's distant peak and thought of the people she loved on Tilden.

Scynn dug the claws of its lower four limbs into Idris' back and fondled his thoughts with its upper two hands.

"You can't deny me! There's nothing I can't have!"

"That's it, fool! Don't you see! The only reason you want me is because you can't have me! If I did what you want, perhaps a few weeks would pass til you grew bored with me and tossed me away!"

"You have two days to reconsider."

"And what if my answer is the same?"

"It won't go well with you and the ones you love."

Kira couldn't back down, Elyon wouldn't let her; "I've given my answer – I won't change my mind!"

Scynn gave a yank and Idris' rage took over - he wrapped his arms around Kira, lifted her up, and cast her over the railing. "You were wrong! It only took a few minutes for me grow tired of you before I tossed you away!"

Elyon was already on the ground waiting. He caught her and lowered her to the soft sand.

Kira felt as if she had only fallen from her bed. She wasn't hurt, but she didn't want Idris to know that. She positioned her head so that she could look up at him and lay still. When she saw him leave the balcony she got up and went down to the docks as fast as she could. A vessel was being made ready to sail back to Tilden – she climbed aboard, unhindered by any of the crew.

The image faded and the sea became blank. Elyon didn't present any more pearls, but proclaimed; "These deeds of the Overlords show to what extent they've aligned themselves with Scynn."

"And what of the Council?" asked the king.

"Kavan has slain all but two of them; Wendel and Linus."

"Then it is time!"

Marland, October of year 303...

Warrick's head hit the marble floor so hard that he nearly lost consciousness. The thud, barely audible to the crowd, was thunderous to him and it blocked out the laughter for an instant. He lifted himself up just enough so that he could caress the back of his skull with his hand - he could feel the lump of the bruise, already at full size, but there was no blood. This wasn't the first time he'd been knocked down by Valena's staff, but he usually succeeded in protecting his head from slamming into the ground. Not so this time – the Overlord's strike, though not unexpected, was too fast. The erupting laughter intensified and made his head hurt even more.

"I'm growing very tired of you and your useless prophecy!" Valena gave Warrick a swift kick in his side. "How many more beatings will it take before you stop proclaiming friendship to Iman?"

Idris and Lachlan sat on their thrones as Valena reprimanded Warrick; it wasn't a new sight for them, and they were almost bored with this recurring scene. About a dozen other Marlanders were in the throne room, they continued to laugh as Warrick rose unsteadily to his feet.

"I won't forsake King Iman. He knows our troubles. Do not doubt in his abilities: he will rescue those who call upon him. He will restore all that has been lost."

"We'll see." Valena returned to her throne, turned and threw her staff at Warrick, then sat down. "Take this, fool! Carry it and know Kavan's power and Iman's impotence. Take it home to Tilden and study the images engraved in it. Return to me in three days and know that every one of them will be marked in your flesh when I beat you with it harder than I ever have before."

Warrick caught the staff but didn't respond.

"You've always been given special privileges because you were one of our liberators. We all hoped that in time," Valena gestured to her companion Overlords, "you'd learn to appreciate the ways of the world and join us. Three decades have passed and you still refuse to let go of hope in Iman. It's becoming difficult for me to see why you should be allowed to live."

"He always gets you so riled up," said Idris. "It's not worth your trouble. Norris, take him away."

A muscular red headed man took Warrick's arm and escorted him out of the throne room.

"Enjoy the next three days, friend of Iman! They may be your last!" Valena called out as they left.

Lachlan chuckled. "What're you going to beat the slaves with now?"

    *   *   *   *   *   *   *   *   *   *   *

Just as there were three individuals who received special recognition in Marland, there were three others who received special loathing in Tilden. And similar to how the three on Marland were called the Overlords, the Tildenian trio were called the *Outcasts.* The Outcasts were not praised, befriended, or feared, and other than their families and a few close friends, Justin, Elson, and Warrick were isolated from the Tildenian slaves and Marlander guardians alike.

To Justin's disappointment, the Tildenians, for the most part, had not forgiven him as Emily had, and they clung to bitterness toward him and hated him. They hated Warrick and Elson as well, but Justin didn't know if it was for the part they played in violating the Renfrew, or if it was because they remained close friends with him. For different reasons, the Marlanders despised the three of them – they couldn't be friends with anyone who didn't serve Kavan and Scynn, and who still clung foolishly to the hope that an aloof Iman would restore the island.

Justin was pleased that the Tildenians had accepted Elana and Bernal, his adopted children through his marriage to Emily, but this came at his expense. Their feelings toward him weren't sour at first, when he came to them in the Marland wild, nor even after the first few years following their return to Tilden. But when they grew into adolescence and were given the choice to work alongside their Tildenian friends, serve the Overlords, or become outcasts like their mother and Justin, they elected to forsake the two people that loved them most and freely entered a life of slavery. Among the slaves, they were constantly bombarded with bickering of how Justin's crime caused them everlasting misery. With blisters on their hands, dirty feet cut by rocks, and sore backs, the common attitude proved contagious – they learned to hate Justin.

Most days, Justin welcomed the guilt, humbly acknowledging his failure as he helplessly observed the oppressors rule over his innocent island friends. But sometimes he wasn't willing to carry the burden. Those who judged him had no comprehension of the circumstances that led him to the Renfrew - they didn't discover its secret place; they didn't gaze upon the sparkling red water; they didn't see Durwin and Baldwin drink from it; they didn't know how it empowered to fly! Though he told them such things, they couldn't fully comprehend the situation he'd been in, he knew, and he doubted that most of them would have resisted drinking if they'd been there.

But it didn't matter. What's done is done - there's no undoing it. Just focus on the present, one day at a time, he told himself. Anything he could think to do to make amends with the Tildenians he did: spreading hope that aid from King Iman would come as Elyon promised; encouraging Elson and Warrick to share their visions; and lighting the evening fire for the Tildenians in the center of Bentleigh for warmth, cooking the day's end meal, and (for some) a symbol that Elyon hadn't forgotten them.

The thing he did most often and most intensely, though, was not a physical act at all, but an attitude, an exercise of his soul – he prayed, pleading silently with all his might for King Iman to fix what he'd broken. Somehow he knew that the king could hear his petitions. Carollan had known his thoughts, certainly King Iman and Elyon could, he reasoned. He spent a good portion of many nights sprawled face down on the floor, begging for his island friends to be saved from this corrupted world of Overlords and pain and toil and death.

Often those prayer sessions began with him being awakened by familiar stinging visions. Nightmares frequented Justin, memories of the departure from the island; of finding Evelyn's body in the Renfrew's empty riverbed; and the most intense one – the images of his friends struggling against falling into the void. Indeed this dream had never stopped occurring, nor had it faded in strength. As a precursor to the nightmares, a scene usually came to him; a vast, even infinite, dark cloud that shielded the world from sunlight.

It had been nearly a week since Justin had the other dream, the pleasant one, of Mount Rigid.   It was the first dream he had that gave him hope. He had other dreams too, just as everyone did; quirky ones manufactured by his subconscious, the sort where things that happen don't make sense and fade away fast and are forgotten. But the other dreams, the ones that kept returning, had substance, and it seemed to him that they were from a source other than himself, and he referred to these as *visions* rather than *dreams*. He held tightly to the vision of Mount Rigid - it made him feel strong; it offered him hope; it made him believe that something was about to happen.

      *   *   *   *   *   *   *   *   *   *   *

"I knew you were going to get yourself in more trouble!" Warrick's wife, Tanya, spewed words mixed with anger and sorrow. "Why did you have to go to the tower? Why did you have to go to Marland at all?"

"Do you think only those on Tilden should be encouraged?" Warrick was firm in his reply, but kept his tone soft in an attempt to be sensitive to Tanya. "Those of us on Marland need encouraging the most! I was only doing what King Iman asked of me."

"But why did you have to go to the tower?"

"I didn't plan on going there – Valena found out that I was in Marland and had me brought up to the throne room."

"And you *had* to remind her that you and Elson and Justin would rule the tower one day, didn't you?" Tanya held the Overlord's staff - a look of disgust emerged on her face as she observed the symbols that decorated it.

"That *is* the vision Elyon gave me." For a second, Warrick thought Tanya's reaction would be to lash out at him with the staff. "Don't you understand me yet?"

"Maybe what Elyon gave you was meant for you to treasure privately, not something for you to brag about to challenge the Overlords! It's not wise for you to provoke them. I may never see you again!" Tears came down her cheeks but she didn't let the emotions crack her voice, she was too angry.

"Some things are worth dying for," said Warrick. "If I had backed down, if I had refused to perform my duty to the king, what would I be? If I choose to keep silent from this day forward, what would I become? My body might go on living, but I would die a different kind of death - my heart and spirit and everything that gives me hope and purpose would shrivel and die, and I would be an empty shell of a man. And then, when I stand before the king to give account for my life, what would I say?"

"I don't want you to go back! I need you!"

"Trust in the power of Elyon and King Iman. The vision will come to pass – I'm not going to die. But even if I do, I'll die remaining faithful to them, and I know that it won't be the end. Remember Lucy, how I saw her with him after she died?"

"Have you ever considered that you might have been hallucinating? Maybe she wasn't real! Maybe King Iman wasn't real!"

"They were real!" Warrick was becoming angry now. "Is that what you've thought all these years? Have you humored me by pretending to believe me? Lucy is alive and with the king! I know it! But even if I'm wrong, … even if it's only a fantasy, that fantasy is the best thing that I know, better than any reality this corrupted world can offer!"

"Then you are a fool!" Tanya threw the staff at Warrick.

*   *   *   *   *   *   *   *   *   *   *

Carollan strolled down the wide main corridor of the castle. Elyon's recent presentation at the sea, demonstrating the extent to which Scynn's corruption had defiled the Overlords, and King Iman's declaration had been cause for a number of Casilda's citizens to surmise what would happen next. Carollan, however, considered himself wise enough to not assume too much about what the king's plans might be, even when circumstances seemed in line with his suspicions; instead of guessing and making assumptions, he made it a point to visit the castle in hope of learning what would be done from a more reliable source. But this morning he was having a difficult time finding Sandor and he approached the lounge opposite the king's throne room for the third time, having circled the large palace thrice without finding the High Captain.

The door to the king's inner chamber opened and a pair of servants emerged. Carollan darted into the lounge, pleased that his small frame was easily hidden from the view of Durwin and Baldwin. The twins walked down the hall and exited the place without speaking to anyone. Like the Outcasts on Tilden, Durwin and Baldwin had grown used to similar treatment from Casildans for having revealed to Kavan the quarry of white marble. In spite of the protests from a number of citizens, including Sandor and Carollan, Durwin and Baldwin retained the right to come and go to the city as they pleased.

"They're up to something," Carollan muttered to himself, but not soft enough to avoid drawing attention from a pair of soldiers nearby.

"What's that you say?" inquired one of them.

"They're up to something." Carollan repeated so that they could hear him clearly, but didn't hang around to explain - he resumed marching down the corridor, quickening his pace, but it still wasn't fast enough – the twins were distancing themselves from him. He took to the air, but only for a moment...

"Carollan! What are you doing?"

Carollan recognized the voice immediately and banked a hard mid-air turn to reverse his direction, once again glad of his small size. "Sandor! Where have you been?" He telepathically shouted, "I've been looking all over for you! The twins were here!"

"In the castle?"

"Not only in the castle, but in with the king!"

"The Master has just begun to move to carry out his plans. We can't let them perform more acts of treason – not now."

"What do you know of the king's plans?"

"The rumors swirling around the city are more than rumors. The Executives have been summoned – I witnessed Elyon meet with them; they are being sent away from Casilda."

"But they've never left the city."

"There are lots of things about to happen that have never happened before," answered Sandor. "Come, we must follow the twins."

"How will we find them?"

"They're not very good at hiding their tracks, remember that they were followed by some who do not possess even a fraction of our skills."

They walked briskly to the nearest castle exit. Flying inside the palace was generally frowned upon, though Carollan had been willing to risk the offense a few moments ago, given his dire need to find Sandor. But now was not the time to draw attention to themselves. They took to the air once past the entrance guard.

The journey from Casilda was not one that could be made on foot, nor by boat, for the city existed in a different realm than the world of the Marlanders and Tildenians. With the bright city behind them, the first phase of their trip was through a pale haze, then came an empty black void, and then a few bright dots came into sight. The dots grew rapidly in size as Sandor and Carollan zoomed past the stars, and at last they came to a unique orb, the one they sought (not that it took them a long time to get there, but because they had to pass countless others before reaching this one). Down they flew into the atmosphere, gazing upon the beauty of the world's green lands and blue waters, pinpointing a spot on the rotating sphere and going straight for it - Tilden on the left, Marland on the right, the South Sea and Corliss Lake straight ahead.

Sandor shot into the water. Carollan followed without hesitation, though he had expected Sandor to pull up and head to Marland, but he trusted his guide and stayed close behind. Large mounds of a broken mass lay on the seabed – remnants of the island, yet they didn't stop. Through the bottom of the sea, into the rock of the world they advanced until they found themselves in an enormous cavern in which no natural light shone and no natural plant grew and no natural creature dwelt.

Sandor's sword was out in half an instant, though no visible foe was present.

"What is this place? How did you know of this?" asked Carollan. He followed Sandor's example and drew his blade and took up his shield as well.

"It's Kavan's lair." Sandor pointed to the ground at four large footprints pressed into the molten floor. "I didn't know of this place until now. I would have never found it I if I hadn't been following the twins."

"What signs did they leave that you found?"

"The wind and sea and rock cried out to me of the path they had taken."

Carollan's admiration for his companion grew. "How can you sense such things?"

"We're all fearfully and wonderfully made, but not made the same. Come, we shouldn't linger."

*   *   *   *   *   *   *   *   *   *   *

Their walking sticks drummed rhythmically into the mountain path as the three friends advanced toward Mount Rigid. Again. Elson and Justin carried the staffs that they'd owned for so long – the one that Justin found near Evelyn's body and the one that Elson carried in memory of his departed father. Warrick left behind his usual staff and carried one that he was almost as familiar with – Valena's ornate staff. In spite of the number of beatings he received from it, there was something about it that enticed him, even caused him to have a slight fondness for it. Seven days had now passed since Justin's vision of Rigid. He'd visited the mountain every morning since, dragging Elson with him for two of the times. Warrick would have accompanied them had it not been for his recent trip to Marland.

"So much has changed since we were together last, and that was only a few days ago," said Justin.

"Certainly not for the better." Warrick's response was sour, and he emphasized his frustration by slamming the staff unnecessarily hard into the ground. "I'm not afraid to die. I only wish I could do it without hurting those that care for me. Tanya doesn't understand anything."

"Don't be too resigned to dying," replied Elson.

"Not everyone who's confronted by death is as fortunate as Kira," challenged Warrick. "I don't think I would survive a fall from the top of the tower."

"What will you do when Idris finds out she survived?" asked Justin.

"I don't know. I can only hope that whatever force protected her then would guard her again," answered Elson.

They came into the small field on the north side at the base of the mountain and Justin stopped. "Don't you see what's happening? Can't you sense that we're near the end?"

"What are you talking about?" snapped Elson.

"I know I'm near the end – I just said I'm going to die." Warrick's look was of one whose words hadn't been heard.

"I'm talking about how within one week something significant has happened to each of us that's changed our lives: I've had a new vision; Elson's wife survived a three hundred foot fall and is sure to be pursued when Idris learns she's alive; and your very life is threatened."

"That's supposed to encourage us?" demanded Warrick. "Let us lift our hands and shout for joy and dance!" he said sarcastically.

"Be encouraged that there's no going back to where we were," replied Justin.

"What's so significant about your dream?" challenged Elson.

Warrick shook his head in frustration, not caring about what Justin had to say.

"It's not just a dream – there's power in what I saw, and goodness. It's given me strength and hope!" Justin's face seemed eerily cheerful as he continued; "Warrick, do you really think King Iman will throw away your life, which you've willingly given to him? Do you think we've spent all this time in service to him, being Outcasts, for nothing?"

"Let me understand. Because of the things that have happened to us this week – which were quite terrible for the most part – you believe it's a sign that the king's aid is finally coming?"

"Yes!" said Justin. "Promises have to be kept!"

Warrick chuckled and shook his head, then let it hang down and closed his eyes as he ventured into a moment of silent reflection, his brown hair dangling before his bowed brow. He opened his eyes and looked at the thing in his hands. "Then I guess I won't need to return this!" He hurled the staff as hard as he could into the woods.

All three men listened carefully to hear it slam into whatever it would strike, but apparently its fall was cushioned by the soft undergrowth of the forest, for no sound was made.

They were startled when a walking flame emerged from the forest with the staff in hand. Elyon walked directly to Warrick and presented it to him; "You'll have to carry this for a while longer."

Warrick received it without question.

"Come, I have something for you three."

"Where?" asked Elson.

"Up."

* * * * * * * * * * *

Sandor placed his hands on the course ledge and stood tall to peer over it; Carollan had to hover a couple of feet in the air to gain the same vantagepoint. Below was a large circular room with four white stone slabs piled recklessly together on top of a mound of red rock. The dark walls were striped by slow moving streams of orange lava that pooled on the floor and flowed randomly across the space to fall into a natural trough in a low shelf on the opposite side of the cavern.

Neither Kavan nor the twins paid any attention to whether they stepped into the magma – it didn't hurt them. When Kavan paced once around his marble throne and reclined against its massive back, it seemed evident to Sandor and Carollan that the meat of the conversation had already been chewed.

"Are you certain of Iman's intent?" Kavan glared at the twins with his eyes and with his mind. He sensed no trickery.

"We have revealed his very words," assured Baldwin.

A smile spread over Kavan's face. "Then I'll be seeing him soon."

The twins departed.

"Traitors!" Carollan silently exclaimed to Sandor. "They must not get away with..." his thoughts turned to an audible scream as an enormous horn pierced him from behind and pinned him against the ledge. His sword fell from his grasp as he wrapped his small hands around the ivory.

"Hello, little champion!"

Sandor turned abruptly to face the assault - he saw that it was Elzib that had spoken and speared Carollan. Two more stood on either side of him – Drimelen and Feloniche. A hundred other of Kavan's horde formed rank behind them.

"Welcome to Marheon, High Captain of Casilda!" said Drimelen.

Sandor held his sword in front of him, deftly slipped his shield from his shoulders and took to the air, hovering in the space above Kavan and his throne.

Kavan, instead of lunging to attack, remained on his royal seat and took delight in watching his horde swarm around Sandor.

"You have no chance for victory here!" declared Drimelen. "Not in our strongest stronghold!"

Sandor knew that Drimelen spoke the truth, ironically. The most he could hope for was to escape. Carollan could offer no aid, for he had already been removed from the scene by Elzib and deposited into some sort of pit, a massive door closed over its opening, held shut by yet more of the horde. He prepared for a long struggle, motivated to get free so that he could come back and rescue Carollan, and he knew he had made a mistake in coming here.

Carollan examined the walls of his prison and saw that they were coated with a black substance. The space was expansive and he flew all around its boundary in search of an area that wasn't coated with glimmerstone, though he was certain he wouldn't find such a spot. Without his sword, he had no chance to break out. Above was the sound of the battle – the cheering and chanting and pounding of the horde as they assaulted Casilda's greatest soldier. Light flashed like repeating lightning, illuminating the cavern with each injury.

"Accursed twins! Durwin! Baldwin! Traitors!" He slammed his fists into the wall.

*   *   *   *   *   *   *   *   *   *   *

All three men were surprised at how easily they ascended Mount Rigid, and each perceived that Elyon was giving them power beyond themselves. When they reached the peak, they stopped to look around and took in the sight of the land and sea far below.

But Elyon didn't pause. Instead, he made his way across the pinnacle and when he saw that the men had stopped, called out, "Come. Keep following."

Justin, Elson, and Warrick watched Elyon continue to ascend, walking into the air over the mountain, up some invisible staircase toward a white cloud that hung in the sky twenty or thirty feet above. They went to the spot where Elyon last touched the mountain and followed him, using their walking sticks to make sure each step was where they thought it should be.

Justin was the first to reach the upper surface of the cloud. He saw Elyon walking about, and was startled to see that they weren't the only ones there.

"It's alright. Come."

Justin stepped tentatively onto the white carpet of air and vapor and was relieved to find that it was solid. He approached Elyon, drawing within a circle of twelve giants – kneeling, living statues, which he observed were identical, varying only in color. He continued toward Elyon, next entering into a smaller circled formed by ten gray figures, expressionless, on ten gray horse-like creatures.

Elson and Warrick followed, equally amazed.

Beside Elyon, suspended in the air, was a familiar ten-sided gem.

Without speaking, Elyon reached his hand into the diamond and clenched his fist. The clarity of the stone subsided as a pale yellow glow filled the gem. The yellow grew darker and turned orange and red. After a few moments, Elyon's flames danced hungrily within, and he relaxed his hand and withdrew it.

"This is the Evanstone, it is King Iman's, given now to you." Ten sides, all of equal size, five sides facing upward, five downward, reflecting flawlessly the firelight within.

"What is it?" asked Justin. "I mean, what are we to do with it?"

"Marland, Tilden, even the whole world has been corrupted by Scynn. The Evanstone can guide you in hindering the work of the beast. There is a battle raging to save what Scynn has claimed.

Sometimes the struggle is perceived by you mortals, sometimes not. The Evanstone sees all, knows all, and despises all things tainted by Scynn - nothing that is corrupt is exempt from its judgement. It is part of me, for you saw that I put myself into it. Show me your staffs."

The men obeyed and held out their walking sticks.

Elyon took up the staffs, not with his hands, but with his mind, and floated them above the mens' heads. "Onyx. Jasper. Emerald."

Three of the statues came forward, black, red and white, and green.

"These twelve beings are the Gemstones. They guarded the island and protected you from Kavan and his horde. They guarded Tilden, resisting Kavan's effort to utterly destroy you all. Know that you were never forgotten."

Onyx, Jasper, and Emerald took hold of Justin, Warrick, and Elson's staffs, respectively.

"Justin," called Elyon, "where did you get your staff?"

"I found it near Evelyn's body, after Scynn took her from me."

"Elson, where did you get yours?"

"I found it on Great Falls, near the place where my father was killed. I carry it in remembrance of him."

"What of yours, Warrick?"

"It's not mine. It belongs to Overlord Valena. She has given me many beatings with it for your sake. It is said that Kavan gave it to her himself."

"Again I declare that you were not forgotten. Whoever honors King Iman will never be forgotten." Elyon turned to the three Gemstones. "Reveal them."

The three statues faced each other and swung the staffs inward, slamming them together in a mighty crash. Wood and bark and sparks flew in every direction as the thunderous sound rumbled through the sky and clouds and into the valleys below. The men stared wided eyed at what remained in the hands of the Gemstones - three shiny, silver steel rods.

"These are the three staffs of my three greatest captains, the ones that were used to call forth the Rivers of Power long ago," explained Elyon. "Two captains remain faithful. Sandor offered you his staff, Justin, when he learned of the cruelty that your wife endured at the hands of Kavan. Gavril willingly offered his to you, Elson, in honor of your father, a man who loves King Iman. Kavan, serving his own purposes, gave his staff to Valena. It's hers no more – it is yours now, Warrick."

Justin, Elson, and Warrick stood silent in awe.

"Use them from now on to move the Evanstone," said Elyon, "nothing else may touch my stone lest it receive its wrath."

Elyon gestured to the riders, "These are the Executives, they carry out the stone's judgement - it is their only master."

The men walked tentatively to the Gemstones, which crouched low so the humans could reach the staffs, then went to the Evanstone. They surrounded it and pressed the staffs into its lower section just below the middle, where the lower and upper halves met in perfectly straight seams.

"Take the stone to the sea," commanded Elyon, "so that it may consider Marland's corruption."

Elzib perched with perfect balance high atop the Bentleigh bell. He looked down on the village. Whips beat the backs of struggling slaves, even pregnant women, whose bellies were swollen from the seed of their husbands, or from a soldier whose lust they had been made to quench. Some Marlanders strutted about brandishing weapons, others stumbled wildly or lay passed out in whatever place they happened to be when the effect of the ale they drank, or the berries they ate, or the herbs they smoked overtook them; Kavan had revealed to Valena another secret of Marland - how to concoct mind-altering potions from the fruits of the land. Elzib drew in a deep breath of satisfaction and basked in his power - all is well on Tilden!

His thoughts turned to Marland and Marheon. Certainly Kavan would have things well in hand on Marland, Elzib had no doubt about that, and he was anxious for the next time they would meet, how would Kavan commend him for a job well done? But he wasn't convinced that Drimelen would succeed in Marheon, especially since neither he nor Kavan was there to help. Sandor was strong and not likely to tire, even with the entire horde in Marheon assaulting him. Would it be enough to contain Casilda's captain? Maybe Kavan had been foolish to leave, and foolish to order him and Feloniche away to Tilden – what matter could be so pressing? But if Drimelen failed, perhaps that would be to his benefit – only Drimelen held a higher rank; if Sandor escaped, perhaps he'd be given an opportunity to replace Kavan's second in command.

A gust of wind blew suddenly from the south, but Elzib remained calm, repositioning himself on top of the bell to face the disturbance. The source of the breeze, a tall, pale, skeletal figure sprinted from the forest and stood before Elzib.

There was no need for Elzib to speak, yet he made it clear to Feloniche that he wanted to know what was happening.

"The Executives are here!" declared Feloniche.

Elzib moved his head slowly from side to side in disbelief.

"I've seen them! They're coming down from Mount Rigid. The Outcasts and Gemstones are with them."

"Impossible! They've never left the king's city – they don't belong here! Their duties are not for this world!"

"Search me! See if I speak the truth!"

Feloniche relaxed his mental guard and Elzib looked into the reservoir of his mind and found the images – ten gray riders on ten gray stallions followed the Gemstones and Outcasts, who were carrying a giant diamond with a fire burning inside.

"Send all our forces down to the sea at once!"

*   *   *   *   *   *   *   *   *   *   *

The silence of the forest was soothing. Alone in preferred isolation, Kira thought of Elson. She had wanted to go with him, but he said Justin was determined to get to Rigid early and there was no way she could keep up. Besides, she had sensed it was important for Elson to be alone with Warrick and Justin.

And she was reluctant for people to see her walking about; she feared that when Idris learned she'd survived he would send for her again, or maybe even come across the water for her himself. Being by herself was best for her survival.

But was survival the best thing for her?

She had felt the question weighing on her recently, but had been able to push it aside. Now, however, there were no distractions to aid her in subduing the depression. Her surroundings were utterly calm and quiet, and scary thoughts bombarded her.

"No! I will not end my life." She said it out loud, angry and scared, desperately hoping the sound of the words would convince her that they were true. She had meant to be firm, for in her mind they were spoken clearly, but she forgot that her speech was slurred, and her stumbling words, instead of strengthening her resolve to live, seemed to support the idea that she'd be better off dead.

"It would devastate my parents," she said, "for their sake I will live."

"But they don't understand you," an inner voice replied, "and you're making life so difficult for them."

"It would devastate Elson," she countered.

"But he'd be free to find another woman – a bride that was beautiful, a bride that he deserves," came the silent response.

Tears formed as she considered that the best thing she could do for Elson would be to die.

"What joy remains for me? What do I have to look forward to?" Her sorrow grew with every question, for she didn't have any answers.

She sensed something coming, and welcomed anything that would delay this bitter contemplation.

Baldwin approached, wondering how best to accomplish his purpose with Kira. He saw that she wasn't alone - a ghastly figure stood over her, groping and prodding her mind. He had brown, hairless skin and orange hair that was long and snarled. His knees bent backward, his elbows bent forward, his face was rearranged so that his mouth was above his nose and his eyes below it; his chosen shape was a rebellious declaration against the one who had made him.

"Out of the way, Loller," ordered Baldwin, "I've got business with the ugly woman."

Loller jumped up, surprised by Baldwin's arrival. He wiped the drool out of his eyes and turned to greet the twin. Baldwin was dressed in the white garb of a Casildan soldier, and on his back he carried one of their shields with the emblem of the eagle. "Where's the other?" he asked, for he expected Durwin to be with him.

"I'm alone."

Baldwin revealed himself to Kira, who up til then had been unable to see the immortals.

"Who are you?" she asked.

The dialogue between the twin and Loller remained one of telepathy, but he spoke out loud to Kira; "Don't you recognize me?"

Kira looked into his face for a long time. He was terrible and pure at the same time. Then she remembered; "You were there that night! You drove us from our homes and pushed us into the sea!"

Loller laughed.

"I removed you from a place that was no longer safe. I'm Baldwin - can't you recognize me?"

Kira shook her head. "You're so different – not at all as I remember you."

"It's you that has changed, not me."

"Why did you interrupt my work? I was making great progress today." Loller grew suspicious; "What do you intend to do with her?"

Baldwin let down his guard so that Loller could see his purpose.

Loller laughed again. "I want to come."

Baldwin nodded, but just then Feloniche came running, shouting that Elzib demanded Loller's presence. Loller obeyed and left, regretfully.

"What do you want from me?" asked Kira.

"I need to take you to meet with someone."

"Who?"

"My master."

"I'm not sure I trust you. Why should I go?"

"Because I'm still your friend."

Kira wasn't certain that she agreed, but consented to go with him.

Baldwin took her and lifted her up, placing her comfortably on his shoulder and began to walk north. He didn't seem to be exerting himself, but they moved very fast, and only a couple of minutes passed until they arrived at the shore of the South Sea. As soon as Baldwin stepped onto the sand, a creature shot out from a breaking wave and came halfway up the beach as if to meet them. In spite of all that had changed, Kira thought this animal remained as amazing as it had ever been. But when Baldwin told her to climb on its back, she became afraid.

"Is the orca safe? Many animals have become dangerous."

"This one has indeed become a killer, but at the moment knows not hunger, nor warmth, nor cold, nor fear; only that it's to take us to Marland."

Kira still wasn't comfortable. "Isn't there another way for us to get across?"

"This is the plan that has been set in place." Baldwin helped Kira get on the whale, then looked up and saw a group of people coming from the south, from Rigid, and another group coming from the southeast, from Bentleigh. He took a seat behind her, in front of the creature's tall dorsal fin, just as an enormous wave flooded the shore. The orca rose up, spun around, and swam out to sea, staying shallow so as to keep Kira's head above water. Baldwin held his shield in front of her to prevent her from being swept away by the force of the water. If there were no delays, he was certain he would deliver Kira in time.

*   *   *   *   *   *   *   *   *   *   *

Wendel leapt back in surprise, his heel caught on the ground and he fell. The man had appeared out of nowhere to stand directly in front of him, and the sticks that he'd been carrying scattered across the ground. The man's expression was commanding, if he was a man, and struck Wendel with fear. When he drew his sword, Wendel wondered whether his days had come to an end.

"Where is your book?" asked Durwin.

"Which book?" Wendel said, for he possessed two.

"The one that contains the history of your people since the island fell."

"Here, I always carry it." Wendel pulled the book from his garments and held it up.

"Bring it. Follow me."

Wendel got to his feet and followed. Though he would likely receive a beating later for not bringing the firewood to Valena, he had greater fear of what would happen if he disobeyed.

When they reached the beach, Durwin stopped and turned around so that he faced north toward the tower. "Read."

"Read what?"

"The entries in your book; read them out loud." Durwin opened the book at random and held it out to Wendel. "You need not read them all now. Begin here and don't stop."

With his back to the breaking waves of Corliss Lake, Wendel began; "*October 1st, year 272: It has been several days since…*"

"Louder!" Commanded Durwin.

Wendel cleared his throat and began again, this time with greater effort; "*October 1st, year 272: It has been several days since Ansen Verrill left Tilden to go to Marland in search of his son, Elson. It has been suggested that…*" Wendel didn't look up from the text again, and read as loud and clear as he could. If he had looked up, he would have seen his friends - all of the Tildenian slaves on Marland, approaching and Gavril following close behind, escorting them. Wendel went on; "*October 13th, year 272: It was learned today that Idris has killed Ansen Verrill. This news was delivered…*"

Gavril positioned the slaves between Wendel and Corliss Lake, while he and Durwin stood in front of Wendel, between him and the tower, with their swords drawn and shields ready. They knew it wouldn't be long before they were confronted.

*   *   *   *   *   *   *   *   *   *   *

The longer Elson and Warrick stared at the diamond, the more in awe they became. Justin, walking in front with his back to the Evanstone, didn't have the opportunity to study it, and he was anxious to stop so that he could look at it again.

But that may have to wait, for when the sea came into sight, so did the spectacle of a vast army, every soldier brandishing a glimmerstone weapon.

Justin halted. Elson and Warrick stopped immediately after. The Gemstones stopped too, but the Executives continued to move forward, splitting into two groups of five to flank the diamond and the others. The fire in the Evanstone grew violent - thunder roared, and flashes of light danced within, reflecting off the perfect walls. The riders lowered long spears as their steeds began to sprint toward the sea.

*   *   *   *   *   *   *   *   *   *   *

Idris rushed up the wide marble stairs at the base of the tower. He had received news of strange events happening on Tilden – news from one of the scouts whose job it was to survey the land across the water with a spotting scope. Valena waited for him in the throne room; she would be there, he knew, attempting to summon Kavan. But he stopped short of the entrance when a voice called out; "What you want is not in there."

Idris turned to see Kavan appear beside the entrance.

"What's happening?"

"It's time for you to receive what you asked for."

Idris waited silently, questioning Kavan with his eyes.

"I'll take you to the Icyandic now."

"What about Lachlan and Valena?"

"They are not to drink from the white river, only you. They've already received all that they asked for. Besides, Lachlan is needed here and I will meet with Valena shortly." Kavan glanced toward the sea.

Idris spun to look there as well and saw that Lachlan had assembled the entire Marland army and was leading it toward a group of slaves that seemed to have escaped and huddled together behind Wendel Wright, who was reading loudly from a large book.

"I won't offer again – come with me now or never again see the Icyandic." Kavan walked north into the woods.

Idris followed Kavan.

$$*\quad*\quad*\quad*\quad*\quad*\quad*\quad*\quad*\quad*\quad*$$

The ease with which the Executives rode over the Marland troops was incredible. The Marlanders had expected a victory, and an easy one, over the horsemen, who numbered less than a dozen. Never before had their glimmerstone been ineffective; they had learned from Lachlan how to manipulate it to beat, crush, cut, grip, lash, poke, slice, and split whatever they wanted. Their weapons moved as swiftly as ever, obeying their imaginations, but the gray figures, and even the beasts that carried them, were impervious to their efforts, so much so that they didn't even attempt to defend themselves. Instead, the riders marched steadily through the

Marlander ranks and drove their spears into them, piercing their hearts. The slaughter was over in a few minutes - no Marlander remained alive on Tilden.

When the last soldier fell, a wave swept onto the shore and dragged the lifeless away as if Tilden itself objected to having to bear the burden of the dead and commanded the sea to clean its shore. The water receded - no Marlander remained on Tilden.

The Executives acknowledged their duty there was done and turned north, for during the fight the Evanstone was exposed to Marland and sensed great corruption there. The lightning within the stone remained intense, and the thunderclaps continued. It ordered the Executives across the water.

Hooves clapped against the surface as the creatures ran over the sea. Unhindered by the motion of the waves, they advanced with great speed. The riders held out their spears, pointing them at the place where corruption was greatest - they headed directly for the tower with intent to collect debts that had come due.

*　　*　　*　　*　　*　　*　　*　　*　　*　　*　　*

Sandor's clothes were ripped to shreds. What remained of his uniform hung in loose loops about him. But his strategy was working: ever since Kavan and Elzib and Feloniche had gone he had a much easier time defending himself. He'd been able to cast Drimelen down onto the lava covered floor several times, not that the lava hurt him, but the reprieve allowed Sandor to move closer to the highest point in the cave, the place where he'd try to make his escape.

The struggle had seen more than two days pass, and Sandor knew that he couldn't keep up the fight indefinitely. Besides, the sooner he got away, the better chance he had at stopping Durwin and Baldwin from committing whatever treacherous deeds they intended.

He gripped his shield with both hands and spun around fast, ramming it into the swarming hive of warriors that surrounded him to scatter them. His shield was scratched and battered, but it remained strong enough. Drimelen had not yet returned from the last time

Sandor had thrown him down, and Sandor shot for the roof. Finally the path was clear!

Relief washed over him as he flew up through the firmament; none of the horde could catch him now. He ascended to the sea, then soared into the air over Corliss Lake.

*   *   *   *   *   *   *   *   *   *   *

"How much further?" asked Kira. Baldwin had been carrying her ever since the killer whale deposited them safely on Marland, far enough away from the tower to avoid the commotion there.

"Just ahead," replied Baldwin. "There."

Kira saw two figures standing in the shadows beside the path about thirty yards in front of her. Panic struck as she recognized them. "Put me down! Take me away from here, take me anywhere but here!"

Baldwin refused to let her go, though she struggled with all her might to get down. "You're no friend to me! You lied – you *have* changed, you're evil!" She pounded her fists into Baldwin's chest.

Idris and Kavan were delighted by her arrival.

*   *   *   *   *   *   *   *   *   *   *

"...*285th year: The Overlords decreed today that the work on the tower shall be increased to finish...*" Wendel's reading continued in spite of the fact that his voice had grown hoarse. Durwin and Gavril remained in front of Wendel with swords drawn and shields at the ready to meet Lachlan and his troops and a number of Kavan's horde that drove them on in a fury. Only Gavril and Durwin were aware of the oncoming horde, as they remained invisible to the mortals.

"This fight is not for us," said Gavril to Durwin.

"How far out are they?" replied Durwin.

"Half a league, and coming fast. The Tildenians are slow – we need to get them away from here," urged Gavril. "Take them. I'll hold off Lachlan and the horde."

Durwin shed his invisibility. "Whoever is loyal to King Iman, follow me and live!" he shouted as he walked past the slaves onto the sea. They hesitated to follow, but when they saw that Lachlan and his forces were nearly upon them they ran to the water, expecting to sink into the waves and thinking that they had a long swim before them. To their astonishment, they floated on the waves, bobbing up and down, struggling to walk behind Durwin, who seemed to be leading them not directly to the south, but diagonally out from the shore.

But Lachlan was there, only a few yards from the stragglers, those among the slaves that hesitated longest to follow Durwin or were slow. Lachlan raised his black and silver sword to begin the killing.

Gavril revealed himself to Lachlan and the other Marlanders.

Lachlan let his first blow fall on the shield of the stranger, the only one who seemed able to offer any resistance.

The horde paused, amused at sight of Lachlan fighting Gavril. But then they saw the Executives approaching and fled.

Lachlan struck the stranger's shield again. His blade carved a deep cut across the eagle's beak. Gavril absorbed the blow but didn't retaliate.

Some of the Lachlan's troops stopped advancing to watch the fight. Others pursued the slaves into Corliss Lake, only to find that they couldn't remain on top of the water like them. Some of them turned back, but some swam on to continue the chase.

"This way! Quickly!" ordered Durwin. "Get clear of their path to the tower!"

The people moved as fast as they could: some tried to hurdle the waves; some laid down on the sea and tried to roll over them; some carefully positioned their feet, not taking a step until they had confidence of solid footing; some crawled on all fours; some moved forward alone; some pulled each other in groups, holding hands and locking arms.

The Executives were close, within a hundred yards. Their spears glinted in the sun. The sound of their approach was like a cyclone.

Linus glanced at the nearest rider. So impressed by the figure was he that he forgot Durwin's instruction to get out of the way. The rider turned to the side and looked at Linus and found him corrupt, guilty. His spear pivoted sideways and reached out to strike...

The rest of the Tildenians managed to get to a safe distance and Durwin declared that they need not race on in panic any longer.

"What are you?" Lachlan slammed his blade once more into Gavril's shield, adding another slash across the eagle's head.

Gavril didn't speak, but placed his battered shield on his back and sheathed his sword as he lifted up from the ground, giving Lachlan a clear view of the Executives. The swimming Marlanders that had been pursuing the Tildenians were already dead – red droplets fell from three of the riders' spears.

The horsemen quit their rapid pace as they reached land, but moved steadily into the charge of the Marland army. Lachlan led the attack and was one of the first to fall, his heart neatly stabbed by one of the spears.

With their leader dead and their numbers dwindling, the Marlander soldiers retreated to join all of Marland's citizens in the tower, for all the people had become afraid and took refuge in the tall building.

     *　　*　　*　　*　　*　　*　　*　　*　　*　　*　　*

"Changed your mind?" asked Idris, cheerfully.

"No! No I have not!" exclaimed Kira. She shook badly and knew that if Baldwin put her down she'd fall.

"Don't be afraid, daughter. You haven't been brought here for them, but to meet with me." Someone else was there. Kira probed in her memory to recall the voice, for it sounded familiar.

"This one's of little value," said Kavan. "Let us have her, after all she is rightfully his." Kavan nodded toward Idris.

"She is of great value," replied King Iman, "and she is mine. Your task is finished here, Kavan – be gone."

Kavan bent down and whispered something to Idris, then left.

"Icyandic! Come forth!" cried King Iman. Immediately the ground split apart and a trench formed, about fifty feet long, ten feet wide, and ten feet deep. It stayed empty for only a few seconds, then a gush of white water sprang up and filled it.

Idris dropped to the ground and strained to reach the rising water.

Neither the king nor Baldwin moved to stop him, but the king warned; "It would be better for you if you didn't drink. This is not what I desire for you."

Idris didn't refrain - at last the cold water touched his lips! The taste was sweeter than anything he had ever known. After several long draughts, for he wanted to be certain that he drank enough to become immortal, he rose to his feet and ran into the woods.

Baldwin sensed that Kira's trembling had subsided and he put her down beside the king and beside the flowing river.

"Go into the water, Kira," said the king, "but don't open your mouth and drink. Submerge yourself and be transformed – I offer you a new life."

Kira went to the edge of the trench and sat down clumsily. She let her legs drop in; they tingled as if cold, but she sensed that the water was warm. She slid forward, trying to inch herself in slowly, but realized she couldn't - she'd have to let go and fall in all at once. She wondered if she should drink the water and glanced up at the Caretaker. His eyes held her gaze and convinced her to trust him. Into the water she went, her mouth closed tight.

The tingling sensation flowed through her entire body - it was invigorating, bordering on sensuous. She was reluctant to leave, but she needed to surface for breath. She swam up and Baldwin lifted her out of the river and placed her before King Iman.

She felt at ease and looked down at her body: her crooked limbs were straight; her skin was taught; her breasts were full and high! "Thank you!" Her speech was clear!

King Iman gave a subtle nod to send the Icyandic back to the depths and the ground came together to close the trench.

"Why did you let Idris drink, but told me not to?"

"Death, though unpleasant, serves a purpose," replied King Iman. He could see from her expression that she wanted a deeper explanation. "Some things that at first seem to be a curse, turn out to be a blessing. Some things that at first seem a blessing turn out to be a curse. You weren't meant to be as you are forever – the Icyandic would've prevented you from experiencing a greater transformation. Remember that I also advised Idris not to drink."

Kira wasn't sure she understood, but if she did, she didn't know if she agreed.

"Go to your husband."

She shuddered, "Who is my husband?"

"The one who loves you more than himself."

"What about Idris? He won't allow me to be with Elson now."

"His rule here is finished. You'll never see him again."

*　　*　　*　　*　　*　　*　　*　　*　　*　　*　　*

Justin, Elson, and Warrick thought the Gemstones had left them when they came down from Mount Rigid. The Gemstones were there, it was only that they had resumed their invisibility. They were obviously aware, however, that the rest of the Tildenians had come down to see what was happening once word spread that they were carrying a large diamond of fire and were being followed by ten mysterious riders.

"Stay back! Don't touch it!" shouted Warrick, remembering Elyon's warning, for the people had gathered around the floating diamond.

Unbeknownst to the Tildenians, a terrific battle raged around them - the Gemstones fended off a large number of Kavan's horde. With the Executives gone, the horde had regained their courage and attacked in full force to destroy the humans, specifically the three who carried the Evanstone.

Justin wanted desperately to know what the Executives were doing; "Keelan," he cried, extending his hand. Keelan promptly handed Justin the spotting scope that was hung over his shoulder. Justin lifted it to his eye and searched the horizon.

*　　*　　*　　*　　*　　*　　*　　*　　*　　*　　*

Valena, having witnessed Lachlan's death from the balcony outside the throne room, closed the doors, barred them shut, and barricaded herself within the upper level of the tower as best she could. Then she dropped to the floor face down and sought her master.

After several minutes without a sign that Kavan would come, she rose and went again to the balcony. From her high perch she saw that the ten riders had spread out and surrounded the tower. Valena could hear faint sounds on the levels below, and an occasional rapping against the doors.

She went back inside and fell to the floor again. This time, Kavan came quickly.

"My lord, I'm trapped!" she exclaimed as she rose to her feet. "Who are these men that have destroyed Lachlan and have no fear of glimmerstone?"

"They are not of this realm. Their strength is beyond the power of the black stone."

"Will you help me?"

"Of course, daughter, would I have come otherwise?"

"What should I do?"

"There's only one way for you to escape their wrath." He drew one of his trident swords and presented it to Valena, gripping the central blade to offer her the handle.

The time had come - all the Marlanders had gone into the tower. The Executives pressed their heels into the stallions' sides and they moved forward. They reached the base of the structure together, and through numerous doorways entered the empty ground level. Inside, they dispersed and began to climb.

The first kill was made on the sixth level, one-fifth to the top. It wasn't long after and the white stairs and walls were covered in streams of blood, red ribbons that fell all the way down and out the open doorways onto the sand.

The muffled screams grew louder, more distinct, and the commotion below more intense. Valena took Kavan's blade, not fully comprehending what he wanted her to do with it.

"There's little time," Kavan warned. "If you want to escape you must shed your flesh. Use the sword to get free; leave your body and come with me."

"Can't you fight them? Can't you destroy them, or at least repel them from the tower – your tower? Will you let it be taken without offering any challenge, and without defending those loyal to you?"

"I could have, my daughter, if you hadn't been so careless as to give your staff away." Kavan's tone became less gentle, less benevolent. "Don't you know that it was used for bringing them here?"

Valena wept and fell at Kavan's feet, still holding the sword. "I'm sorry! I'm so sorry! Won't you fight them now?"

Kavan smiled.

Valena began to understand. "You can't defeat them, can you?"

"You have no more time. Use the sword."

Valena grasped it with both hands, but didn't raise it. "I don't think I can do it. Will you help me?"

Kavan nodded. "Of course."

He lifted her up and led her to her throne. He helped her to sit and took her crown and placed it on her head. He placed his hands around hers so they held the sword together and raised its point to Valena's chest. Kavan pushed the blade slowly through her body until it pierced the back of the throne.

Valena tensed and convulsed and whimpered with pain.

"It'll be over soon, my daughter." Kavan's eyes revealed pleasure, and his ears savored the sound of her blood splattering onto the stone floor. He kept one hand around hers and caressed her brow with his other, not to comfort her, but to experience her death more intimately. Then her spirit abandoned her body and sank to the nether world of the dead.

"She's the last one," a voice called from the balcony, "there will be no more seasonal slayings."

Kavan turned to see Gavril entering.

"Truly, I'm not surprised to see the manner in which you treat your *children*," said Gavril. "Lying to them, leading them into darkness, delighting at their death."

Kavan pulled his sword from the throne and Valena's limp body and confronted Gavril, pleased at having an opportunity to fight the captain.

Gavril didn't draw his sword or reach for his shield. "The Executives won't be slowed by any of those," he nodded to the makeshift barricades that Valena had installed.

"It's not time for me to face them."

"Their current purpose is to kill everything in this place that is corrupt. Do you think they'll excuse you?"

There were no more screams coming from below. In the sudden silence, Kavan's smile and confidence fled. He sheathed his sword and flew from the tower just as all of the doors flew open and the Executives burst in.

*　*　*　*　*　*　*　*　*　*　*

Through the spotting scope, Justin saw his friends coming across the sea – on top of it! He saw limbs flail frantically as they struggled to stay on their feet. They employed various maneuvers to move on top of the water in pursuit of a magnificent figure in white linen. And on their faces, he saw smiles. He'd seen this before. Many times before!

Then he understood! The images of his nightmare were coming to fulfillment, only his friends weren't in danger as he'd always perceived; they were safe and free - the oppression was over!

He lowered the scope and looked out over the sea with naked eyes to see the dancing dots of people far away. Deep down, a laugh began to gurgle upward. The first chuckles were quickly replaced by a stream of loud bursts. Never had he laughed with such joy! He had heard this before. Many times before!

Then he understood the visions further! The laughter of the dream that he'd always thought evil was not – it was his own! His laughter grew stronger at the realization.

Warrick came and took the scope from Justin's hand and lifted it to his eye to see what had given his friend such merriment.

Elzib was outraged that his forces weren't able to get to the humans - the Gemstones were too fast and too strong. Though they were unable to fly, bound to the earth, they swatted ferociously at the horde with their long, solid limbs, keeping them away from the people gathered around the Outcasts and the Evanstone. The Executives had slain the Marlander soldiers, all of them, and Kavan wouldn't be pleased. Elzib felt that his only hope for redemption lie in defeating the Gemstones and killing the Tildenians. With the Executives gone, he thought it a possible task.

Elzib shifted his focus angrily toward Marland and wondered what Kavan had done when he learned that the Executives were approaching. Did he fight? Or flee? Had he been captured, or worse? Was he free to join the battle on Tilden? Elzib scanned the sky and saw no sign of his coming. Instead, he saw a group of people walking on the water. He saw the one leading them…

"Baldwin!" he bellowed. In a split second he realized the humans could see the king's servant. "Traitor!"

Elzib cast off his invisibility – if Baldwin could be seen, then so could he! The people on the beach turned as one to face him, fear strangling their hearts.

Justin's laughter died.

Onyx, still out of sight to the humans, stood between them. Elzib crouched down, then sprang at the black Gemstone. Onyx grabbed the ends of the two long horns.

That was exactly what Elzib wanted – he dug his feet down and with his thick legs spun about as fast as he could. Onyx didn't have time to release his grasp and was cast aside.

A clear path before him, Elzib searched for a valuable kill; two worthy victims were in range. He leapt forward, grabbed Emily and Tanya and held them high in the air. He savored the moment and anticipated their deaths.

A blow to his belly sent him tumbling back. The two women were flung further away from their friends, closer to the trail that led back to Bentleigh. Loller and Feloniche went for the girls, but Topaz and Sapphire stopped them and threw them into the sea. Elzib kicked Onyx off and rose to pursue Emily and Tanya. Onyx attempted to follow but was immediately engaged by the swarming horde.

Without perceiving the presence of their protectors, and seeing Elzib coming at her, with nowhere else to go, Emily sprinted up the trail. Tanya, a strong runner, followed and soon took the lead. They knew it hindered them, but they couldn't help looking back to see if the monster was still chasing them.

It was!

Elzib's girth was more than the path could accommodate, and he smashed into trees on both sides, bending them wildly or snapping them if they refused to flex.

The sound of cracking lumber behind them gave the women a sense of the power that their predator possessed and inspired them to move faster with renewed energy. Tanya was getting far ahead of Emily; she wanted to stop and wait for her, but fear prevented her.

Elzib knew he could take them at anytime, but was enjoying the chase. The high-pitched shrill screams invigorated him, but he accepted the fact that if he delayed too long, someone might come and spoil the fun. He increased his speed.

Tanya turned and saw that Elzib was dangerously close to Emily, almost within reach. Running forward while looking behind, Tanya's foot caught on a stone; she stumbled ahead several steps but couldn't maintain her balance – she fell.

Emily came upon her fallen friend in a few seconds and stopped to help her up.

Elzib was there – he was upon them!

They had no chance to flee, and they knew it; they squeezed one another and braced for pain and death.

Elzib could taste their fear, could almost feel their warm blood flowing down his long horns. A couple more seconds and they would be skewered on them, then he would return to the sea with their bodies on his spikes to show their husbands! Only two tiny, insignificant trees stood between him and the women. He reared up on his heels and lunged forward.

The trees bent over until their trunks touched the ground, but didn't break. Elzib couldn't reach the women. He was surprised when the trees righted themselves and pushed him backward. He couldn't get his horns out, they were sunk in deep. He pushed against one tree while pulling on the other, then tried the opposite. He pulled back as far as he could, trying to rip the trees out of the ground. They remained in place. He pushed them over in every direction – they sprang up straight every time, and with each movement bark fell away and revealed that they weren't trees at all, but tall steel shafts smeared all over with black streaks! Elzib let out a loud lowing sound to call for help. He tried to reach the girls again, but they were still too far away.

Emily and Tanya crawled up the path to increase the distance between them and the monster.

Elzib kicked and pulled and hit and surged and dropped and spun, but he was stuck. He called out again.

Warrick, Justin, and Elson, arrived. Warrick ran to Tanya, Justin to Emily. They all stared at the shafts that had been trees, then at Elzib, trapped, and were amazed.

Sandor landed beside the struggling Elzib. "Will you slay him, my Lord?"

The humans could see Sandor, but they didn't know who he had spoken to until they heard the crackle of flames; "I don't take pleasure in the death of anyone." Elyon appeared, he had been standing beside the women. He looked down at the Tildenians; "It's safe now. Go back to the others beside the sea."

They obeyed, making sure to stay far away from Elzib's thrashing as they went.

After they had gone, Sandor spoke again; "What shall be done with him? Take him back to Casilda and keep him with the others?"

"Where were you?" asked Elyon.

"I was trying to stop the twins. I followed them to Marheon. They had some part to play in this didn't they! I'm too late! What treachery did they accomplish?"

"They only did what I told them to," rebuked Elyon. "You may be my greatest warrior, but you don't know the details of all my plans."

Sandor felt very foolish; he looked at the condition of his uniform and was embarrassed. "Carollan went with me – he couldn't get free."

Elyon nodded; he knew already.

"Why didn't you tell me?" asked Sandor.

"I wanted you to learn two valuable things: humility, and the location of Marheon."

"I now know them."

"Take Elzib back to Casilda, but don't leave him there. Take him and all of the captured horde to Marheon and lock them in the pit. The prince will go with you, and he'll oversee Carollan's release, for he has the key to the pit and will hand it over to you."

  * * * * * * * * * * *

The horde fled when they learned of Elzib's capture, leaving the twelve Gemstones as the only invisible beings on the Tilden coast. The people rejoiced as they were reunited with brothers and sisters, fathers and mothers, sons and daughters, and friends; those who had come from Marland and finally arrived after the long walk over the sea.

And Thalassa's Crown came into sight, that magnificent vessel, sailing in from the west, ship and crew in plain view for all to see. It anchored and Gavril came onto the land and instructed Justin, Elson, and Warrick to bring the Evanstone on board so that it could be brought to the tower.

The Outcasts and their families boarded the ship, while everyone else rushed to find other boats so they could follow. Gavril delayed departing until he saw that the people were assembled, then he gave the order to sail.

They weren't more than half a league out when a fiery comet sailed overhead, a blazing orange ball that filled the sky like a second sun. It was too bright to view directly for longer than an instant, but in quick glimpses the people thought they saw a black figure within.

Elyon focused on the tower and made straight for it, soaring over the trees into the wide open expanse above the water. But he didn't intend to go alone: when he summoned Onyx, the Gemstone lifted into the sky into Elyon's embrace like a piece of iron drawn to a strong magnet.

"It's time for you to recover a portion of what was stolen from you," said Elyon. "First gather what you find at the shore, then inside the tower, then go to the cave behind Great Falls."

"It will feel good to be more complete," replied Onyx.

"Begin with this." Elyon presented a small glossy black sphere and handed it to Onyx. "From the trees – the women are safe, and Elzib is captured."

"I'm honored that you used me."

Elyon released Onyx as soon as he was over Marland. Onyx landed solidly on the sand, while Elyon crashed into the ground, abandoning his human shape to become a consuming fire, spreading all across the land and into the tower.

Bodies were scattered all over – the remains of the Executives' harvest. Not only those who had been slain on Marland, but also those who died on Tilden, for the sea had been made to deposit them on Marland, their weapons also. These were what concerned Onyx – they were grafted with his flesh, stolen by Kavan long ago. Elyon's fire caused the glimmerstone to soften, and Onyx wiped the black material from the weapons and adsorbed it into his body.

The Tildenians watched the inferno from the water. They were certain there'd be nothing left of Seton but ash, and expected the tower to topple over at any moment. But as they drew closer, the flames subsided and the tower remained. A blizzard came in from the east and from the west, delivering a heavy snow upon the land.

By the time Thalassa's Crown arrived, nearly a foot of snow had fallen, and, except for the tower looming high above, the place looked as if it had never before been inhabited. There were no docks, no homes, no buildings whatsoever, save the tower. There was no sign of a battle – no blood, no rotting flesh, and no pieces of bone. Not even the steel of the weapons remained. The snowstorm subsided and the sun came out.

The blizzard had not been kept from inside the tower, and the floors and stairs were covered with several inches of snow, the deepest spots near openings to the outside. Kira stood alone in the center of the lowest floor. There were no footprints in the snow around her, and she wore the same brown skirt and laced top that she had worn the day she married Elson beside the ash tree. And the seven yellow ribbons that Elson had given her had been recovered and were wrapped around her neck and arms and legs. She wasn't cold or frightened, for King Iman had told her to go there and wait. Even during the fire and the wind, and with a black stone giant walking around, and then the snowstorm, she had stood firmly in place with a sense of peace from knowing that as long as she obeyed her king, there was no safer place for her.

"Kira!" Elson recognized her immediately and ran to her, abandoning his place at the Evanstone. "Kira!"

"Elson!" Kira, also, when she saw Elson enter the tower, ran across the snowy floor and fell into him. Tears of joy dripped down her cheeks, leaving moist streaks on her perfect skin. Elson tried to push her away so that he could look upon her beauty, but Kira resisted, not wanting to be parted from him in the least.

Six years later...

The grass tickled the soft undersides of Kira's bare feet. She craved the sensation and pushed down, but this bent the blades of grass over and the ticklish feeling disappeared altogether. She lifted her feet slightly so that the blades became erect again and the sensation returned. The morning sun was beginning to strengthen, and she reminded herself not to bask too long in its rays. There was no evidence to give her reason to worry about the sun giving her wrinkles - her skin was as smooth and supple as it had been when she was a little girl, a trait that she credits to having been submerged in the Icyandic, but she wasn't invulnerable to being burned.

She wasn't the only one who seemed impervious to aging — acquiring years without suffering physical attrition was something all those who had lived on the island experienced. Again, this was thought to be due to their exposure to the white river. For those who had been born after the island disappeared, however, this was not the case. Some of them were now approaching forty and were beginning to show signs that their bodies were failing. Wrinkled skin, creased around the eyes and mouth, loss of hair among the men, sagging breasts among the women, were a few indicators that they were not as strong and healthy as those who had once been called islanders. It was ironic that some people that appeared to be the youngest were, in fact, often the oldest, a phenomenon credited to their long-time exposure to the Icyandic. Kira looked around at her friends and wondered if her beauty would last beyond theirs, given her unique exposure to the river, and if so, would they become envious of her?

A butterfly fluttered past, and she rose to pursue it as gracefully as she could in spite of her round belly that was more than a half dozen months ripe. It would be her and Elson's second child. "Shane, come see the butterfly!" Her first born, a boy, now three years old, ran from a group of children to join his mom and trapped the insect in his hands.

Kira had been fascinated with butterflies her whole life, but especially since her transformation in the Icyandic. The process that a caterpillar undergoes, shedding a shape that is unsightly and cumbersome to obtain one that is glorious and beautiful, was something that she had experienced herself and treasured. But even more than the transformation of her past, she believed the metamorphosis of the butterfly was a model of what was yet to come, and that she would be transformed again into something that would make her current body pale in comparison.

"Be careful. Don't hold it too tight."

Shane obeyed and moved his cupped hands apart to make sure the delicate winged creature was unharmed. When he saw that it was, he closed his hands over it again and looked to his mom for instructions of what to do next.

"Go show the other children," she suggested. Shane ran off and Kira waddled back to the cove and saw that Conroy and Keelan had arrived and reclined beside their wives, Allison and Megan, respectively.

"Isn't this beautiful?" Amara said as Kira sat down next to her.

"Except for the island, this is my favorite place," responded Kira. She looked up at the waterfall cascading from the middle of Great Falls, and at the white walls of the steep gorge on either side, then down at the clear water in the pool at the base of the falls, then at the incessant waves dancing over Corliss Lake, and finally at the spectacular tower.

Megan brushed aside strands of straight, golden-yellow hair that the breeze placed in front of her eyes, and noticed the smile on Keelan's face, a slightly mischievous grin that spread across his cheeks. She looked down at her belly, for she was also with child, wondering if it had become exposed. They had been married for over twenty years and had seven children, though he may not have sired them all, but this would be their first born into a life of freedom, and as such carried a new excitement. "What?" She couldn't help smile in return. "What are you smiling at?"

Keelan didn't answer.

Megan turned to Conroy, who had joined Allison and placed his arm around her; "Why is my husband smiling so?"

Conroy rolled his eyes. "Enough already. If you don't tell them, I will."

Keelan stood up and held his arms out. "I'm pleased to announce that the first annual Tournament of Marland Games will be held in August!"

"This August?" asked Bethany.

"This August!" Keelan was ecstatic. It was well known that he'd been spearheading a campaign for a number of years to recommence what had been the Tournament of Island Games.

"It won't be the same," replied Amara. "What's the point?"

Keelan's smile shrunk a little and he looked to Megan, who wore an *I-told-you-so* expression. "Nothing's the same?" With a well-practiced response, he said; "Do we not still have arms and legs and hands and feet? Can we not still run and jump and swim and throw? Do we not still have muscles and minds and eyes and hearts and lungs? Of course we do – we have all these things still! Then I say let's use them to the best of our ability! Let's celebrate who we are and what we can do!"

"Lots of people are moving away," said Amara.

"All the more reason for having the games. What could be better for reuniting us once a year?" Keelan's smile was back to full size. "But there is something we need."

"What?"

"Signs!" Keelan looked at Conroy.

Conroy and Allison's son, five-year old Garrick, came from playing with the other children and fell into Conroy's lap. Hot and sweaty, he took up a cup of water and gulped it in a thirsty frenzy. Distracted by Garrick, Conroy had been oblivious to Keelan's stare.

Keelan observed that Conroy hadn't perceived the hint and asked directly; "Conroy, will you make new signs for the games?"

Conroy looked down at Garrick and drew a hand across the top of the child's head to straighten messy hair. "Would you like to learn how to carve wood?"

Garrick's excited nod settled it – he and his dad would provide signs for the games.

Onyx stood on the north wall of Great Falls' gorge and looked down on the happy people. He was pleased that this particular group stayed, but many others had left, spreading out across the world, now that freedom afforded them the option. Some left to get away from the place of tragedy; some left to go search for new mysteries of the world. Whatever the reason, a large portion of the people had gone.

Onyx had come to realize that it was because of this that he and his companions had been separated. Of the twelve, he was the only Gemstone who remained nearby: Elyon had instructed them to spread out so that they could protect the entire world. It was Elyon's order that Onyx remain to watch over Bentleigh and Seton. Seton had been given a new name, however, Sutton, meaning *southern settlement*, because it was the southernmost city in the vast country of Marland, and because the people desired to rid themselves of all that remained of what Idris had established.

Though scattered to the ends of the world, the stone guardians were not required to perform their duty by themselves - they were in constant communication with each other, as always, and King Iman had sent troops from Casilda, too many to count, to aid them in resisting Kavan and his horde and their raging hatred.

Onyx turned toward the tower and saw that Carollan was near, a sight that gave him comfort, for he desired to go to Tilden but didn't want to leave without making sure Marland was in good hands. None of Kavan's horde had been seen for some time, but Onyx guessed it wouldn't be long before some dastardly scheme was put into action by the fallen ones. And Scynn, always lurking, managed to keep a strong grip on the mortals, even with the Evanstone present, and came often to manipulate minds and fuel wrongful desires of any who allowed it.

With a bound, Onyx leapt from the pinnacle of the mountain and fell invisible into Corliss Lake and sank rapidly to the bottom. Striding along the seabed, he kept a cautious eye for the enemy. The waters were not patrolled as much as the land and skies, and it was good for him to venture here, he realized; perhaps he should perform more routine surveys of the sea. But he arrived at Tilden without crossing any adversary and stepped onto the path that wound up to Bentleigh.

It was wider now, mostly due to Elzib's rampage, but the Tildenians had also widened it from the spot of Elzib's capture southward to the town. The passage, now more a road than a path, made it easy for the statue of King Iman to be relocated from the seashore to the place where it now stood, between the two silver shafts that had ensnared the monster. When the Evanstone was placed in the upper level of the tower, the people on Tilden became envious and desired to have a monument of their own to celebrate what their king had done for them. The statue seemed the perfect thing – it was already there, and after Conroy made repairs to it as best he could to mend blemishes that had been the result of the Overlords' casting it face down and dancing on its back all night following the assault, the people were very satisfied with it. The surrounding area was cleared and the road made to encircle the statue so that anyone who traveled between the sea and Bentleigh would pass by the memorial. Onyx walked past it, offering only a sideways glance at the graven image of his master.

The old bell still hung in the town's center. During the reign of the Overlords the Tildenians had been permitted to ring it while mourning the death of one of their own. And so to them the sound had grown bittersweet, recalling feelings of pain and hope at the same time, for some thought the sound would carry to the dwelling place of King Iman and that he would come and take away the spirit of the departed to a place of peace and beauty, perhaps back to the island. For this purpose the bell was still used, though if they could see what Onyx saw they would know that there was no need to summon the king – his servants were everywhere. More importantly, Elyon was there.

*   *   *   *   *   *   *   *   *   *   *

Six years is a long time to be alone, and Idris silently scolded himself for staying away until now. His trust in Kavan is what betrayed him, he knew, for he saw no reason to believe the warning his master had whispered in his ear - that King Iman's rage would consume him if he stayed in Marland, and that he should flee far away as fast as he could and wait for Kavan to meet him.

But Idris had not seen Kavan since. The disapproving expression that he'd seen on King Iman's face after he drank the white water, however, gave him reason to stay away. At least it did until Scynn found him again and restored an old vision in his mind. Slowly his attitude toward the king changed from fearful to cautious, then from cautious to disbelieving. Fearless and angry, he now marched toward Seton, only slightly aware that Scynn walked beside him step for step.

What should he have to worry about? He was immortal. There was nothing that could harm him; even Iman himself had no power to destroy him, if he was even still around. And if Iman was gone, he'd assert himself over the mortals and recover his title of Overlord straight away! Soon he'd be back, triumphant, ruling over all from atop the tower. And this time Kira would be with him. No, he had nothing to fear, nothing to lose by returning.

He took a moment to take in the spectacular view surrounding him. A pair of lofty mountain ranges flanked him, rolling south as far as he could see. Flowers were everywhere, fully blossomed, bearing petals so large he thought their stems should have been bent beneath them. He turned around to look to the north, from where he had come; the forest was dark and ominous and for a second he was afraid. Then he became angry that the woods frightened him and he considered chopping down all the trees: it would be very satisfying, he thought, to punish them, and it seemed a good idea to increase the boundary of the beautiful valley, but he was impatient to reach Seton and proceeded forward.

Strange happenings seemed afoot, though, as he noticed the mountains to the east and west seemed larger, steeper, and more rigid. He looked back at the forest again; the trees appeared taller than before, and darkness dominated.

Idris quickened his pace.

But the mountains grew impossibly tall impossibly fast!

He turned east and started to run, thinking that route would offer the quickest exit. But the faster he ran, the steeper the slope became!

And then he realized that the mountains weren't getting taller – he was getting lower; the valley was sinking!

He stopped running and watched.

Only a short time passed until he was surrounded by walls, which had been the valley floor moments before, and the flowers extended toward him horizontally. High above he could see an opening shrinking; the patch of blue sky grew smaller and the flowers pressed against him and tickled his face.

He fended off fear – he was immortal!

The circle of light shrank to a speck and then disappeared as rock ledges came together overhead. Unharmed, he smiled at the ridiculous event, until he realized he had no way of getting out.

*   *   *   *   *   *   *   *   *   *   *

The next day was cloudy. Justin looked out from the balcony on the top level of the tower and thought about the time when clouds were friendly; soft, round puffs of white that filled the sky over the island as decorations. These were different kinds of clouds, these were the kind he saw in visions. They were dark gray, more black than white, and gave Justin the impression that they carried a mean verdict against the land, which they executed by blocking precious sunlight.

Tired of the sullen scene, he went back into the room that housed the Evanstone, the very room that the Overlords had used for their throne room. The large diamond hovered in the center of the space, high enough so that its central seam was level with Justin's chest. As always, streams of yellow, red, and orange danced within the gem. Justin still found the mysterious sight captivating; sometimes he gazed into it for hours.

It was unusual that he was bored. Most days the people required his attention to resolve the issues of their lives, for he, along with Elson and Warrick and their families, had been given the responsibility of governing the people. Elyon instructed that at least one member of the ruling families was to be with the Evanstone, and only members of the royal families were permitted there without being summoned for judgement. So had it been since the day the tower became theirs.

Though bored and lonely, Justin was fully aware that he wasn't alone. All ten Executives surrounded him, standing guard, evenly spaced along the perimeter of the room. Their stoic faces were gray and still, ever staring with dark eyes, and it seemed as if they'd turned to stone, for when they weren't carrying out an order from the Evanstone they never moved. The creatures they rode were gone, Gavril had taken them away on Thalassa's Crown. They came to life easily enough, Justin knew, for he had seen them react to the Evanstone's detection of disobedience many times to send them into action to punish the guilty. He had learned that judgment wasn't a pleasant thing, but he also understood its benefit, for without penalty a criminal might not be deterred. He was glad for the Evanstone and the order it established, but things still weren't good, and it was still his fault.

One haunting memory made this undeniable. Nearly a year had passed, but the pain of the tragedy remained. The circumstances of that day had been similar to this one; he'd been alone with the Evanstone and clouds separated the land from sunshine mercilessly. A young girl, five years old, wandered too far up the tower while searching for her parents. For some reason, the guards at the entry had been away from their posts, and Pollina entered unhindered. The fire within the Evanstone flared immediately and Justin saw the nearest Executive react. She was laughing as if she was being playfully chased when the spear was driven sideways through her tiny heart. Death came so quickly that her face still wore the smile as she collapsed onto the stone floor.

Justin had been angry that he didn't know her name at the time. He remembered clearly the faces of her parents when he found them and presented them with Pollina's broken body; that was something he'd like to forget. Warrick and Tanya had done everything they could to comfort the grieving couple. Having lost Lucy years before, they felt most qualified to guide them through the sorrow and told them that time would ease the anguish.

Justin felt a growing concern for the new generation, that since they hadn't experienced island life themselves, this corrupted world would be all they knew and they might become content with less than was meant for them. But a world where death reigned because of Scynn's presence was no place for Justin, and he longed for the king to send a new gift, a better gift, that would restore all that had been lost.

The sun was still high and Justin grimaced at having to wait a couple more hours until Elson came to relieve him from his post. Without purpose he wandered past a couple of the Executives and stared up at their blank faces. He took care not to get too close, though he doubted he was ever out of reach of their long spears, even when he stood in the center of the room next to the Evanstone.

He went over to the jewel and looked inside it, as he often did. He tried not to look at his reflection, for the gem seemed to always show him disfigured with flaws that he believed didn't exist. It was the same for all who examined themselves using the diamond. His eyes were drawn to a particular ribbon of yellow that revolved in a tiny orbit around a dull red form, and he was struck with a new sense of wonder. Though he'd spent years with the stone, and though he'd gazed into it so much that he thought he should know everything about it that could be known, he suddenly felt exposed to a new and unknown depth of the Evanstone. Without realizing what he was doing, he reached out and touched the diamond. It felt cold and hard, and the smoothness of the surface was unmatched by anything he'd ever felt – except for the stone pillar on the island.

A blade coated with crimson came into focus at the bottom of his view, followed by a sharp stinging in his back. Justin's mind went blank and he fell to the floor beneath the Evanstone. His heart became still as blood flowed from the wounds left open where the Executive's spear had been.

Sight returned to Justin. He was alive, without his body, which he saw bent unnaturally at his feet. He wasn't alone: two of the king's servants were there, wearing white uniforms and shields slung across their backs; he recognized them at once. Between Durwin and Baldwin was an even more impressive figure. Her flowing yellow hair and emerald eyes were intimately familiar.

"Come with me." Evelyn approached Justin and held out her hands and smiled.

"How can I still live?"

"Your spirit lives on because you have been forgiven. This is not true for everyone. Your body will be recovered later. Come with me," she said again.

"Where will we go?"

"To a place more magnificent than Iman's Isle."

"Is it far?"

"Yes."

"How will we get there?"

"We'll fly."

Epilogue

Silence. Never before, nor ever since, has there been such silence. The street was lined on either side with spectators, packed from the palace all the way to the eastern gate, for everyone wanted to see if he was going. Servants of the king, people who had been welcomed into the city, even the four palace guards had come to witness the departure, to see if, by his expression, they could gain a sense as to if he was really going to do it?

Magnificent structures towered over the procession of one, brilliant white buildings crafted with patient precision. Normally, sounds of jubilation echoed off their walls and danced around their ornate pillars, but not today. Today the people were quiet, downcast, watching him leave, filling in the street behind him, but being careful to not get too close, and willing, with the power of their minds, their footsteps and their pressing against one another to create no noise. And they didn't.

The king had issued the challenge some time ago for all to hear, for any to answer - but there was only one who could. And that was the purpose of the public challenge, everyone knew, not to summon a volunteer, but to emphasize to all that there was none but him, the one walking steadily down the street alone. He could do what must be done, there was no doubt about that, but would he? Would he really be willing to go through with it, to the end, until it was finished?

Everyone wanted him to - the king, citizens of Casilda, and most of all, a man and woman in the front of the crowd near the gate. They were kneeling, their hearts filled with intense sorrow and intense joy all at the same time. The man drew nearer to the couple. Tears ran down their faces and they began to shiver uncontrollably. He glanced at them for a moment as he walked, not stopping, though, never stopping, and told them with his thoughts that everything would be all right, that he would not fail.

Their emotions became unbearable and they fell forward, prostrate on the white marble street, their faces pressed into it as he reached the opened gate and turned and spoke, shattering the silence; "Watch for my return. I'll come soon." Then he departed the white city, the place of the king, his home. And Casilda was silent again.